DATE DUE

OC 24			
FE 08			
MR 28			
FE 27			
OC 10			

Books by Judith Miller

FROM BETHANY HOUSE PUBLISHERS

*with Tracie Peterson

POSTCARDS *from* PULLMAN ∗ 2

WHISPERS ALONG *the* RAILS

JUDITH MILLER

BETHANYHOUSE
MINNEAPOLIS, MINNESOTA

Whispers Along the Rails
Copyright © 2007
Judith Miller

Cover design by Dan Thornberg, Koechel Peterson & Associates

Scripture quotations are from the King James Version of the Bible.

Published by Bethany House Publishers
11400 Hampshire Avenue South
Bloomington, Minnesota 55438

Bethany House Publishers is a division of
Baker Publishing Group, Grand Rapids, Michigan.

Printed in the United States of America

Paperback: ISBN-13: 978-0-7642-0277-3 ISBN-10: 0-7642-0277-4
Hardcover: ISBN-13: 978-0-7642-0441-8 ISBN-10: 0-7642-0441-6

Library of Congress Cataloging-in-Publication Data

Miller, Judith, 1944-
    Whispers along the rails / Judith Miller.
        p.   cm. — (Postcards from Pullman ; 2)
    ISBN 978-0-7642-0441-8 (alk. paper) — ISBN 978-0-7642-0277-3 (pbk.)
    1. British—United States—Fiction. 2. Young women—Fiction.
3. Railroads—Employees—Fiction. 4. Industrial relations—Fiction.
5. Depressions—1893—Fiction. 6. Pullman (Chicago, Ill.)—Fiction. I. Title.

    PS3613.C3858W49   2007
    813'.54—dc22   2007023745

In memory of my mother

GLADYS E. McCOY
(June 16, 1914–February 8, 2003)

With a grateful heart for
the memories she created,
the laughter she shared,
the faith she lived,
and the love freely given.

JUDITH MILLER is an award-winning author whose avid research and love for history are reflected in her novels, many of which have appeared on the CBA bestseller lists. Judy and her husband make their home in Topeka, Kansas.

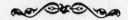

He that speaketh truth sheweth forth righteousness:
but a false witness deceit.
—Proverbs 12:17

CHAPTER ONE

Pullman, Illinois
March 2, 1893

In the hush of Olivia Mott's third-floor bedroom, the click of the metal latches on her Gladstone traveling bag echoed in the early morning silence. She tugged on the handle and lifted the pebbled leather bag from atop her bed. The travel case, with its double-stitched leather handle and linen lining, had been costly, but if her work for the Pullman Palace Car Company was going to require riding the rails, one good piece of baggage was a necessity. Her heart fluttered at a rapid pace, and she clasped her palm to her chest. *Fear? Excitement? Gloom?* A mixture of all three, she decided.

With a jab of her moonstone hatpin, Olivia secured her narrow-brimmed felt hat into place. She hoped it would prove substantial enough to hold her coffee-colored curls in place.

Greeting Olivia with a cheery good morning, Mrs. Barnes pointed her toward the kitchen. "I've prepared a breakfast fit for a queen. You don't want to begin your new position on an empty stomach." The older woman waved Olivia onward.

The smell of hearty fried food wafted across the kitchen, and her stomach roiled. "I believe a cup of tea and one slice of your nicely browned toast would be the most that I dare eat this morning, Mrs. Barnes." She lightly tapped her fingers on her stomach. "I'm a bit nervous, and I fear a heavy meal won't sit well."

Mrs. Barnes pushed a wayward strand of graying hair behind one ear. "You may be sorry once you depart Pullman and your stomach growls in protest." Her eyes shone with disapproval. "You're too thin, dear. No one would ever guess that you're an assistant chef in a fine hotel."

The landlady's reminder that Olivia would soon leave the familiarity of her newfound home in Pullman was enough to send Olivia's spirits plummeting. She'd been living in Illinois for only a year now, and though she'd had a bumpy beginning, her life had recently settled into a satisfying routine.

When Chef René, her kind mentor and the executive chef of the Hotel Florence, had suffered a serious heart attack last November, he had adamantly insisted Olivia replace him as executive chef until his health would permit a return to his duties. And though the chef's unexpected affliction had caused Olivia great sorrow and concern, it had also given her four additional months in Pullman before beginning her new work assignment on the rails.

She and Fred DeVault had used that added time to work toward rebuilding their friendship. They still remained on tentative footing but had made slow, steady improvement. Four months ago, they'd exchanged no more than terse greetings. Now they enjoyed talking to each other and even shared an occasional hope or dream. They discussed most everything nowadays—everything except their future together. For the last month, Fred had made a point of sitting beside her in church, and he'd even invited her ice-skating on two different occasions.

Olivia could only hope that her upcoming absences from Pullman wouldn't destroy the progress they'd made. She feared a sense of estrangement would divide them each time she returned, and they might never move beyond this point. If only she didn't have to go out on the rails—*if only*.

But Chef René had now returned to the kitchen, so her reprieve had come to an end. Today she would depart on her first journey riding the rails with Mr. Thornberg, the supervisor who had been assigned to instruct and prepare her for the evaluator position. She prayed Mr. Thornberg would be a patient man. She would feel more comfortable if the company agent, Mr. Howard, had arranged for her to meet Mr. Thornberg prior to their departure. Beginning this new position was frightening enough, but seeking out a stranger in the Chicago train station might be impossible. Though Mr. Howard had given her a sketchy description of him, Olivia thought there would be more than one man with thinning gray hair, a mustache, and a navy blue suit. When she mentioned that fact, Mr. Howard assured her Mr. Thornberg would be waiting by the third ticket counter along the west wall of the station. She doubted it would be so simple.

Downing the last sip of her tea, Olivia pushed away from the table and hoped Mrs. Barnes wouldn't notice she'd eaten only a few bites of the toast. "I'm not certain when I'll return, Mrs. Barnes, but I have my key to the house."

The older woman glanced at the plate. "You've not finished your toast. There's plenty of time before the train arrives. Do sit down."

"I must be on my way, Mrs. Barnes. I promised Mrs. De-Vault I'd stop for a brief visit to bid her and Fred good-bye. I don't want to disappoint her."

Mrs. Barnes seemed to momentarily weigh Olivia's response. "Well, in that case I won't detain you. I'm certain she, too, will miss you while you're away."

Olivia detected a hint of jealousy in Mrs. Barnes's remark, but she didn't respond. With a fleeting kiss to the older woman's cheek, she strode down the hallway, picked up her bag, and departed, thankful Mrs. Barnes hadn't followed. The woman suffered frequent attacks of melancholy since her daughter's marriage and subsequent departure, and Olivia couldn't bear a tearful good-bye. Mr. Barnes had likely hoped Olivia's presence in their home would prove a cure for his wife's bouts of loneliness, but that hadn't occurred, for much of Olivia's time was consumed at work or visiting with Martha, as well as with Fred and Mrs. DeVault.

Olivia shifted the heavy bag into her right hand and crossed the street. In all probability, she'd packed far more than she would need. Mr. Howard had been unable or unwilling—she remained uncertain which—to tell her exactly how long she'd be traveling with Mr. Thornberg on this first journey. She swallowed the lump of fear that was rising in her throat. *This will be a good experience with an array of new and exciting events.* She repeated the phrase aloud, but it didn't help. Instead, the lump increased in size, and she wondered if she would be able to keep down the toast she'd eaten only a few minutes earlier.

It was difficult to believe her life had changed so dramatically in only a year. From a scullery maid in London's Lanshire Hall to assistant chef at the Hotel Florence in Pullman, Illinois, she'd made quite a leap for a young woman of twenty-two years. And now this new endeavor had been forced upon her. Unlike her position in the hotel kitchen, she hadn't asked for this latest job. She didn't want to leave her duties in the hotel for even short periods of time. The mere thought of spending days on the rails, sleeping and dining in the Pullman railroad cars and evaluating services for possible improvement, boggled Olivia's mind. She was completely unqualified for such work, yet she'd had no say in the matter. Mr. Howard and Mr. Pullman had selected her for this job, so she couldn't refuse—not if she wanted to remain employed in Pullman—and she *did*. Fred lived in Pullman. And where else would she, a woman with only one year of training, be hired to work as an assistant chef?

"This will be a good experience, and Mr. Thornberg will be nice." The warble in her voice confirmed the fact that she'd not yet overcome her fear. Not in the least. She climbed the front steps and knocked on the DeVaults' front door. Surely Mrs. DeVault would have some words of wisdom that would assuage her fear.

Olivia took a backward step as the door swung open and Fred greeted her. She didn't fail to note the sadness that shone in his eyes. He took the valise from her hand and sat it near the door. Grasping her hand in his own, he led her down the hallway toward the kitchen. "Mother was beginning to worry. She expected you a little earlier. I think she was hoping for more time to visit."

"Mrs. Barnes insisted I eat something before leaving the house."

"You're rather pale," he said. "You shouldn't travel if you're sick."

Mrs. DeVault immediately scurried across the room and placed her palm on Olivia's forehead. "Oh, my dear, you're as white as winter's first snow. Are you ill?"

"I believe it's fear more than anything physical." Olivia sat down on one of the kitchen chairs and rested her chin in her palm. "I know I shouldn't be frightened, but if I don't excel at this new position, I'll likely find myself unemployed."

Mrs. DeVault poured a cup of tea and set it in front of Olivia. "Drink your tea, dear." The older woman took a chair beside her. "I don't mean to make light of your fears, but you must trust God. Worry serves no purpose, and if you permit it, your fears will consume you. Just place your trust in God, my dear." She grasped Olivia's hand in her own. "He is with you everywhere, Olivia. Talk to Him."

Olivia's hand trembled as she lifted the teacup to her lips. She took a sip and returned the cup to its saucer. "I know you're right, Mrs. DeVault, but I often forget. I'll do my best."

Fred quietly finished his breakfast while his mother continued to offer sage words of advice. Though he said nothing, Olivia didn't fail to notice his gaze flitting back and forth while his mother spoke to her.

Olivia glanced in his direction. "Do you ever forget about trusting God, or is it just me?"

He wiped his mouth with a worn cloth napkin. "Sometimes I forget, too."

Mrs. DeVault laughed. "Fred forgets because he thinks God

is too busy to take care of matters without an assist from him. Isn't that right, Fred?"

Fred grinned and shook his head. "No. I believe God can take care of things, and I do trust Him, but most of the time I'm in a hurry to make things happen."

His mother laughed. "Right. God doesn't adhere to Fred DeVault's time schedule." She patted Olivia's hand. "You're going to do just fine out there on the railroad. I hope you get to see lots of new and interesting places that you can tell me about when you return."

Olivia forced a smile and agreed to give Mrs. DeVault a full report upon her arrival back in Pullman. When a train whistle sounded in the distance, Olivia pushed away from the table. "I had best be on my way. I wouldn't want to miss the train. That would certainly be a poor beginning to my new position." She did her best to sound brave.

Mrs. DeVault grasped her hands and offered a prayer for safe travel and a speedy return, then motioned for Fred to hurry and finish his coffee. The two women walked down the hallway, Fred soon following after them.

"You wait right here for a minute, Olivia. I have something for you to take along with you." Mrs. DeVault hurried upstairs while Fred donned his cap.

He glanced toward the clock in the parlor, and Olivia felt a twinge of guilt. "You're going to be late, aren't you?" She knew he was expected at the training center in Kensington, where he'd begun helping some of the jobless and unskilled workers develop a trade.

"The fellows will get by without me for a few minutes. There are others who can keep things moving along until I get there.

Besides, seeing you off is more important."

Her heart skipped a beat at the kindness of his words and the gentleness in his voice, but before she could respond, Mrs. DeVault returned with a small Bible in her hand. "I know you have your mother's Bible, but I thought it would be too large to carry around with you." She handed the Bible to Olivia. "So tuck this one into your suitcase. Now, the two of you had best be off to the train station."

Fred retrieved the Gladstone bag while Olivia embraced his mother. The older woman wrapped her in a hearty squeeze. "Take good care, my dear. Remember, I'll be praying for you."

Olivia whispered her thanks for the Bible as well as the promised prayers; she knew she would need them both. After one final good-bye, Mrs. DeVault sent them on their way.

Olivia tucked her hand in the crook of Fred's arm and looked up at him. How she wished she had a picture of him to carry along with her. For now she'd have to memorize his features: his dark wavy hair, the sparkling blue of his eyes, and the angular shape of his chin. She tightened her hold on his arm and enjoyed the feel of his muscles flexing beneath her fingers.

"I'm going to miss you, Olivia."

"And I will miss you, too. I only hope Mr. Thornberg will be a kind man and train me quickly so I may return." Her voice cracked with emotion. She must change the topic, or she would surely cry. "How are the young men progressing at the center?"

"Some of them are doing exceedingly well. I'm very proud of the progress they're making."

"Have you had any success in locating positions for them within the Pullman Car Works?"

He shook his head. "Sad to say, we're not. However, I've

formed a small group of men who have begun to seek positions for some of the fellows we're training. If we can't locate jobs for them here in Pullman, then we're going to search out other possibilities." He grinned. "Some will need quite a bit of help preparing for interviews and the like, but I think they have more hope now that they know we're going to help in that regard, too."

"That's a wonderful idea. When did all this begin? You haven't said a word about any of this to me."

"I wanted to be certain the idea would go over well with the others before saying too much. John Holderman was excited by the plan, and he's already made two trips into Chicago to survey possibilities. We even hope to help relocate the men who lose their jobs here in Pullman."

Fred's enthusiastic desire to help the young men succeed was clear, and Olivia couldn't help but admire his generous spirit. Even though he'd been unable to secure a glass-etching position—his expertise—for himself, he remained willing to help others achieve their dreams.

Fred could move from Pullman and likely find employment elsewhere. However, his mother had grown to enjoy the small community of friends and longed to remain in their comfortable flat. Fred wouldn't deprive his mother of those things. The death of his father years ago had caused them both a great deal of suffering. Back then Fred had vowed to spare his mother any further unhappiness if and whenever he could. Olivia knew he'd not break his word.

She squeezed his arm. "From all accounts, you're making excellent progress."

"I can't deny a sense of satisfaction each time one of those fellows masters a new skill."

"I'm sure that's what Chef René experienced each time I met with success in the hotel kitchen. I do dislike leaving him alone on the very day he's returning to work."

Fred laughed. "He's not what I'd call *alone*. He'll be surrounded by kitchen boys and scullery maids."

She joined in his laughter. "You're right on that account. He'll probably long for peace and quiet by day's end. Besides, I'm certain Mr. Howard will check on him frequently."

"Your Mr. Howard does seem to check on the people he cares for, doesn't he?"

She raised her brows. "He's not *my* Mr. Howard. You continue to believe he has feelings for me, don't you?"

He grinned and nodded. "Absolutely. I had hoped he would give up; then again, he'd be a fool to give up so easily."

Olivia didn't know whether to be flattered or annoyed by Fred's remark. She'd made every attempt to assure him that she neither encouraged nor desired Mr. Howard's advances, but his position as company agent created difficult situations for her. And the fact that he lived next door to Mr. and Mrs. Barnes didn't help. Sometimes she thought Mr. Howard purposely waited until she left the house and then hurried outdoors to join her. For a time, she'd even exited through the rear of the house in order to elude him. But Mr. Howard had caught on, or Mrs. Barnes had secretly shared the information with him. The older lady continued to think Olivia and Mr. Howard would make the perfect couple. Unfortunately, Mr. Howard seemed to agree. Olivia had done her very best to squelch his interest, but she'd not been successful.

Her efforts to convince Fred she had no romantic interest in Mr. Howard had also failed. She tugged on his arm and came to a halt in front of the train station. "Any interest I have in Mr. Howard is no different from your own. He holds my future with this company in his hands, but he doesn't hold sway over my personal life. In fact, Mr. Howard isn't even aware of my travel schedule."

"What makes you so certain?"

"When I inquired about the length of my journey, he said he had no idea since Mr. Thornberg was in charge of the arrangements."

Fred pulled open the front door of the train depot and followed her inside. Had they not been within hearing distance of the ticket agent and several passengers, she would have continued their discussion, for she wanted to dispel his concerns before leaving. With Fred by her side, she stepped to the ticket counter.

The agent handed her a ticket. "Mr. Howard came over last night and paid for your ticket, Miss Mott."

Fred's eyebrows knit close together. "I thought you said Mr. Howard was unaware of your travel schedule."

She could hear the doubt in his voice. "He knew when I was scheduled to depart. He merely arranged for my pass. Other than that, he's left matters in Mr. Thornberg's hands." She stuffed the train pass into her purse and stepped toward one of the benches, her heels clicking on the Minton tile floor. "Come sit down with me." She hoped to use these final moments to set Fred's mind at rest and make certain there had been no misunderstanding.

A group of travelers entered the station, and soon the waiting area overflowed with boisterous laughter and conversation. There would be no opportunity for a private talk amid the turmoil. A shrill whistle announced the arriving train, and Fred angled his body forward to look out the far window. He glanced back at her. "That's your train. Let's make our way through this crowd and wait by the side door."

Olivia didn't hear the approaching footsteps and started at the touch on her shoulder.

"I'm sorry. I didn't mean to frighten you."

Samuel Howard stood behind her. His glance momentarily shifted toward Fred. Olivia saw Mr. Howard's eyes darken and his features harden. When he stepped to her side, she noted the leather traveling bag in his hand.

"Are you taking this train, also?" Olivia's gaze traveled from the bag upward to his eyes.

His smile appeared forced. "Why, of course, Olivia. I'm going with you. And I believe that's our train." He nodded toward her Gladstone bag. "I assume that's yours." Without waiting for an answer, he grasped her arm. "Come along, Olivia. We don't want to miss our train."

There had been no opportunity for fond farewells. There hadn't even been time for a hasty good-bye. Olivia glanced over her shoulder while she hurried alongside Mr. Howard. Fred had stepped outside onto the platform. She couldn't be certain if it was pain, anger, or perhaps disbelief that now shone in his eyes.

CHAPTER TWO

Olivia pressed her nose to the train window and scanned the crowd. She needed one last glimpse of Fred. *There!* He'd moved to the far side of the station. She strained forward and willed him to look in her direction. He turned around, and Olivia's heart pounded in a jarring rhythm. If only he would look at her, surely he would see her dismay. But he didn't look up; instead, he trudged back inside the depot. Each time she thought the two of them might heal their scars from the past, something happened and reopened the wounds. And most of those occasions seemed to include Mr. Howard.

Fred was once again walking away rather than moving toward her. How she longed to run after him, force him to listen, make him aware she'd known nothing of Mr. Howard's plans to accompany her on the train. But there would be no opportunity for explanations this day.

Once Mr. Howard settled beside her and the train had departed for Chicago's Van Buren Street station, Olivia turned toward him. "I'm somewhat confused, Mr. Howard. When we spoke yesterday, you advised me that I was to meet Mr. Thornberg in Chicago. You even gave me specific instructions where to meet him."

"And a description so you could easily identify him," Mr. Howard added. "I received word from Mr. Pullman early this morning that Mr. Thornberg had taken ill and would be unable to accompany you. When I stopped next door this morning, Mrs. Barnes informed me that you had already departed. I believe she said you'd gone to bid *Mrs.* DeVault good-bye."

Olivia stiffened at his comment. She owed him no explanation, and she'd give him none. "Am I to assume that you then volunteered your services?"

He chuckled softly. "Mr. Pullman and I agreed that, given the delay already incurred due to Chef René's medical condition, we didn't want to postpone your training any longer. There really was no one else available. And, of course, I am pleased to be of service to both Mr. Pullman and to you. I believe you'll find our journey enjoyable as well as instructive. Not that I'm as well versed as Mr. Thornberg, but I certainly do know the rules."

"I'm sure you do, Mr. Howard."

He frowned and tapped the notebook he had removed from his pocket. "The test will be to see how well *you* learn them. Mr. Pullman has high hopes for you, Olivia. I trust you won't disappoint him."

Olivia's primary concern was avoiding the loss of her position as assistant chef at the Hotel Florence rather than preventing Mr. Pullman's disappointment, but she realized the two went hand in hand. For that reason, she knew she must do her best.

Mr. Howard handed her the leather-bound notebook. "You may use this to keep your notes."

"Notes?" She wasn't certain she'd have so many fresh ideas that she couldn't remember them before returning to Pullman.

"You will need to keep detailed notes, Olivia." He leaned a bit closer. "I will refer to you as Olivia while we're traveling, and you should refer to me as Samuel. That way the employees will think we are . . . uh, related."

"Why do they need to believe we're related? What possible difference could it make?"

"Think of this as a type of charade or playacting. We don't want any of the attendants to suspect that we work for Mr. Pullman. Otherwise, they would likely treat us with more preference, and it wouldn't be a fair evaluation of the services offered to our customers."

She wasn't certain that she believed him, and he apparently detected her uncertainty.

"Consider the following: Mr. Pullman enters the dining room of the Hotel Florence. Do you not warn the entire staff that you expect them to perform at their very best? Do you not attempt to offer the very best plate of food to him?"

Olivia had to admit Mr. Howard was correct. Undoubtedly she would want to impress the company president. On the days when Mr. Pullman arrived at the hotel, she or Chef René made certain the kitchen staff knew of his presence. "Yes, but he is the—"

He held up his index finger. "And we are his representatives. For that reason alone, the staff will not perform in their usual manner if they know we are on board this train. Trust me. I know what is best."

There wasn't time for further discussion, for they had reached the Van Buren Street station. Olivia walked alongside Mr. Howard as he approached the ticket counter. She was surprised to see him pay for the tickets. Mr. Pullman issued passes to many of the employees who traveled while performing business for the company. Once she was traveling on her own, she wondered if she would be expected to bear the expense of her train tickets. If so, her wages would quickly diminish. Once they boarded the train, she would inquire.

"We'll be departing from track eight in only a few minutes." With a suitcase in each hand, Mr. Howard led the way.

She would have been more than content to carry her own baggage, but Mr. Howard insisted. No need to argue, as he wouldn't listen. Mr. Howard expertly wound his way among the throngs of passengers, occasionally glancing over his shoulder to make certain, she assumed, he hadn't lost her in the crowd. He didn't allow for the fact that his legs yielded a much longer stride than her own, and by the time they stopped beside one of the dark green railcars, she was out of breath. The Pullman name was stenciled in large gold letters above the windows. She could only hope that they had reached their destination. "Is this our train?"

Mr. Howard nodded. "There should be a porter and conductor on the platform to load our luggage and help us aboard."

Before she could respond to his assessment, attendants suited in navy blue jackets, pants, and caps marched onto the platform, each of them heading for a specific railcar. A conductor and porter approached them, the conductor rather stern and the porter offering a welcoming smile that revealed an even row of ivory teeth. Olivia smiled in return.

Mr. Howard appeared unimpressed as he dropped their cases onto the platform. "It appears service isn't what it used to be in these Pullman cars."

The porter immediately hustled to Mr. Howard's side and retrieved their baggage while the conductor offered a profuse apology. "Reassignment of several employees delayed our ability to arrive on the platform a full hour in advance, sir. I do apologize. This is an uncommon occurrence, but to make up for any inconvenience, we would be pleased to offer you and your traveling companion a complimentary meal in our dining car."

After hearing the conductor's profuse apologies and receiving an offer of a free meal, Mr. Howard appeared appeased. The conductor punched their tickets for the first portion of their journey and assisted them onto the train. Once seated, Mr. Howard motioned toward Olivia's bag. "You need to write this information in your journal, Olivia."

She hadn't even had an opportunity to absorb her surroundings, but she removed the journal from her purse. With the notebook perched on her lap, she looked at him. "What am I supposed to write?"

He glanced around before leaning closer. "Didn't you take note of the men's names on their uniform badges? You must always take note of employees' names, Olivia. The porter is Hoover and the conductor is Franklin." When she didn't move quickly enough, he touched her pencil. "Write down their names and the fact that they were not present on the platform an hour prior to departure. Also note that when I complained of poor service, we were offered an apology and two free meals for our inconvenience."

After jotting down the information, Olivia closed the journal. "Will the cost of our meals be deducted from their wages?" Olivia certainly didn't want to eat a free meal at the expense of other employees.

Mr. Howard shook his head. "You need not concern yourself over that issue. Was the step properly positioned when you boarded the train?"

Olivia bobbed her head. Surely it must have been in the proper position, for she'd not experienced any difficulty. She didn't want to admit she hadn't the vaguest notion *where* the proper position might be.

He narrowed his eyes. "Have you studied the training manual I gave you last month, Olivia?"

"I've read through a portion, but I wouldn't say I've actually *studied* it." She wilted at the intensity of his gaze. "To be honest, I haven't had a great deal of time of late. You may not recall, but my cousin Albert and Martha, who supervises the maids in the hotel—"

"I *know* who Martha is, Olivia. Get on with your story." He was, quite obviously, annoyed.

"Their wedding is approaching—April the twenty-second, to be exact. Martha has requested my assistance with the preparations. I'm to be her attendant, you know."

He arched his brows. "And?"

She fidgeted with the lace collar that circled her neck. The adornment was the only touch of femininity she had added to her navy blue traveling suit. The fabric scratched her neck, and now she wished she had chosen her plain white shirtwaist instead. Mr. Howard's stare remained unwavering. "And I've been busy helping Martha with her wedding plans, so I haven't had sufficient time to study the book in detail."

Mr. Howard rested his head against the plush tufted upholstery and tapped his fingers on the armrest. "I don't want to appear overbearing on your first day, Olivia, but it seems you don't have a clear understanding of the importance of this new position." He patted her hand. "Well, we can't change past decisions, but we'll obviously need a more extensive training period. I had scheduled a round trip from Chicago to New York. Under the circumstances, I don't believe that will prove sufficient."

Her chest caved like a deflated soufflé. The progress she and Martha had made thus far would be of little consequence if she had to remain away from Pullman for an extended period. Olivia's throat constricted as an unexpected and frightening thought entered her mind. "We *will* return prior to the wedding, won't we?"

"That will depend entirely upon you, Olivia. If you learn quickly, we should be back in Pullman with time to spare. But if you have difficulty comprehending what is expected . . ." Mr. Howard's words trailed off in a silent warning.

He had located her Achilles' heel. Whether she wanted to wrestle with learning the rules contained in the inch-thick porter's manual or not, she would do so. She couldn't disappoint Arthur and Martha. She'd begin studying right now. While Mr. Howard stopped the porter and asked him a question, Olivia dug in her handbag and removed the manual. She wanted Mr. Howard to realize she was serious about learning. Maybe then he would reconsider, and they could return home earlier than planned.

The porter ambled off, and Mr. Howard glanced at her hand. Before she could say a word, he snatched the book from her and shoved it inside his jacket. "What are you doing?" He hissed the words in her direction, anger flashing in his eyes.

The man's irrational behavior was disconcerting. "I was going to study. I thought you wanted me to learn the rules."

"Not here. Not where the porters and conductors will see you. They'll know we're spot—employees. Why else would we have a company manual?" He glanced about and removed the book from his jacket. "Put this away and do not remove it unless you are in the privacy of your berth with the curtain drawn. Do I make myself clear?"

She bobbed her head and quickly tucked the book back into her purse. A lump had risen in her throat, but she forced it down. She didn't want to cry in front of Mr. Howard. And she certainly didn't want to provoke him further. Rather than look in his direction, she studied the car's interior, the stained-glass windows inserted above each plain window, the intricate designs carved into the rosewood panels that concealed the upper berths until nighttime descended, and the beautifully etched mirrors. The opulence of the cars gave testimony to Mr. Pullman's penchant for details and excellence.

The conductor inched down the aisle checking tickets, and Olivia recalled Mr. Howard's recent purchase in the train station. "Will I be expected to purchase tickets when I travel? I had assumed there would be some sort of pass I would carry."

Mr. Howard didn't appear annoyed by her question. "When you are traveling, you will be given money to purchase your tickets. Although the company issues passes to certain employees and an occasional customer or friend, a pass would alert the staff that you are either a friend or employee of the Pullman company."

"I see." She didn't understand the need for secrecy, for she doubted whether a porter would treat her with more deference with or without a pass, but she didn't say so. There was little doubt Mr. Howard preferred undisputed acceptance of his explanations.

They had traveled for nearly half an hour when Mr. Howard tipped his head closer. "Signal the porter and advise him that you're experiencing an upset stomach."

Olivia opened her mouth to protest, but after one look at Mr. Howard's steely eyes, she signaled the Negro porter. The man's skin shone like fine ebony. He looked first at Mr. Howard, who nodded.

"Yes, ma'am, how can I help you?"

"Do you have something that might settle an aching stomach?"

"We can't give out medicine, ma'am, but I'd be pleased to bring you a cup of tea and some dry toast if you think that might help." He offered a look of sympathy.

Olivia wasn't certain if she was supposed to agree to the tea, but the warm drink sounded inviting even if her stomach wasn't upset. "Thank you. Tea would be most helpful, though I don't believe I'll try the toast." With an unwavering smile, the porter rushed off to do her bidding.

Mr. Howard nodded toward her pocket. "Check your timepiece to see how long it takes him."

Olivia withdrew the small pocket watch and clicked the tiny hasp. She hadn't wanted to accept the gift, but Mr. Howard had insisted. He'd said it was imperative she be continually aware of the time. And she supposed that was true. She wouldn't want to miss a train, but it seemed as if Mr. Pullman should provide the necessary equipment to his employees. She would never be expected to supply her own knives to carve meat in the hotel kitchen. Why should she be expected to purchase a watch? Or, in her case, why should Mr. Howard purchase the item? When she had questioned him, he had shrugged and explained that many employees were required to furnish their own tools.

The porter returned with her tea. Before she could add cream, Mr. Howard leaned closer. "Check the time, Olivia. How long did it take him?"

"Seven minutes." She snapped the lid of the watch into place and picked up the cream.

"It should take no longer than five. Do make note of that." He glanced at her teacup. "You may drink your tea before adding the notation to your journal."

The noonday meal proved a prolongation of Mr. Howard's criticisms. While Olivia thought the service impeccable, Mr. Howard found fault with everything, from the water spot on his spoon to her overfilled cup of tea. "Beverages should be poured no higher than a half inch from the top of the glass or cup. Make a note."

Those seemed to be his favorite three words. She wondered if she would have any empty pages in the journal by the time they returned to Pullman.

When seven o'clock arrived and Mr. Howard made no move toward the dining car, Olivia's stomach growled in protest. "Will we not be taking the evening meal aboard the train?"

He glanced over the top of his book. "Yes, but I requested the latest service available for our supper." He removed a needlepoint bookmark from the seat and slipped it between the pages of his book. Olivia wondered if his deceased wife had stitched it for him—perhaps a birthday or anniversary gift. She didn't have time to contemplate the possibility for long. "You should remember this, Olivia. It's best to have the porter reserve you a table for the last seating of the day. That way you'll be able to make certain all menu items remain available, even at the end of the day, a matter that is of great importance to Mr. Pullman." He tapped her journal. "If you think you might forget, you should make a note to yourself."

"I feel certain I can remember, Mr. Howard. I can certainly empathize with the chef if a shortage should occur. There are times when no matter how much planning goes into ordering and such, one comes up short. We've been known to have an occasional misstep at the hotel, too." She noted the creases between his eyebrows deepen and immediately realized she shouldn't have offered such information. Upon their return to Pullman, he'd likely take Chef René to task. She wanted to add that it had occurred only once or twice but feared she'd make matters worse.

Thankfully, the porter arrived several minutes later and announced their table was ready. Olivia hoped all would go well, although Mr. Howard appeared intent upon finding something wrong at every turn. The dining car attendant held her chair and unfolded her napkin, all the while maintaining a broad smile. Olivia thought his face must ache by day's end. He announced the specials in a crisp, clear tone, inquired what they would like to drink, and handed them each a pristine menu. The water glasses were filled to below the half-inch mark, and there didn't appear to be any spots on the silverware.

They completed the meal without incident, and Olivia sighed with relief when Mr. Howard stated they would return to the sleeper car. "I want to return to our car in time to observe the porter making down the beds."

Rather than observe the porters stretching sheets across the pull-down beds, Olivia wanted to crawl into one of them and hide from Mr. Howard and his constant admonitions. She followed him down the narrow corridor, through the vestibule that connected the railcars, and back into their sleeper, where the porter was hard at work near the far end of the car.

While the porter popped an upper berth from the ceiling and folded down the opposing seats below, Mr. Howard droned on. "Three to five minutes per bed maximum, linens crisp and tight, pillow toward the engine, and draperies properly affixed." The list went on and on. "I'm certain you believe my manner overbearing, Olivia, but while we're traveling, you must remember I am acting as your supervisor rather than a suitor or a friend."

Olivia swallowed hard, forcing herself to remain silent. She considered Mr. Howard neither a friend nor a suitor, but she dared not say so. Mr. Howard had been abundantly clear that contradiction would not be well received. Fortunately, the porter soon arrived at their end of the car, and Olivia was able to crawl into one of the curtained cocoons for the remainder of the night. She rested her head on the starched white pillowcase and knew these hours behind the forest green curtain would be her only respite throughout this journey.

CHAPTER THREE

Pullman, Illinois
March 2, 1893

Without a backward glance, Fred strode away from the train depot, confusion clouding his thoughts. He wanted to believe Olivia had told him the truth. Had she actually been unaware Mr. Howard would be her traveling companion? *Traveling companion*. The very idea made Fred's blood boil. His irritation mounted when he recalled Mr. Howard's possessive grasp of Olivia's arm. There was little doubt the man considered Olivia much more than an employee. And the angry glare he'd directed at Fred had been palpable. How could anyone interpret Mr. Howard's actions as anything other than a man staking his claim? Mr. Howard considered Fred his romantic rival.

The idea stopped him in his tracks. He couldn't possibly compete with Mr. Howard for Olivia's affections—or anything else, for that matter. Mr. Howard possessed every advantage: he could control his own work schedule, he had the income with which to woo Olivia in a fine manner, he lived next door to her, and he could offer her a life filled with anything she desired.

During the past months, Fred and Olivia had nurtured their fragile friendship, both of them hoping to restore their earlier bond. At least that's what he had thought. Today, feelings of doubt were creeping to the forefront of his mind. Had Olivia actually been working late on the nights when she said she couldn't see him? Or had she been with Mr. Howard? Several months ago, Fred's mother had mentioned an opening at a nearby rooming house, but Olivia had declined, giving the excuse that Mrs. Barnes might spiral into a state of melancholy. Now Fred wondered if Olivia's refusal had more to do with Mr. Howard than with Mrs. Barnes and her health. Did Olivia care for Mr. Howard?

Fred attempted to force the thoughts from his mind, but they nagged at him like an irritating itch. He'd attempted to keep his feelings for Olivia somewhat guarded, but if he was going to protect his heart, he must further tighten his armor. He kicked a pebble down the street, exasperated by this latest turn of events. Mr. Howard's true concern should be directed toward the unrest that simmered beneath the surface in the town he'd been hired to manage rather than toward Olivia. Fred doubted whether the man realized how many residents harbored resentment for the inequities that took place in the Pullman Car Works or in the town of Pullman itself, the nation's latest so-called utopian community.

He turned up his collar against a stiff cool breeze and suddenly realized he'd forgotten his sketches. For nearly six months he had been working with Bill Orland, who had genuine design talent. The two of them had developed several ideas for glass etchings, yet there was no opportunity to see the designs produced. Other than the actual design and an explanation of the etching process, the training couldn't be done within the confines of their small training center. They didn't have access to the necessary acid baths or grinding tools needed to complete the process. Unfortunately, the same held true for many of the crafts they wanted to teach the men. Yet all of the men who volunteered their time were doing their best to develop innovative ways in which to help those who longed to better their lot in life. The idea remained sound, but they'd all accepted the fact that for true apprenticeship to occur, one needed to be within the confines of the workplace or have access to all of the tools and equipment.

Today, however, Fred was excited to have a bit of news for Bill Orland. Information Mr. Godfrey, Fred's supervisor, had passed along last evening. Bill and his family had been struggling to make ends meet since his layoff from the car works. He had chosen to live in Kensington, where the rent was lower, but that decision had cost Bill his job. Though the company denied the practice, it was a well-known fact that workers who rented accommodations outside of Pullman were the first to be laid off. Fred hoped today's news would help Bill regain financial stability for his family.

His quick stride had turned into a loping jog by the time he bounded up the front steps and entered the front door of the redbrick row house. "It's only me, Mother. I forgot my sketches."

A near collision with his mother brought him to an abrupt halt in the hallway. "Since you're here, come and have a cup of coffee."

"I'm already late." He knew his mother would want details

of his seeing Olivia off, but right now he needed time to sift through his feelings.

She frowned. "I won't see you again until morning. I know your volunteer work at the training center is important, but I'm anxious to know how things went between you and Olivia." She motioned him toward the kitchen. "The poor girl was in a frazzled state, what with worrying over locating Mr. Thornberg and not knowing how long she'd be away. Was it a tearful good-bye?"

There would be no escape. He sat down while his mother pulled a cup-and-saucer from the cabinet and filled it with the steaming brew. She placed it in front of him and waited, her eyes filled with anticipation.

"Olivia safely boarded the train. There were no tears. In fact, there was no farewell. Mr. Howard appeared shortly before departure time and whisked Olivia down the platform and onto the train."

His mother dropped into the chair across from him. "Mr. Howard? He was going to Chicago?"

Fred poured a dollop of cream into the coffee and stirred, the spoon creating a small whirlpool in the center of his cup. "Chicago and wherever else this journey takes her. Mr. Howard will be acting as Olivia's traveling companion. That's as much as I heard before he hurried her away from my side."

"But I thought Olivia said . . ."

He sipped his coffee and stared into the distance. "We both know what she *said*, Mother, but that's not what occurred. She appeared surprised when Mr. Howard arrived, but who can know for certain?"

His mother frowned. "What is that supposed to mean? Surely you don't think she knew Mr. Howard was going to be traveling with her. She's been doing her best to discourage the man."

Fred shrugged and gulped the coffee. "I don't know what to think. I do remember Olivia's list of lies. I've worked hard to move forward, but I can't deny this makes me wary." He glanced at the clock and downed the remains from his cup.

His mother patted her palm on the table. "You can't rush off. Tell me more."

"I need to be on my way. Besides, there's nothing more to tell. Olivia is gone, and Mr. Howard along with her."

His mother pushed aside her coffee cup and leaned her arms across the table. "There must be a simple explanation for all of this. I don't believe Olivia knew Mr. Howard would be traveling with her."

Fred shook his head. "Believe whatever you wish, Mother. I've told you all I know. I'm going to the training center. I just hope Bill hasn't given up on me and gone home." He gathered up his sketches and pushed away from the table.

His mother followed him down the hallway. "You should give her the benefit of the doubt, you know."

He turned, bent forward, and kissed her soft weathered cheek. "You've made your point very clear. I will give the matter additional thought, but one thing is certain: I'll not make the same mistake twice."

"What does that mean? That you're going to close the door on her when you've only opened it a mere crack?"

He shrugged. "It means I'll give the matter additional thought. When Olivia returns, we'll have to see what happens."

Without giving her time for further comment, he hurried off. His mother's remark hadn't surprised him. All along she had remained Olivia's staunch supporter. It had been his mother who had continued to study the Bible and pray with Olivia, and it had been his mother who had convinced him that Olivia had changed her life. Likewise, it had been his mother who had encouraged him to restore his relationship with Olivia. He had agreed to offer his hand in friendship, but he hadn't planned to lose his heart to her again.

The tower clock struck ten o'clock when he pushed open the door of the training center. He glanced around the room and waved to John Holderman, who was doing his best to explain the bolt department of the Pullman Car Works. How much more effective it would be for the men to actually see the process and watch the men at work. Perhaps one day they'd be able to convince their supervisors or Mr. Pullman to permit such an experience. But for now, they must do their best to simply acquaint the men with the type of tools and machinery they would be expected to use should they be hired.

During his time here at the center, Fred could once again use his creative talent. While several of the men taught the higher mathematics and scientific theory necessary in their endeavors, Fred nurtured creativity in his few students. Bill Orland's talent had emerged like cream rising in a pail of fresh milk. His drawings were rich and textured, the type that would lend beauty and artistry to either clear or silvered glass.

Fred spotted Bill hunched over a table near one of the windows. He stared over his shoulder at the drawing of a crane on a marshy bank. "Beautiful work, Bill."

Bill glanced up from his drawing and grinned. "Thanks."

"I thought you might be gone before I arrived."

He brushed the thatch of dusty brown hair away from his

eyes and glanced toward the clock. "I don't have to leave until noon today, but I was beginning to wonder if you were coming in."

Fred dropped onto a chair beside him. "I had some personal business to attend to, but I wanted to talk to you about some news my boss mentioned last night before he left work."

Bill placed his pencil on the table and turned. "From that grin, I expect it's good news. Did you get assigned to the glass-etching section?"

Fred shook his head. "No, this is something for you. I'm not positive it will work out, so don't get your hopes too high—you might not want to mention it to your wife just yet."

"Well, what is it?"

Fred kneaded his hands together while he explained what Mr. Godfrey had told him about a glass-etching business in Chicago. "Seems the owner's health is beginning to fail, and he needs help with the business. Mr. Godfrey knows I've been unhappy and thought I might be interested."

"Well, aren't you?"

"I can't leave Pullman, Bill. My mother . . ."

Bill nodded. "I understand. You've got to look out for her best interests, too."

"If you could go to work for this man and learn the trade, you might be able to purchase his business someday." Fred could barely contain his excitement. If he couldn't have such a dream for himself, he wanted it for Bill. "I thought we'd take the train in to Chicago next week and meet with him. What do you think?"

"I think I'd be a fool if I didn't at least take a look. When do you want to go?" Bill's eyes shone with excitement. "It's going to be hard to keep this news under my hat."

Fred understood. When men were laid off or fired from their jobs, they struggled with issues of pride and depression. Seeing their wives forced to take in sewing or clean houses didn't bolster the men's feelings of self-worth, either.

"How about Thursday? And let's take those drawings with us. I want Mr. Lockabee to see your work. I think he'll be impressed." He patted Bill on the shoulder. "Looks like John's completed his lecture, and I want to talk with him for a few minutes."

Bill wouldn't be concentrating on his drawings the remainder of the morning, and Fred couldn't blame him. This was a rare opportunity. Bill was already hurrying across the room to share the news with several of the other men.

John nodded toward the group as Fred approached. "What's all that about?"

After Fred's quick explanation, John hollered congratulations across the room. Bill pumped his arm in the air, and Fred laughed at his enthusiasm. "Don't get him too excited. I don't want him to end up disappointed if it doesn't work out."

"Looks to me like the Lord's got His hand in this one. Think about it. How often does something like this happen?"

"It's the first time I know of, and I couldn't be more pleased for Bill. We've all been worried over his situation. The church has been helping out, but with more and more men being laid off, the benevolence fund is being stretched to the limit."

John scratched his head. "His own business—that's really something. I hope it works out for him."

"Chicago is wide open for the taking. Not much competition and high demand with all the construction and wealth. I'm hoping Bill can do some of that fine artwork on the doors and windows of those fancy mansions along Prairie Avenue."

"He'll need to convince only one of those women that she needs his artwork, and the rest will follow suit. Seems they like to do their best to keep up with one another." John glanced around the room. "It would be wonderful if we could see the rest of these fellows have the same opportunity."

"This center is a wonderful thing, John, but what we truly need is a place where the men can get their hands on the machinery. We're not giving them the real training they need."

John shuffled his notes and stacked them on the table. "We're giving them more than they had when they walked in the door, and most will be better-equipped than their counterparts, Fred. But I like the idea that you're looking to find alternatives for training the men. While you're in Chicago, maybe you can find us a benefactor to equip the training center."

The two men laughed. They both knew that unless someone like George Pullman or Philip Armour finally realized the advantage of financing a manual training center, it wouldn't happen. Only when one of the wealthy tycoons saw the profit to be gained by having a ready supply of skilled workmen would a fully equipped school open.

CHAPTER FOUR

Chicago, Illinois
March 2, 1893

Charlotte Spencer, daughter of the Earl and Countess of Lanshire, raked a comb through her snarled hair before she fell back against her pillow. She lacked both the energy and inclination to continue with her toilette. Enveloped in a cocoon of lethargy, she'd done no more than perform the absolute necessities of life for the past month—or had it been longer? She'd lost track of time.

One thing was certain: she'd soon need to make plans for her future. She had paid for her room rent through the end of February, or was it March? She couldn't remember. Unlike the first four months following her clandestine departure from Pullman, these last months had been no more than a blurry existence. In retrospect, those first months had been rather enjoyable. She'd taken a room at the Palmer House and whiled away her afternoons shopping at Marshall Field's emporium and enjoyed taking her meals at Chicago's finer restaurants—until she had realized her funds were running low and she'd been forced to find a more economical place to reside.

Shortly after leaving Pullman, she had sold the remaining pieces of her mother's jewelry, the pieces she'd stolen before she and Olivia had set sail from London a year ago. London—that part of her life now seemed so distant. Had it truly only been a year? Strange that a scullery maid who had worked in the kitchens of Lanshire Hall shared her darkest secrets. Charlotte hadn't even known Olivia until a few nights before they set sail for America. Olivia had been fleeing the unwanted advances of Chef Mallard, head chef of Lanshire Hall, while Charlotte had been running toward the man who she thought would marry her and give her unborn child the name he deserved.

A sigh escaped Charlotte's dry lips. She longed for a cup of tea. Surely the hotel clerk would bring her meal before much longer. She rested her palm across her forehead, hoping to will the dinner tray to her door. But when the clerk didn't arrive, her thoughts soon returned to Olivia and the town of Pullman. Both she and Olivia had arrived at their destination with plans for the future, albeit plans based upon a foundation of lies and deceit. Charlotte believed her own deceit had been repaid in full measure, for she'd suffered the humiliation of Randolph Morgan's rejection. He had denied having fathered her unborn child and declared her no more than a common harlot. Randolph was interested in protecting his future with his wife and children—the family he had failed to mention to Charlotte when they'd first met at her family home in London.

The stench from the street below seeped through a crack in the windowpane, providing an odious manifestation of her current life along with a reminder of the privileged life she'd abandoned in England. Her conduct during that first encounter with Randolph Morgan in London had been unbefitting a woman of nobility, and the confrontation with Randolph after arriving in Pullman hadn't gone well, either. He had made his position quite clear: he had no intention of changing his marital status, not even for the daughter of the Earl of Lanshire. She shuddered at the memory.

So many memories from her short time in Pullman. What of her child? Had Olivia kept him, or had she freed herself of the responsibility and taken little Morgan to an orphanage? What did Olivia think of her behavior, she wondered. "Surely she realized the child was better left in her care," Charlotte muttered. "What would I have done with him?"

A hammering knock sounded at the door and interrupted her one-sided conversation. "Just leave the tray on the floor outside my door."

"I need to talk to you, Miss Spencer."

She rolled to one side and forced herself to a sitting position. Another loud knock. "Give me a moment, please. I'm coming." She padded across the wood-plank floor on bare feet. She'd likely have a splinter in her foot before she reached the door, but the clerk's impatience was obvious.

With her body positioned against the door, she turned the key and opened the door a crack. The door pushed against her hip, and she shoved back as the clerk attempted to wedge his foot in the opening. Her heart thumped in an erratic cadence. Peering into the dank hallway, she said, "What do you want?"

His weight held the door tight against her body. "I need your rent. You're already two days overdue. I've slipped three notes under your door. Have you read them?"

She glanced down. Her bare foot rested on a piece of paper. "No, but I'll read them once you leave."

He sighed. "I can't leave, Miss Spencer. I got to have the money."

Her pulse quickened at his demand. She needed time to think. "I've been ill, and I'm not properly dressed. If you'll leave my supper tray, I promise to come down first thing in the morning and pay what I owe you."

"How much longer you planning to stay? A few days? A week? A month? What?"

His persistent behavior annoyed her, yet she did not dare appear unfriendly. "I fear I may be required to depart your establishment and find something less expensive. Have you any recommendations?"

Once again he sighed—this time much louder. "Are you talking cheaper or free, Miss Spencer?"

She cleared her throat. "Free might prove the best solution."

"You ain't gonna try and do me outta what you already owe me, are you, 'cause I can take this supper tray downstairs and have it for myself."

"No!" She assumed her most regal tone. "I wouldn't consider such subterfuge."

"Right." He hesitated a moment longer. "You can pick up a list when you come down to pay your final bill." He stepped away.

His movement, combined with Charlotte's weight against the door, caused it to unexpectedly slam shut. She hoped he wouldn't misconstrue the incident. Having the hotel clerk angry would only multiply her problems. When she could no longer hear his footfalls, she opened the door. Thankfully, he had left the tray. She carried it to the other side of the room and placed it atop the marred and stained chest of drawers. She wondered if her parents had ever stepped inside a place such as this. Just as quickly she pushed the thought from her mind and lifted the domed lid from the tray. Gravy had already begun to congeal atop the meat. She touched the green beans. Cold—all of it. But her growling stomach would not be denied.

She sawed through the stringy piece of meat, uncertain of its origin even after she'd tasted a bite. What did it matter if she died of food poisoning? The world would be better off without her. She finished the meal, every cold bite and every lukewarm sip of tea, before returning to her bed. She sat on the edge of the sagging mattress and dumped the contents of her purse onto the worn coverlet. After counting her remaining money, she scanned the three notes left by the desk clerk. It appeared she would have sufficient funds to pay her bill if the price hadn't gone up too much come morning. She couldn't afford another day's rent—of that, there was no doubt.

With as much effort as she could muster, Charlotte pulled her valise from beneath the bed. She'd need to be packed and checked out early, for she couldn't risk being charged for another day. Her reflection in the mirror indicated a good deal of time would be required for her toilette.

———

The thunder and pounding rain that had kept Charlotte awake for most of the night had stopped by early the next morning. She longed to remain abed yet forced herself from beneath the dirty coverlet and prepared to meet the day.

When she had finally dressed and fashioned her hair, Charlotte dropped to the side of the bed, exhausted. She needed to rest before she could trudge about the mucky streets seeking another place to call home.

Only moments later a knock sounded at the door. "Are you still planning to check out today, Miss Spencer?"

"Yes. I'll be down to settle my bill momentarily. I need to gather my belongings, and I'll be on my way."

"I'll have a list of possible lodging and your bill when you come down."

She could hear the relief in his voice and wondered if he had thought she would sneak off in the night. Truth be told, she'd considered the idea but only for a moment, for she didn't know where to begin looking for a place to stay. The man had probably slept with an ear toward the door in case she attempted to slip out.

"No doubt he's as tired as I am." She shoved her hairbrush and the few remaining items into the bag. After a final glance around the room, she headed downstairs. She'd not miss this place.

With his hands folded and a halfhearted smile on his lips, the clerk stood waiting for her at the counter. He unfolded his hands as she drew near and slid her bill across the scarred wood. She placed her valise on the floor and opened her purse. After paying the bill, she'd have barely enough for a small breakfast.

The clerk snatched the money from her hand as though he feared she might change her mind and return the cash to her handbag. He quickly slipped it into a drawer and then handed her a paper. He pointed to several names at the top of the sheet. "These here are some folks I know who live in Packingtown out behind the stockyards and meat-packing plants. They might be willing to let you stay a few days until you can find work." He straightened his shoulders and nodded toward the list. "The rest of them places lend a hand to immigrants and folks who ain't been able to find work. None of 'em is much to speak of 'cept maybe Hull House, but something is better than nothing."

After reviewing the list, she asked for directions to one of the places he'd called a settlement house. She waited while the clerk sketched a scanty map on the back of the paper. Though a settlement house sounded most unpleasant, living with strangers in a hovel behind the meat-packing plants held absolutely no appeal. The stench from the streets outside the hotel would be nothing compared to the choking smells of the stockyards and slaughterhouses.

Charlotte absolutely couldn't go to Hull House, for she had met Jane Addams on one of the woman's trips to London two years ago. During her visit, Charlotte had been among a group of four women who had discussed Miss Addams's ideas for working with the immigrants and the impoverished. Truth be told, Charlotte hadn't actually contributed to the conversation. She'd listened but had found the entire topic rather boring. Though she doubted Miss Addams would remember her, she dared not take the chance.

Map in hand, she picked up her valise and headed toward the door. "Thank you for your kindness."

"You be careful out there, miss. Wouldn't want nothing bad happening to you."

Charlotte nodded and hoped she could follow the directions. The man's warning sounded ominous, so she looked up and down the street before starting off, though she didn't know how she could possibly protect herself. The area surrounding this hotel was seedy at best, but she now wondered if she was off to seek housing in an even more frightful area of the city.

Her feet had begun to ache by the time she made the final turn onto Ashland Street. Fortunately, the map had taken her to an area lined with neat cottages, two-story frame houses, and well-manicured yards. She checked the house number and hoped the clerk hadn't given her an incorrect address. The neighborhood appeared to be one for private homes rather than for a settlement house.

She tapped on the front door. Several minutes passed before a tiny woman with gray hair fashioned in a tight knot appeared and greeted her. Not certain whether she'd actually arrived in the right location, Charlotte pointed to the paper. "I've been told this is a settlement house where I may receive room and board free of charge."

The woman stared at her with judicious blue eyes. "That's not entirely true, my dear, but do come in and we'll talk." She pointed to the corner. "You may place your bag over there."

Charlotte did as instructed and then followed the woman into the parlor. The furniture was worn, but the house was tidy and clean. Charlotte doubted that she could find a speck of dust anywhere.

The older lady pointed to the divan. "Have a seat and I'll explain the rules."

"Rules?"

The woman gave an emphatic nod. "I'm Mrs. Priddle, the owner of this house. When my husband, Charles, died over ten years ago, I decided to lend a helping hand to women and children in need. This is not, however, a place where you will receive free room and board." Mrs. Priddle settled back in her chair. "I'm a staunch believer in helping those who are also willing to help themselves."

This wasn't what Charlotte had envisioned. She wanted to be assigned a room where she could hide away until she decided what to do about her future. A place where she'd be left to herself and her meals would be delivered twice daily. "But I don't have any money to pay. That's why I've come here."

Mrs. Priddle nodded. "I suspected as much. Those with money don't arrive on my doorstep. Tell me about yourself. Let's begin with your name; then you can tell me a bit about your abilities."

"I am La—Charlotte Spencer. My abilities? Well, I can embroider and needlepoint fairly well. I play the piano and can sing, though my music teacher wasn't overly impressed with my voice." She looked heavenward. "Of course, I can read and write."

"Cleaning? Gardening? Cooking? Laundry? Do you have ability in any of those areas?"

Charlotte slowly shook her head. "I'm afraid not."

"You are obviously from England, Miss Spencer. From what you have told me and my own observations, I am guessing that you have led a privileged life. That, of course, is none of my business. There is no requirement to reveal your personal history, but if we both agree that you will live here, I'll need your assurance that the police will not come knocking on my door to locate you."

Charlotte considered whether Olivia or her parents might send the authorities to find her, but quickly dismissed the notion. She'd been gone from Pullman for seven months. If people had been looking for her, they would have ceased their search long ago. Unless Olivia had contacted her parents while they were visiting in Pullman, they'd have no idea Charlotte had ever set foot in this country.

"What are your rules, Mrs. Priddle?"

The older woman smiled, and the wrinkles deepened around her eyes. "I was coming to that. First, residents of Priddle House must earn their keep, either by performing the tasks I mentioned earlier or by working outside the home and contributing their earnings to aid in the maintenance of the house. Second, you are responsible for the upkeep on your own clothing, unless you prefer to pay one of the other Priddle House residents to perform such duties. Third, since you will share your room with others, you are expected to be courteous and neat. Fourth, you must attend the daily Bible studies, one at noon and one in the evening. If you work outside the house, you attend only the evening session. If you work in the house, you have the privilege of attending both."

Charlotte wasn't certain she considered attending two Bible studies each day a privilege, but she wouldn't argue that point with Mrs. Priddle. And she didn't know what work she could perform that would qualify her for admittance.

"Well, Miss Spencer, now that you've heard my rules, do you wish to move in to Priddle House?"

"I would very much like to remain here, and I can assure you that the police will not come looking for me." Charlotte folded her hands in her lap. "I fear I have little to offer in the way of domestic assistance. I've never been employed."

"Tut, tut. We can take care of that as long as you're a willing worker. Nothing I appreciate more than a willing worker, Miss Spencer." The older woman squared her shoulders. "And I believe I have the perfect solution for you. Several of my educated ladies such as you have gone to work at the dry goods stores on State Street. Have you heard of Marshall Field and Company, Miss Spencer?"

"Yes, I'm somewhat familiar with the store you're referring to, but I doubt . . ."

The knot of hair perched atop Mrs. Priddle's head wobbled precariously as she shook her head. "No room for doubts. Trust me. I'll have you a position in no time."

"But I don't—"

The clock on the mantel began to chime, and Mrs. Priddle held her index finger in the air. "Come along. It's time for Bible study. We meet in the dining room before we eat our dinner."

Charlotte silently followed along. She wasn't interested in the Bible study, but she certainly wanted the dinner that would follow. She hadn't eaten since last night, and her stomach had been growling in protest for the past half hour.

Mrs. Priddle waved her arm in a wide arc. Apparently the ladies weren't arriving quickly enough. Charlotte watched as six ladies scurried into the room and took their places at the table. One carried a toddler on her hip. All of them offered nervous smiles, as though they were uncomfortable at the sight of a newcomer.

"Ladies, this is our new resident, Miss Charlotte Spencer." Mrs. Priddle nodded toward the woman holding her child. "You'll be sharing a room with Ruth, Sadie, and Fiona." She tipped her head slightly. "Sadie is Ruth's daughter. Fiona is at school; you'll meet her later this afternoon. I'm sure you'll find her a delight." Mrs. Priddle completed the introductions and then opened her Bible. The others followed her lead. Charlotte glanced around the table and wondered what these women would think of her when they discovered she didn't own a Bible. That hadn't been among Mrs. Priddle's rules, yet she wondered if she'd be ousted even before she'd unpacked her few belongings.

The Bible study went on longer than Charlotte had hoped, but the hearty meal served afterward was worth the wait. After saying grace—the third prayer since sitting down at the table— Mrs. Priddle announced they would be having beef stew. Charlotte decided the dish would have been more aptly described as vegetable stew, for she discovered only one small piece of meat in her two servings. Still the flavor was good. Several of the women viewed her with wide-eyed stares when she had consumed a second helping of the hearty stew, but she'd been hungry enough not to care. And the biscuits were as light and fluffy as the ones Olivia used to make on Sunday mornings.

Thoughts of Olivia vanished when Mrs. Priddle tapped her arm. "If you've eaten your fill, I'll show you to your room. You can unpack and get settled."

Charlotte wiped her mouth, nodded to the ladies, and followed Mrs. Priddle to the entry hall, where she retrieved her valise. With her stomach full, she decided a nap would do nicely. When they reached the top of the stairs, Mrs. Priddle entered the second door on the right, which opened into a bright cheery room with cotton lace curtains at the window and more furniture than Charlotte had ever seen in one room. There were two full-size beds, a child's iron bed, two chiffoniers, a wardrobe, and a trunk at the foot of each bed. Very little of the threadbare carpet could be seen, for the overabundance of mismatched furniture.

"Which bed will be mine?"

Mrs. Priddle pointed to the bed on Charlotte's right. "You'll share this bed with Fiona."

Charlotte gulped. "Share?"

Mrs. Priddle didn't seem to notice Charlotte's distress. "We attempt to place no more than two in a bed, but it's sometimes necessary to increase to three." She smiled and glanced at Charlotte. "But never more than three. You may hang your dresses, skirts, and shirtwaists in the wardrobe. The two top drawers of the oak chiffonier are assigned to you. Make certain all your belongings are placed inside the drawers each morning before you come downstairs for breakfast. I encourage tidiness throughout the house."

Charlotte placed her valise atop one of the trunks. She hadn't planned on having to share a bed. Moreover, she thought the idea rather abhorrent. Possibly some other arrangement could be made. "Perhaps Fiona could change beds and sleep with Ruth. I'm unaccustomed to sleeping with another person, and I fear my tossing about will keep the girl awake. I don't want her falling asleep during her school lessons on my account."

Mrs. Priddle chuckled. "You need not worry about Fiona. The girl has had any number of residents share this room with her. She sleeps through most anything—even young Sadie's crying."

In her worry over Fiona, Charlotte hadn't considered the wails of a baby that might occur during the nighttime hours. Listening to Morgan's cries had nearly caused her to come undone. How would she be able to tolerate listening to someone else's child?

Mrs. Priddle patted her shoulder. "Don't fret. You'll become accustomed to the nighttime noises. Soon you'll be able to sleep through most anything, just like the rest of us."

Though she wanted to disagree, Charlotte remained silent. Obviously nothing she said would change Mrs. Priddle's decision. She unlatched the hasp on her valise and gazed longingly at the bed. The moment her clothes were hung in the wardrobe, she would enjoy a nice long nap. She might not sleep tonight, but at least she would get some rest this afternoon.

With purpose in her step, Mrs. Priddle returned to the hallway. "Once you've unpacked, do come downstairs. Until we locate a position for you in town, you can help Nettie in the kitchen. She can always use some extra hands." Without a backward glance, she disappeared.

Charlotte clenched her jaw. Hadn't Mrs. Priddle heard her say she didn't know the first thing about cooking or cleaning? More important, she didn't want to learn any of those tasks. Nothing in her longed to prepare food, wash dishes, or make beds. She found the mere thought of those chores most distasteful. Though she considered languishing over the process of unpacking, Ruth's arrival with baby Sadie quickly changed her mind. It was apparent there would be no privacy in this house.

CHAPTER FIVE

Chicago, Illinois
March 9, 1893

For an instant, Charlotte thought she might suffocate. She clasped a hand to her chest, unable to believe Mrs. Priddle's announcement. She forced herself to inhale a deep breath. She'd been here only three days, and now Mrs. Priddle expected her to begin work at Marshall Field's department store. She had hoped the matriarch of Priddle House would find some sort of less-taxing work for her. Charlotte had suggested the possibility of teaching one or two piano lessons each week. But her suggestion had been dismissed when the older woman pointed out they lacked a piano and the income from such lessons would be minimal. She'd waved a dismissive hand and declared a position in town would be best. And now Mrs. Priddle's expectations had been fulfilled. A job had become available this very day.

"Are you certain?" Charlotte croaked.

"Indeed, my dear. Answered prayer; that's what it is. The Lord knows we need additional funds, and He's sent you to fulfill that need. The money you'll be contributing is going to help immensely." Mrs. Priddle chirped about the room with a dustrag in one hand and a broom in the other.

Charlotte didn't want to ruin Mrs. Priddle's moment of joy, but the woman's announcement hadn't filled her with the same emotion. Instead, a quiet desperation wrapped around her like a heavy shroud. She stepped closer and touched Mrs. Priddle's thin arm. "I'm not certain you should be counting upon a paycheck just yet. Won't it be necessary for me to interview for the position?"

Mrs. Priddle flipped her feather duster in the air. "An educated young woman such as you will have no problem with an interview. Mr. Field will be pleased to count you a member of his staff." She ran the dustcloth across the oak mantel. "I told you the store gives preference to women who live here. We'll all be praying for you, as well."

How could Charlotte argue with those observations and comments? "There is one final problem, Mrs. Priddle."

The woman turned from her dusting. "And what would that be, my dear?"

"I don't have the proper clothing. I believe the ladies who work in the department store wear dark skirts and shirtwaists or simple dresses or suits. What few dresses I have would be totally inappropriate."

After replacing the two matching candlesticks to the mantel, Mrs. Priddle waved Charlotte toward a hideaway beneath the stairs. "We have what I refer to as our community closet. Clothes that have been donated for circumstances such as this."

Mrs. Priddle opened the door. Clothing of all sorts and sizes hung from a pole that had been installed down the length of the expanse. The gray-haired woman pushed aside several items and then removed a gored brown skirt made of panama cloth and a white waist of corded madras. The detachable collar was topped by a small lace tie. She held the items in front of Charlotte. "These will be perfect. And I believe they'll fit just right. Go upstairs and try them while I see what else I can find."

Charlotte didn't argue, for the woman had already buried herself back inside the closet. She trudged up the steps and did as she was told. The clothes were common—more common than anything she had ever worn. The skirt was large around her waist. For a moment that surprised her, but she had lost considerable weight since departing Pullman. Now she would fit into all those beautiful dresses she'd left with Olivia. She removed the brown skirt and thought of her cashmere and lace gowns with a twinge of regret.

She carried the skirt across her arm and returned downstairs. "The skirt is too large, but the waist fits."

Mrs. Priddle poked her head from between several dresses. "Ruth can alter the skirt. I found several more for you to try. Thank the good Lord for donations. Just think where we'd be if we didn't have these clothes."

Charlotte knew exactly where they'd be. She could remain within the confines of the house, avoiding work at the department store. Clothes in hand, she marched upstairs, remaining there for the rest of the day, except for supper and Bible study, of course.

Morning arrived all too soon, and Charlotte hadn't slept

well. Sadie had cried a great deal, Fiona's sleep had been restless, and Charlotte's personal unhappiness had contributed to her lack of sleep. She reluctantly donned the white shirtwaist and brown skirt. Fiona declared her beautiful, but Charlotte knew better. She looked like the other female salesclerks she'd observed. Granted, men occupied more of the sales positions, but women were beginning to take their place behind the counters of Chicago's many department and dry goods stores.

Mrs. Priddle and the other ladies were already at the breakfast table when she arrived in the dining room. They smiled at her with an expectancy that was disconcerting—as though their very welfare depended upon her. In a small way, she supposed it did. A rather formidable thought, since no one had ever depended upon her before. Except for her infant son, Morgan. And she'd certainly let him down. These ladies would soon learn that she didn't handle responsibility well.

Before she departed, Mrs. Priddle and the ladies gathered in a circle and prayed for her. Charlotte's silent prayer was in direct opposition. She expected God would listen to Mrs. Priddle. She was, after all, the epitome of that perfect woman they'd been reading about in Proverbs, chapter thirty-one. Charlotte wished they'd soon complete that particular chapter, for she'd not be planting a vineyard, weaving cloth, or receiving respect from her family. The entire topic caused her extreme discomfort. The only good thing about going to work would be her escape from the requisite noonday Bible class.

After finishing her breakfast, she departed with written directions tucked in her skirt pocket. Mrs. Priddle had suggested a pair of more serviceable shoes, but Charlotte had insisted upon wearing a pair of her own. Four long blocks from home, she wished she had taken the older woman's advice. No doubt she would have several blisters before arriving at her destination. Charlotte stopped at the corner and withdrew the directions from her pocket. From all appearances, she'd traversed less than half the distance. If she'd had a few more coins, she'd hail a carriage.

When she finally reached the corner of Washington and State streets, she had been walking for at least half an hour. Did Mrs. Priddle truly expect her to do this every day? Surely the older woman didn't want her to brave this distance in the rain or cold weather. Finally Charlotte walked through the front doors of the familiar department store, and one of the many greeters stationed inside immediately approached to assist her.

"I'm here to apply for a job."

The man offered a warm smile and quietly informed her to take the elevator to the third floor. "Turn right. Midway down the hall you'll see a door with the word *OFFICE* stenciled in gold-leaf letters. You may enter without knocking."

Charlotte thanked him and walked to the elevators. Once outside the office door, she waited, gathering her courage. She wanted to turn and run. Several minutes passed before she forced herself to turn the knob and walk inside the room.

A rather austere-looking man, appearing to be nearly as old as her father, looked up. "May I help you?"

"I've come to apply for a position as a salesclerk. Mrs. Priddle said I should mention she sent me."

The man's features softened a bit. "How is Mrs. Priddle?"

Charlotte took a step closer. The name Charles Sturgeon was engraved on a silver nameplate on the man's desk. "She's doing very well. Thank you for inquiring."

"Name?"

"What? Oh, Charlotte Spencer. I must warn you I have no sales experience or any other work experience. I've never been employed."

He traced a finger across his mustache. "We train our staff, Miss Spencer." He nodded toward a chair. "Do take a seat."

While he pulled several pages from his desk, she followed his instruction and sat down.

"I assume you can both read and write." He didn't wait for an answer before pushing the papers across the top of his desk. "Fill these out. I'll return shortly."

Charlotte worked her way through the questions, though she wasn't completely truthful. She certainly didn't intend to list her parents' names on the application as next of kin. Instead, she scribbled the word *deceased* and inserted Mrs. Priddle's name as the person to contact in case of emergency.

She'd completed the forms and had waited only a few minutes when Mr. Sturgeon returned with a tall, thin woman in tow. "Miss Spencer, this is Mrs. Jenkins. She is the supervisor in ladies' accessories. We currently have an opening in her department. You'll find Mrs. Jenkins can answer any questions you may have regarding your employment. She will also take charge of your training."

The woman appeared pleased by Mr. Sturgeon's remark.

"Come along, Miss Spencer. We'll go into the department office, and I'll explain your hours of work, your pay, and tell you what is expected of employees working in Mr. Field's establishment."

They walked down the hallway for a short distance, made a left turn, and entered another office, where Mrs. Jenkins told

Charlotte that she would begin her working career this very day and would be scheduled to work four days per week. "If you do well, we will increase your schedule to six days per week."

Mrs. Jenkins didn't realize that increased work hours wouldn't act as an incentive for Charlotte to perform well. "What time do I report to work, Mrs. Jenkins?" Charlotte longed to hear that she'd work only four or five hours per day.

"You will be working from nine o'clock each morning until six o'clock in the evening, with a half hour for your lunch. There is an employee cafeteria where you may purchase your meals at a discount, though you are not required to eat there. There is a music room and gymnasium for the use of all employees, and Mr. Field also grants generous vacations to his employees." She sat a bit straighter as she mentioned the added benefits. "Mr. Field is a forward-thinking man who wants to provide his employees with every opportunity to strengthen both body and mind."

Charlotte had heard those same comments about George Pullman when she'd lived in his so-called utopia. Apparently wealthy capitalists enjoyed the idea of being considered progressive. "Other than the benefits you've mentioned, I've not been told what my pay will be, Mrs. Jenkins."

The older woman shifted in her chair. Questions regarding pay seemed to cause her discomfort. "As a trainee working four days per week, you will receive five dollars. Please don't advise the other trainees, as they are paid one dollar less. Mr. Field pays a dollar extra to Mrs. Priddle's girls."

So that's how she would now be known: one of Mrs. Priddle's girls. Indeed, her life had taken a dramatic change over the past year.

Mrs. Jenkins stood. "I believe now we're ready for a tour of the building."

Charlotte did her best to appear impressed, nodding and smiling when Mrs. Jenkins paused at each feature. Not that the store wasn't impressive, but she had whiled away endless hours in Mr. Field's emporium during those first few months after fleeing Pullman. She'd consumed luncheon in the tearoom, rested in the lounges, read magazines in the library, and visited the writing room and the parlor. Today she was taken for her first visit to the nursery, as well as the meeting rooms provided for women's organizations. Mr. Field even offered stenographic service, telegraph and telephone offices, and a checkroom for coats. Nothing had escaped the capitalist's vision for keeping customers within the confines of his vast domain. He had combined the beauty of frescoed ceilings, monoliths, and splashing fountains with every possible convenience. Wealthy women could occupy their entire day with shopping, meeting friends for tea, attending meetings, and reading magazines. Apparently many of them did.

As they traversed the store, Mrs. Jenkins brought up Henry Selfridge, the head of retail. "You may hear a few of the employees refer to him as 'Mile-A-Minute Harry.' Though I don't approve, the moniker suits. He bustles through the store at an unbelievable pace at least a dozen times a day. You won't fail to notice him." She lowered her voice. "He's the one who developed the concept of our Budget Floor in the basement of the store." Her admiration of his marketing genius was obvious. Along with the wire bustles, pug-dog doorstops, oriental rugs, and fur-lined cloaks, Mrs. Jenkins didn't fail to mention the store's recent expansion, the twenty-three large elevators, twelve separate entrances, and the newfangled revolving doors. There was little doubt the female supervisor held Mr. Field and Mr. Selfridge in high esteem.

"And here we are back in accessories. You will be working the glove counter, Miss Spencer. Be sure to keep your counter well polished. Mr. Selfridge leaves his initials on any counter bearing dust." Mrs. Jenkins motioned a young lady forward. "Miss Lathrop, this is Miss Spencer. For the next several weeks, she will be working the glove counter on Monday, Wednesday, Friday, and Saturday. I'll be here at the counter with her throughout the day. You may return to handbags."

Miss Lathrop didn't speak to Charlotte and barely acknowledged Mrs. Jenkins's instructions. After a tight-lipped glare in Charlotte's direction, she turned on her heel and marched toward her assigned section. Charlotte followed Mrs. Jenkins behind the counter. "Miss Lathrop appeared unhappy. I'm willing to work elsewhere in the store."

"This isn't Miss Lathrop's station, although I know she hoped to make it her own. She wanted to be permanently assigned to gloves, but she isn't meeting expectations." Mrs. Jenkins reached beneath the counter and rearranged several pairs of black kid gloves. "Miss Lathrop is one of those employees who hasn't quite grasped Mr. Field's motto."

"Motto? I don't believe Mr. Sturgeon mentioned a motto."

Mrs. Jenkins beamed. "'The customer is always right.' In other words, give the lady what she wants."

"And the gentleman, also?"

Mrs. Jenkins frowned and wiped an imaginary speck of dust from the countertop. "Of course we want our gentleman shoppers to be treated with the same dignity and satisfaction, but you'll quickly discover the retail store caters to women. Men seem more comfortable in our wholesale store."

"I'll do my best to remember Mr. Field's motto." Charlotte decided Mrs. Jenkins took her work much too seriously.

"Ah, and speaking of Mr. Field, he's approaching our counter now. His daily tour of the building is more deliberate than Mr. Selfridge's hurried circuit." The supervisor tipped her head closer. "Mr. Field wants to be assured his customers receive the utmost care and courtesy while shopping. Each woman should consider shopping in his store an *experience*."

Charlotte forced a smile. "I'll keep that in mind, also."

Mrs. Jenkins squared her shoulders and stood at attention as Mr. Field stepped to the counter. "No customers this morning, Mrs. Jenkins?"

"I'm certain we'll have more than our share in short order, Mr. Field."

Mrs. Jenkins sounded apologetic, as though it were her fault a host of women weren't thronged around the counter begging to purchase a pair of gloves.

Mr. Field appraised Charlotte with his steel gray eyes. "And who is this young woman? I don't believe we've met."

The store's owner was an impressive man—trim, with close-cut, chalk white hair, a full mustache, and dressed in an elegant hand-tailored suit. He reminded Charlotte of a Continental diplomat rather than a merchant in this booming city.

In her attempt to impress the man, Mrs. Jenkins tripped over her words and completely forgot Charlotte's name. A look of utter desperation shone in her eyes, and Charlotte instantly took pity upon her.

"Good morning, Mr. Field. I am Charlotte Spencer, one of

Mrs. Priddle's girls. Mrs. Jenkins has been kind enough to accept me as a suitable candidate for employment in the glove department. I am looking forward to her excellent training. She's already informed me of your motto."

He beamed at Mrs. Jenkins. "Excellent! I can always depend upon Mrs. Jenkins to offer our employees fine training. There were those who questioned my wisdom when I decided to promote a woman into a supervisory position." He glanced toward a wealthy customer standing near a counter filled with detachable lace collars and cuffs. "If you ladies will excuse me, I believe I see a customer in need of assistance."

The moment Mr. Field turned away, Mrs. Jenkins visibly wilted. "Thank you for coming to my aid, Miss Spencer. Whenever Mr. Field appears, I become tongue-tied. Thankfully, Mr. Selfridge interviewed me for the supervisor position, or I would never have been considered." She led Charlotte to the end of the counter and lifted several boxes of gloves atop it. "I do hope you won't repeat any of this to the other clerks."

Charlotte shook her head. "I wouldn't consider such a thing."

"Good. Now then, let's begin. I'm going to show you the necessary steps for pricing gloves."

By day's end Charlotte was uncertain if she would make it home. Earlier in the day she had removed her stockings in the female employees' rest room and had located several blisters on each foot. And standing throughout the remainder of the afternoon hadn't helped. Amidst the throng of other employees, she hobbled out the front door. She'd arrived on the corner of State Street and Washington when someone grasped her elbow.

"Use this money to take a carriage, Miss Spencer." Mrs. Jenkins pressed several coins into Charlotte's hand before proceeding down the avenue, head high and the feather on her hat waving in the late afternoon breeze.

CHAPTER SIX

Pullman, Illinois
Thursday, March 9, 1893

Fred arrived at the train depot several minutes early and sat down on the same bench he and Olivia had occupied the previous week. The exchange with his mother this morning had been brief. While she prepared his breakfast, he had explained the reason for his trip to Chicago. He had considered discussing the glass-etching business with her days ago, but he knew his mother would fret.

After seeing the concern in her eyes this morning, he knew he'd made the correct decision. He had carefully explained that his only interest was to promote Bill and his abilities, but she didn't appear convinced. One day they might be forced to move from Pullman, and he wondered how his mother would react. Minutes later, the door to the depot swung open, and thoughts of his mother's fears vanished from his mind.

Bill ambled toward him with a broad grin and his sketches tucked under one arm. His hair was slicked down, and he wore his Sunday suit. Obviously he hoped to make a good impression. Fred wondered if he should have done the same. He didn't know what time they would return to Pullman or if he would have sufficient time to go change before work, so he'd worn his work clothes. They were clean, but that's the best he could say about them.

Fred noted the hesitation in Bill's eyes and quickly explained his choice of attire. Bill immediately relaxed—until they reached Chicago. As they stepped off the train, his shoulders stiffened. Fred hoped Bill would regain a sense of calm once they arrived at their destination. With a nod of his head, he directed Bill toward the front doors of the train station, hailed a cab, and gave the driver an address on South Water Street.

"Here we are," Fred announced as they stepped down from the cab. He gave Bill an encouraging pat on the shoulder. "Shall we go in?"

Bill grasped him by the arm. Fear shone in his eyes. "I can't remember the man's name."

Fred laughed and pointed to the signage on the brick building. "Lockabee. Mr. Jacob Lockabee." He looked into Bill's eyes. "There's no reason to be frightened. He'll be fortunate to have someone with your talent. Now come along and let's see what's in your future."

The ringing of a small bell over the front door announced their arrival at Lockabee's Design and Glass Etching Shop.

"Be with you in a minute." A raspy, distant voice came from somewhere at the rear of the building.

Fred motioned toward the far side of the room, and the two men sat down on a wobbly bench beneath the front window and waited for the owner to appear.

Bill hunched forward. "Hope it doesn't take him too long. I don't want you to be late getting to work."

"I have plenty of time." Fred slapped the younger man on the back. "Remember, there's no need to be nervous."

They both looked up as a stoop-shouldered man with white hair and glasses entered the room. He glanced back and forth. "Gentlemen? How can I help you?"

Fred stood and extended his hand. "Mr. Lockabee, my name is Fred DeVault and this is Bill Orland. We live in Pullman. I believe you know my supervisor in the electroplating department, Lawrence Godfrey."

Mr. Lockabee pushed his glasses up on his nose. "Ah yes. You must be the fellow he mentioned. So you're interested in coming to work for me?"

"Not me. I'm unable to move from Pullman at the present time. That's why I've brought Mr. Orland." The two men nodded at each other. "Bill's an excellent artist. His work lends itself to glass etching better than any work I've seen in years. He's much—"

Mr. Lockabee waved toward the folder tucked beneath Bill's arm. "That your work?"

Bill placed the folder on the counter. "Yes, sir."

"Well, let's take a look. No need talking. I find a man's work speaks for itself." Mr. Lockabee opened the folder and examined the first drawing. "Uh-huh." He methodically worked his way through the sketches, occasionally glancing at Bill as he turned a page. When he finished, he closed the folder and leaned on the countertop. "You've got a lot of talent. I could sure use someone like you. How much experience have you got with etching?"

Bill's smile vanished, and Fred was certain Bill was already counting himself out of the running. Fred tapped the folder. "He's done every one of those drawings without any formal training. I've been trying to teach him the glass-etching process, but it's been nearly impossible without having the equipment. I have years of experience, but I'm not working as an etcher at the present time, and there's no apprentice program in the Pullman etching division right now."

"Right now?" Mr. Lockabee arched his brows. "You think they're going to begin some hands-on training in the future?"

Fred shook his head. "Never can tell what will happen down the road."

Mr. Lockabee nodded. "I'd sure like to hire you, Bill. You've got some real talent, and Mr. Godfrey probably told you I've got some health problems. I need someone who can step in and help with the etching, too. My orders are running behind."

Bill picked up the folder, obviously preparing to depart, but Fred grasped his arm. "What if I come in with him for a few hours each day to help train him? Then would you consider hiring him?"

Mr. Lockabee scratched his head. "You'd be willing to do that?"

"I would. I can't promise to make it every day, but I'll do my best." Fred grinned and looked at Bill. "Besides, he's a bright man and needs the work. He has a wife and children to feed, and that alone is incentive enough to make him a good employee. It's not going to take him long to learn the trade. He's got the process in his head, just needs practice."

Mr. Lockabee settled on a stool behind the counter. "Then I suppose we better discuss your wages, Mr. Orland. That is, if you're willing to accept the job."

"Oh yes, sir—and call me Bill. I'm more than willing." He clasped Mr. Lockabee's hand and pumped it up and down.

Mr. Lockabee explained his former living quarters were located on the third floor of the building. "They're not bad. My wife and I lived up there for a few years before we bought our house. Of course the place needs a good cleaning, but maybe your wife would be willing to take on the task. If you want to find somewhere else to live, that's fine by me, too."

"Oh no! I mean, upstairs here would work out well for us. We've got a place over in Kensington we rent by the week. We could move in tomorrow."

Mr. Lockabee laughed. "Like I said, the place needs some cleaning. There's a grocery down the street where you can stock up on food and supplies." The old man turned toward Fred. "You think fifteen dollars a week and a place to live is fair until he's able to turn out etchings without supervision?"

Fred gulped. He wondered what the man would have offered him had he been applying for the position. "I'd say that's very fair, Mr. Lockabee."

"Good. And I'm going to pay for your train fare in and out of the city, too, Fred. Wish I could offer to pay you for your training time, but—"

"No need. I offered my services. Your willingness to pay for my train fare is more than generous."

Mr. Lockabee extended his hand to Bill and then to Fred. "You tell Lawrence I appreciate his sending you fellows my way. You're an answer to prayer, and that's a fact. My wife has been worrying herself sick. She'll sleep better tonight knowing I've found some help."

Fred wanted to inquire about the possibility that the business might be for sale, but he supposed it didn't matter. He wasn't in a position to make an offer, and Mr. Lockabee likely wanted to see how Bill worked out before he discussed future possibilities for the business. In any event, the wage was high enough that Bill might be able to save a portion of his wages and be prepared if the opportunity arose.

Their return to Pullman was filled with lively conversation. Bill's excitement was contagious and his appreciation obvious. Before they parted company at the train depot, Bill grasped Fred's hand. "I want you to know that I'm going to split my wages with you, Fred. I won't argue. Unless you agree, I'll go back and tell Mr. Lockabee I won't accept the position." Fred began to shake his head, but Bill stopped him. "I mean it, Fred. You'll either agree to accept payment, or I'll call a halt to the arrangement."

Fred chuckled. "Well, I don't want this opportunity to slip by. I'll agree that you can pay me while I train you. We'll argue about the amount later. Now I believe I'll head for home. I've got several hours before work. A short nap would be good. I'm sure you'll want to visit the training center and tell everyone your good news."

Bill enthusiastically agreed before the men shook hands and walked off in opposite directions.

Fred doubted he'd have time for a nap. His mother would want to hear every detail of the trip and receive assurance from him that nothing in their lives would be changing in the imminent future.

The moment he entered the house, she hurried downstairs. "I was changing the beds, but I've time to sit down for a visit before you go to work."

He nodded and continued toward the kitchen. "How about a piece of that apple cake and a cup of coffee?"

Once he'd taken a seat at the table, the questions came in rapid succession until finally he shook his head. "Can we stop long enough to eat our cake?"

She offered an apologetic smile and pulled up a chair. "Of course."

After only one bite of the cake, a knock sounded at the front door. Fred motioned for his mother to remain in her chair. "I'll go." He went down the hallway and opened the front door.

"Olivia! What are you doing here?" His abrupt question startled her, and she took a backward step. "I'm sorry. Do come in. I wasn't expecting to see you."

She hesitated and then smiled as his mother scurried down the hall. She'd obviously heard the sound of Olivia's voice.

"Olivia! How good to see you. Step aside, Fred, and let her in the door."

He backed away as his mother took charge, ordering him to place Olivia's bag by the hall tree and embracing the young woman in a warm hug. Though he had anticipated Olivia would return within the next week, her arrival caught him off guard. He'd not yet decided upon a plan of action—how to ask the questions for which he needed direct answers. And he wasn't certain his armor had been tightened enough just yet.

"Come join us. We were having cake. Fred, scoot your chair down a bit so there's room for Olivia."

He moved the chair and Olivia sat. His mother cut another

piece of cake, and the three of them surrounded the table like a happy family.

His mother didn't waste any time. "Olivia, do tell us all about your journey. Fred said Mr. Howard accompanied you. That must have been a surprise. And I didn't think you'd be gone so long." She leaned closer. "Martha will be relieved to see you're back. She's been fretting over the wedding plans."

Olivia occasionally glanced in Fred's direction while she related that her training had been extended by Mr. Howard since she'd not studied the manual he'd given her.

"And what of Mr. Thornberg?" Fred asked.

"Once we boarded the train, Mr. Howard explained that Mr. Thornberg had taken ill. He'd sent word of his illness to Mr. Pullman, and Mr. Pullman directed Mr. Howard to supervise my training."

It seemed strange to Fred that Mr. Pullman would be involved in the decision to train one of the young female employees, and he wondered if Mr. Howard hadn't planned to conduct Olivia's training from the very beginning. If so, had Olivia known of the arrangement all along? Unless Olivia misspoke, there'd be no way to prove that. He hoped he was wrong, but he would be mindful.

Maybe a few properly phrased questions would get the answers he needed to hear. "Now that you've begun your training, Olivia, exactly what is it you're doing? I'm somewhat perplexed by why Mr. Howard believes you are the one person who can perform the requisite duties."

Olivia swallowed a bite of the apple cake. "I'm assessing methods to save money and find ways to better serve the passengers."

"Truly? Why doesn't the company simply ask the passengers if the services are adequate? Mr. Pullman has enough spotters riding the trains to keep the waiters and porters on their toes. Those poor men dare not make an error, I'm told."

Olivia shrugged and met his gaze. "I don't know anything about spotters. Mr. Howard didn't mention such a position. I can only tell you that Mr. Pullman wanted an assessment from a woman's perspective. He thought my work in the hotel would permit me to judge food preparation as well as other amenities provided on his coaches." She pointed her fork to the cake and turned toward Mrs. DeVault. "I believe this cake would be well received at the hotel if you'd be willing to share the recipe with me."

His mother beamed at the compliment and nodded her agreement. She patted Fred's hand. "Tell Olivia about Bill Orland's good news."

He tapped his finger across his lips. "I'm letting Bill and his wife have the pleasure of spreading the news—except to you, Mother."

Olivia arched her brows. "I'll look forward to hearing the news when it becomes common knowledge. How have you been, Fred?"

He dropped his gaze to the table. The warmth in her eyes made it difficult to concentrate. "Fine. A few more layoffs at the car works. Otherwise there's nothing to report."

His mother took a quick sip of her coffee. "Will you be required to make any more trips before the wedding, Olivia? Martha is in dire need of your help."

"I don't know. Mr. Howard said he would need to go over the notes I made and discuss them with Mr. Pullman. I did mention the wedding to Mr. Howard. I'm hopeful he'll have an answer by week's end." Olivia pushed her chair away from the table. "I had best be on my way. I'm quite weary from the trip and must unpack. I hope to spend a few minutes visiting with Chef René and then go to bed." She removed a small timepiece from her pocket and clicked the hasp. "And you must soon depart for work, Fred."

He watched as she closed the timepiece and returned it to her pocket. "I didn't know you owned a pocket watch."

"Samuel gave it to—" She stopped midsentence and locked gazes with Fred.

He broke eye contact and watched her shove the timepiece inside her pocket. *Samuel?* Olivia and Mr. Howard were now on a first-name basis? And he was giving her gifts? Fred's armor tightened.

"He said it was imperative I have a timepiece for my new position, so I may keep proper notes and be on time to meet my trains and to . . ." her voice drifted into a stammered silence.

"I see," Fred said with a brief nod. "If you'll excuse me, I must go upstairs and take care of something before I depart for work. I'm pleased you made it home safely, Olivia." He didn't wait for a response. Instead, he pushed away from the table and was down the hallway and up the stairs before his mother could object.

He remained in his room while his mother escorted Olivia to the door. Once the front door closed he hurried back down the stairs. His mother stood in front of the door with her arms folded across her waist and a frown on her face. She was unhappy with his manners. Fred passed by her and headed toward the kitchen.

His mother followed close on his heels. "There was no need for you to run upstairs. You could have given her an opportunity to explain."

Fred had hoped to pick up his belongings from the kitchen table and make a hasty exit out the rear door. "She did explain—didn't you hear? That fancy timepiece was a gift from *Samuel*." His voice cracked.

"Mr. Howard insisted she accept it," his mother defended.

"Did you not notice she slipped and called him by his given name? Tell me, have you ever heard *me* refer to any of my supervisors by their given names?"

"No, I haven't. But have they ever insisted you do so?" When he didn't respond, she shook her head. "Of course they haven't. But Mr. Howard has insisted that she refer to him as Samuel when they are alone."

Fred didn't doubt that Mr. Howard had made such a request. The man's behavior reinforced what Fred already believed: Samuel Howard had more than a passing interest in Olivia. What bothered him more was the ease with which she'd spoken Mr. Howard's given name. It had slipped over her tongue without any sign of hesitation.

His mother shot him a look of disapproval. "She assures me that she's done everything in her power to discourage Mr. Howard's advances and that she doesn't care for him in the least. She can't control his decisions. I fear you jump to conclusions because of what's occurred in the past. Go and invite her to join us for dinner after church on Sunday." His mother filled a basin with hot sudsy water and began to wash their coffee cups. "And if the Spirit moves you, you can apologize to her, too."

"I suppose I should try to get the issue resolved."

His mother wiped her hands on the frayed dishcloth. "Well, that sounds promising."

He chuckled and pointed toward the clock. "I'll stop and ask her on my way to work. If I leave now, I should have time."

His mother's smile was evidence he'd made her happy. He jogged down the front steps and wondered if his decision would please Olivia. After the way he'd rushed out of the kitchen only a short time ago, she might turn him down. He hoped she'd be at the hotel. Since she mentioned wanting to go to bed early, he wouldn't want to disturb her at home. The thought of stopping at the Barneses' house held little appeal, especially the possibility of coming face-to-face with Mr. Howard.

He lengthened his stride. If Olivia had already left the hotel, he'd ask Chef René to deliver his message. Feeling unexpectedly lighthearted, he rounded the corner and stopped. Olivia and Mr. Howard were strolling arm in arm toward the entrance of the Arcade. As they turned to enter the building, Olivia glanced in his direction. He noted her look of surprise before he turned and walked away. So much for her weariness and going to bed early.

March 23, 1893

Fred glanced at the clock tower as he walked between the iron gates leading into the car works. No need to hurry. He had at least twenty minutes before he must report to his electroplating job in the iron machine shops. Whistling a soft tune, he strode alongside the steel tracks that carried flatbeds of lumber and supplies, as well as the partially assembled railroad cars, into the Pullman Car Works. Once inside, the shells moved from one department to the next for further assembly. At one shop, electrical wiring; at another, mahogany woodwork or silver cuspidors; at another, the etched-glass windows, until finally the car rolled out of the building a completed and luxurious Pullman sleeper car.

The building stretched and yawned in a seemingly unending cavern that reverberated with the sounds of pounding machinery and shouting voices. Fred waved at several workers on his way through the bunk and sash division of the painting department. Odors of perspiration and varnish combined and filled the room with a scent all its own.

Drying racks held the doors, blinds, sashes, and bunks that daily arrived from the woodshop after having received an initial coat of stain. Tomorrow the pieces would have shellac or varnish applied and then be left to dry for an additional two to four days. When he neared the far drying racks, Fred stopped short. Angry voices rose above the din of the machinery.

There was no doubt that Mr. Vance had reached his boiling point. The shop supervisor's face had turned as red as a beet. "If you don't quit questioning my work assignments, you're going to find yourself looking for work elsewhere."

Mr. Vance's angry warning didn't deter Harlan Ladner, a long-time employee in the paint shop. Usually a quiet man, Harlan's outburst surprised Fred, and he edged behind one of the drying racks.

"What you're doing isn't fair. Since we're being paid by piecework rather than daily wages, two or three of us shouldn't always get the assignments that take the longest to complete. You give the jobs with a quick turnover to those same fellows every day. None of them been here near as long as us." Harlan waved toward a group of men a few feet away who were rubbing shellacked blinds with pulverized pumice stone and water.

Mr. Vance clenched his jaw. "Are you hard of hearing, Ladner? I said *I* decide who does what work around here."

Harlan remained undeterred. "We got families to feed just like them, but they take home a third more in wages because you give them the jobs that need fewer coats of paint or less sanding."

"*Fred!* What are you doing down here?" a voice hissed in his ear.

Fred jumped and turned like he'd been jabbed with a hot poker. *Mr. Howard!* He'd not heard him approach.

"Pa-passing through on my way upstairs," Fred stammered.

"You weren't passing through anywhere. You were standing in the shadows eavesdropping. What is it you find so interesting?" Mr. Howard's voice had escalated, and the tables turned. Instead of Fred listening to Mr. Vance argue with Harlan, the workers were now listening to Mr. Howard's invective. The company agent lifted his gaze toward the other men. "Get back to work! This doesn't concern you." The men instantly turned away.

Fred tightened his fingers around his lunch pail and felt the metal handle cutting into his palm. He shouldn't have stopped. "I'm going to be late for my shift if I don't get over to the elevator."

Mr. Howard grasped Fred's arm. "There's no reason for you to be in the paint department unless your supervisor sends you down here. Do I make myself understood?"

Fred nodded.

Mr. Howard released his arm with a thrust. "Get on upstairs and count yourself lucky I'm not reporting you to your supervisor."

Fred didn't know why he should count himself lucky; what was there to report? He'd not committed any offense. However, he'd not argue the point with Mr. Howard. The sounds of snapping belts and whirring machinery greeted him when he stepped off the elevator on the third floor. He didn't chance stopping until he arrived in the electroplating department.

Fred nodded to Mr. Godfrey on his way to the closet at the far end of the room. He hung his cap on one of the hooks and shoved his lunch pail onto the shelf. He made a mental note to advise Harlan Ladner about next Sunday's union meeting. Fred had never seen any of the men from the paint shop at their meetings. There was little doubt that the men performing piece-work had an additional set of unresolved issues.

Fred waited outside the gate early the next morning. He wouldn't attempt to walk through the paint department again today. He'd jotted down the union meeting details, and when Harlan approached, Fred pulled him aside and slipped the paper into his hand.

"I know you don't have time to talk, but this is about a union meeting. Read it and talk to some of the other men—just be certain you can trust them. See if they'd like to attend, too." Fred patted Harlan on the shoulder. "We'd like to see you there."

Harlan gave the paper a fleeting look before shoving it into his pocket. He didn't indicate whether he'd attend or not, but Fred had done what he could. Having men from the paint department who were dealing with unfair work assignments could only help to strengthen their cause—especially since there had been recent talk of switching all departments to the piecework method.

Amidst his mother's protests, Fred hurried her out of church immediately after the Sunday morning service. If he was going to arrive at the training center before the rest of the men, he didn't have time to wait until she completed her usual after-church visiting. She continued to object while they walked home, but he knew that in spite of her protests, she'd have his noonday meal on the table soon.

Long ago he had explained his Sunday afternoon meetings as nothing more than one way the men could come together and discuss ways to improve the training center and to help one another. She'd accepted his explanation without question, yet sometimes he wondered if she suspected there was more to them than that.

While his mother donned her apron, Fred raced upstairs and changed his clothes. As expected, his meal was waiting when he returned downstairs. He ate much too hastily to suit his mother, but she finally ceased her warnings.

"Just remember that if you end up with a stomachache, it's due to your poor eating habits and not my cooking," she said.

Fred grabbed his hat and walked down the hallway. "You are absolutely right. I won't place an ounce of blame on you," he called over his shoulder.

He was the first one to arrive at the building a short time later, but soon the training center filled with many men interested in bettering their working conditions at the car works. At two o'clock sharp, Fred shouted above the laughter and talking and called the group of men to order. Except for the sound of chairs scraping across the concrete floor, the noise subsided and the men turned their attention toward the front of the room. The turnout was better than expected. Fred was pleased to see that Harlan and several other new faces were among those in the crowd. He thought they were all from the paint department. He'd ask Harlan later. For now, he requested the men address their grievances.

Several men aired complaints regarding the recent hiring practices. Then a man sitting beside Harlan waved to be recognized. Fred nodded to him and he stood.

"If you think you got it bad now, just wait 'til you switch over to piecework." He looked around the crowd as he spoke. "I'm telling you, the supervisors play favoritism, and some of us can't make anywhere near the same wages we was getting on weekly wages. It's going to take a strike to settle what's going on inside the car works."

Fred didn't fail to note the looks of alarm from several quarters. Mr. Rose jumped up from his chair and lifted a fist overhead. "Don't go talking strike. It'll get us nowhere. We tried to get the company to make concessions back in 1886, and we got nothing to show for that one but more debt. A lot of you fellas wasn't around then, but let me tell you what happened: The company locked them iron gates and wouldn't even talk to us. Pullman and his board of directors was prepared to keep them gates locked instead of meeting even one of our demands." He looked around the crowd. "We was just like you fellas that are raring for a strike. But they knocked the wind out of our sails. When they finally unlocked the gates, we returned with the same work conditions, the same pay, and more debts. Took us a long time to dig outta that hole."

"One thing's certain, whatever we decide, we need to be united," Fred replied.

One of the more recent employees jumped to his feet. "We hear what you're saying about previous attempts to bargain, Mr. Rose, but there comes a time when we have to stand up for ourselves, too. The company has proved its loyalty is to the stockholders, not to the employees."

Fred permitted the men time to speak their minds, and though they'd not arrived at any decisions or remedies, the workers appeared thankful to have the opportunity to be heard. If not by company officials, at least by one another. He asked for volunteers to assist in the training center and was pleasantly surprised when several men agreed to lend their services several evenings a week. As had become their practice, they passed a hat to collect funds to help those who had recently been laid off and were struggling to make ends meet. Though the collections were never enough to meet the needs of all those affected, each family was thankful for help, no matter how small the gift.

Once the meeting dismissed, most of the men remained to visit for a few minutes. Fred cut through the crowd to shake hands with Harlan. He hoped to gain more information about piecework assignments in the paint department. "Thanks for coming, Harlan." Fred shook Harlan's hand. The man had a firm grip.

"Several of us wanted to see what you had in the way of organization, so we decided to check things out." Harlan grinned at the semicircle of men surrounding him.

Fred nodded toward the back of the room where a stranger stood in a far corner. "That one of your fellows, too? I've never seen him before."

Harlan turned his head and followed Fred's line of vision. "Nope. Never saw him before." He turned toward his fellow workers. "Any of you know who he is?"

Only one man nodded. "Ain't that Mr. Vance's cousin that he brought to the shop last week?"

The rest of the men narrowed their eyes and looked again. "Might be," one said. "Yep. I think it is. What's he doing here?

You think he's taking a job in the car works?" The question was posed to no one in particular.

"Naw. Didn't Mr. Vance say he lived back east and was here for a visit?"

"How would I know? Mr. Vance don't talk to me."

"Well, he don't talk to me neither except when I do something wrong. But I heard him talking to Mr. Howard when they was walking through the department."

Fred's stomach churned, and he grasped Harlan by the arm. "Who all did you tell about this meeting?"

"Just these men that are with me." Harlan glanced around the semicircle. "You fellows tell anyone else about this meeting?"

Fred saw that he'd likely offended several of the men with his question. "Sorry, men, but we can't be too careful. We take care to keep information about our meetings quiet, but word sometimes trickles back to management. We try to close any gaps as soon as possible. There have been too many men involved with union organization who have lost their jobs."

Panic shone in Harlan's eyes when he withdrew an empty hand from his jacket pocket. "I've lost the note you gave me. I had it right here in my pocket. I know I did." He tried the other pocket and then the pants pockets. "Maybe it's at the house."

"You think maybe you dropped it at work and Mr. Vance picked it up?" one of the men asked.

Harlan once again thrust his hand into his pocket, obviously hoping the note would magically reappear. "You think we'll all be fired come morning?" Dread laced Harlan's words.

Fred's earlier comment had caused a greater depth of alarm than he'd intended. "The young man may have simply happened by and stepped inside. I'm not certain when he first entered the meeting. I'm glad you fellows decided to attend. If anything comes up at work tomorrow morning, let me know."

Harlan glumly agreed. "My wife wanted me to stay home with the family this afternoon. Seems like I should have given in to her."

"Ain't nothing happened just yet, Harlan. Besides, we all know something has got to be done to get things changed around in our department."

The men continued talking, and by the time the workers from the paint shop departed for home, the panic had subsided and they were on a more even keel. Fred visited with several other groups, especially those charged with the benevolence fund. They had to decide how much each family would receive. He hoped there would be enough to go around.

When he finally closed and locked the door to the training center it was nearing five o'clock, and the sun was dropping into the western horizon. His mother had expected him an hour ago. He lengthened his stride while jumbled thoughts of the meeting invaded his mind. A branch cracked and he instinctively looked around, sucking in a breath of air. *Mr. Vance's cousin!* The young man was hiding in the shadows of the tree-lined street.

Fred considered calling out to him but immediately thought better of the idea. A confrontation would serve no purpose. Had Mr. Vance sent the young man to spy on them? Perhaps there was more need for worry than he'd expressed to the men.

He uttered a prayer for the men and their jobs—and one for himself. If problems arose, Fred could be the first one to lose his job. Mr. Vance's cousin didn't know Fred's name, but it wouldn't take long for Mr. Vance or Mr. Howard to figure out exactly who had been in charge of the meeting this afternoon.

CHAPTER EIGHT

Chicago, Illinois
April 10, 1893

Charlotte hadn't planned on the likes of young Fiona Murphy when she arrived at Priddle House. But then, she hadn't planned on sharing a bedroom or working at Marshall Field's retail store, either. At times she thought standing on her feet all day was somewhat easier than answering the ongoing questions of the ten-year-old girl who shared her bed each night. The moment she returned home from work, Fiona attached herself like an appendage—one that walked and talked and craved Charlotte's undivided attention.

Charlotte did her best to answer the girl's questions, though she'd quickly tired of repeating the same details of the retail store and its personnel. More times than she cared to remember, she'd described Joseph Anderson, a doorman at the Washington Street entrance who met the carriages of the wealthy women arriving each morning at Marshall Field's. Fiona didn't mind the nightly replication. The girl simply wanted to be noticed and, quite obviously, needed a mother's love.

During Bible study each evening, Fiona would plant herself beside Charlotte and share her Bible. Thankfully, Fiona knew the books of the Bible, for Mrs. Priddle expected each of them to follow along while she read the evening's Scripture. Had Charlotte been required to perform the task, she doubted there would be much time remaining for Bible study each night. Fiona had her own method for remembering the location of each book. Charlotte quickly decided learning Fiona's method would be more difficult than simply doing as Mrs. Priddle advised: begin with the first two and add two more each day.

Charlotte hadn't been diligent in her pursuit and thus far hadn't mastered the books of the Old Testament. While Fiona praised her progress each week, Mrs. Priddle wasn't nearly as impressed.

When they had completed their study for the evening, Charlotte was anxious to go upstairs and prepare for bed. Her feet were swollen and her back ached.

"Before we dismiss, I'd like to see how we're all doing memorizing our Bible verses and books of the Bible." She turned her bright blue eyes toward Ruth. "Why don't you begin, Ruth? Then you can take Sadie up to bed while the rest of us take our turns."

Though Mrs. Priddle's offer to Ruth was couched as a suggestion, they were all aware the proposal was actually a command. Charlotte had thought the method strangely familiar until she finally remembered it was the same approach her nursemaid had used when she was a young girl. Ruth complied with Mrs. Priddle's request, rattling off her verses one after another without a mistake. The moment she'd uttered the final word, she quickly retreated upstairs with Sadie riding on her hip. Ruth had memorized the names of the books of the Bible long ago, for she'd arrived at Priddle House while still pregnant with Sadie.

From time to time, Mrs. Priddle would surprise one of the ladies and have her recite a verse she'd learned weeks ago, a test to see if she still remembered. Charlotte shivered at the thought, but at the rate she was progressing, she need not worry overmuch. One by one, Mrs. Priddle listened to the verses and dismissed each lady in turn. Only Fiona and Charlotte now remained.

"You're next, Charlotte. Let me see. According to my calculations, you should have already memorized the names of all sixty-six books of the Bible, but as of last week you still hadn't mastered the Old Testament." Mrs. Priddle's Bible rested on her lap, her hand resting on the leather cover. "I hope to be pleasantly surprised this evening."

No doubt Mrs. Priddle would be surprised, albeit not pleasantly. Fiona offered an encouraging look. Charlotte stumbled along until Mrs. Priddle called a halt to the effort. "Fiona, I want you to work with Charlotte every evening once you've completed your school lessons. This is important, Charlotte. You'll be able to locate Scripture much more quickly once you've memorized the books of the Bible."

Fiona enthusiastically bobbed her head, but Charlotte silently groaned. Once Fiona completed her recitation, Mrs. Priddle dismissed the two of them with a caveat to study diligently. Fiona grasped Charlotte's hand and marched alongside her up the stairs. "This will be great fun. You can help me with my lessons, and I'll help you memorize."

"Indeed. Great fun." Charlotte dropped onto the side of the bed. "Your method doesn't work for me, Fiona."

Ruth lifted Sadie into her iron crib and then sat down beside Charlotte on the patchwork quilt. "I used music to help me learn the titles. Have you tried that?"

"No. Is there some special tune?" Charlotte was willing to try anything to avoid Fiona's memorization method.

Ruth shook her head. "No, just find any tune that works for you and sing." A blush colored her cheeks. "Sounds rather silly, doesn't it?"

"No. Your method might work. I used to play the piano, and I enjoy music. I'll try that. Thank you, Ruth."

Fiona jumped up from the small writing table, where she'd begun to write her spelling words. "Piano? You play the piano? Will you teach me? I've *always* wanted to learn to play the piano. Oh, please say you will." Delight shone in the girl's eyes.

"In order to teach you, we'd need a piano, Fiona. Otherwise, I'd be pleased to give you lessons. I'm terribly sorry to disappoint you."

Charlotte immediately mourned the refusal. Fiona didn't ask for much, and Charlotte would have enjoyed granting the girl's wish. Fiona had endured more difficulties than most people twice her age, and Charlotte marveled at her ability to maintain a cheerful outlook. At the age of five, the girl had suffered the death of her father, a drunk, Mrs. Priddle had said; then Fiona's mother had contracted tuberculosis. Had it not been for Mrs. Priddle's kindness, she'd be living in an orphanage. Though surprising to Charlotte, Fiona counted herself fortunate to be living here, attending school, and memorizing Bible verses.

"Maybe one day we'll have a piano and I can learn." Her soulful look disappeared almost as quickly as it had arrived.

While Fiona continued with her spelling lesson, Charlotte returned downstairs. With Mrs. Priddle's tin of glue, old pieces of wrapping paper, and a pair of scissors, Charlotte pieced together a long, thin piece of paper. Using a book edge, she drew narrow lines to resemble the piano keys. While leaving the white keys untouched, she carefully inked in the black keys of a piano keyboard. When she'd finished the project, she rolled it up and carried it upstairs. Fiona turned as Charlotte walked in the room.

"Lessons completed, Fiona?"

The girl bobbed her head. "Almost. Then we can begin thinking of a tune for you."

Charlotte unrolled the piece of paper across the bed and watched the excitement sparkle in Fiona's eyes. "A piano!"

"Well, not quite. We'll have to sing the notes instead of having the piano play them, but I thought I could teach you the keys so that when you're able to take lessons one day, you'll already know the keys and how to place your fingers."

Fiona knelt down at the side of the bed and perched her fingers over the make-believe keys. "Oh, Charlotte, thank you! You're the very best friend in the world. This is a wonderful present." Her eyes glistened as she looked up at Charlotte. "Come and see, Ruth."

Ruth stepped to the side of the bed and squeezed Charlotte's shoulder. "It is lovely, Fiona. I'm sure that one day you'll become a fine pianist."

Ruth leaned close to Charlotte's ear. "That was a lovely gesture. You're a kind person, Charlotte."

Charlotte winced at the praise. She was neither a kind person nor a good friend, and she'd prefer Ruth and Fiona not think of her as such. They'd expect her behavior to reflect those qualities in the future, and Charlotte was certain they'd be disappointed.

Wanting to divert attention away from herself, Charlotte pointed to the keys and began to explain the layout of the white keys and the black keys. "First you need to learn the letter names of the notes."

She knew Fiona would be a quick study. The girl memorized her weekly Bible verses in one sitting. They worked together, plotting out a tune for the books of the Bible while Charlotte named and hummed each note as she struck the key.

"Who taught you how to play the piano, Charlotte?"

"I had a tutor who lived at our home in London when I was a youngster. She taught me all of my school lessons, as well as piano and needlework." The girl attempted to besiege her with questions, but Charlotte pointed to the paper keyboard. "Roll up the paper. It's late and we'll not be able to get up in the morning."

Ruth had already gone to sleep by the time Fiona and Charlotte were preparing for bed. As Fiona snuggled beneath the covers a short time later, she rested her hand atop Charlotte's arm. "Thank you, Charlotte. I don't miss my mother quite so much with you around."

Fiona's sweet words were offered in love, yet they served to remind Charlotte of her own child. A reminder that she'd deserted little Morgan without as much as a backward glance. "Go to sleep, Fiona. Go to sleep."

Charlotte attempted to follow her own instruction to Fiona,

but sleep wouldn't come. When it finally arrived, her dreams were filled with images of Morgan and then of her own childhood in Lanshire Hall, with piano lessons and Ludie brushing her hair. And a baby crying. But the cries weren't from Morgan. Sadie had awakened and was crying for Ruth to feed her.

———————

The following Sunday, Charlotte removed a dark brown skirt from the wardrobe and placed it on the bed alongside one of her three shirtwaists. Thankfully, Ruth had offered to launder and press Charlotte's clothing in exchange for needlework lessons. Charlotte's evenings were consumed with piano, needlework, and singing the books of the Bible.

"Why don't you wear one of your pretty dresses to church, Charlotte?"

Fiona stood in front of the wardrobe, caressing a chiffon silk gown with lace insets and a hand-ruched bodice. The dress was an extravagant purchase she'd made at Marshall Field's while still living in style at the Palmer House months earlier. "It's not suitable for church. That gown is intended for more important occasions."

"What's more important than God?"

Charlotte grinned. "Well, nothing, really. I should have said that the dress is for more formal occasions, such as a party or dancing."

Fiona continued to cling to the silk skirt of the gown. "I think God likes pretty dresses, too. He won't care if you bought it for a party but decided to wear it to church instead."

Charlotte picked up the white shirtwaist. "This suits my life

97

right now, Fiona. Even if the dress were appropriate, I wouldn't wear it."

"Why? It's so pretty."

"Because it reminds me of the past and my life before I came here. Now stop asking questions and let's get dressed. Otherwise Mrs. Priddle will be thumping the broom handle on the ceiling, and we'll miss breakfast." Charlotte didn't give Fiona time to argue any further. She shoved her arms into the shirtwaist, fastened the row of buttons, and stepped into her chocolate brown skirt.

Church attendance was mandatory for the residents of Priddle House. Though Mrs. Priddle didn't specify which church the women should attend, she made certain they all warmed a pew on Sunday mornings. "We must replenish our hearts and our souls." Mrs. Priddle uttered the same statement every Sunday morning as they departed for church. The services were much different from what Charlotte had been accustomed to in London yet somewhat similar to the ones she'd attended in Pullman.

She hadn't listened to very many of those Sunday morning sermons in Pullman. Now, however, she clung to every word, for during Sunday dinner Mrs. Priddle enjoyed what she called a time of reflection and discussion. Charlotte called it a quiz. After dozing off during her initial visit to First Methodist Church, Charlotte now paid strict attention. She had quickly learned that missing one of Mrs. Priddle's discussion questions was met with the assignment of an additional chore, something Charlotte planned to avoid in the future. She'd been required to wash all the pots and pans for a full week, and her fingernails still suffered from the endeavor.

Fiona squeezed into the pew and sat down between Charlotte and Mrs. Priddle. The pianist struck the chords of the first hymn, and Fiona moved her fingers along the top of the pew in front of them, playing an imaginary keyboard. Surprisingly, Mrs. Priddle didn't object.

After the service Mrs. Priddle grasped Charlotte's arm and then motioned Fiona to walk on ahead. "If you like, I could ask the reverend if you could bring Fiona down here one evening a week and give her lessons on the piano. Do you think that would help?"

Charlotte pulled the older woman into a warm embrace. "Oh, Mrs. Priddle, would you? She wants to learn so much."

Mrs. Priddle grinned. "Well, she'll not produce any sound out of that piece of paper or the back of a church pew. I'll see what I can do, but don't say anything. We don't want to get her hopes up and then be disappointed."

"I promise I won't say a word. When will you ask him?"

"You're as impatient as a little girl." Mrs. Priddle glanced over her shoulder. "I'll go back and ask him now. Tell the rest of the ladies I'll be along shortly."

Charlotte hurried to join the others. She hoped Mrs. Priddle would return with good news and could hardly contain her excitement as she fell in stride alongside Fiona. This would be a good day!

CHAPTER NINE

Pullman, Illinois
April 22, 1893

Olivia wrapped a warm shawl over her flannel nightgown, shoved her feet into the worn slippers at her bedside, and padded to the window. She uttered a silent prayer, thankful to be back in her bedroom and not riding the rails, where her movements had been confined to the small bedchamber or narrow aisles. Not that the accommodations provided on the Pullman cars were lacking. Indeed, they were quite lovely, but after traversing the countryside for nearly two weeks, Olivia was luxuriating in the freedom of space that her rooms permitted. With a slight shiver, she traced her finger over the frosted ice crystals caused by last night's sudden dip in temperature. The sun would soon melt the crystallized design, and by midmorning the unexpected freeze would be all but forgotten. She pulled the shawl a bit higher around her neck.

Olivia leaned back and flexed her weary shoulders. She had worked late into the night stitching the final seed pearls to the train and hem of Martha's ivory wedding gown. Her effort was a special gift to Martha, who had become distraught after learning the seamstress at Dunbury's Dress Shop had contracted a severe case of pneumonia and wasn't expected back to work for at least another week.

In the morning's light, Olivia examined her handiwork. It had been tedious and exhausting, but it had been worth the effort. The gown was stunning. Yet by this time tomorrow, the wedding ceremony and reception would be a mere memory, and she could relax.

At the moment, though, there was little time to dwell on thoughts of tomorrow. Too many tasks awaited completion before she could depart for the church. With the help of both volunteer kitchen staff and friends, the largest room on the upper floor of Market Hall had been converted into a reception area, artistically arranged with flower-bedecked tables to seat the many wedding guests who would attend the brunch following the noon ceremony.

Pulling an old shirtwaist and skirt from the walnut wardrobe, Olivia quickly donned them. Chef René had offered to bake the wedding cake, but she'd kindly refused him. Cakes, especially those needing the decorative touches required on a wedding cake, were neither his specialty nor his favorite type of creation.

Although the doctor had declared the chef had made a return to full health, Olivia still worried he might suffer another relapse if he didn't get adequate rest. He had, however, surprised her by creating a magnificent ice carving for the center of the bride's table. Carefully stored in hay and hidden away at the icehouse near the Calumet River, the carving had thrilled

Olivia when he'd taken her to see it yesterday: a magnificent depiction of kissing lovebirds sitting atop a fluted heart.

He had declared the rendering an artistic expression of love. She had agreed. The carving *was* beautiful, but Olivia would have preferred a fluted heart *without* the kissing birds. Chef René had once professed he wasn't easily caught up by the trappings of weddings and love, but Olivia knew that wasn't entirely true, for his carving had captured the very essence of a young couple in love. She secretly wondered if he had ever longed for marriage and children.

She knew better than to ask. His personal life remained private. On several occasions she'd attempted to draw him into a discussion of his early years in France, but to no avail. Perhaps one day he would consider her a worthy confidante, but for today she must concentrate on the wedding.

After pinning her hair into place, Olivia descended the front stairs of the Barneses' residence. The move to the older couple's home had proved a good one for her, and she'd become quite fond of them—except when Mrs. Barnes took on the role of surrogate mother or matchmaker. Olivia's foot had barely landed on the bottom tread when she heard Mrs. Barnes approach from the kitchen.

There was a purposeful stride to the woman's step. Her graying chignon bounced in synchronized movement as she drew near. "Olivia! Don't you even consider leaving this house without a proper breakfast."

Olivia paused, surprised by Mrs. Barnes's commanding edict. Though her landlady issued advice from time to time, she was generally kind and soft-spoken, not given to issuing ultimatums, especially to a houseguest or boarder. Normally Olivia would have hearkened to such a strong admonition, but not this morning. Too many details required her attention.

Most important, the wedding cake awaited her final touches. Both the cake and ice carving would be delivered to the reception hall during the wedding ceremony. The mere thought made her uneasy. When she'd voiced her preference to oversee the entire process, Chef René had laughingly pointed out the impossibility of such a maneuver. "*Non!* You are a member of the wedding party. It is not possible."

She had grudgingly conceded that he was correct. And last evening had been filled with sewing on seed pearls rather than cake decorating.

Olivia turned toward the hall tree and stopped short. "Where is my coat?"

Mrs. Barnes appeared pleased with herself as she primly folded her arms across her chest. "I've put it away for safekeeping until after breakfast. You'll not have time to eat before the wedding, and I don't want you to faint as you walk down the aisle." She placed her palm against her own cheek. "Just think of the embarrassment if you should faint when you're standing in front of the wedding guests. Not to mention that you would ruin the ceremony! Martha and Albert would not be pleased."

Hopeful she could outwit the older woman, Olivia decided to take the offensive. "Being forced to rush around at the last minute is an even more likely cause of fainting. And I don't want you to be filled with self-recrimination because you forced me to use up precious time eating breakfast."

Mrs. Barnes was undeterred. "I'll take my chances. Come along." She tugged Olivia's arm.

No sense taking up more precious time arguing, Olivia

decided. She'd eat a few bites and be on her way. "Please return my coat to the hall tree. I don't want any further delays once I've completed my meal."

While Olivia hurried toward the kitchen and scooped a spoonful of scrambled eggs onto her plate, Mrs. Barnes remained behind. Olivia hoped the landlady was fulfilling her request. Moments later the older woman scuttled into the room and surveyed Olivia's plate. Without asking, she placed two slices of crisp bacon and a fluffy biscuit on Olivia's plate. "There now. That should hold you until the wedding brunch is served."

Olivia gobbled down the eggs, but the moment the older woman turned her back to wash the cooking utensils, she wrapped the bacon and biscuit in her napkin. Thankful Mrs. Barnes continued to chatter while she washed the dishes, Olivia silently pushed away from the table and tucked the napkin and its contents into the pocket of an apron hanging on the nearby hook. She tiptoed back to her chair and declared she'd best be on her way.

Mrs. Barnes spun around to examine the green-rimmed china plate. Her eyebrows scrunched together and her lips formed a tight line. "You ate much too quickly. You'll have a stomachache before you reach the hotel." She pointed a soapy finger in Olivia's direction. "And I won't take the blame for your upset stomach. Food that hasn't been properly chewed is a direct cause of improper digestion and stomach complaints."

"I promise not to hold you accountable." Olivia squeezed Mrs. Barnes's shoulder. She didn't like deceiving her, but precious minutes were ticking away. Moving down the hallway quickly, she grabbed her coat and turned toward the kitchen.

Shoving her arm into one of the sleeves, she called, "Is Mr. Barnes going to deliver—"

Mrs. Barnes bustled toward her. "No need to holler, my dear. I'm right here. Horace and I will bring everything to the hotel by ten o'clock. The gown and veil, along with your dress and toiletries—we'll bring everything you've set out in your room."

Dressing at the hotel had initially been Olivia's idea, and Martha had immediately agreed they would save time by doing so. Besides, they could help each other with their dresses and hair. Surprisingly, Mr. Billings, the hotel supervisor, had arranged for them to use one of the unoccupied guest rooms on the second floor at no charge.

Both Olivia and Martha had worked in harmony to make certain today would be an unforgettable event. Olivia hoped that Albert and Fred were doing the same for each other. Mrs. DeVault had been an ever-present help, but they had all agreed her assistance would be of greater value at home, where she could make certain the men arrived at the church on time and properly attired.

Mrs. Barnes clucked her tongue as she followed Olivia down the hallway. "You had best hurry along, or you'll not have time to decorate the cake."

Olivia sighed as she leaned sideways and glanced at the clock in the parlor. She buttoned her navy blue coat and pulled on a pair of warm gloves—no need for the lamb's-wool muff today. And by afternoon she wouldn't need the heavy coat or gloves, but last night's chill remained in the air. Why hadn't Mrs. Barnes been worried about the time when she was forcing breakfast upon her a half hour ago? After a final wave to her landlady, Olivia rushed toward the hotel. Although living in the upper rooms of the Barneses' house had caused its share of problems, residing in close proximity to her work would prove key today. She'd need every available minute between now and the wedding.

As expected, Chef René met her at the kitchen door. He pointed at the Seth Thomas clock hanging on the far wall. "Were you taking a beauty sleep this morning?" He didn't await her response. "I didn't know what to think. First I am thinking I should prepare the cake icing. Then I am thinking you said you wanted to prepare it yourself. Next I am thinking if you don't get here, there won't be enough time. Then I am thinking—"

She held up her hand. If she didn't stop him, this could go on for the remainder of the morning. He took her coat while she quickly explained her difficulty in escaping without first eating breakfast.

"How could Mrs. Barnes detain you for such a thing as breakfast? Does that woman not realize you work in a hotel kitchen? We *have* food!"

His waving arms reminded her of one of the policemen she'd seen directing traffic in downtown Chicago. It seemed Chef René was going to provide a touch of drama to her already hectic schedule. "I'll go downstairs to the pastry kitchen and work so that I don't interfere with breakfast for the hotel guests."

His brows knit into a frown. "Breakfast has already been served in the dining room. You may work here." He patted his palm on one of the large worktables. "It's better to work in the upstairs kitchen so we don't have to carry the cake upstairs after it has been decorated. What if you should trip?"

She didn't argue, but they both knew his reasoning was illogical. When the cake was delivered to Market Hall, it would be carried up a flight of stairs to the reception room. Though Olivia would have preferred the reception be hosted in the rooms above the Arcade, she had been alone in her reasoning. Martha, Albert, and Fred thought Market Hall the perfect location. The serving staff would be required to navigate a staircase in either place, but the stairway in the Arcade was much wider. There would be less chance of mishap. But she'd held her tongue and bowed to the bride's wishes.

Before returning to her rooms last evening, she had frosted the layers using a special fondant recipe. Now she must mix only enough frosting to add the decorative touches that would transform the cake into a beautiful creation. During the earlier hubbub, there hadn't been time to think, but now, while placing the final touches on the cake, her thoughts began to wander.

Though she had hoped to assist with more of the wedding preparations, Olivia had done her best to help while still maintaining her traveling schedule. She had been deeply honored when Martha had chosen her to act as her sole attendant for the ceremony. But along with the thrill had come a longing. She wanted to continue working as a chef, yet she ached for a life beyond her work—a life she could share with someone who would love and cherish her. Someone who would view her with the same adoration she saw in her cousin's eyes each time Martha entered a room. In truth, she desired more than just *someone*: she wanted Fred. Unfortunately, he didn't appear to harbor the same desire. His interest in reestablishing their relationship had cooled considerably since she'd begun her training on the rails.

After selecting one of Chef René's metal decorating tips, Olivia slipped it into the canvas pastry bag. She spooned the thick decorator's icing inside and carefully squeezed until a small frosting star appeared. She circled the bottom layer of the cake with stars and then surveyed her work. It would do.

Using the same precision, she continued with the next round while she anticipated standing across from Fred during the ceremony and walking down the aisle on his arm. Would he be stiff and distant? She hoped not. For this one day, she prayed he'd gift her with his quick smile and affable personality, that he would remove the wedge of formality that had separated them over the past weeks. She refilled the pastry bag and once again began to pipe the frosting.

If only she could return to those early days when they'd first met—the Sunday afternoons canoeing on Lake Calumet and sharing a picnic lunch afterward, the long summer evenings when she'd cheered him on during the baseball competitions at the athletic field. She ached for the times with Fred that she'd once considered quite ordinary events.

But what of *today*? One of the kitchen boys had mentioned seeing Fred walking with Mildred Malloy on several occasions. Olivia didn't know if it was true, but she couldn't help wondering if Mildred would be sitting in a church pew awaiting his arm once they'd completed their formal duties as wedding attendants. Would she sit beside him at the reception and enjoy his company while Olivia sat alone, feigning a smile? She forced herself to push the thought from her mind and concentrate on the cake.

Chef René lumbered down the steps and through the doorway as she placed the final rosette on the cake. He walked around the table, eyeing the cake from every possible angle before grunting his satisfaction. "*Bon!* You have created a magnificent cake." He pointed toward the clock. "Now you must get dressed. Martha is already upstairs waiting for your assistance."

Olivia reached for a knife to make one final adjustment, but Chef René lightly slapped her fingers. "*Non!* There is insufficient time. Besides, the cake is already perfect. Go on now."

She raised up on tiptoe, brushed his cheek with a fleeting kiss, and then hurried from the room. How thankful she was for this gentle giant of a man.

The prearranged carriage arrived at the hotel, and Chef René escorted Martha and Olivia to the front door. "You both look beautiful." When Olivia opened her mouth to speak, he touched a finger to his lips. "Please! No more instructions. I am capable of handling the few remaining details. I will see both of you at the reception hall."

This man possessed more talent than any chef in all of Chicago, perhaps the entire country. Any bride would be ecstatic to have him oversee the details of her wedding, yet Olivia couldn't help herself. She stopped just outside the door to remind him of the mints.

"Did I not *make* them? I will not forget the mints, or the cake, or the ice sculpture, or any of the food. *Please!* Go, before you are late for the ceremony." Shaking his head, he turned and trudged back inside without giving her an opportunity to issue any further reminders.

Olivia and Martha arrived at the church on schedule, well before any of the invited guests. They made their way to the anteroom off the front vestibule, where they would await the sound of the chosen organ chords before beginning their entrance into the church. While Martha hurried to the waiting room, Olivia peeked inside the sanctuary. An array of fresh flowers and greenery had been beautifully arranged by Mr. Jordan, the talented nurseryman in charge of the Pullman greenhouses and longtime acquaintance of Chef René. Tall tapers in brass candelabra flanked either side of the sanctuary, and Mr. Jordan had fastened beribboned white gardenias and greenery to the end of each pew. Inhaling deeply, Olivia was certain she could smell the sweet scent of the gardenias and pale yellow roses that had been forced to bloom prematurely in the muggy warmth of the town's huge greenhouses. The decorations were exquisite.

"Martha! Don't you want to see the church?" Olivia's voice echoed throughout the cavernous vestibule of the Greenstone Church.

Stepping to the doorway of the anteroom, Martha shook her head. "I'd rather be surprised. Now come in here before someone sees you."

Within moments of closing the door, the muted voices of the arriving guests seeped beneath the polished cherry door of the anteroom. The excitement was nearly too much to bear. Olivia examined the row of buttons on Martha's gown one final time. "It sounds as though the ushers have already begun to seat the guests. It won't be long now, Martha." Olivia grasped her friend's gloved hand in her own. "I didn't realize these final minutes would be so unbearable. I don't know how you can remain so calm." Olivia's mind raced as she attempted to recall whether she'd informed Chef René to send extra serving trays from the hotel kitchen. "I've done my best to remember all of the details."

Martha pushed her veil aside and drew Olivia into an embrace. "I know you have, Olivia. In truth, I feel somewhat guilty. There were times when I know I should have done far more to help, but even with your required traveling, you were always one step ahead of me. Not that I minded."

It was true that Olivia had taken over many of the plans, but she had enjoyed the experience. She was, after all, accustomed to making arrangements for parties at the hotel, whereas Martha had never before attempted such a massive undertaking. Now Olivia could only hope that everything would proceed according to schedule.

CHAPTER TEN

The chords of the organ music wafted through the open doors of the Greenstone Church and mingled with birds chirping in the nearby trees. An early spring—or so it appeared. Fred could remember years past when layers of snow remained on the ground during late April. Today, however, the skies over Pullman and Lake Calumet were clear and blue; not a sign of gray could be detected overhead.

Fred grasped Albert's shoulder and glanced heavenward. "Looks as though the weather has cooperated with you, my friend." He turned at the sound of approaching footsteps. Malcolm Overby stood nearby waving him toward the street. After a promise to return quickly, Fred hurried toward the young man. "What are you doing here, Malcolm? You're missing your classes over at the training center."

The young man shook his head. "Ain't no use. Training or not, things ain't gonna get no better for us, Fred. My friend Paul got laid off yesterday. Word is, there's gonna be big layoffs coming soon. Especially in the freight department. I won't be around long enough to finish my training. If I get laid off, I'm gonna have to look for work somewhere else—maybe go back to Pittsburgh. Can't afford to stick around here and wait things out. Going through all this work trying to learn a new trade ain't gonna help."

"I'm surprised at you, Malcolm. I never figured you to be someone who would quit so easily." Fred hoped his comment would stir some passion in the younger man.

He shrugged his broad shoulders. "You know how it goes around here. Bachelors in Pullman and married men living outside of Pullman are the first to be laid off. I'm living in Pullman, but I ain't got no woman lined up to marry me."

Fred nodded. He did know the procedure for layoffs within the company. And he also knew the depression that had been forecast to plague the country would tighten its grip on those least able to bear the burden. The wealthy men like George Pullman might experience a slight sting from the economic downturn, but their wives would continue to shop at Marshall Field's, and they'd still escort their families abroad for fanciful, meaningless excursions. Meanwhile, the men who labored in their factories would be laid off without so much as a backward glance. And in Pullman it would be bachelors first. As head of a household and the only support for his widowed mother, Fred's status was considered equal to that of a married man— unless layoffs moved to the next level. In that event, he would be one of the first to go if and when cuts were made in the electroplating section. A chilling thought yet a fact of life for the common laborer as well as for the skilled craftsman. Frugal by nature, Fred's mother placed money in a savings account at

Mr. Pullman's bank each week. Her protection against such an event.

"You've not yet been laid off, Malcolm. My advice is to go to the center and gain as much training as possible. Don't give in to defeat." He nodded toward Albert. "I've got to get back to the church, but we'll talk tomorrow." He clapped Malcolm on the back and watched for a moment before returning to Albert's side.

Albert tipped his head toward Malcolm. "What was that all about? Malcolm looked like he'd lost his last friend."

"Just about. A friend who works in the freight department was laid off yesterday. I'm growing concerned with the number of recent layoffs. None of this bodes well for any of us. If we're to survive, I think we're going to have to unionize or strike. Or both," he added.

"This is my wedding day, Fred. Could we put aside such talk for today?" Albert didn't wait for an answer. Instead, he grasped Fred's arm. "Come on, or the guests are going to think I'm going to leave Martha standing at the altar without her groom."

Fred followed alongside Albert, and the two of them took their assigned places at the front of the church. After several minutes, the preacher nodded at the organist. The rear doors of the sanctuary opened, and the chords of the processional swelled in anticipation of the bridal party's entrance. Fred watched as Olivia slowly proceeded down the aisle. She peeked at him from beneath her long brown lashes. There was no denying she was a vision to behold in the pale yellow gown. Compared to the creamy daffodil shade of her dress, his black serge suit and gray tie seemed downright drab. Even the glossy sheen of his freshly polished shoes wasn't as vivid in her presence. He had dampened and slicked down his hair in an attempt to control the unruly waves, while her coffee-colored curls remained perfectly arranged beneath a yellow silk hat that matched her gown to perfection. He attempted to look away, but he'd been unable to force his gaze from her. He'd noticed every detail of her flawless appearance.

Once Olivia had taken her place in the front of the sanctuary, Martha followed, her gown falling in perfect ivory folds as she proceeded toward her groom. Flanked by Olivia and Fred, the couple faced Reverend Loomis. The minister's bald pate shone beneath the flickering light of the candelabra. With practiced ease, Reverend Loomis led Albert and Martha through the ceremony, adroitly guiding them as they said their vows. No doubt the preacher had long ago memorized the wedding service. Not once did he glance down at his notes or Bible.

Finally Reverend Loomis looked toward Olivia—her cue to take Martha's flowers and Fred's signal to hand Albert the wedding ring. Fred reached into his pocket, retrieved the ring, and slipped it into Albert's hand. Several guests in the front pews twittered and elbowed one another while Martha held the outstretched bouquet. Fred looked toward Olivia. She appeared lost in her own private thoughts.

Suddenly the preacher grabbed the flowers from Martha's hand and thrust the bouquet in Olivia's direction. His sudden movement stirred Olivia to action. She clutched the floral arrangement to her chest and sent an apologetic look in Martha's direction. An unexpected wave of emotions assailed Fred. On the one hand, he understood Olivia's embarrassment, yet her careless behavior during this important event provoked him. Surely she should be able to remain attentive for the exchange of nuptials between her cousin and her best friend! Likely she was absorbed with thoughts of *Samuel* rather than the wedding at hand, he decided.

Moments later the minister pronounced Albert and Martha man and wife and then presented them to the congregation. The young couple walked arm in arm toward the rear of the church. Fred stepped to the center of the aisle and crooked his arm. Thankfully Olivia had remained alert during the final minutes of the ceremony. With his shoulders as rigid as the iron gates that guarded the Pullman Car Works, he escorted Olivia to the rear of the church.

The moment they entered the vestibule, he lowered his arm and extended his hand toward Albert. "My congratulations, Albert. I know you're going to have a life filled with happiness."

The two men stood nearby as Olivia stepped forward and embraced Martha. "The ceremony was beautiful. I'm sorry I didn't take your bouquet on cue." Regret filled her voice as she released Martha.

Albert winked and drew near. "You were probably daydreaming about your own wedding. Am I right?"

She glanced in Fred's direction. "I believe I'll have to find a steady suitor before I can daydream about a wedding."

Fred absently straightened his tie, careful not to look her in the eye. "Is that so? I believe the entire town is merely waiting for an announcement that you and Mr. Howard will soon wed."

Olivia stiffened her shoulders. "Then they'll wait a very long time. Mr. Howard and I are not courting."

Fred couldn't be certain if he'd detected pain or anger in her eyes, but he decided against a verbal response. This was not the time or place. He shrugged his shoulders and excused himself.

"I'll go make certain the carriage has arrived to transport us to Market Hall."

Greeting visitors at the reception rather than in the church vestibule was the latest fashion; at least that's what Martha had advised. Fred hadn't even considered what might be fashionable in wedding planning. He'd given the driver explicit instructions and was pleased to see the horse and carriage coming to a halt in front of the church. After a quick wave to the driver, he returned to the vestibule and motioned the others forward.

Once they were seated in the carriage, Olivia leaned close. "I didn't see Mildred at the wedding."

"Surely you're aware Mildred is working at the hotel. Otherwise, she would be in attendance." Apparently someone had seen him in Mildred's company and passed along the information to Olivia. Though Mildred was a nice enough young woman, Fred had no romantic interest in her. However, he didn't plan to share that bit of information with Olivia—or with anyone else, for that matter.

"And would you have been her escort?"

"As I said, she couldn't attend so I see no need to further discuss the matter."

His response was enough to halt any more questions, and she turned away to stare out the window.

———

"Olivia!" Martha leaned into the carriage and tapped Olivia's shoulder. "Do quit your daydreaming and come along."

Olivia hadn't even noticed that the coach had come to a halt outside Market Hall, and she'd been completely oblivious when the others had exited the carriage. However, once her feet touched solid ground, only a moment was needed to gather her thoughts. Without waiting for the others, she hiked her skirts and hastened off toward the main entrance of Market Hall. By the time she'd raced up the stairs, perspiration dotted her forehead and she was panting for air.

Chef René clucked his tongue. "Such unladylike behavior, Miss Mott. Are you so afraid I cannot cater this small wedding reception? Is that why you rush like an unruly child?"

His question stopped her in her tracks. "No." She gasped for another breath of air. "I simply didn't want you overexerting yourself."

"Ha! We both know that is only partially the truth. You also want to prove yourself."

"This has nothing to do with proving myself. This is my cousin's wedding, and I want to make certain everything is perfect."

The rotund chef crossed his arms on his broad chest. "And *I* can't ensure perfection? Is that what you're saying?"

"No. You are much more qualified than I." She sighed. They were wasting time arguing while, from the top of the stairway, she could see the cake was not yet on the table.

He followed her gaze and held up a warning finger. "The cake is arriving as we speak. I will see to it."

Olivia took one step backward, teetered, and then lunged toward Fred as her foot slipped off the top step. Had it not been for Fred's quick reflexes, she would have toppled down the steps. Instead, they stood locked in an embrace at the top of the stairway as Olivia attempted to regain her balance. She grimaced in pain while clutching Fred's shoulders. "I believe I've sprained my ankle."

Fred held her, his hands grasping her waist. "I believe Mr. Howard is racing up the stairs, either to rescue you or to punch me in the nose. From the scowl on his face, I'd guess it's the latter. I do hope you'll save me from an altercation. I'd dislike ruining my new suit and possibly losing my job at the same time."

Before she could respond, Mr. Howard was at her side. "What are you thinking, DeVault? Miss Mott is not some trollop to be manhandled. Release her immediately!"

"No! Please, don't let go." She dug her fingers into Fred's shoulders.

Mr. Howard's complexion resembled the redbrick houses that lined the streets of Pullman. "*What?* You want to continue making a spectacle of yourself in front of all these people?" His teeth were clenched, and the muscles along his jaw quivered when he spoke. It was obvious he didn't want the wedding guests to overhear him confront her. Mr. Howard wouldn't want to make a spectacle of himself.

Olivia continued to cling to Fred's shoulders. "I've sprained my ankle and am unable to stand on my own."

Mr. Howard smoothed an invisible wrinkle from his double-breasted vest. "I'll fetch a chair for you." He glared at Fred as though he had caused the entire incident. "*And* a physician."

Mr. Howard snapped his fingers at one of the kitchen boys, and soon a chair was placed in the receiving line so Olivia could sit down and the entire wedding party could continue to greet the guests. They made an interesting spectacle: Martha, Albert, and Fred standing side by side while Olivia rested on a chair with her ankle wrapped in ice-packed toweling and her foot propped on an overturned bucket. *Lovely!* Only Chef René appeared unconcerned with her situation. He seemed utterly pleased that she'd been temporarily restricted to a sitting position. She was glad they'd provided her with a view of the stairway, so she could see the guests as they arrived.

Catching a glimpse of Ellen Ashton ascending the steps, Olivia brightened. She waved her friend forward, wishing she could rush to meet her. She hadn't expected Ellen to attend. Olivia hadn't noticed her during the wedding ceremony and wondered if she had only just arrived in Pullman.

Ellen arched her brows as she approached. Olivia forced a smile and hastened to explain her predicament. "I'm certain I'll be fine by the time we've greeted the final guests. I don't intend to remain seated throughout the entire day."

Ellen glanced at the mound of damp cloth surrounding Olivia's ankle and shook her head. "With all that wrapping, it's difficult to guess how much swelling has occurred. But please don't worry about me." She grasped Olivia's hand. "I'm sorry I didn't arrive in time for the wedding. Father requested I complete a few things at the office, and I missed the earlier train."

Fred leaned down close to her ear. "Perhaps you'd like to introduce your friend, Olivia." He nodded toward the increasing number of guests that had begun to form a line behind Ellen.

She squeezed Ellen's hand. "It appears we're detaining the other guests, but if you like, you can come and stand nearby."

Ellen shook her head. "No. I'd only be a distraction. I'll go in and mingle with the other guests until you've finished your duties."

Walking into a gathering of strangers would be frightening to some, but not to Ellen. Olivia's new friend was poised, educated, charming, and never appeared to be at a loss for words.

"In that case, let me introduce you to Fred DeVault. Fred, this is my friend Ellen Ashton. Martha and Albert agreed I should invite her to the festivities. Ellen lives in Chicago."

"Pleased to meet you, Miss Ashton. You did say *Ashton*, didn't you?"

Ellen offered him a fleeting smile and a quick nod as she continued down the receiving line. Fred stared after her as she approached Martha. He was obviously taking more than a casual interest in Olivia's guest. He shifted his position and leaned forward, clearly eager to hear each word she exchanged with the wedding couple.

Even after Ellen had walked into the reception hall, he'd followed her with his eyes. Now, several minutes later, he surveyed the room, probably hoping to catch another glimpse of her. And how could Olivia blame him? Ellen possessed a magnetism that went far beyond her beauty or intelligence. Like a moth to a flame, people surrounded her wherever she went. At first Olivia had been taken aback by the number of people who were drawn to Ellen. But now she'd grown accustomed to such behavior. Yet she hadn't expected Fred's overt reaction. She hadn't anticipated the possibility that he could be so easily enamored.

When the line of guests had finally thinned, Martha grasped Albert's arm and the couple prepared to enter the reception hall. Fred stooped down beside Olivia. "By any chance is your friend Ellen Ashton related to Montrose Ashton—the Chicago lawyer?"

Olivia sighed. She thought he had squatted down to assist her or inquire about her ankle. Apparently he was even more interested in Ellen than she had initially suspected. The fact that Fred knew of Montrose Ashton certainly surprised her. "Yes, he's her father."

Fred arched his brows. "How is it that you happen to count the Ashtons among your acquaintances?"

His question annoyed her. While they should be joining the bridal party in the reception room, he was quizzing her about Ellen Ashton. The very idea! She shot him a critical look and then unwrapped the towel and dried her ankle.

"Could you help me into the other room? If not, would you locate someone who is willing to do so?" She realized her tone was strident, but it had the desired effect. Using his arms to brace her weight, Fred helped her up and then wrapped one arm around her waist to steady her while she tested the ankle.

He pointed toward her foot. "Try to take a few steps while I'm still holding on to you."

With slow uneven steps, they made their way toward the doorway, Fred embracing her waist while Olivia hobbled alongside him. As they continued into the room, her ankle gained strength, and with each step she became more secure. Thankfully, the pain had noticeably diminished. Pleased with her progress and anxious to discover if all was in readiness, Olivia scanned the room for a glimpse of Chef René. Instead, she locked gazes with a frowning Mr. Howard, who was shouldering his way through the crowd.

Mr. Howard's nostrils flared as he came to a halt in front of them. "Why didn't you send for me? While the doctor wrapped your ankle, I distinctly told you to send for me when you wanted to move from the chair."

She didn't recall his saying any such thing, but then, she'd been busy responding to the doctor's questions while he had probed and examined her leg. He stared at Fred's hand clasping her waist, and anger flickered in his eyes. The three of them remained frozen in place while the chattering guests made their way to the gaily decorated tables.

Olivia was uncertain how long they continued standing in the middle of the room. She'd yet to respond to Mr. Howard's question. It was Fred who finally spoke. "I believe Martha is motioning for us to join them at the head table. We don't want to detain these hungry guests." That said, he stepped forward and forced Mr. Howard to move aside.

While Fred maintained his hold around her waist, Mr. Howard moved to her right and accompanied them across the room. She was certain they made quite a strange sight to those watching, but she didn't care. Fred's attentive behavior delighted her, though she surmised his intent was more to annoy Mr. Howard than to be in her company. Once Mr. Howard took his place with some of the other guests, she would properly thank Fred for his assistance. Perhaps on this auspicious day, the barrier that had formed between them would dissolve.

As the trio approached the bridal couple, Martha wedged herself between Mr. Howard and Olivia. She dipped her head, keeping her lips close to Olivia's ear. "Mr. Howard and Fred will be seated on either side of you. I had hoped to seat Ellen to your left, but Mr. Howard insisted. What was I to do?" The folds of her lacy veil rippled as Martha shrugged her narrow shoulders. "Ellen will be seated on Fred's right, but at least the two of you will be in close proximity."

Olivia couldn't imagine a worse scenario. Both men hastened to assist her to her seat. Mr. Howard won, and Fred turned to assist Ellen. Thankfully Chef René hadn't disappointed her. Everything had been completed to perfection—except the cake. The ice sculpture glistened in the center of the far table, but the wedding cake was nowhere in sight. She waited until she spotted him in the doorway and motioned him forward. He shook his head, and she read his lips as he formed the words *not now*.

Unwilling to be deterred, she leaned toward Mr. Howard. "Would you please ask Chef René to step over here for a moment? It's urgent that I speak to him."

Mr. Howard appeared pleased to do her bidding. Moments later, he returned to the table with Chef René following in his wake. "How may I be of assistance, Miss Mott? The servers need my direction." The chef's formality and tone signaled his displeasure, but Olivia remained undeterred.

"*Where* is the wedding cake?" She spoke in a whisper, not wanting to draw the bride's attention to a possible problem.

Chef René tightened his broad lips into a thin line. "The cake will be presented in due time. I must see to serving the brunch at this particular moment. The cake is not needed until after the guests have eaten. Now, if I may be excused?"

"But it *has* been delivered from the hotel kitchen?" She knew he had expected no more than a nod—a silent acceptance of his terse response. But even the chef's irritation hadn't proved enough to counter her persistence.

He pulled a shapeless cotton towel from his waist and wrung it between his thick fingers. There was little doubt she had tried his patience to the extreme. "The cake will be presented at the proper time." His tone resonated in a low, even timbre that precluded further discussion.

The man was downright exasperating! Why didn't he answer

her with a simple yes or no, instead of leaving her to worry? The moment an opportunity presented itself, she'd ask one of the waiters.

Unfortunately, when the waiter drew near to serve the fruit cups, Mr. Howard thwarted her chance. With his shoulder pressed against her, he leaned close and whispered, "Who is that attractive woman sitting beside Fred? I don't believe I've seen her before."

Mr. Howard's breath tickled her ear. His propinquity disturbed her, and she shifted in her chair. Her change of position produced a hairsbreadth of space between them. People were watching, and she didn't want to give an appearance of intimacy with the company agent. If she could believe Fred's comments, talk was already circulating about town, and she didn't want to give wings to such rumors. Local tittle-tattle was *one* thing Mr. Pullman and the company agent couldn't control. They might be able to enforce regulations regarding wallpaper choices, the manner and location for hanging one's laundry, or the proper attire for strolling in the park, but whispered rumors were beyond their reach. And if there was one topic the locals enjoyed more than any other, it was discussing the superiors who enforced Mr. Pullman's countless rules.

His question prompted Olivia to cast a fleeting glace to her right, where Fred and Ellen were deep in conversation. A knot of jealousy welled in her chest. Their fruit cups remained uneaten, with the decorative mint leaves still resting at perfect angles atop the pineapple wedges. There was little doubt that Ellen had piqued Fred's interest.

Mr. Howard's lips grazed her ear. "Are you going to tell me who is sitting beside Fred, or must I go and introduce myself?"

"Ellen Ashton."

Mr. Howard's spoon slipped from his fingers and clanked as it hit the table. "Did you say *Ashton*?"

Why did everyone request clarification of Ellen's surname?

CHAPTER ELEVEN

Fred couldn't believe his good fortune. Ellen Ashton, the daughter of Montrose Ashton, had been assigned a seat beside him. But he was annoyed that Samuel Howard had somehow managed to obtain a seat at the bride and groom's table—alongside Olivia, of course.

No matter what the occasion, Mr. Howard consistently used his power and influence to insert himself whenever and wherever it served his purpose—even the wedding reception of a hotel maid and skilled laborer from the electroplating division. Mr. Howard wasn't in attendance today because he wanted to celebrate the nuptials of valued employees. Rather, his presence was based upon his own desire to control Olivia. At least that's what Fred had concluded the moment he saw the company agent walk into the church.

On the other hand, there was the possibility that Olivia desired Mr. Howard's presence and had requested this seating arrangement. Either way, Fred was pleased to be seated next to

Miss Ashton. She could provide a rare insight into her father's determination to help unionize the workingmen of Chicago. He wondered if Mr. Howard had any idea that the daughter of Montrose Ashton was sitting only a short distance away from him. If so, he'd masked his vexation. At the moment, Mr. Howard and Olivia were engrossed in a rather one-sided conversation. Perhaps he was warning her against associating with the young woman.

From all appearances Olivia's attention would likely be solely directed at Mr. Howard this day. Fred's mother had suggested he offer Olivia an opportunity to detail her working affiliation with Mr. Howard. But each time he attempted to speak to her, her interest was directed toward Mr. Howard. After several endeavors, he gave up and turned his complete attention to Miss Ashton. Fred could now honestly inform his mother that his failure to communicate with Olivia hadn't been entirely his fault.

Ellen Ashton proved to be a most interesting young woman. Well traveled and educated, she had little difficulty entertaining him in an unaffected manner with tales of her journeys abroad. But it was her father's law practice and reputation for aiding the unions that truly interested Fred. When Ellen inquired about his work in Pullman, he used the opportunity to advantage. After a brief explanation of his tiresome duties, he lowered his voice. "How much do you assist your father with his unionization work, Miss Ashton?"

Her hazel eyes sparkled with a hint of surprise. She tilted her head and met his gaze. "Why is it you inquire, Mr. De-Vault?"

He leaned closer. "May I trust your ability to keep our discussion confidential?"

She peered over the rim of her coffee cup. "By all means."

"There are a number of workers who are interested in unionizing. As you likely know, we'd lose our jobs if anyone heard us even mention our intentions. I had hoped your father might help us in our efforts."

She leaned back in her chair as though she found the conversation tedious, but once the waiter had removed her plate, she lowered her shoulder and leaned in. "I don't believe this is the proper place to discuss strikes and unionization. If an opportunity arises where we can visit privately, I'd be pleased to answer your questions."

Fred exhaled, pleasantly relieved that he hadn't misjudged Miss Ashton. He'd make certain they had an opportunity to speak privately before she departed. There were many questions he'd like to pose. Perhaps she'd have the answers; perhaps she wouldn't. Either way, he was now a step closer to Mr. Ashton and other union supporters who could help their cause.

Glancing at the bridegroom, he wondered if Albert would continue to support the local effort now that he was married. Most of the union support came from the single men, workers who didn't have others relying upon their wages. Fred considered his own position. He didn't have a wife and children depending upon him, yet he supported his mother. A sobering fact that was never far from his mind. If something happened to him, she'd be left in dire straits. If they owned a home in nearby Kensington or Roseland, she could take in boarders and support herself. But like most Pullman employees, he rented from the company. And if he were terminated, he would lose the right to live in Pullman.

Truth be told, his involvement in the union movement jeopardized her well-being more than his own. He could find work and support his mother outside of Pullman, but if he were to disappear or meet with an unexpected accident, she would suffer dearly. And shocking disasters occurred all too frequently among the laborers who attempted to organize. Only last week he'd heard of three deaths—all men who'd been actively working to unionize Marshall Field's employees in Chicago.

Since the Chicago Haymarket Square bombing in 1886, when workers had rallied and gone on strike demanding an eight-hour workday at the McCormick Works, men like Pullman, Armour, McCormick, and Field had donated large sums of money to stamp out what they considered subversive movements by their workers. And woe to the man who spoke of collective bargaining to these powerful men. George Pullman was reported by the Knights of Labor to be the most persistent and malignant of the capitalists. An enemy determined to eradicate unionization at any cost. After dealing with both the threat of strikes and actual walkouts on several previous occasions, George Pullman had been clear: he would take a hard line against his workers.

While ignoring the needs of the men who labored to make them wealthy, these bastions of capitalism salved their consciences by aiding in the construction of the cultural centers that would bear their names. All in an effort to maintain their own fame and to prove Chicago the equal of any eastern city. These men had more money than they could ever spend in a lifetime, yet they refused to even discuss the possibility of wage increases or proper hiring practices. The very idea caused a smoldering fire to burn in Fred's belly. The workers and their families deserved better. These were the issues he longed to one day discuss with Montrose Ashton.

———

When Olivia confirmed that Ashton was Ellen's last name, Mr. Howard appeared shaken. Olivia studied his pasty complexion. "Are you ill? If you need to leave, please don't feel obligated to remain on my account." Frankly, she longed to have him depart. She still didn't know how he'd managed to obtain a seat next to her at the bride and groom's table.

"No, I'm fine." As if to prove the validity of his response, he picked up his spoon and ate a piece of fruit. He swallowed the chunk of apple before continuing his inquiry. "How do you happen to know Miss Ashton?"

The intensity of his dark-eyed stare was disconcerting, and Olivia shifted in her chair. She thought his question intrusive yet felt compelled to respond. "I met her several months ago in Chicago."

He waited, his mahogany eyes turning a shade darker. "And?"

"And I enjoy her company." Perhaps her curt response would call a halt to his unwelcome interrogation.

Undeterred, he continued to hold her in his brooding stare. "And her father, Montrose Ashton, you know him, as well?" He didn't wait for her response. "I believe you dropped one of his business cards in my office some time ago."

Olivia hesitated and then recalled the incident. She'd gone to Mr. Howard's office in November of last year to discuss her new position with the company. She had dropped the business card while removing a handkerchief from her pocket. Mr. Howard had picked up the card and returned it to her. When she had avoided his questions as to how she happened to have Mr. Ashton's card in her possession, Mr. Howard had become quite agitated. Moreover, his present behavior was similar to what he'd exhibited back then. Strange that both Fred and Mr. Howard would mention Montrose Ashton. As in England, she supposed solicitors were considered public figures of a sort, but there were many solicitors and barristers in a city the size of Chicago. Why the interest in this particular one?

Whether Mr. Howard knew Mr. Ashton or not, she disliked his intrusion into her personal affairs. The fact that the Earl of Lanshire had selected Mr. Ashton as his solicitor prior to leaving the country and had directed Olivia to contact Mr. Ashton was none of Mr. Howard's business. Not that she had anything to hide, but she considered the matter private.

Mr. Howard cleared his throat, still waiting for an answer. Olivia rearranged the napkin that lay across her skirt. "I have met Mr. Ashton on one or two occasions, but my friendship is with Ellen. Our association has nothing to do with any sort of business. We enjoy visiting museums, chatting over a cup of tea, or visiting with friends."

Surely that should be enough explanation for her inquisitive employer. And she'd managed to tell the truth. She didn't mention that Ellen sometimes assisted in her father's law office. Ellen likely knew of Lady Charlotte's disappearance and Morgan's birth, although the two of them had never discussed the matter.

The two of them had met and formed their unlikely friendship when Olivia had followed the instructions contained in the Earl of Lanshire's missive. A simple command that had directed her to make contact with Mr. Ashton. She and Ellen were as different as night and day. While Ellen was educated, worldly, and certainly wasn't required to work to support herself, Olivia was the exact opposite. But for some reason, they had been drawn to each other. After Olivia had completed her first meeting with Montrose Ashton, she and Ellen had gone to tea at a small shop near the law office.

When Ellen discovered Olivia's discomfort in getting about the city, she had taken it upon herself to become Olivia's tour guide of sorts, introducing her to the variety of stores, museums, and a host of her friends and acquaintances. She had enjoyed their ventures to visit Jane Addams at her settlement house, where she offered a variety of assistance to the impoverished immigrants flocking into the city. A challenging conversation could always be found at Hull House. Truth be told, Olivia wouldn't mind escaping to Chicago or Hull House right now—anyplace where she could avoid Mr. Howard's piercing stare.

Glancing down the table, she motioned for a waiter who was removing the empty fruit dishes. "Could you tell me if the wedding cake has been delivered from the hotel?"

The waiter nodded toward the door. One of the kitchen boys from Hotel Florence was inching his way across the room in a single-handed attempt to carry Olivia's culinary creation to the serving table. Olivia inhaled a giant breath. Her gaze darted across the room to Chef René. He had spotted the lad and was signaling him to wait.

The chef lumbered across the room like an ominous thundercloud. Scowling at the kitchen boy, the chef carefully grasped one side of the cake board, and together they gently placed it upon the table. The moment the cake was in place and surrounded by greenery and a few yellow roses, Chef René motioned the boy to one side of the table and grasped the young man's ear in a tight pinch. The lad danced on tiptoe as he accompanied the chef toward the kitchen. Along with a painful ear, the young man would suffer a good dose of the chef's ire, for the kitchen boy hadn't followed the prescribed serving procedures for employees of Hotel Florence.

Olivia relaxed in her chair, certain that nothing more could go amiss this day. By early afternoon, her positive outlook began to fade. Plans to resolve her misunderstandings with Fred during their time together at the reception now appeared doomed to failure. Instead, she'd been forced to respond to Mr. Howard's insistent questions while Fred and Ellen sat with their heads tipped close together, talking continually. Olivia wondered if they had even tasted their food. Several times she'd heard them laughing, as though they'd shared some fanciful story. She had expected Ellen to leap from her chair and leave at the first opportunity. Surprisingly, she had stayed, appearing engrossed in conversation and oblivious to the departing guests.

Olivia was about to interrupt the two of them when Chef René strode toward her, mopping his brow. "This is the first opportunity I have had to offer my apologies. All your hard work and then we nearly have the cake . . ." He pointed toward the floor. "I did not realize the boy had taken your creation from the kitchen. You know we have procedures in place to avoid such occurrences."

Olivia held up her palm to halt his apology. "It is forgotten. The lad was attempting to help. I'm sure he'll follow procedures in the future." She touched a finger to her ear. "His tender ear will help him remember."

The chef heaved a sigh. "I don't know if I would be quite so forgiving, but I suppose all is well . . ." He massaged his forehead as though the process would help him recall the rest of the saying.

"That ends well?" Olivia grinned as she completed the sentence.

"*Oui*! All is well that ends well. I had best get back and oversee the workers before some other misguided soul attempts to assist me." The chef turned and marched off, his toque bouncing side to side in rhythm with his footsteps.

Mr. Howard lightly grasped her elbow. "It appears most of the guests are preparing to depart. I do hope you'll permit me to escort you home."

Olivia shook her head. "Thank you for your offer, but I plan to spend the remainder of the day with Ellen."

"Really?" He arched his brows. "Miss Ashton is otherwise occupied, and I'm sure Mr. DeVault will be more than pleased to see her to the train depot."

Olivia stepped to one side and freed her elbow from his hold. "Ellen is here at *my* invitation, not Mr. DeVault's. I wouldn't consider such an idea."

"No? Well, it appears Miss Ashton isn't of the same mind." He looked toward the door. Olivia turned in time to catch a glimpse of Fred and Ellen walking arm in arm toward the stairway. She wanted to run after them or, at the very least, call out

Ellen's name. But she didn't want to appear unladylike and cause a spectacle.

"*There* you are!" Martha wended her way through several remaining guests and clutched Olivia's arm. "Come and bid me good-bye." She pulled Olivia alongside her and turned her back toward Mr. Howard. "Ellen asked me to tell you that once you've changed out of your dress, you should meet her at the restaurant in the Arcade."

"And Fred?"

Martha's face wrinkled into a slight frown. "Oh! You thought . . ." She giggled. "Fred offered to escort her to the restaurant on his way home."

Though it seemed somewhat odd Ellen hadn't waited, perhaps she'd wanted to avoid interrupting Olivia's conversations with Chef René and Mr. Howard. A million questions came to mind, but Martha certainly wouldn't have the answers. "Are you and Albert departing for your overnight in Chicago?"

"As soon as I've changed into my traveling suit and we've picked up our bags. Albert tells me he managed to purchase two tickets to the theater this evening. And we're going to dine at the Palmer House restaurant."

Olivia had been so busy worrying about Fred and Ellen that she'd completely forgotten her duties as Martha's wedding attendant. "Come along. I'll help you change so you can be on your way."

"No need. I have someone to assist me." Martha glanced over her shoulder toward Albert.

"Oh, of course! What a ninny I am—already forgetting you now have a husband to help you with such matters." Olivia's cheeks grew warm with embarrassment. The sight of Albert unfastening the row of pearl buttons on Martha's gown was more than Olivia cared to imagine.

Martha chuckled and gathered Olivia into a warm embrace. "Thank you for all your hard work. I couldn't have managed without you. I'll contact you as soon as we return home."

The two young women bid each other farewell, and Olivia remained at the far end of the reception hall, watching as Martha returned to Albert's side. She secretly hoped Mr. Howard had located someone else to visit with during her brief absence. She glanced over her shoulder and sighed as she saw him approach.

"They make a good couple. Martha will help your cousin achieve his full potential."

Mr. Howard's observation made their marriage seem more a business arrangement than a mutual commitment of love. Olivia realized that those of noble birth, as well as those of wealth, were often forced into arranged marriages. Personally, she abhorred the idea of a loveless marriage. "This wasn't a business contract. They are simply two people in love who want to spend their lives together."

"Of course, of course. I didn't mean to imply otherwise, but a good wife can certainly have a stabilizing influence on a man seeking to make his way in the world." He lightly touched her arm. "May I escort you home so you may change out of your gown before meeting Miss Ashton?"

She jerked to attention. He couldn't possibly have overheard her discussion with Martha. Only one of the scullery maids had been close enough to hear. He must have slipped the girl a few coins for the information. How dare he! "And how would *you* know of my plans to return home before meeting Miss Ashton?"

He didn't flinch. Nor did he lie. "I paid the scullery maid. Highly improper, but surely my unacceptable behavior proves how much I desire some time with you—even if only a few minutes."

She stared at him, speechless, longing to think of some off-hand rejoinder, but nothing came to mind. His honesty had completely disarmed her.

He crooked his arm. "May I take your silence as agreement? We *do* live next door to each other."

Mr. Howard appeared quite smug, as though he'd decided she couldn't possibly find a reason to refuse him. Unfortunately, he was correct. She took his arm and, with only a slight limp, descended the stairs. What difference could it make? They were two people walking in the same direction. If the town gossips wanted to link them romantically, she couldn't stop their idle chatter. And there was little doubt several of the women doing their shopping were scrutinizing more than the fresh produce as they passed by. Olivia could feel their stares even after they'd left the building.

Once outdoors, she savored a sense of relief and inhaled the sweet scent of the budding flowers and trees that lined the walkways of the town. The lovely prelude to spring quickly erased thoughts of the formidable looks they'd received from the shoppers inside the market. If only she could now free herself of Mr. Howard's company and join Ellen at the Arcade restaurant.

CHAPTER TWELVE

While they walked toward the Arcade, Fred and Ellen continued to chat. He had been pleased when she agreed there was a need for further unionization among workers. It was when he'd mentioned his concerns over his mother's well-being that Ellen had been quick to warn him about what he already knew: his involvement in the labor movement could spell disaster for him as well as for his mother.

Fred squared his shoulders. "When the time comes, I'll need to take a stand alongside the other men. Such choices are difficult, but unless we're committed to the cause of creating better conditions for everyone, I fear change will not happen within the company. No doubt there will be families who suffer."

Miss Ashton quickened her step to keep pace. "Unfortunately, the fear of retribution is a strong weapon of the capitalist. I don't believe the common workingman is a coward. Instead, he feels compelled to shy away from the labor movement for the sake of his family. One can't fault a man for honoring his personal obligations."

The ostrich plumes that trimmed the crown of Miss Ashton's scallop-edged hat waved in the light spring breeze. Fred thought the hat somewhat fanciful, but he was no expert on women's apparel. And given the number of flower- and ribbon-bedecked hats he'd observed at the wedding reception, he didn't suppose Miss Ashton's was any more extreme than most. It did seem a bizarre contradiction to her astute remarks, though.

He hastily forced aside his thoughts of Miss Ashton's attire. "There's truth in what you say, but if we're to succeed, we must lay down our fears and learn to use every advantage to promote our position." He glanced around. "We'll be forced to change opinions about this town. Outsiders come here and think we've been given a virtual utopia, although nothing could be further from the truth."

"Do you find strong support for the labor movement here? My father believed that few were willing to rally behind the Knights of Labor. He would be surprised to discover otherwise."

Fred's excitement mounted as Ellen explained her father's zeal for offering his legal expertise to the labor movement. Like Fred, Mr. Ashton desired to see every worker gain a decent wage and tolerable employment conditions. "There are many who want to see conditions improve. How far the workers are willing to go is another matter altogether. Since everything must be cloaked in a veil of secrecy, it's difficult to speak in terms of numbers or degrees of commitment." They came to a halt outside the Arcade entrance. "Be assured there are others like me—especially the single men. Eventually I believe the discontent will become intolerable and fears will be pushed aside in favor of justice."

Two women carrying shopping baskets on their arms drew near, and Ellen instantly redirected their conversation to a more neutral topic. "You say the restaurant is down the hall and to the right?"

"Yes, but you needn't go in just now. Olivia won't be arriving for a while yet." He motioned toward a bench across the street. "Your friendship with Olivia surprises me."

She walked alongside and joined him on one of the benches near a neatly trimmed cluster of rosebushes. "We're quite different yet similar in many ways, too. We both have deep concern for the downtrodden. While Olivia shies away from such concepts as labor movements, she offers help in other ways. She offers a helping hand when and where she can. She's even gone with me to Hull House and met with Jane Addams."

"Exactly what brought Olivia to your father's office, Miss Ashton? For the life of me, I can't imagine why she would visit a Chicago lawyer. You know, I thought Olivia believed Chicago a formidable place. I'm amazed to hear she's ventured into the city so frequently."

A gentle breeze off Lake Calumet tugged at Ellen's silk jacket. "I'm not at liberty to discuss Olivia's personal business affairs, but if you're genuinely interested, I suggest you ask her."

Fred adroitly caught a misdirected rubber ball and tossed it back to one of the young boys playing nearby. "If you don't want to discuss Olivia, what about Jane Addams? Correct me if I'm wrong, but I've heard that Miss Addams is a staunch supporter of George Pullman and is one of those admirers I spoke of earlier. She's been quoted as saying others should emulate his generosity toward the workingman. Obviously, Miss Addams has misinterpreted Mr. Pullman's motives and actions."

"Jane and I don't concur on everything, but we do agree there are a multitude of people flocking into Chicago who need assistance. And she's reaching out to them in an effort to help. To be honest, Jane doesn't discriminate. She seeks financial assistance for her projects wherever she can find it." Ellen glanced toward the young boys tossing their ball. "Quite frankly, I agree that there are some good things to be said for this town. Whether the good outweighs the bad is a matter of opinion. I can tell you that Jane prefers to believe this town is the altruistic endeavor of a benevolent man, and neither of us will ever convince her otherwise."

Fred leaned forward and rested his forearms across his thighs. "If she worked for the company and lived in this town, she might decide otherwise. Perhaps if she'd talk to a few of the residents who have departed Pullman to live elsewhere, Miss Addams would have a more accurate idea of what it is like to live in a repressive environment."

"Is that how you feel about Pullman?"

He noted her surprised tone. "There's no denying the architecture in Pullman is pleasing to the eye, but this community doesn't warm the heart. The people who live here have no ownership in the town. We're simply pawns who bring it to life in order to fulfill George Pullman's dream. It's rather sad when you think about it."

Ellen raised her parasol against the bright afternoon sun. "I don't doubt there are many who would concur with your assessment, but Olivia hasn't conveyed that idea to me. On the contrary, her views seem to align more with those of Miss

Addams—at least regarding the benefits of the living conditions and amenities provided to the citizens."

Fred straightened and leaned his weight against the back of the wooden-slatted bench. "We all have diverse expectations, and Olivia has experienced a somewhat different circumstance than most. From the day she arrived, Mr. Howard has been her advocate. Even her current living quarters go beyond what any other employee of her class enjoys. But enough about that." He shifted on the bench. "Do you think your father would consider meeting with some of us who are interested in supporting a labor movement?"

"I'm sure he would, but I'd urge you to be very careful. The last Pullman employee who met with my father was greeted with his termination papers when he returned home. I'd venture a guess that it was Mr. Howard who handed him his papers."

Fred gave her a lopsided grin. "And I'd likely agree with you. There's very little that gets past him."

"Then I suggest you postpone any plans to meet my father. Mr. Howard is aware we've spoken at length today. He saw us talking at the reception, and there's little doubt he observed us leave the building together. If there are those who are willing to gain favor by reporting the activities of their fellow residents, Mr. Howard will surely have someone watching your every move for weeks—perhaps months—to come." She lowered her parasol and withdrew a card from her purse. "If you should decide you want to meet with my father in the future, he can be contacted at this address. In the meantime, I suggest you use caution in choosing those you draw into your confidence. Sometimes those we suspect the least can do us the most harm.

And now I should go to the restaurant and await Olivia."

Ellen stood and Fred offered his arm. She shook her head. "No need to accompany me inside. I'm sure you'd like to return to the reception and bid Albert and Martha farewell. I can find the restaurant on my own."

He slipped the card into his jacket. "It's been a genuine pleasure, Miss Ashton." He patted his pocket. The stiffness of the card beneath his fingers provided a sense of hope. "I look forward to meeting with your father one day in the future."

"I'll inform him of our visit today, Mr. DeVault."

Fred remained beside the bench for a moment and watched as she crossed the street and passed by two men outside the Arcade. They looked in his direction, and he considered Ellen's earlier warning. Had she been speaking of Olivia when she mentioned caution about drawing others into his confidence? If so, Miss Ashton need not worry on that account. The few words that passed between them nowadays could be numbered on one hand. He had thought to rectify that strained situation today, but Olivia's earlier preoccupation with Mr. Howard and her current plans to meet with Miss Ashton had prevented any opportunity for that.

He strolled down the tree-lined avenue, his thoughts returning to Olivia and her association with Ellen Ashton. Did Miss Ashton suspect Olivia of some covert behavior? Surely not. Yet the reason for their association remained a mystery to him. Perhaps Olivia had confided in his mother. He knew the two women visited frequently in the evenings when he was at work—at least on those evenings when she wasn't keeping company with Mr. Howard. His jaw tightened at the thought of Olivia sharing her time with Samuel Howard.

He turned the corner and hurried down the street just in time to escort Martha and Albert to the train station in their rented carriage. After bidding them a safe journey and sending them on their way to Chicago, he turned the horses toward the large Pullman barns. The barns reflected yet another of the many rules and regulations to keep the town of Pullman flawless for the frequent visitors. All horses and carriages were to be housed within the confines of the Pullman barns rather than maintained at the home of a resident. What a silly rule! People living in other communities parked their carriages in the front or rear of their homes, but Mr. Pullman considered any such conveyance a distortion of the aesthetics of the town. Therefore, no horses or buggies lined the streets of Pullman.

Fred jumped down from the carriage, turned the reins over to the stable boy, and watched as the manager added several figures and handed him a cost sheet made out in Albert's name. The amount would be deducted from Albert's next paycheck. One thing was always certain in Pullman: one's pay wasn't deposited in the bank until all obligations to the company had been paid in full. Fred surmised Albert's paycheck wouldn't amount to much next week, what with rent for the couple's apartment, fees for the reception hall, and the cost of renting the horse and carriage. A heavy burden for such a young couple.

He'd walked only a short distance when he noticed one of the men who'd been standing outside the Arcade a short time ago. Now the man was seated on a bench across the street and held an open newspaper on his lap. Fred's spine stiffened and his hands clenched at the sighting. Was the man following him? The remainder of the way home, Fred listened for the sound of footsteps. When he finally arrived at the front door, he glanced over his shoulder. There was no sign of the man, but he still wasn't sure he hadn't been followed.

He attempted to forget his worries about the man when he entered the house. Any sign of distress and his mother would question him for the remainder of the evening. He could blame his preoccupation on Albert's departure, for it was going to be strange having his friend living elsewhere. He'd enjoyed having someone his own age rooming with them, and the extra money had certainly helped with expenses. Perhaps he and his mother should seek another boarder. Recalling Malcolm Overby's mention of layoffs earlier today, Fred wondered if they would have any success finding another renter. Or, if his mother would agree to the risk, they could offer accommodations to one of the small families that might be left homeless by the layoffs.

The clanking of pans signaled his mother was at work in the kitchen, and Fred continued down the hallway. She glanced up from the worktable. "You look like you're carrying the weight of the world on your shoulders."

"Not quite." He pulled a chair away from the table. "Mind if I ask a few questions?"

She swiped her hands down her apron front. "Not if I can keep on working while we talk." Without waiting for a response, his mother began sorting through a basket of snap beans. When the wedding festivities had ended, she'd obviously stopped in Market Hall to purchase some of the produce raised in the Pullman greenhouses during the winter and early spring—another reason she enjoyed living in the town.

"Far be it from me to keep you from preparing food." He

settled on the chair, hoping to gather his thoughts for a moment.

"I thought you were going to have a chat with Olivia today. Instead, you were busy conversing with that Ashton woman every time I looked your way."

He straightened his shoulders. "And did you notice that Olivia was busy talking to Mr. Howard? How was I supposed to get a word in edgewise?"

"*Humph!* That sounds like an excuse to me."

He didn't want to argue with his mother. "Samuel Howard isn't someone I care to offend. You'll recall that he wields a good deal of power in town?"

"I know that! But you could have tried a little harder."

Fred did his best to assume a soulful look. "I decided it would be better to wait until she wasn't in Mr. Howard's company. I'll talk to her after church next Sunday." His response appeared to appease her. "By the way, has Olivia ever indicated why she visited Mr. Ashton's offices?"

His mother dropped her knife on the worktable and studied him. He clenched his jaw, hoping that he could remain steady under her close scrutiny. Still maintaining her fixed gaze, his mother sat down opposite him, her dinner preparations seemingly forgotten for the moment.

"Did you ask Miss Ashton that same question?"

He sucked in a breath. Her piercing stare wouldn't permit him to look away. "I did."

"And? What did she tell you?"

"She suggested I ask Olivia if I really wanted to know."

His mother gave an approving nod. "Good for her. I wasn't so sure I liked Miss Ashton, but there's obviously more to her than meets the eye. She seems to know how to hold a confidence."

Fred rested his forearms on the table. "So there *is* something secretive in nature about Olivia's visit to Mr. Ashton. I thought so. Otherwise, she'd have told Martha or Albert, and I'd already know what was going on. There's no need to keep me in the dark. You know I can keep a secret."

His mother chuckled. "I suppose you learned that from me, didn't you? Thing is, I don't know any more about Olivia's visits to Mr. Ashton than you do. And even if she had confided in me, you know I wouldn't break my word."

"You think maybe Mr. Howard's got her doing some kind of underhanded dealings for Mr. Pullman? Olivia would be a perfect pawn. I doubt she even knows Mr. Ashton offers legal help to the unions, but you can bet both Mr. Howard and Mr. Pullman keep a close eye on what he's up to." He leaned back and folded his arms across his chest. "You think maybe they're using Olivia to gain information about the men involved in unionization? I mean, what earthly reason could Olivia have for needing a lawyer? I hope she hasn't agreed to get involved in something that could prove dangerous for her."

His mother's chair scraped on the floor as she pushed away from the table and stood. "I think your imagination has gotten the best of you, son."

Fred rested his chin in his palm, amazed at his mother's naïve attitude. Olivia likely shared his mother's view, unless she'd willingly agreed to play the role of a needy woman seeking legal advice while acting as a spy for the company. Would she have agreed to befriend Ellen Ashton in order to gain information for Mr. Howard? Perhaps he had convinced her that unionization would ultimately harm the residents of Pullman and she'd become an agreeable participant in an evil plan. He wouldn't put such an idea past someone like Samuel Howard. In spite of the warmth in the kitchen, a chill coursed through his body.

CHAPTER THIRTEEN

Chicago, Illinois
May 3, 1893

Charlotte took her position behind one of the glass cases that displayed an unending variety of Parisian-made kid gloves, interspersed with delicate linen handkerchiefs and beaded evening bags. After only a few days in the store, she had suggested the arrangement as a method of increasing sales in their department. Both Mr. Selfridge and Mrs. Jenkins had lauded the idea and given their approval. Days later, Mr. Field noted the increased revenue in their department and had praised Mrs. Jenkins for her innovative concept. When the older woman had attempted to deflect the commendation to her subordinate, Charlotte had demurred. Though Charlotte hadn't considered the matter of any great consequence, the selfless act had resulted in Mrs. Jenkins's ongoing gratitude. This morning the older woman smiled and waved to Charlotte as she hastened toward the front of the store.

A double row of carriages had already begun to form outside

153

the Washington Street entrance, each carrying a woman of means who awaited the pleasure of entering Mr. Field's vast cathedral of stores. The moment the doors were unlocked, the ladies of the upper class began to enter, each one being met by an official greeter. They entered and strolled the aisles at a leisurely pace. Nothing was hurried in this vast emporium that catered to the discriminating tastes of the wealthy. Marshall Field's dry-goods establishment had been created for them to enjoy the freedom of unaccompanied visits to a place in the city where they could fill their days with shopping, visiting, enjoying tea, and reading. All the comforts of home were available between their visits to the dress salons and fitting rooms.

In contrast, women such as Mrs. Priddle would shop at the Boston Store, a department store that catered to the common crowd. The older woman considered the life of the wealthy to be unimaginative and boring. Charlotte hadn't disagreed with Mrs. Priddle's assessment. To do so would require too much explanation. However, her previous life had prepared her for the foibles of the affluent customers she now served each day.

Charlotte had learned the names of the wealthy women who typically spent three and four days a week in the store, especially those who had a penchant for accessories and were always anxious to see the latest arrivals in her department. She was opening the display case to replace the current array of gloves with the latest shipment when Mrs. Pullman approached her counter. Though Mrs. Pullman frequently shopped in the store, she'd stopped at her accessories counter on only one other occasion. Her eldest daughter, Florence, had been with her, and Mrs. Jenkins had taken charge. But Charlotte had remembered Mrs. Pullman's face and now greeted her by name.

"If I may be of assistance, please let me know, Mrs. Pullman. I will be happy to serve you." That said, she stepped back. Never rush the customer. Allow her time and space to enjoy the shopping experience, and she will make a purchase—one of Mr. Field's rules.

Mrs. Pullman continued to examine the gloves and then tapped the glass. "May I see that evening bag?"

Charlotte removed the beaded reticule from the case. It was one of her favorites. Though she deemed it a poor choice for a woman of Mrs. Pullman's years, she remained silent. Mrs. Pullman opened the clasp and turned the bag over several times, examining the handwork, and then looked into Charlotte's eyes. "What is your opinion of this evening bag?"

Charlotte hesitated. "I am personally quite fond of the bag, Mrs. Pullman. Is it a gift for your daughter?"

Mrs. Pullman smiled. "How did you know?"

"I saw her when the two of you were in the store several days ago. When you asked to see this bag, I thought of her. I'm certain she would be delighted to receive it."

Mrs. Pullman handed Charlotte the evening bag. "Then I shall see that she has it. Now, I believe I'll need a lovely handkerchief to tuck inside, don't you think?"

Once the woman had decided upon a delicately embroidered handkerchief, she departed, off to evaluate newly arrived merchandise throughout the store, enjoy a cup of tea, or visit with the other dowagers. Charlotte wrapped the gift according to the store's exacting instructions and then called for a bundle boy.

With the package tucked snugly beneath his arm, the boy

rushed off as though the very world depended upon his immediate delivery of the beaded handbag and handkerchief. Truth
be told, his world *did* depend upon that very thing, for if Mrs.
Pullman should arrive at her carriage before the package, his
termination would be immediate.

Mrs. Pullman's early morning purchases had created a void
in the display case, so Charlotte searched for the perfect
replacements. She unwrapped several evening bags that had
come in the latest shipment and decided upon a bag of black
silk with an unusual decoration in a Japanese embroidered
design. The bag was edged with black ribbon, a crystal fringe,
and a black ribbon draw. A perfect replacement, for it was
entirely different from its predecessor. Yet another of Mr. Field's
rules. Charlotte closed the case as Mr. Selfridge bustled past
her counter at a rapid pace.

The sound of an irritable young girl soon captured Charlotte's attention, and she turned. Her breath caught as she
locked gazes with the man escorting her. The young girl yanked
on his arm while the man continued to stare at Charlotte. She
didn't fail to detect the fear in his eyes. *Randolph Morgan!*

With fingers trembling and stomach roiling, she attempted
to remain calm and absorb the sight of him surrounded by his
wife and children. At least she assumed the woman was his wife
and the two young girls his daughters. One couldn't be certain
with Randolph, she told herself. Just as quickly, she pushed
aside the thought. Randolph would never escort anyone other
than his wife and children into one of Chicago finest stores. He
might be willing to provide support for a secluded mistress or
to escort a woman of nobility while visiting a foreign country,
but far be it from Randolph Morgan to enter Marshall Field's

fine emporium with anyone other than his wife. He wouldn't want to be ostracized from Chicago society.

Randolph's present intentions were obvious: he wanted to avoid Charlotte at all costs. She observed his attempt to turn his daughter in the opposite direction, but the girl was headstrong, determined to make her way to the gloves and handbags in Charlotte's glass case.

The possibility of humiliating him in front of his family created a sense of delicious pleasure for a moment—until she saw the little girl's adoring eyes as she tugged on her father's hand. He stooped down in front of her. Though Charlotte couldn't hear the conversation, she was certain he was making his best argument against shopping in the accessories department. Meanwhile, Mrs. Morgan had sauntered off to examine a sumptuous array of veiling in the next aisle and appeared not to notice the unfolding drama. Randolph rubbed a thumb across the little girl's plump cheek—a stray tear, perhaps?

The girl reminded her of Fiona. They were likely close to the same age and bore the same fair complexion. She wondered if Randolph's daughter played the piano. The child continued to gaze longingly toward the counter and offered Charlotte a winsome smile. An unbidden remembrance of their Bible study from last evening overwhelmed her. Mrs. Priddle had read from the book of Matthew and then talked about Jesus and the illustrations He had used in teaching His disciples. Mrs. Priddle had talked about feeding the hungry and visiting the ill and how each act of kindness we performed for one another was the same as if we'd done it for Jesus. What was it she'd said? True believers reflect the love of Jesus in how they treat others. Yes, that was how she'd put it. Charlotte considered the pain

Randolph had caused her and the longing she continued to feel as she watched him with his family. Although Mrs. Priddle's words were easily spoken, they'd not be so easily followed. Yet whom would she hurt the most? His children? His wife? Randolph would bear some of the pain, but would it be worth the damage she would inflict upon his wife and children, who had done nothing but love him?

The little girl managed to slip away. Before Randolph could stop her, she was standing in front of Charlotte's counter and pointing at a pair of dainty gloves. With an air of expectancy and delight shining in her eyes, she asked if she might try them on. Charlotte slid open the glass door as Randolph approached.

"There you are—they may be a size too large, but I have a smaller size if your father approves the purchase." She didn't look at him. She couldn't.

"What has she talked you into, Randolph? Not another pair of gloves. Really, Margaret, you don't need more gloves. Let's go upstairs, and we'll see about a new dress." Mrs. Morgan turned and retrieved her other daughter by the hand. "Vivie wants to go upstairs."

The gloves sagged on Margaret's small hands like burlap bags. They were several sizes too large. The girl removed them, and Charlotte expected her and her father to walk away. Instead, Randolph smiled at his daughter and asked for a smaller size. "A young lady can never have too many gloves. Isn't that right, Margaret?"

The little girl nodded enthusiastically as Charlotte handed her the gloves. Her annoyance obvious, Mrs. Morgan returned to the counter with their younger daughter at her side. "I suppose if we're going to spend time in accessories, you can show me that evening bag."

Charlotte removed the black silk bag from the counter. "Our new shipment of bags arrived yesterday. I placed this one in the display case only a few minutes ago."

Mrs. Morgan appeared pleased by the revelation. "How many do you have in stock?"

Charlotte understood. Mrs. Morgan didn't want anyone else to have the same bag. "It's the only one—an original. You'll not see a duplicate, either here or abroad."

"Good. I'll take it." She glanced down at Margaret, who had slipped her hands into the soft kid gloves. "And I suppose we'll take those, too. What about you, Vivie? Do you want some gloves?"

The younger girl wagged her head back and forth while Margaret removed the gloves and handed them to Charlotte.

"We're going to have lunch in the tearoom. Do you get to eat in the tearoom every day?" the girl asked.

"Really, Margaret! I doubt the salesgirl is interested in our luncheon plans." Mrs. Morgan grabbed Vivie's hand. "I'm going to take Vivian upstairs to begin looking for a dress. I trust you two will come along once you've taken care of the bill, Randolph?"

"Yes. We'll join you shortly."

Charlotte tallied the bill while Margaret continued to stare at her. "Well? Do you eat in the tearoom every day?" she whispered.

"No, I don't eat there often. If I ate there every day, it would no longer be special, don't you agree?" She handed the bill to Mr. Morgan, careful not to touch his hand. The amount would be added to his account and the statement sent at the end of the month.

Margaret's brow furrowed. "I suppose you're right. But I like to eat there when we come shopping."

"I'm sure you do. It's a wonderful place. And I suggest the chicken potpie. It's my very favorite."

Margaret beamed. "It's my favorite, too. And the lemon cookies."

Charlotte agreed. "An excellent choice."

Randolph's shoulders relaxed. The fear in his eyes had been replaced with curiosity. "Thank you for your kind assistance."

"You're welcome. Do come again, Margaret," Charlotte said.

For the present, she'd shown Randolph Morgan as much kindness as she could. Charlotte hoped her actions had given him evidence of her newfound faith. She watched Randolph envelop the little girl's hand. He beamed at the child with an undeniable adoration, a poignant reminder that little Morgan had neither father nor mother in his life.

Fred had ceased his daily visits to Lockabee's Design and Glass Etching Shop two weeks ago when it had become evident that Bill Orland had gained an excellent working knowledge of the etching process. Bill just needed more confidence in his ability, and that would come with additional practice. He was a quick study and had rapidly acquired the necessary skills to manage the day-to-day operation of Mr. Lockabee's shop. Fred had promised he'd return once a week to answer any specific questions or to help with a special project, but Bill didn't really need him. Fred planned to completely withdraw as Bill's instructor by the first of next month. Bill's self-assurance would increase once Fred completely stepped out of the picture.

While he ambled down the street toward the train station, Fred decided the benefits of helping Bill had far outweighed any of the inconvenience. Granted, the frequent trips to Chicago proved taxing at times, but seeing Bill and his family flourish had been worth it.

"Fred! Hold up!" Waving his hat overhead, Harlan Ladner loped across the street and fell into step alongside Fred. "You have a few minutes to talk?"

"I was heading into Chicago, but I can catch the next train if need be."

Harlan shook his head. "I can't be late for work, but I wanted to fill you in on what's been going on in the paint shop."

Thus far there had been no repercussions from the meeting back in March, and Fred continued to hope that the incident wouldn't deter the men in the paint shop from aligning themselves with those who favored unionization. Neither Harlan nor the other men had appeared at the meeting in April, and Fred hadn't pursued the matter. He understood their fears. They'd come around when the time was right.

Fred had expected Mr. Vance to retaliate prior to this time. "Something new happening in the paint shop or more of the same treatment? Has Mr. Vance said anything?"

"I'm sure he knows something. He's been cold as ice. The man never cracks a smile, and nothing's changed with the work assignments. If anything, he's showing even more favoritism toward those new hires. It takes everything I've got to keep from telling him off." Harlan shoved his hat back on his head. "My wife tells me I better learn to keep my mouth shut, or we'll be looking for a new place to live."

Fred nodded as they continued on. "I think your wife is as set on staying in Pullman as my mother."

"Now, that's the truth. The women sure do like it here." He glanced over his shoulder. "You remember that fella that turned up at the meeting in March?"

"How could I forget?"

"Mr. Vance told us the fella was his cousin and only here for a short visit, but it seems he's still in town. I didn't think too much about it, but one of the other men heard Mr. Howard and Mr. Vance talking the other day."

Fred and Harlan came to a halt across the street from the train depot. "Talking about what? Mr. Vance's cousin?"

"Exactly. Seems he's not really Mr. Vance's cousin."

"What makes you so sure?"

"Mr. Vance said his wife didn't like having a stranger living in the house with them and wanted to know how much longer the fella was going to be in town. Sounds kind of suspicious, don't you think?"

Fred scratched his head. "It does. I'll do some checking around and see if I can discover any information. We missed you at the last meeting."

"To tell you the truth, I think it's better if we stay away until we figure out what's going on. If Mr. Vance is having us watched, it will only cause trouble if we show up at the meetings." He clapped Fred on the shoulder. "Our not being there doesn't mean we don't support taking a stand sometime in the future. And we'll come back to the meetings once we figure out exactly what's going on."

"John Holderman tells me that some of you have been coming over in the evenings to help with training. I know the men appreciate it."

"It's the least we can do. Mr. Vance did ask me how come several of us had taken such an interest in going to Kensington." Harlan grinned. "I asked him how he knew where we were spending our time."

"Good for you! What'd he say?"

"Said he'd had business over in Kensington on several occasions, and every time he was headed in that direction, he saw one or two of the men from the paint shop." Harlan laughed. "Funny thing is, I think he expected me to believe him. What business would Mr. Vance have in Kensington?"

"None that I know of," Fred replied.

The train whistle sounded in the distance, and Harlan glanced toward the clock tower. "I better get going or I'm going to be late for work. I'll let you know if any other information comes my way."

"And I'll do the same." Fred waited until Harlan departed and then hurried across the street.

He rushed to the ticket counter and purchased a round-trip ticket to Chicago. With only minutes to spare, he exited the depot, darted down the platform, and boarded the train. After dropping into a window seat, Fred considered Harlan's news. He hadn't wanted to express concern over the information Harlan delivered. Yet it appeared the company hoped to discover more information than the supervisors or resident gossips could provide. Did Mr. Howard plan to infiltrate the town with men hired to spy on the employees? A chilling concept.

CHAPTER FOURTEEN

May 5, 1893

Olivia squirmed in her seat as the *Pennsylvania Limited* rolled eastward toward New York City. This first trip on her own had caused both a good deal of fear and a surprising sense of exhilaration. At the moment, she was uncertain which emotion had taken hold of her, for she could feel the uncomfortable stares of the gentleman sitting across from her. She had attempted to avoid him, to no avail. The man would periodically depart for the dining car or perhaps the smoking car, return, and take the seat opposite her. She'd given thought to expressing her concerns to the porter but decided against the idea. What if the man was an important railroad investor and she insulted him? His perfectly pressed suit and polished shoes bespoke a man of means. She pulled out her notebook and added to the notations she'd begun earlier in the day. There was little to write, for other than the gentleman seated across from her, she'd found nothing about which to complain. The staff proved attentive, the coach luxurious, and the scenery interesting.

Keeping her head bowed, Olivia peeked from beneath her thick lashes and attempted to steal another glance at the man. He grinned in return, and she felt a flush of warmth rise in her cheeks. She wanted to look away, but the sparkle in his midnight blue eyes held her captive.

He leaned forward a mere inch or two and tipped his head. "Matthew Clayborn of Chicago." His introduction was clipped and crisp. "And *you* are?"

"O-Olivia Mott—Miss Olivia Mott—of Pullman." She stammered out the reply and immediately wished she could shove the words back into her mouth. This man was a total stranger, yet she'd given her name and place of residence. Mr. Howard said she should never identify herself as a resident of Pullman. Olivia wasn't certain why it mattered, but he'd been quite emphatic about that particular point.

Mr. Clayborn pointed toward her notebook. "You're a woman after my own heart—a writer." He raked his fingers through his sandy blond hair. Several strands on either side of his head protruded in disarray.

Though she attempted to stifle a grin, Olivia's efforts proved ineffective. After she touched a hand to the side of her head, Mr. Clayborn immediately followed suit.

He continued to finger-comb the sides of his hair. "Bad habit, especially after visiting the barber's chair. Those concoctions they use can make your hair stand straight on end. Is that better?"

Olivia giggled at his unaffected nature. Given his clipped introduction, she'd expected the opposite. "Perfect."

"Tell me about your writing, Miss Mott. Are you a novelist? Or perhaps you write for a newspaper? Another Nellie Bly?"

Olivia had heard stories of the famous Nellie Bly and her feats. Miss Bly was a woman who was afraid of nothing. A woman willing to challenge and champion the causes of equality and human rights through her many courageous deeds and newspaper articles. "I'm neither a reporter nor a novelist. Merely a woman writing in her journal."

"Really?" Before she could snap the book out of reach, he stuck his finger between the pages and peered at her notes. His icy blue eyes stabbed her with a sharp look. "Your journal doesn't appear to contain the musings of a traveler, Miss Mott. You seem to be jotting down the notes of a reporter. I do understand your reticence to admit the nature of your employment, but there are those of us who are a bit more enlightened than the average man. I personally admired Nellie Bly's determination and grit. She was willing to suffer to bring about change and help others." He tapped his finger atop the Bible resting beside him. "An imaginative mind could draw a rather simple analogy between Nellie Bly and Jesus, don't you think?"

Olivia frowned. She wasn't accustomed to making such comparisons, since she was only beginning to learn the truths of the Bible. Perhaps Mrs. DeVault would understand such an assessment, but a newspaper reporter, even one as noted as Nellie Bly, didn't seem at all comparable to Jesus. "I'm afraid I don't share your depth of knowledge, Mr. Clayborn."

He chuckled. "Most believe I have no depth of knowledge— at least where the Bible is concerned. And my analogy *is* rather weak, but Miss Bly willingly suffered when she went into that mental institution. Through her articles, she created change for those living inside the walls of those facilities. On a much deeper level, Jesus suffered and died for us so that we might have eternal life. Through the Bible, He leaves us His story so that we may change our own lives and spend eternity with Him." He shrugged. "Not a very eloquent summation, I fear."

Olivia tucked the journal into her valise. "There is a vague similarity, yet I doubt whether you need worry about a preacher asking you to prepare his sermons."

"Point taken."

They both glanced toward the far end of the coach where the taunting laughter of a young boy continued to grow incessantly louder. Olivia watched the porter, who was dutifully caring for the child while his parents enjoyed themselves in another car. Olivia estimated the boy to be four or five, certainly old enough to understand proper behavior. The lad had made a game of yanking off the porter's cap, tossing it upon the floor, and hollering with delight. With each episode, the porter silently picked up his hat, brushed it off, and returned it to his head. Olivia wondered how long the older man would suffer the child's rude behavior before correcting him.

Mr. Clayborn gave a long, low whistle. "That porter certainly has more patience than I could ever muster. That youngster needs the strong hand of discipline properly applied."

Olivia covered her mouth to stifle a laugh. "I'm certain the porter agrees, though you could never tell by looking at him."

He shook his head. "Sad, isn't it?"

Olivia arched her brows, hoping for further explanation.

He nodded toward the porter. "That the staff members are forced to accept rude behavior from their passengers in order to make a living." He shifted closer. "*Tips*, Miss Mott. These men must accept all form of ill-treatment if they are going to receive the tips they need to support their families. They can't possibly live on the paltry wages George Pullman pays them."

Olivia met his steady look. How had he come to know the amount of wages paid to Pullman employees? She didn't know if she should trust Mr. Clayborn, and her imagination suddenly took flight. Was this a test? Had Mr. Howard placed this man in her path to see if she could capably handle her new position? If so, she'd failed miserably. Already Mr. Clayborn could report that she'd informed him she lived in Pullman. He had also been able to peruse some of her notes without much difficulty.

He pointed to her valise. "Those notes you're making. I don't for one minute believe you're merely writing a daily journal. A lady's journal would consist of musings about the beautiful scenery or interesting traveling companions she'd met. That's not the type of writing I observed in your book."

"You saw only a few scattered entries, Mr. Clayborn." She lifted her head to a jaunty angle. "And might I add that your behavior is nearly as rude as that of the mischievous child sitting at the front of the coach."

He rocked back in his seat as though she'd slapped him. "I apologize. You see, I'm a news reporter myself, and I thought I'd found a like-minded soul. Please forgive my prying, but it's a trait of reporters. It's what we do, how we gather information for our stories."

She narrowed her eyes. As if he'd been reading her thoughts, Mr. Clayborn reached into his suit jacket, retrieved a card, and offered it to her. Mr. Clayborn's name had been printed in bold black letters on the thick stock paper. Directly beneath his name, Olivia read the words "Reporter, *Chicago Herald*." It appeared Mr. Clayborn was who he proclaimed, yet she still remained suspicious of the man.

"And what news article are you writing, Mr. Clayborn?"

He winked and inclined his head in her direction. "We're not supposed to give out that kind of information, Miss Mott. I don't want another reporter to get the scoop first."

"Scoop?" The only scoop she knew about was the one she used to ladle sugar or ice cream. Why a reporter would fear someone else would get a scoop first, or even want one for that matter, seemed an odd thing.

"Scoop. Story. We don't want someone else to beat us out of our story."

This man certainly had a strange way of talking. Perhaps he *was* a reporter. It seemed all professions had their own vocabulary and special phrases. She didn't understand some of the terms Fred and Albert used when they spoke about electroplating, and they didn't understand many of her cooking terms.

She decided to inquire a bit further. "And how long have you worked for the Chicago newspaper, Mr. Clayborn?"

"Five years. Before that, I reported for the *Pittsburgh Dispatch*—the same paper where Nellie Bly got her start." His chest swelled as though that piece of information would somehow make him more important in her eyes. "And please call me Matthew."

"We barely know each other. I don't—"

"Who is going to know, Miss Mott—*Olivia*? I don't know another passenger on this train, and I'll wager you could say the same. And you can rest assured the porters and wait staff in the dining cars aren't going to tell." He unfolded his long legs and tapped his index finger on his pursed lips. "Secrets. Pullman porters know better than to speak about anything that happens in their car. They know how to keep secrets. And if they don't, they're soon out of work."

The parents of the unruly child were strolling back to their seats. Olivia watched as the father flipped a coin with his thumb and forefinger. Prisms of golden sunlight poured through the windows, and the porter's ebony face glistened. He jumped forward and adroitly snatched his tip midair. The little boy wailed in protest, and Olivia watched his father dig another coin from his pocket and hand it to the child. Olivia turned away.

"In a few more years, they'll wonder why their son has become completely unmanageable."

Olivia scooted back into the cushioned seat. "In my opinion he's already incorrigible, but I'm certainly no expert on child rearing."

"Nor am I. And seeing that child's unruly behavior makes me wonder if I ever want to be." Matthew turned his attention toward her valise. "Exactly what takes you to New York, Olivia? Perhaps a holiday? Or possibly an assignment for the Pullman newspaper? Pullman does have a newspaper, doesn't it?"

She nodded. "A weekly publication—primarily local news."

Matthew rubbed the shadow of blond stubble on his jaw. "You've set my investigative instincts on edge with your secretive nature. Thus far I've concluded you are unmarried, and therefore you are employed in some manner by the Pullman Palace Car Company." Before she realized what was happening, he leaned forward, grasped her hand, and turned it over in his own. "Not a laundress. Your hands are much too soft."

She yanked her hand away. The man would not relent. He didn't need to be a news reporter or have investigative talent to realize she wasn't married. She'd introduced herself as Miss Mott, and he'd examined her hand. He could see that she wore no wedding band. And it was common knowledge that only employees and their families could live in Pullman. What could she say? She didn't want to fall back into her old habit of lying. Such behavior would be a genuine disappointment to Mrs. DeVault—not to mention the Lord! Finally she beckoned him forward. "If you promise not to reveal my identity, I'll tell you."

He rubbed his hands as though they were conspiring to commit a dreadful crime. "Your secret is absolutely safe with me."

She hoped she wasn't making a terrible mistake. "I'm the assistant chef at Hotel Florence."

He rocked back in his seat and laughed. Not a mere guffaw, but a robust belly laugh!

Olivia folded her arms across her waist and glared as tears pooled in his eyes and slowly trickled down his cheeks.

Continuing to laugh, he reached into his pocket and extracted a handkerchief, dabbing his cheeks with the linen square. He looked up and met her angry stare. Immediately, his laughter came to a halt. "I'm sorry. I've offended you with my reaction, haven't I? Surely you expected I would laugh at your response." He waited a moment, but when she said nothing, his smile vanished. "You didn't really expect me to believe you're a chef at Hotel Florence, did you?" He slapped his palm to his forehead. "You *did* expect me to believe you. And now you're angry because I don't believe your little fabrication."

"Fabrication!" Her chin jutted forward as she squared her shoulders and sat up straight. "You're accusing me of lying when I've told you the truth, and you think I shouldn't take umbrage at your insulting behavior?"

"Please don't be offended, Miss Mott, but I have personal knowledge that Hotel Florence employs a rather rotund French chef—a *male* French chef. You, Miss Mott, are neither French nor a man."

His smug look of satisfaction served only to irritate her further. "How astute you are, Mr. Clayborn. You are correct on those accounts, but your reporter's instincts have failed you. You do not *listen*. I said I was employed as the *assistant* chef at Hotel Florence. Chef René is the executive chef. He is, as you say, both French and a man."

He eyed her suspiciously. "I'm still not convinced, Miss Mott. A female chef—*assistant* chef—would be a rather forward-thinking idea even for a city the size of Chicago or New York. But in Pullman? Hard to believe."

"Not so difficult as you may think, Mr. Clayborn. Innovative men such as George Pullman produce change." She pointed to the upper berths that were hidden away behind carved rosewood marquetry. "Only a few years ago men such as yourself wouldn't have imagined sleeping on a train that offered comfortable beds and electric lights. Nor would you have entertained thoughts of the vestibules, dining car, barbershop, or the library and smoking car that are available on this very train. His progressive ideas have greatly benefited the public."

Mr. Clayborn laughed. "The public has not benefited nearly so much as George Pullman. His passengers and employees have made him one of the wealthiest men in this country, Miss Mott, yet it's obvious you are quite smitten by the man."

"Not by the man, but by what he has accomplished, Mr. Clayborn."

"On the backs of his workers, Miss Mott."

They were moving headlong into another disagreement. Mr. Clayborn's argument closely resembled what she'd heard from Fred when he talked of worker unionization. "Not all of us ascribe to such beliefs. There are many happy residents in Pullman."

He gave her a sidelong glance. "We've digressed from our original discussion, Miss Mott, but I'd enjoy continuing our talk in the dining car. With your expert knowledge of food, I'm certain you'll be able to help me with my dinner selection. Will you join me?"

She didn't fail to note his intonation. His invitation was a challenge, one she would not refuse. "I would be delighted, Mr. Clayborn, but I don't dine at five o'clock. I plan to wait until seven." She would see just how anxious he was to put her to the test.

He rubbed his hands together. "Done! Seven o'clock suits me just fine."

CHAPTER FIFTEEN

Two hours later the steward met Olivia and Mr. Clayborn at the door of the dining car, his broad smile revealing an even row of white teeth that matched his starched cotton jacket. Except for the fact that he wore a pair of neatly pressed navy blue pants rather than black trousers, he could have passed for the steward at Hotel Florence.

The waiter's attire differed from that of the steward only in the long white apron that dropped to the top of his shiny black shoes. And while the porters were ebony skinned, the complexion of the dining car attendants was a shade lighter. Perhaps another one of Mr. Pullman's many rules.

Olivia immediately took note of the sumptuous table settings. The pristine white tablecloths had been starched and pressed to perfection. Each table had been set with the specially manufactured Calumet china. Each dish bore the distinctive Pullman name printed in midnight green and rimmed with dual bands of midnight green and brilliant gold. A crisp white linen napkin lay neatly folded atop each dinner plate. Polished silver and fine glassware twinkled in the radiance of sunlight that spilled through the window. A variety of greens and fresh flowers were perfectly arranged in crystal vases and centered on each table. The steward held their chairs and then motioned their waiter forward.

Careful to secure a folded linen towel around the pitcher to catch any drips, the waiter filled their goblets with ice water, handed each of them a menu that set forth the evening's dinner offerings, and silently disappeared to permit them adequate time in which to make their choices.

Mr. Clayborn perused the list for a moment. "What do you suggest, Miss Mott?"

"I don't know your food preferences, but I plan to order the French slaw, double lamb chops with mint jelly, asparagus with cream sauce, and duchess potatoes. I believe I'll decide upon dessert after I've finished my meal." Her mouth had already begun to water in anticipation of her selections. She glanced across the table and pointed at the menu. "I see they have blue points on the half shell. Do you enjoy oysters?"

He shook his head. "Not particularly. They're rather slimy in my estimation. I prefer more common fare."

She nibbled at her bottom lip to keep from laughing. Obviously Mr. Clayborn was going to test her prowess. Little matter, given the numerous choices on the menu. "Then I suggest the stuffed turkey, mashed potatoes with gravy, marrowfat peas, and perhaps a serving of pickled beets or lobster salad au mayonnaise."

He contemplated her choices for a moment, exchanged the marrowfat peas for sugar corn, and disregarded her suggestion for the lobster salad. Perhaps he didn't like seafood of any type. The waiter beamed an approving smile, though Olivia was certain he would have done so regardless of their dinner choices.

The waiter looked at Matthew. "Coffee with your meal or afterward?"

"Both," Mr. Clayborn responded. "I'm certain I'll be ordering a slice of apple pie with the New York ice cream for dessert, too."

"Yes, suh. I'll be sure to hold a piece of that apple pie just for you." He nodded and departed to place their order.

Mr. Clayborn removed a notebook and pen from his pocket and relaxed in his chair. "Tell me, Miss Mott, exactly what is the difference between a marrowfat pea and a plain old pea." He poised the pen as though anxious to make note of her response.

She giggled. "There is a very distinct difference. The marrowfat pea is much larger than a regular pea."

"I believe I can remember that without writing it down." He tapped his pen on the table. "And cold custard à la chantilly?"

"Cold custard with sweetened whipped cream, sometimes flavored with vanilla bean. I believe you are testing me, Mr. Clayborn."

He tucked the notebook back inside his jacket pocket. "I know so little about food that you could tell me anything and I wouldn't know if I'd received the proper answer. Then again, I could always go and ask the chef."

She perked to attention. "You know the chef on this train?"

He nodded. "I know the stewards, porters, cooks, buffet attendants, barbers, waiters, and conductors who work on this train."

"And how can that be?"

He laughed. "Now I think you are testing *me*, Miss Mott." He took a sip of his water. "I travel frequently and use the *Pennsylvania Limited* whenever possible. In time you get to know the employees."

Olivia wasn't certain she believed him. The waiter hadn't acted as though he'd ever seen Mr. Clayborn before this evening. When Olivia mentioned that fact, he appeared unruffled.

"A Pullman employee would never approach a passenger in a familiar manner." He held a finger to his lips. "Secrets. Remember? If you wish, I'll prove that I am known by the staff aboard this train. Indeed, I'd enjoy making a wager with you."

She arched her brows. "I don't believe in gambling, Mr. Clayborn." What kind of woman had he taken her for?

"Not even if I can arrange a meeting with the chef and a tour of the kitchen?" He grinned. "No money involved, Miss Mott."

She hesitated. If there was no money involved, perhaps the wager would be harmless enough. "Then what are the terms of your wager, sir?"

"If I secure a meeting with the chef and tour of the kitchen, you agree to travel as my companion for the remainder of the journey—except during the nighttime hours, of course."

The offer was too good to reject. Their private berths would be ready within the hour, and arrival in New York was scheduled for eleven o'clock tomorrow morning. His wager would entail visiting with him for only a few more hours. What could be easier? The man was excellent company—except for his inquisitive nature. "Yes, of—"

He held up his index finger. "There's more."

Her lungs deflated in a weary sigh. She should have known. His offer had seemed too good to be true. "What else?"

"At any other time when we may be traveling aboard the same train, you'll agree to this same arrangement."

She frowned, and a small V formed between her brows. "You can't be assured that we'll always be assigned to the same coach."

"But *you* can. I just happened to notice you carry a special pass, and that pass allows for seat reassignment." With a lopsided grin, he nodded toward her purse. "I imagine just one flash of that gold card you carry would send any Pullman conductor scurrying to change your seating assignment."

Olivia cringed and wondered if anyone else might have observed the gold card. Mr. Howard had advised her to keep the card well hidden and to use it only in an emergency. Otherwise, she was to use cash like most other passengers. For a fleeting moment she wondered what else Mr. Clayborn had observed. First her notes and now her pass card. The way he'd been sticking his nose into her business, it was a wonder the man's well-shaped snout hadn't grown by several inches since boarding the train. However, she doubted whether they'd ever encounter each other again, and she desperately wanted to examine the kitchen and speak to the chef.

Before she answered, the waiter was at their table. With crisp military precision, he placed white china plates atop the patterned chargers and refilled their coffee cups from the silver server. The elegant arrangement of the food would have pleased even Chef René. After only one bite of lamb chop, her decision had been made. "I'll agree to your wager, Mr. Clayborn."

"Once your meal was served, I was certain you'd have little

difficulty with your decision. The food on this train is by far the best I've ever eaten, and believe it or not, I've dined in some elegant restaurants."

There was no smugness in his voice, only a deep appreciation for the meal he'd been served. They conversed little throughout the meal. After a bite of the asparagus, Olivia pointed her fork toward the vegetable and rolled her eyes toward heaven. "Perfect."

Mr. Clayborn grunted his agreement while forking another bite of stuffing. "You should try this next time. You won't be disappointed. It's every bit as good as it looks."

While he later devoured his warm apple pie topped with ice cream, Olivia enjoyed a slice of pineapple cake topped with a sumptuous fruity glaze. Though she was overfull and unable to completely appreciate the cake's subtle flavor, she couldn't resist even the final bite. She leaned back in her chair and yearned to loosen her corset lacings.

As if he'd read her mind, Mr. Clayborn unbuttoned his jacket. "Now then, let me see if I am going to win this wager that we've agreed upon."

He signaled for the waiter, who silently approached and leaned forward. She couldn't hear what Mr. Clayborn was saying, but the waiter bobbed his head several times and then straightened. "I'll be right back with your answer, suh."

"He's going to see if he can gain permission from the chef and the conductor for our visit." Mr. Clayborn eyed the silver coffee pitcher that remained on the table. "More coffee?"

Olivia shook her head. If she attempted to swallow even a mouthful of liquid, she would surely burst. Within minutes the waiter returned and bent forward to speak with Mr. Clayborn.

She leaned a bit closer, hoping to discover what the waiter had to say, but her efforts proved futile. If she was going to succeed in her investigative endeavors, she'd best learn a few of Mr. Clayborn's tricks. The waiter straightened and stepped back to assist Olivia with her chair.

"Both the chef and conductor have agreed that we may visit the kitchen." He pushed away from the table and stood. "Even your *pass* wouldn't gain you entry to this kitchen."

The pride in his voice reminded her of a small child anxious to taunt a playmate. Olivia didn't tell Mr. Clayborn, but she wouldn't have ever considered using her pass to request a visit to the kitchen. Mr. Howard had advised her to blend in with the other passengers and never draw attention to herself. Unfortunately, she had remembered the latter portion of that admonition too late. So much for remaining inconspicuous. Not many people requested visits to the kitchen and even fewer were granted the privilege. She doubted whether the dining car staff would soon forget her, but it was too late to back out. Moreover, such behavior would only serve to gain further unwanted attention. The moment they stepped away from the table, a buffet attendant silently approached.

The snap of a crisp tablecloth cracked through the air as they walked down the aisle. Moments later, Olivia glanced over her shoulder. Their table had already been reset to accommodate another duo of hungry travelers. She ought not be surprised. There was little time for dallying on Mr. Pullman's railcars. The movement of every dining car employee had been calculated to speed the hordes of hungry passengers through the dining car while still conveying a sense of elegant dining at a leisurely pace. And through it all, the employees never stopped smiling.

Olivia wondered if the waiters, behind those gleaming smiles and polite comments, longed to dislodge those diners who remained long after their meals had been completed. If the porters and waiters were as dependent upon their tips as Mr. Clayborn indicated, they must surely dislike the passengers who lingered. Yet each of the employees continued to smile. What rule was it that required smiles and hospitality at all times? She couldn't remember the number, but obviously the men had taken that one to heart.

Mr. Clayborn stepped to one side and gently grasped her arm, propelling her forward. "Miss Mott, I'd like to introduce you to the chef of the *Pennsylvania Limited*, William Richmond." He gave the chef a sideways glance. "Correct?"

"That's right, Mr. Clayborn. Pleased to meet you, miss." The chef continued working while he spoke. He turned a fat juicy steak and nudged one of the cooks to stir the cream sauce. Olivia followed his gaze as it darted about the tiny kitchen. Four men stood back to back without a hairsbreadth between them. She thought of Chef René. He could never cook in such a kitchen. Even absent the other men, she doubted he could fit in the narrow space. Looking about, Olivia marveled at the variety of conveniences that had been fitted into the compact space.

"I'm amazed you can prepare a meal in this small work area."

The chef laughed, his limp toque drooping to one side. "Economy of space. Every canister and tool has its proper spot, and woe to the man who moves anything from where it belongs." He proudly pointed out the three-tiered range. "One for baking, one for broiling, and the other for boiling water and meeting any other cooking needs." He pointed to the shelves and cupboards on either side of the range where the kitchen equipment and supplies were maintained. "Plenty of storage space if everyone keeps things tidy, and we even got this fine carving table connected by pipes to the steam boiler. Keeps the food good and hot." A waiter arrived with additional orders, and the chef waved the man forward. "Sorry, but that's as much time as I can offer right now. Too many orders coming in."

Olivia thanked Chef Richmond profusely for his time. Before they departed the dining car, Mr. Clayborn pointed out the side door. "Food can be loaded to the kitchen by using this side door." He grinned and buttoned his jacket. "Or unloaded."

"Unloaded?"

He hesitated. She must have sounded overly interested, for his demeanor turned suspicious and he appeared to be searching for the proper explanation. "Right. Whatever needs to be accomplished—loading or unloading. Soiled linens and the like."

She didn't pursue the topic. Quite obviously he was avoiding her question. His response was downright silly. Why would they load and unload the dining room linens near the kitchen when the task could be accomplished much more easily at the far end of the train where the items were stored? No need to pursue the matter right now. He'd already expressed misgivings about the notes she was keeping. She had best not appear too curious, but she'd make note of his comment in her journal. If the linens were actually being loaded into the kitchen, time and effort could be saved by using the far door.

Mr. Clayborn opened the door to the vestibule that connected the dining car with the next railcar. "Would you like to stop in the library car before settling in for the night?"

During her training journeys on the rails, Mr. Howard had advised her that the library, also known as the concession car, was a social gathering spot where men could enjoy a cigar, a glass of port or whiskey, and a newspaper. She remembered his cautionary words: *"Most women don't enjoy the atmosphere or amenities offered in the library car. You would seem out of place. The ladies find the parlor car more to their liking."* Although her appearance might be overlooked since she was in the company of Mr. Clayborn, she knew that, at least for the present, she was not expected to share any cost-saving ideas regarding operation of the library car. And if Mr. Clayborn visited the library car and she returned to the sleeper, there would be ample opportunity to write in her journal.

Once they'd passed through the vestibule, she glanced over her shoulder. "I believe I'll return to the sleeper, but please feel free to visit the library without me."

She sighed with relief when he heeded her suggestion. There was little doubt Mr. Clayborn's acquaintance had been an asset, but she needed time alone when she could let down her defenses. She hadn't anticipated the presence of someone like Matthew Clayborn. The strain of weighing each word had proved difficult, and she hadn't been adept at maintaining secrecy. Within no time Mr. Clayborn had managed to discover she lived and worked in Pullman, was an assistant chef for the Hotel Florence, and was keeping notes in her journal. Thus far, she didn't consider herself much of a success at this new venture.

The porter was preparing the beds when Olivia returned to the sleeper. She sat down on the opposite side of the car while he folded down two opposing seats to form the lower berth and popped the upper berth from the ceiling. He glanced over his shoulder and tipped his hat. "I's gonna have this here bed made down for you in no time."

With the other passengers off to the dining car, parlor car, or library car, Olivia settled into the brocade-upholstered seat and continued to observe the porter's agility. While humming an unfamiliar tune in a soft resonating tone, he clipped the curtains to a carved wooden rod that traversed the length of the car and affixed the headboard. Within a period of less than three minutes, the blankets, pillows, and linens were tucked, folded, and aligned with faultless precision. She mentally calculated the length of time she utilized when making her bed each morning, and she didn't have to set up the bed or climb a ladder to accomplish the task. She could offer no insight that could possibly help in saving time or money with this particular task.

While the porter continued making down beds, Olivia pulled out her notebook and jotted her observations. It didn't take long. She did write down her question regarding unloading and loading linens in the kitchen car, and she noted the excellent service in the dining car as well as the agility and kindness of the porters before she snapped the book together and returned it to her valise.

Once she'd closed the curtains to her berth, Olivia struggled to disrobe and don her nightclothes and soon discovered the procedure was no easy task in the cramped space. She wondered how two people of any size could possibly accomplish the feat without causing bodily harm.

As the other passengers slowly made their return, she heard murmured complaints from several men who were unhappy to find that their beds had already been made down, along with the cries of the undisciplined child at the other end of the coach. It seemed that he didn't want the day to come to an end, either.

Before closing her eyes, she silently prayed—mostly for herself. This job wasn't something to which she had aspired. Already she knew it wasn't a position that would bring her any joy. Perhaps if she could discover an abundance of time- and money-saving ideas during her first few journeys on her own, Mr. Howard would see fit to reinstate her as the full-time assistant chef at the hotel.

The next morning, Mr. Clayborn greeted her with an invitation for breakfast. She accepted his offer, and once they were seated in the dining car, his lips curved in a lopsided grin. "How did you sleep last night?" The waiter poured steaming coffee into their china cups and handed each of them a menu.

"Not particularly well, though through no fault of the accommodations. We *did* have a rather noisy group in our car, don't you think?" A variegated whirlpool appeared as Olivia stirred a dollop of cream into her coffee.

He laughed and spooned sugar into his coffee cup. "I've been on worse. You wouldn't believe some of the tales I've heard the porters tell when they're back in the smoking car shining shoes."

"What kind of tales? You've captured my attention, Mr. Clayborn."

He shook his head. "They are stories I would never repeat to a lady. Suffice it to say, I don't know how the porters maintain their composure in such distasteful situations. I fear I would be an utter failure."

Olivia wouldn't ask for additional details. Even if his stories would provide her with further information for the company, she'd not embarrass herself or Mr. Clayborn. Best to change the subject. "How long will you remain in New York?"

He rested his elbow on the table and cupped his chin. "I'm not entirely certain. Depends on where my story leads me. I never purchase my return ticket until I've completed my work. Could be tomorrow, could be next week." He shrugged his shoulders. "It's part of the reason I remain single. Like a lot of the men who work on these trains, I keep a difficult schedule. And difficult schedules don't make for a happy family."

"But you told me last night that most of the men are married."

"They are. I know of one who has a wife at each end of the line. If he ever gets transferred to a different route, it will wreak havoc on both ends." With a flick of his wrist, Mr. Clayborn snapped open his napkin and placed it across his lap.

She expected to see a spark of humor in his eyes, but one look told her he hadn't spoken in jest. Unless they were conferring about an ancient biblical figure, Olivia didn't care to discuss the idea of multiple wives with Mr. Clayborn. "You snapped that napkin with the same agility I observed last night when the porter made down the beds."

He cupped his hand to his mouth and leaned closer. "The

waiters refer to the porters as sheet shakers or pillow punchers." He grinned. "Sure does get the porters all riled up."

Olivia considered the staff at the hotel. Did they have unkind names for the cooks or maids? If so, she'd not heard them. "And do the porters have a name for the waiters?"

Mr. Clayborn was silent until the waiter set their breakfast plates before them and retreated as quietly as he'd arrived. "A rather offensive term, but they've got one."

Olivia stared after the angular waiter for a moment. "With all these men working in such close quarters, it's a shame they must resort to uncivil behavior."

Mr. Clayborn picked up a biscuit and slathered half of it with butter. "You are, Miss Mott, quite naïve. Do you not realize a pecking order exists among these men?"

Mr. Howard had explained the hierarchy of the workers, but she'd paid little attention. There were, after all, superiors in every line of work. Unless, of course, you had attained the level of George Pullman, Philip Armour, or Marshall Field. Perhaps rank mattered more than she realized.

"Let me explain." Matthew withdrew a piece of paper from his pocket and drew tiny squares. "Up here you have the conductor. He's always Caucasian. Below that, you have the porter—always Negro, always dark-skinned, and usually tall and thin so he can easily reach the upper berths and make down the beds. The porters are required to use special blue blankets and pillows for themselves to guarantee they aren't confused with those of the white conductors. At their district offices, two sign-in windows are maintained: an indoor one for conductors, an outdoor window for porters. More important, the work of the porters entails what you've already observed, as well as some things you likely won't see. There's the heavy lifting, caring for the sick and elderly, acting as nursemaid to undisciplined children, making down beds, polishing shoes, ironing, scrubbing toilets, escorting inebriated travelers to the rest room and cleaning up their messes—the list goes on and on. As for the conductors, they collect tickets and occasionally lift a bag, but mostly they issue orders to the porters. Much like a private in the army, the porter must follow his superior's order without question."

Olivia recalled reading in the rule book that a porter must never question a conductor's orders. She equated the concept to her years of employment at Lanshire Hall. She had been unable to question Chef Mallard's authority, and he had taken advantage of his position. Likely some of the conductors did the same. Little wonder the porters grew increasingly unhappy.

Mr. Clayborn pointed back and forth between the squares he had drawn to represent the conductor and porter. "The disparity in pay is hard for the porters to accept. They must rely on their tips, while the conductors receive much higher wages. But the most difficult part is the fact that no matter how well a porter performs his duties, he'll never achieve conductor status."

"I can see where that would cause resentment."

Mr. Clayborn sipped his coffee. "Mm-hmm. And then there are times when only a couple of Pullman cars are attached to the train instead of ten or twelve. Rather than using a regular conductor, a porter is assigned as porter-in-charge. He takes over the duties of conductor, but his pay remains the same. Not particularly fair, do you think?"

Olivia considered her instant promotion to Chef René's

position when he had suffered his heart problems. Though her pay hadn't increased, she knew that the experience of assuming his duties might one day help her achieve her goal of becoming an executive chef. But that wasn't the case for the porters.

"Though the pay issue may be unfair, even greater inequality exists since the porters *can't* be promoted to the position of conductor." While they were finishing their breakfast, Mr. Clayborn continued with the explanation of the squares and lines that he'd drawn on the piece of paper.

Olivia didn't find the chain of command in the dining car much removed from that of the hotel kitchen. "A great deal depends upon the person at the top of the chart, don't you think? If the chef treats his assistants with dignity and value, the attitude flows downward. The same holds true with a conductor."

"I believe that it really begins *above* what I've drawn on this chart, Olivia. In this instance, it depends upon Mr. Pullman and how much he values his employees. Is acquiring more wealth than one man can possibly need in a lifetime more important than paying workers a livable wage?"

Olivia recalled a passage in the Bible that she and Mrs. DeVault had discussed several weeks earlier regarding a workman and his wages. The conversation had stemmed from Fred's constant talk of the need for unions in order to gain better wages and working conditions. Although Mrs. DeVault hadn't spoken ill of Mr. Pullman or the company, she had turned to Scripture and said she believed what it said. Olivia wondered if God would approve of the manner in which Mr. Pullman handled his enormous wealth. She doubted whether He would be pleased. "I agree that a fair wage should be paid, but I don't think that you and I or even all of these workers combined can do anything in that regard. As you said, Mr. Pullman has the final say in such matters."

Their porter entered the dining car holding the hand of the disobedient child who'd been traveling in their coach. The dark-skinned man received a kick to the shins as he lifted the boy into his chair. Without a word, he brushed the scuff mark from his pant leg.

Mr. Clayborn tipped his head toward the porter. "That's a prime example of what I'm talking about. No employee should be expected to suffer such treatment. If these giants of industry don't change their ways, their employees are going to rise up against them. They'll unionize and strike."

His warning reminded Olivia of Fred.

CHAPTER SIXTEEN

Pullman, Illinois
May 13, 1893

The smell of frying bacon wafted up the stairs, and Fred inhaled deeply. It had been some time since he'd forced himself out of bed so early on a workday morning. By seven o'clock this evening he'd likely be sorry, but right now he felt invigorated. He could almost think of himself as an employee who lived a normal life: one who rose early, worked the day shift, and came home to eat supper and enjoy the evening hours with family and friends. It hadn't been so very long ago that he'd been one of those men living a normal life, yet it seemed ages since Mr. Godfrey had changed his shift. He remained on the list of employees seeking a return to the day shift, but from all he had heard around the department, that prospect seemed unlikely.

His silk tie brushed across the back of his hand as he flipped and twisted it back and forth to form a perfect knot. His mother had given him the tie for his last birthday. At first the checkered pattern had seemed out of place hanging alongside the solid navy blue and black ties in his closet, but it had soon become his favorite. He stared in the mirror and gave one final tug at the length before donning his navy blue suit jacket. There was a spring in his step as he entered the kitchen and greeted his mother.

She tipped her head to receive his peck on the cheek. "Don't you look handsome this morning! You're in good humor for someone who's had so little sleep."

"At least for the moment." He picked up the coffeepot and helped himself. "Breakfast smells inviting. I'm glad I remembered to leave you a note saying I'd be up early this morning."

With a chuckle, she handed him a plate filled with crisp bacon, fried eggs, and warm biscuits. Fred waited while she filled a plate for herself and sat down opposite him. His mother nodded: his signal to give thanks for their breakfast. Neither of them would argue the point that his mother's biblical knowledge surpassed his own, but she expected him to give thanks for their meals when he was present. The day after his father's death, she had insisted Fred assume the empty chair at the head of the table. Along with that seat had come both the privilege and the responsibility of thanking God for their many blessings as well as for their meals. But that, too, had changed when he'd been switched to the late shift. Offering grace at breakfast this morning clarified how much he'd missed sharing this morning ritual with his mother.

"Are you going to keep me in suspense throughout breakfast or tell me what gets you out of bed so early this morning?" His mother wiped the corner of her mouth with one of the frayed cloth napkins she considered good enough for every day.

He had hoped she wouldn't ask. "I'm going into Chicago."

Keeping his head lowered, he concentrated on his breakfast.

"For?"

"For a few hours."

"Don't you play silly games with me, young man. You know what I'm asking." She'd taken on that same tone she'd used when he was a boy, the one that never failed to intimidate him.

He forced himself to remember he was no longer a child. "I'm going for business. I'm not at liberty to reveal any more, so please don't ask." His mother was as tight-lipped as any woman he'd ever known, but telling her he planned to go into Chicago and discuss unionization or anything vaguely related to the topic would only send her into an ear-bending lecture. The less she knew, the better. If she should be questioned about his involvement in union activities, she could offer a forthright response.

She drummed her fingers on the tabletop. "Not at liberty, or don't want to tell me?"

He swallowed the last piece of his biscuit. "Both." He pushed his chair away from the table. "Sometimes the less you know, the better." He carried his plate to the sink and returned to kiss her on the cheek. "If I don't move along, I'll miss the train. I should be home by two o'clock at the latest."

She followed him down the hallway and grasped his arm before he could depart. "Don't jeopardize your future here in Pullman."

The fear in his mother's eyes plagued him as he walked to the train depot. For a brief moment he considered returning home, but as the train belched and wheezed into the station, he knew he couldn't—not even for his mother. Some things in life were greater than oneself or even than the desires of one's mother.

He boarded the train and stared out the window as the train picked up speed. The iron behemoth quickly traversed the stretch of isolated prairie that divided the outskirts of Pullman from the burgeoning fringes of Chicago. In a short time the stubby grass and wild flowers would no doubt be replaced by numerous large buildings like those that lined Chicago's bustling streets. His mother's deep regard for the city of Pullman baffled him. While most of the neighborhood women wanted nothing more than to move into a home or apartment where they could plant a row of pansies along the front walk without first obtaining permission, his mother's desire was to remain in the strict confines of Pullman. What he regarded as unwarranted control, she considered stabilizing. Amazing!

He realized her fears stemmed from having been evicted from their home after his father died. Being forced to live with relatives until he'd been old enough to support the two of them had been difficult, and he didn't discount that fact. But he'd attained manhood years ago. Even if he lost his job and they were forced to move from Pullman, he could find employment that would pay more than enough to rent a suitable apartment. He'd welcome the opportunity to look for something else right now. But he wouldn't. Unless terminated from his position with the company, he would yield to his mother's wish and remain in the town she now called home.

The high pitch of the train's whistle announced their imminent arrival in Chicago. Fred wiped his sweaty palms on his knees and wondered if he should have adhered to Ellen Ashton's advice. His mother had always accused him of being much too impulsive as a boy. She thought he'd outgrown the trait, but he knew he'd likely never be one of those men who quietly weighed all the consequences of each decision before moving forward. He was prone to follow his instincts. Sometimes it worked and sometimes it didn't, but he had only himself to blame when caught shortsighted. He fervently hoped this wouldn't be one of those times.

Since leaving home he'd checked the address on Montrose Ashton's business card several times. He had planned to hire one of the hansom cabs outside the station, but the kindly directions received from a fellow passenger changed his mind. He followed the man's advice and turned left for two blocks and then made a right on Arundel Street. It was more an alleyway than a street, but he quickly located the building. Goldleaf signage on the front window proclaimed the office of Montrose Ashton was located within. A harsh-sounding buzzer announced his entrance. An unoccupied wooden desk faced the front door, and several empty chairs lined the wall. He closed the door, approached the desk, and hoped Ellen would materialize from the adjacent room.

He cleared his throat and waited. No response. With a glance toward the door leading to the other room, he tugged at his collar. He should have made an appointment. "Anyone here?"

"Who's there!"

Fred started. The words were more of a command than a question. He edged a bit closer to the doorway. "Fred. Fred DeVault." He waited for a response. Perhaps further explanation was needed. "I'm an acquaintance of Miss Ellen Ashton."

The sound of wood scraping on wood was soon followed by

heavy footsteps. A long shadow fell across the floor, and soon Fred was face-to-face with a broad-shouldered, white-haired man holding an open book in one hand and an unlit cigar in the other. The gentleman's piercing blue eyes flickered with confidence. "Do I know you?"

Fred extended his hand. "No, Mr. Ashton, but I met your daughter in Pullman. At a wedding."

"How do you know I'm Montrose Ashton? I could very well be Mr. Ashton's law partner or his clerk." He tucked the tip of the cigar between his lips and waited.

"I merely assumed that you—"

The man removed the cigar from his mouth. "Assumptions are usually the first step to grievous error, young man. Better to ask questions than to make assumptions." He obviously decided to take pity on Fred, for he waved his cigar in the air. "Oh, never mind. I'm Montrose Ashton. And you are Miss Mott's beau."

Mr. Ashton continued to hold the book and cigar. Not knowing what to do and feeling somewhat the fool with his hand hanging in midair, Fred slowly lowered his arm. "Not exactly."

"*Humph!* Then I don't know who you are, and I haven't time for unscheduled appointments." He snapped the book shut and turned to leave.

"Wait!"

The lawyer skewered him with a fiery glare. A tactic the older man had likely developed while passionately arguing cases to a jury.

"*Excuse me?*" The question cut through the air like an unsheathed sword.

Fred's shoulders slumped. "I am well acquainted with Olivia—Miss Mott, that is. We are friends, but I'm no longer her *beau*."

Mr. Ashton looked him up and down and dropped his book onto the desk. "My daughter says otherwise. Which of you is correct?"

"I am averse to disputing your daughter's word. I will merely say that I am well acquainted with Miss Mott." Fred took a step forward and hoped Mr. Ashton wouldn't toss him out on his ear. "I do hope you will agree to see me, even if only for a brief visit."

Mr. Ashton grabbed his book and waved Fred forward. "Oh, come on in here. Ellen told me you'd likely darken my doorway before a month had passed. She said you're the impatient sort. She was right."

Fred dropped into the chair opposite Mr. Ashton's desk. He hunched forward. "Did your daughter tell you about my interest in the unionization of Pullman workers?"

He shoved the cigar into the corner of his mouth and leaned back in his chair. "She told me the two of you talked." He clenched the cigar between his teeth as he spoke. The thick Havana bobbed up and down like an unwieldy baton.

"I think I'd be a good contact for you, Mr. Ashton."

"Do you? And why do you think I'd need some sort of contact in George Pullman's thriving utopia?"

Mr. Ashton didn't seem nearly as intelligent as Fred had anticipated. The man should surely understand the advantage of having men willing to help organize from within the company. He laid out his plan as simply and succinctly as possible. Though Ellen hadn't mentioned any such problem, he wondered if her father had begun to lose his edge.

The older man yanked the cigar from between his lips and stuck it into the narrow opening of a silver bud vase that seemed strangely out of place on his cluttered desk. He leaned forward until his chest rested atop the desk, and Fred wondered if he was going to pillow his head on his arms and take a mid-morning nap.

Instead, Mr. Ashton arched his neck and peered directly into Fred's eyes. "You, Mr. DeVault, are a very dangerous young man. If my daughter hadn't vouched for you, I would have thrown you out of my office the moment you mentioned George Pullman and unionization in the same breath."

Fred reeled at the remark. Wasn't this the man who had staunchly defended the rights of workers to unionize? The man who made speeches about downtrodden immigrants and traveled the country speaking in public forums? "I . . . I don't understand."

"No, of course you don't. You're young and impetuous. Didn't my daughter warn you about visiting this office so soon after the two of you were seen together in Pullman? Did you even bother to take heed of your surroundings or ascertain if you were being followed?" He didn't wait for an answer. "No, you did not. And why didn't you? Because you are an impulsive young man. And, of even greater concern, you are impatient." He flattened his palms on the desk and pushed until his torso returned to an upright position.

Fred didn't understand. Nobody had followed him—at least he didn't think so. "Why the concern? Everyone knows of your involvement with the unions."

Mr. Ashton slapped a hand to his forehead. "It is not *me* I worry about, Mr. DeVault. It's you and all of the other men and their families who live in Pullman. If you have no concern for yourself, please remember you place others in jeopardy by your impulsive behavior. My daughter tells me you have a mother. Did you think of her welfare when you boarded the train this morning? Does she support you in a unionization movement?"

Fred shook his head.

"Your eyes speak volumes, Mr. DeVault. I can see your mother knows nothing of our meeting this morning."

"She knows about my beliefs, but she tends to worry over-much." Likely an unconvincing response, but he thought the lawyer's concerns a tad histrionic. "How am I jeopardizing others, Mr. Ashton?"

"If word circulates that talk of strikes or unions is resurfacing, you can expect George Pullman to dig in and strengthen his hold on the company as well as the town. In that event, it will take even longer to make progress. Our object is to clear away obstacles, not create them. Rule number one: Don't underestimate the enemy, Mr. DeVault."

"And rule number two?"

"Realize there are others who know more than you. Be willing to learn and follow their instructions."

Fred was afraid to ask what rule number three might be. He'd been put in his place already. Thankfully, he was saved from further humiliation when the buzzer on the front door announced someone had entered the outer office. Mr. Ashton touched his index finger to his lips. Fred nodded. Obviously the lawyer took secrecy to the extreme.

The older man pushed away from the desk. "I'll be right with you," he called.

"It's just me, Father."

Fred glanced over his shoulder, pleased to hear Ellen's voice. Perhaps her presence would lighten the conversation.

Mr. Ashton dropped back into his chair. "Come and see who's here in my office."

Ellen entered her father's office carrying a small bouquet of pale yellow daffodils and a red rose surrounded by several stems of fern. "Fred!" Her surprise faded to a look of concern. She dropped the flowers on top of the desk and motioned to her father. "I'll return in a moment."

The two men waited, their silence broken only by the tapping of Ellen's shoes as she crossed the tile floor and the metal clacking of the door lock snapping into position.

Mr. Ashton's bushy eyebrows raised high on his forehead. "Problem?" he inquired when Ellen returned to his office.

"Possibly. On my return I noticed a man standing near the front door. I thought he looked familiar but couldn't place him until I saw Fred here in your office."

Her father scooted forward. "And?"

"I don't know his name, but he attended the wedding reception in Pullman. Did someone come with you?" She hesitated. "Or were you followed?"

Mr. Ashton scowled and yanked his cigar from the bud vase and pointed it at Fred. "You see? I do know what I'm talking about." He turned his attention to Ellen. "The two of you are going to have to leave this office arm in arm. Is the man well dressed?"

Fred wondered what difference it made what clothing the man wore, but even more, he wondered who it could be. In all honesty, he thought Ellen was quite mistaken. A part of him wanted to rush outside and confront the man. Most likely he was a complete stranger who lived in Chicago and had never before seen Fred or Ellen. He'd probably already departed.

Ellen shook her head. "No. His clothing is intended to reflect he's a workingman, but I noticed his shoes. Well polished and expensive. His hair and mustache are well trimmed— probably best described as a ruddy brown shade. He appears to be in his early forties."

Her father beamed. "I'm pleased to know you put your observation skills to good use." Reaching into his pocket, he withdrew more cash than Fred earned in a week. "Use this. Go someplace expensive. A business establishment where this fellow will appear out of place. The restaurant in Palmer House would be fine." He turned his attention to Fred. "And don't turn around to see if he's following. Let Ellen take the lead. She knows how to handle these situations."

"Yes, sir. But don't you want me to attempt to identify the man?"

"I want you to do exactly as I've said. If Ellen thinks there's an opportunity for you to take a look at the fellow, she'll let you know. Otherwise, you keep your eyes on *her*. Act like you're a young man smitten by my beautiful daughter. Can you manage that?"

"Well, yes, of course, but . . ."

Mr. Ashton didn't give him an opportunity to finish his sentence. Instead, he had turned his attention to Ellen, who was slipping the single rose into the bud vase. "Where am I going to put my cigar if you stick that flower in there?"

She raised her brows and smiled. "The trash?"

Her father growled as Ellen gathered the bouquet of daffo-dils from his desk, but she merely offered him a sweet smile as she walked from the room and glanced over her shoulder. "Let me put these in a vase of water, and then we'll leave, Fred."

CHAPTER SEVENTEEN

Fred listened carefully. He wanted to prove himself to Mr. Ashton, for right now there was little doubt the older man considered him more of a detriment than a benefit to any union movement. Fred and Ellen departed the law office walking close together, laughing and talking in hushed voices until they reached the corner of State and Monroe streets. Although it appeared Ellen was entertaining him with a humorous anecdote, she was actually directing him toward the hotel entrance.

This marked Fred's first visit to Palmer House. Though his initial inclination was to gawk at the luxuriant surroundings, he forced himself to appear nonchalant as they entered the building. Well-dressed businessmen and wealthy visitors swarmed the lavishly appointed lobby. Surrounded by the conspicuous display of crystal chandeliers, gilded cuspidors, and marble floors, powerful men brokered trades and exchanged the day's news within the confines of the opulent hotel. While cigar smoke circled over their heads, these defenders of power delighted themselves with their wealth.

Ellen tugged him toward the far end of the lobby, where they turned a corner and neared the entrance of the hotel restaurant. A uniformed steward greeted them with a look of disdain until Fred recalled Ellen's instruction and slipped the man a crisp dollar bill. It seemed a large sum for merely seating them at a table, but Fred didn't argue. Nor did he object when Ellen nodded for him to sit on the far side of the table. Once the steward handed them their menus, he silently retreated and Ellen leaned close.

"Once I begin to read my menu, lean toward me and glance over my right shoulder. Tell me if you recognize the man seated in the gold-brocaded chair facing the restaurant entrance."

"Is he wearing the work clothes you described to your father?"

She shook her head. "No. Somewhere along the way he has acquired a suit jacket and tie, but it's the same man."

Fred wondered how the man had accomplished such a feat, but Ellen didn't appear surprised in the least. Once she leaned back in her chair and concentrated on the menu, he did as she had instructed. The scent of her perfume greeted him like a spring bouquet as he tipped his head close to her shoulder.

"Do you see him?" Ellen's breath grazed his ear, and he momentarily lost his concentration.

He leaned back and picked up the menu. A moment later he pointed to one of the offerings. "I've never seen that man before in my life. And I don't think he was at the wedding reception. I've met all of Albert's friends. We work in the same department as well as play baseball and row on the same teams. I have *never* seen that man."

Ellen chuckled softly and tapped the menu as though they'd been discussing their luncheon orders. "Why don't you signal for the waiter? You mustn't be late for work. Do you plan to take the one-thirty train?"

Instinctively Fred searched the room for a clock. "Yes. I begin my shift at three o'clock, and I'll need time to change clothes." He continued to scan the room.

"There are no clocks in here, Fred. The establishment expects guests to linger over their meals. That fact aside, the wealthy want to give the illusion they aren't constricted by time schedules like the rest of the world, yet most of them are more regimented than the working class, at least the men are. Their wives are another story entirely." She clicked open a small brooch and checked the time. "It's almost noon. Would you prefer that we merely ordered coffee?"

He shook his head. "Wouldn't that appear odd so close to the noon hour?"

"Yes, but you being late for work would appear even more unusual." The waiter arrived at their table and stood at attention, his uniform as crisp as that of any soldier prepared for inspection. Ellen smiled up at the man. "What would you suggest? We must meet a one-thirty train."

The waiter's chest swelled with pride, especially after they accepted his recommendation. While they ate their meal in the stateliness of their surroundings, Ellen directed their conversation away from discussion of unions or the gentleman in the lobby. "Did anyone know you planned to come to Chicago this morning, Fred?"

He shook his head and swallowed a bite of creamed peas. "No one except for my mother, and I didn't tell her who I planned to visit. She wouldn't mention my plans." Given the fact that the gentleman remained in the lobby, he felt obliged to vouch for his mother's trustworthy nature.

She wiped the corner of her mouth with the linen napkin. "Not Olivia?"

"No." He jerked his gaze away from his plate and met Ellen's inquiring eyes. "My mother said Olivia departed on Monday. She's back out on the trains—without Mr. Howard this time, I believe."

"I realize it's none of my business, but don't you think it's time you and Olivia aired your differences regarding Mr. Howard?"

He stared at her, dumbfounded. Had Olivia confided in Ellen? How much had she told, he wondered. The thought annoyed him. He didn't like the idea of the two women discussing his personal life over tea and biscuits.

"Please don't be offended, but I don't think this is a discussion the two of us should be having. Didn't she tell you she was leaving?" He stabbed several peas with the tine of his fork.

Ellen rested her palm on the table. "I apologize for my intrusion, Fred. You're absolutely correct. The status of your relationship with Olivia is none of my business. I'll do my best to refrain from such inquiries in the future. However, it's obvious you care for each other." She offered him a half smile. "In response to your question, no, I didn't know Olivia was departing. The last we talked, she hadn't been given any date when she would be going out again. I hope all goes well for her. I know she'd prefer to be in the kitchen with Chef René. Both he and your mother have been wonderful mentors for her, don't you think? In differing areas, of course."

"I suppose they have." The waiter returned and removed

Fred's plate. The remark further reinforced how much Olivia had likely confided in Miss Ashton. "I didn't realize you and Olivia had developed such a close friendship. It appears there's little the two of you haven't discussed."

A soft ripple of laughter escaped her lips. "We may come from completely diverse backgrounds, but we formed a friendship the first time we met. She's a lovely young woman who's overcome difficult circumstances. I truly admire her. Olivia tells me she was immediately drawn to your mother and her kindness. There's little doubt your mother has been a genuine inspiration to Olivia, what with teaching her about the Bible and such."

"They have become good friends," he admitted.

Throughout the remainder of their meal, Ellen acted like a woman in love. She batted her lashes, laughed, and patted Fred's hand while chatting about meaningless topics. When they'd finished their meals, Fred signaled for the waiter, paid their bill, and then pushed away from the table. The waiter thanked them profusely and offered to hail a carriage, but Fred declined. The generous tip Ellen had instructed Fred to leave the man had likely been the primary motivation for his final offer of assistance. As they passed through the lobby, Fred forced himself to keep his attention focused upon Ellen rather than on the man seated in the mahogany- and gold-brocaded chair.

"You performed magnificently, Fred. I was afraid you'd be distracted and look toward our recently acquired friend."

He smiled at the reference. "I doubt he's a friend, but he's become as constant as my shadow." Fred could see the man's reflection in the gilded mirror as they walked out of the hotel.

Once again, he was following behind them.

Ellen slipped her hand into the crook of Fred's arm. "I'm guessing he's going to follow you onto the train. He may or may not get off in Pullman. Please don't let him think you've noticed him. If he thinks you've spotted him, they'll replace him. Better we know who we're looking for."

With a forced smile, Fred pointed into the window of a jewelry shop. "They?"

"Whoever has him following you. There's no way of knowing exactly who within the company has hired him to track your movements. I'm going to accompany you to the train depot. Before you board the train, I want you to kiss me."

He stopped in his tracks, and Ellen tugged him forward. "We must make this appear genuine, Fred. If they believe we're romantically involved, you won't draw as much suspicion from the company."

At Ellen's instruction, Fred waved for a carriage, and soon they were on their way to the Van Buren Street station. He could only hope they would manage to lose the man in the confusion of traffic as they traversed the busy streets and passed the fork of the river harbor. But the stranger likely knew where they were headed.

Fred's thoughts were a jumble by the time they arrived, though Ellen remained perfectly calm as they stepped across the threshold. "Have you already purchased your ticket?"

He nodded. "Maybe he's not here."

"Who?" Her eyes immediately reflected recognition and she smiled. "Oh, you mean our new friend. Never doubt that he's here. And even if we don't see him, we can't take any chances. I'll attempt to make our farewell as painless as possible."

From her ease with their predicament, Fred could only assume she was an old hand at situations like this. He wondered if he would ever reach that point. He hoped he wouldn't have to find out. If he was going to become instrumental in the cause—the term Mr. Ashton liked to use—he'd best learn to adapt. Shortly he'd have an excellent opportunity to prove his malleability.

They joined the throng of passengers jostling to and fro, some headed for the ticket counters while others rushed toward the barbershop, restaurant, or fruit stand within the miniature domed city. Weaving through the crowd as if she'd done it every day of her life, Ellen led him across the concourse and onto the proper platform where they waited. Moments later, the conductor called a familiar "All aboard!"

Before he had time to further consider his own actions, Ellen raised up on tiptoe and clasped her arms around his neck. He had planned a brief peck on the cheek. Instead, she kissed him full on the lips. Startled by her unseemly behavior, he attempted to take a backward step. Undaunted, her lips remained firmly affixed to his own as she grasped his collar so tightly he thought he might strangle.

When she finally released him, she rested her palms against his chest. "I'm sorry, but I fear we would have lacked believability if I had permitted you merely to peck me on the cheek like an old married couple." She touched her gloved finger to his cheek. "Look into my eyes as though you're sorry you must leave me."

He did as she'd told him. Her eyes twinkled, and he suddenly realized she was enjoying his discomfort. Without further thought, he swooped her into his arms and kissed her soundly.

When he finally released her, she nearly toppled backward. Grasping her shoulders, he held her firmly in place. "Careful. I wouldn't want you to fall over while we're in the midst of proving our love for each other."

She gaped at him and he cupped her chin, gently pushing her lips together. "You don't want to appear surprised by your beau's enamored behavior." He glanced up, noted the man waiting nearby, and once again pulled Ellen into an embrace. "He's waiting for me to board the train. When shall I return to Chicago?"

She shook her head. "I'll come to Pullman. Let's wait until a week from Sunday. Perhaps Olivia will be back, and I can visit with her also. I'll plan to arrive on the two-o'clock train, if that's agreeable."

He walked toward the train and blew her a kiss. "Until then, my dear." After boarding the train, Fred made his way down the aisle and dropped onto one of the seats. He scooted across to look out the window and wasn't surprised to see Ellen still standing on the platform. She waved until the train pulled away from the station. He smiled and decided she had likely remained in place and waved until the train was completely out of sight. Ellen was the consummate actress, he decided.

————

The conductor passed through the car proclaiming, "Shee-ca-go, Shee-ca-go." Olivia sighed with relief, pleased she would soon be back at work in the hotel and enjoying what she'd come to consider her normal life. With luck, she could make the train to Pullman and be home within the hour. The train braked and slowed as they entered the glass-domed depot. She peered out the window and then jerked around in her seat. Her hat cocked to one side and nearly slipped from her head as she pressed her nose against the window and continued to stare. Surely not! Yet she knew her eyes hadn't deceived her. Fred and Ellen stood locked in an embrace on a nearby platform. He was kissing her with undeniable ardor.

Her heart pounded in her chest and reverberated in the distinct thump of a battle cadence. Maintaining her watch, she inched closer to the window and hoped the sight had been no more than an optical illusion. Without warning, the train lurched to a halting stop. Her face collided with the cold resistance of the thick unyielding glass. A searing pain rushed upward through her face as she watched Fred smile while Ellen waved. Olivia backed away from the window and rubbed her nose.

Droplets of blood trickled onto the jabot of her shirtwaist, and she grasped for her handbag. Blood rushed from her nose like a fount while she dug in the recesses of her purse for a handkerchief. Passengers filed down the aisle, more intent upon detraining than lending aid to a young woman with a bleeding nose. A porter escorting an elderly woman glanced down and immediately drew near. He seemed to yank a clean white towel from out of thin air.

"What happened to you, miss?"

Olivia pointed to the window. "I was watching the scenery and struck my face when the train came to an unexpected stop."

He nodded sympathetically. "You sit right here." He glanced toward the old woman clinging to his arm. "I'll send someone to help you right away. They'll get you all cleaned up afore you get off the train."

Before she could object, the dark-skinned porter gently directed the old woman forward and disappeared from sight. Olivia leaned her head against the back of the seat, but her effort did little to stanch the flow of blood. With the porter's towel still pressed to her nose, she stood, determined to board the train to Pullman and confront Fred. She'd moved to the aisle when a conductor with another porter in tow appeared and thwarted her escape.

The conductor eloquently yet firmly advised that he could not permit an injured passenger to detrain without lending aid. "Why, what would folks think if you stepped off this train in an injured state? I've sent for a doctor to examine you and make certain you've not sustained permanent injury." He glanced at the porter. "What's her final destination?"

She didn't want to admit to these employees that she was a resident of Pullman. That would be breaking Mr. Howard's admonition against such a disclosure. "I noted a friend boarding the train to Pullman. I must detrain so that I may speak with him before he departs." Her frustration mounted at the conductor's intrusive behavior, and she decided that if these two men didn't soon release her, she'd admit to most anything. She must board the train to Pullman.

The conductor solemnly shook his head. "No need to hurry, miss. The train to Pullman departed a couple minutes ago. There's another one heading for Pullman in a half hour. If we get this bleeding stopped, maybe you could take that one and meet up with your fellow."

"He *isn't* my fellow, and I don't want to wait half an hour."

The porter placed a damp cloth on her forehead and another at the base of her neck. "You jest pinch your nose like this." With his thumb and index finger, the porter pinched the bridge of his nose. Moments later he nodded toward the window, which revealed a tall man carrying a physician's bag hurrying toward the platform. "Here come the doctor now."

"I don't need a doctor. I need to get off of this train."

The porter offered another sympathetic nod. "Mm-hmm, I knows you got lotsa things needin' your attention, miss, but we's jest tryin' to help you. We don' want none of our Pullman passengers gettin' off this here train lookin' like they been in some kinda battle." He offered her a toothy grin.

"I do appreciate your kindness, but I am—"

"Step aside, porter. I'll take over." The physician pushed his way between the porter and conductor and sat down opposite Olivia.

The physician's abrupt comment had startled Olivia, but if the doctor's command offended the porter, he gave no indication. He immediately stepped aside but remained close at hand, obviously prepared to follow any additional orders. She glanced at the imprint on the porter's shiny name tag. *Bernard Samson.* She would remember his name and offer several fine comments about this man in her notebook. At least a little benefit might be derived from this disastrous event.

Throughout the next fifteen minutes, the doctor offered little more medical expertise than she'd already been given by the porter. When the bleeding finally ceased, the doctor left, and she was permitted to detrain. While she waited on the platform, the porter hurried inside the station to purchase her ticket to Pullman. He had recalled her desire to reach the town and had offered the additional kindness without prompting.

He returned with the ticket in one hand and a cup of ice

and a white handkerchief in the other. After handing her the ticket, he nodded toward the stains on her shirtwaist. "This here ice might help to get the blood out afore it has a chance to set in too good."

She placed a coin in his hand. "Thank you for your kindness, Mr. Samson."

He grinned and tipped his cap. "Oh, you's most welcome, miss. You jest give that there cup to the conductor on the Pullman train and he'll bring it back on his next run." He turned as a shrill whistle sounded in the distance. The porter pointed toward the inbound train. "Looks like that's your train to Pullman."

She stared after him for a moment. While humming a soft tune, he tucked the coin into his pocket and headed inside the giant station as though he didn't have a care in the world. Mr. Pullman was fortunate to have the likes of Bernard Samson working in his employ.

Once her train had arrived and she'd settled into her seat, Olivia considered all she had observed a short time earlier. Seeing Ellen and Fred in a public display of affection remained difficult to digest. The very idea seemed incomprehensible. She wanted to believe it wasn't them, but as she replayed the scene in her mind, she couldn't deny their identities. There had been few people waiting on the platform, and she'd been able to observe them without any distraction. Other than a well-dressed gentleman with a mustache and reddish brown hair, Fred and Ellen had been the only ones waiting near the Pullman train platform. After Fred's kiss, the two of them had parted, and Ellen had remained on the platform, waving after him while the dapper gentleman brushed by and followed Fred toward the train. She remembered every minute detail that had unfolded before her eyes. Except for the unknown gentleman, she abhorred all that she'd seen.

The fact that she'd missed Fred's train was likely a good thing. What benefit would have come from a confrontation? He would have told her what she already knew: she had no hold on him. He was a single man, free to spend his time with whomever he pleased. And if Ellen Ashton pleased him, what right did Olivia have to voice an opinion?

Ellen's beauty and charm surpassed that of any woman Olivia had ever known. In truth, Olivia had been surprised and flattered by Ellen's offer of friendship. She'd also been suspicious at first, apprehensive that someone of Ellen's stature could have a genuine interest in befriending a lowly hotel cook. But Ellen had quickly allayed Olivia's doubts and proved to be an ally, someone Olivia could trust. At least that's what Olivia had thought until an hour ago. Ellen's betrayal cut even more deeply than Fred's behavior. After all, Olivia had told Ellen of her deep feelings for Fred. She had divulged how she hoped one day to see their relationship restored to one of mutual trust that could possibly lead to marriage. Yet knowing Olivia's deepest desires had not curtailed Ellen's obvious desire to count Fred among her numerous conquests. Didn't she have enough men seeking her company? Why did she feel the need to pursue the one man who had captured Olivia's heart?

She continued to blot the smudges of blood from the jabot of her stained shirtwaist. Obviously the discoloration would require more than ice.

What, she wondered, would be required to conquer the pain in her heart.

CHAPTER EIGHTEEN

Olivia handed her cup of melting ice to the conductor as she stepped off the train in Pullman. She briefly considered stopping to see Mrs. DeVault, but one glance at her timepiece indicated the possibility Fred might still be at home. She'd not take a chance on coming face-to-face with him, not now, not in her present state of mind. Better to gather her bag, stop by the hotel to greet Chef René, and go home, where she could rest before supper. Once Chef René knew she was back, he would expect her to return to her regular morning routine. The thought pleased her and a slight smile tugged at her lips, the first since she had spied Fred and Ellen in each other's arms in Chicago.

She opened the depot door, surprised to see Mr. Howard cloistered in a far corner speaking to the well-dressed gentleman she'd seen standing on the platform at the Chicago train depot. When he looked up, Mr. Howard's shoulders immediately flexed to attention. He whispered in the gentleman's ear, patted him on the back, and strode toward her with a defined purpose to his step.

While the man exited out the rear door, Mr. Howard walked toward her. "I've been waiting for you."

She gestured toward the rear of the depot. "Truly? I thought you were engaged in a private conversation with the gentleman who is now standing outside the depot. Who is he? I don't believe I've seen him in Pullman before."

The forlorn sound of a train whistle howled in the distance, and Mr. Howard glanced toward the tracks leading into Pullman. "He works for a competitor, but we've recently become acquainted. We're considering the possibility of hiring him away from his current employer. He's waiting on the train that's arriving."

He hadn't answered her question. She still didn't know the man's name. The stranger was obviously a man of means, and should he be hired, he would no doubt become a member of management.

"When did your new acquaintance arrive in Pullman?" Olivia wasn't certain why she pursued the matter, but something in Mr. Howard's response made her question his honesty.

He gave her a sidelong glance as he reached for her bag. "Yesterday morning. Why do you ask?"

She shrugged. "Merely curious. He looked somewhat familiar. Is his name Herbert Williams?"

Though the weather was far from warm, beads of perspiration now dotted Mr. Howard's forehead. "No. His name is Geoffrey Townsend. And just where do you believe you may have encountered Mr. Townsend?"

How should she respond without lying? "I suppose somewhere during my travels."

"That may be. Mr. Townsend does travel extensively. Now,

tell me about your journey. I'm anxious for a full report." Before she could respond, he pointed toward her shirtwaist. "Do you realize your jabot is stained? I am extremely disappointed that a porter or conductor didn't discreetly mention the matter to you. I hope you've taken down names so that we may deal with this issue." He grasped her elbow as they neared Pullman Avenue. "This is exactly the type of careless and irresponsible service we must correct."

Olivia stopped in the middle of the street and waved a gloved finger in his direction. "You have no idea what has occurred, yet you are immediately willing to condemn the very employees who did the most to help me during a difficult circumstance." Her response was more boisterous than she'd intended.

Mouth agape, he stared at her. "What has come over you, Olivia?" As a carriage approached, he motioned her forward. "Come along. We'll discuss this matter in detail—in a *much more* civil tone."

She shrank at his reprimand. If she continued with her current behavior, she'd likely be unemployed before morning. Yet she'd encountered her friend and Fred kissing on the train platform, received a bloody nose, been lied to by Mr. Howard, and chastised because her jabot was stained—all within less than a two-hour period. As far as she was concerned, it was little wonder she'd lashed out at him. Unfortunately, her foolhardy behavior had resulted in an outcome she hadn't anticipated: she'd be required to remain in Mr. Howard's company and go over her notes.

Her heart fluttered at the thought. Mr. Howard wouldn't approve of the hastily scribbled notes she scratched out each night. Well, *almost* every night. During her week away, there had been a few evenings when she'd completely forsaken the task and merely gone to sleep. There was little doubt he expected to review well-detailed daily reports within the pages of her journal. Hadn't he told her as much when they'd been on their training journey? And though Olivia had intended to rewrite her hastily jotted comments into a neat and precise account, the task had not yet been completed. In fact, she'd not even begun.

She touched her fingers to the back of her neck. "Please forgive my rude behavior. I'm weary from traveling, and I believe I have a headache coming on." Her remark was true enough. She was quite tired, and if Mr. Howard should insist upon examining her notes before morning, she would surely suffer a terrible headache!

He gave her a sidelong glance and finally agreed she should rest. "I had considered accepting Mrs. Barnes's invitation to supper, but if you're feeling unwell . . ."

"Thank you for your compassion and understanding, Samuel. I believe having this first afternoon and evening to rest will permit me to return to work completely refreshed tomorrow morning."

There was little doubt her response disappointed him, but nevertheless he escorted her to the Barneses' porch and placed her baggage near the front door. "I shall expect to meet with you in my office tomorrow morning at eight o'clock. If your headache should disappear, I'm next door and can be quickly summoned."

His smile appeared strained, and there was a false cheerfulness to his words. Olivia hoped she hadn't angered him overmuch, but her refusal had been necessary. The evening would prove disastrous if she presented him with the incomplete journal.

———

The clock had chimed midnight by the time Olivia had completed rewriting her notes and prepared for bed. Though she had planned to eat supper and immediately return to her room, Mrs. Barnes's pitiful demeanor had held her captive until nine o'clock. Finally Olivia had insisted she could remain in the parlor no longer. Even at that late hour, Mrs. Barnes had been visibly disappointed when Olivia had taken her leave and retreated up the stairs. Thankfully, she'd completed over half of her task before the supper hour. Otherwise she'd still be writing.

Olivia dropped into bed, knowing her prayer time would be brief this night. Indeed, she'd nearly fallen asleep at her writing desk before donning her nightgown. The sweet scent of the crisp linens filled her nostrils as she tucked the sheet beneath her chin. Although Mrs. Barnes could prove taxing at times, the woman always tried her utmost to provide care and comfort. Olivia must remember to thank her in the morning for the fresh linens.

The rustling of tree branches whispered through the open bedroom window, and Olivia uttered a prayer of thanks. After long and wakeful nights listening to the sundry noises and commotion aboard the trains, she was pleased to return to the safety, peace, and comfort of Pullman. Her eyelids grew heavy and she drifted to sleep, hoping she'd completed her final journey on the rails.

Olivia's dreams were invaded by clanging bells and the acrid smell of smoke. She coughed and rolled to her side, but loud shouts and the clatter of horse-drawn wagons fully awakened her. Rubbing her eyes, she forced herself to sit up on the side of her bed.

A shout from below jerked Olivia to attention, and she rushed to the window. Across the street and behind the iron gates, flames shot toward the heavens. Through the haze of smoke it was impossible to see if the fire burned in one of the Pullman buildings or farther down the line at the Allen Paper Wheel Works, where the paper cores were constructed and dried before they were fitted into the steel train tires. A blaze would spread quickly with the vast amount of paper stored at the wheel works. But if the fire caused either building to shut down for any length of time, the entire community would suffer.

Several taps sounded at her door and Olivia turned from the window. "Mrs. Barnes?"

"Yes, my dear. I wanted to assure you that we are safe. May I come in?"

Olivia padded across the wool rug and opened her bedroom door. "Has Mr. Barnes gone to help?"

The older woman nodded. "Yes. He left a half hour ago and didn't think the fire was out of control before the fire wagons arrived. Let's pray there isn't extensive damage." They approached the window, and the two of them stood quietly, watching the scene unfold below them.

Olivia squinted her eyes and stared at the clock across the room. Two o'clock. She'd been in bed only two hours. The men and wagons worked in concert throughout the following hours until the fire had been extinguished. In the darkness it was difficult to evaluate how much damage had occurred. But no matter the damage or lack of sleep, she would be expected in the hotel kitchen by five-thirty. At the sound of the downstairs door, Mrs. Barnes bid Olivia good-night for the second time and hurried off to greet her husband.

Mr. Barnes had returned home, his clothes sooty and smelling of smoke. That was the report Olivia received when she came downstairs less than an hour later. From all appearances, Mrs. Barnes hadn't gone back to bed. Perhaps she'd nap once Mr. Barnes departed for his office. In spite of the fire and their lack of sleep, all employees would be expected to report for work at their regularly scheduled time. And most of them wouldn't complain. After last night's fire, they'd be thankful to still have a job. Misfortune in the workplace seemed to have that effect upon the workers. No matter the depth of dissatisfaction, folks sobered and seemingly cherished their jobs when disaster struck, at least for a while.

A short time later Chef René waved Olivia forward as she approached the hotel. He stood just inside the kitchen door, resting his beefy hands on his hips. Rather than offering a cheery greeting, he frowned and pointed toward the second floor of the hotel. "Mr. Pullman arrived an hour ago. Mr. Howard went to Chicago to tell him of the fire, and he insisted upon returning to see the damage for himself. He wants his breakfast served at seven o'clock. Then he will go across the street and examine the damage from last night's fire. I assume you, too, were up most of the night?"

"Yes. I doubt there were many folks able to sleep through all of the commotion. I only wish I had gone to bed earlier." She exchanged her flower-bedecked hat for the familiar white toque and placed her journal in the nearby closet with her purse. At least she was prepared for her meeting. Perhaps with Mr. Pullman here it would be cancelled and her efforts would be for naught.

While Chef René prepared Mr. Pullman's breakfast, Olivia reviewed the breakfast orders gathered from guests the preceding evening. She wondered if they would all arise at their prearranged time given their interrupted sleep. The kitchen staff must be prepared for either event. Most of the food would remain tasty in the special warming ovens. She slipped into her former position with ease and agility, happy to be preparing sausage and griddle cakes rather than a wordy report. Before she'd had time to worry overmuch, the appointed hour for her meeting with Mr. Howard arrived. She replaced the toque with her hat and, with the journal tucked under her arm, waved to Chef René, who offered a sympathetic smile in return.

She passed several unoccupied desks in the outer offices and was surprised to see that even Mr. Howard's clerk, Mr. Mahafferty, was absent from his desk. Voices drifted from inside Mr. Howard's office. Likely going over duty assignments with his clerk, Olivia decided as she settled into a nearby chair.

The voices grew increasingly loud, and from his tone, one of the men was apparently angry. Though she didn't want to be accused of eavesdropping, ignoring the shouted questions and demands proved impossible. She wanted to depart yet worried Mr. Howard would appear and expect her to be prepared for their meeting. Indecision caused her to remain affixed to the chair.

"I'm telling you that I expect answers, Samuel! I've only just completed rebuilding Market Hall after last year's fire and now this. Seems too much of a coincidence to me. I think there's something amiss. If this type of destruction continues, there will be severe ramifications for me and my stockholders. Do you realize what it costs each time I'm forced to rebuild? I will not stand idly by and see profits diminish. This town is intended to make a profit, and you had best see that it does!"

Olivia gulped. It was *Mr. Pullman* in Mr. Howard's office! She gripped the chair arms and attempted to push herself upright. Unfortunately, her legs failed her, and she shrank into the cushioned chair. Heavy footsteps paced the floor inside the office. If only she could disappear. The pacing ceased and she held her breath while Mr. Howard responded. Unlike Mr. Pullman's utterances, Mr. Howard's words were muffled and indistinguishable.

Then Mr. Pullman spoke again. "I believe the workers continue to align themselves into unions. They're not foolish enough to meet within the confines of the town, but every fiber of my being tells me that there is trouble in the offing. I do not want further embarrassment during the Columbian Exposition, Samuel. You must keep this town under control. We have guests arriving from all over the world. Am I making myself clear?"

"Absolutely. Though I don't believe this fire was intentional, you can depend on me to uncover any wrongdoing that may have occurred."

Once again Olivia could hear the thumping of footsteps traversing the inner sanctum. The pacing stopped.

"That's exactly my point," Mr. Pullman said. "You're beginning your investigation with the belief that the fire was accidental. I want you to begin with the belief that it was intentional and try to prove my hypothesis incorrect."

Olivia wondered if Mr. Pullman was leaning over Mr.

Howard's desk as he issued his commands. Before she could further consider the thought, she heard the scraping of chairs on the wooden floor, and Mr. Howard whisked open the door. She couldn't be certain who appeared the more incredulous— Mr. Howard or herself. If her presence surprised Mr. Pullman, he gave no sign. He merely nodded and continued on his way.

Mr. Howard glanced at his door and back at Olivia. "You heard?"

"Not everything," she whispered. "I arrived at eight o'clock for our meeting and didn't know what I should—"

He waved his hand and silenced her. "I should have sent word that I would be detained. And I should have made certain the door was closed." His gaze settled on the journal tucked beneath her arm. "Since you've been waiting all this time, do come in, and let's get started."

As he sat down behind his desk, Olivia noted Mr. Howard's complexion had turned a pasty shade of gray. "Did the fire cause much damage?"

"No. The alarm sounded quickly, and the firemen responded with great haste. A few minor repairs and no injuries. All's well that ends well."

From what she'd overheard, Mr. Pullman didn't seem to be of the same opinion, but she didn't argue. "I'm certain the workers will be relieved to know their jobs haven't been compromised by the fire."

He nervously tapped his pen. "There are those who believe it is the workers who are attempting to wreak havoc in order to gain Mr. Pullman's attention. Have you not heard such rumblings, Olivia?"

"I've been out on the trains, Mr. Howard. How would I be

privy to such comments? Besides, that theory makes no sense. The workers need these jobs to support their families. If they destroy the factories, they destroy their own livelihood. It is a preposterous notion."

Mr. Howard leaned back in his chair and rested his head. "I find that you can't always judge situations or people so simply. Sometimes the people you least suspect are the very ones who betray you." He pointed to her journal. "Shall we begin?"

She shivered at the chill in his voice. Did he think she had something to do with the fire? Why would he think such an outlandish thing? Hadn't he indicated to Mr. Pullman he thought the fire had been an accidental occurrence? Mr. Howard's behavior baffled her.

CHAPTER NINETEEN

Chicago, Illinois
May 17, 1893

Charlotte applied the finishing touches to her hair and smiled into the mirror. Who would have thought that the spoiled daughter of the Earl of Lanshire would one day learn to coif her own hair, and in such a becoming fashion, too? "All things are possible, even hairstyling," Charlotte mused while backing away from the looking glass.

Ruth grinned at Charlotte as she tiptoed across the room toward baby Sadie's crib. "I can't be certain, but I don't believe the Bible passage you're quoting refers to hairstyling."

With a shrug, Charlotte pinned a small brooch to the neckline of her dress. "Perhaps not. But that verse has certainly made me realize that with God all things *are* possible. Even hairstyling," she added with a grin. She picked up her purse and fluffed Sadie's downy curls as she passed by. "You and Sadie have a good day."

"You too, Charlotte. I hope you meet your sales quota before noon."

"Thank you, Ruth. I hope having all these folks in town for the Exposition is going to help all of us meet our quotas. The Merchant Prince isn't happy when sales don't meet his expectations."

Ruth arched her brows. "Prince?"

"That's the moniker the press and some of the store employees use when mentioning Mr. Field. The title fits him well. He reminds me of some—" She stopped midsentence, realizing she'd nearly offered information about her noble birth.

Ruth frowned. "Who does he remind you of?"

"Oh, no one in particular, just some of the wealthy men I met years ago. I'd better hurry." She rushed out the door and downstairs before Ruth could question her further.

With a quick good-bye to Mrs. Priddle, Charlotte hurried outside. As usual, one of the green delivery wagons bearing the words *Marshall Field & Company* awaited her. After her first week at the glove counter, Mrs. Jenkins had gone to Mr. Field and made the travel arrangements on Charlotte's behalf. Now, each morning and each evening, she rode to and from work in one of the special delivery wagons. She doubted the benefit was afforded to many other employees, for the driver always went to the rear of the store, parked the wagon, and then assisted her down. The first day he advised her she was always to enter the store through the Washington Street entrance rather than the rear doors used by the delivery personnel. Except for the deliverymen, she'd never seen any other employee ride in one of the wagons. No one had ever mentioned the privilege, nor had they questioned her. And who would question Mr. Field's decision?

She hurried around the corner and waved a gloved hand at

the doorman. "Good morning, Joseph."

He tipped his hat and gave a small salute. "Good morning to you, Miss Spencer."

Joseph Anderson never ceased to amaze her. He remembered the name of every employee and every shopper who had ever passed through the doors of the emporium. Mr. Field would be delighted if every employee in the store possessed a memory such as Joseph's. One of the first instructions Charlotte had received from Mrs. Jenkins was that she work to develop a keen memory, especially for names and faces.

And Charlotte had done her very best. She'd even written down names along with customers' choices, using her newly acquired memorization technique of musical tunes to help her recall the items. She walked down the aisles that had begun to feel more familiar with each passing day.

After Charlotte had placed her hat and cape in the storage closet provided for employees, Mrs. Jenkins beckoned her forward. "Mr. Field is waiting to meet with us."

An involuntary gasp escaped Charlotte's lips. "Is something amiss?" Try as she might, Charlotte could think of nothing she'd done that would necessitate a visit to Mr. Field's office. Such meetings usually resulted in dismissal, or so she'd been told by several of the salesclerks. Not only would the lack of funds for Priddle House cause undue hardship, but Mrs. Priddle would be embarrassed if one of her "girls" should be dismissed.

Apparently Mrs. Jenkins sensed her fear, for she squeezed Charlotte's shoulder. "No need for worry, my dear."

Charlotte attempted a smile, but her lips wouldn't cooperate. Mrs. Jenkins remained the epitome of decorum as she knocked on Mr. Field's door and then led Charlotte into the palatial surroundings. Mr. Field motioned them forward, a prince on his throne. Thoughts of her early morning conversation with Ruth flitted through her memory as she approached the mahogany desk.

"Be seated, ladies." Mr. Field tugged one end of his white mustache between his index finger and thumb while he waited until they settled into the luxurious armchairs. Looking directly at Charlotte, he began to speak. "As your supervisor, Mrs. Jenkins is required to report frequently upon your progress. Let me say that I am impressed, Miss Spencer. Mrs. Jenkins, Mr. Selfridge, and I concur that you are an excellent employee. You have demonstrated a higher quality than we normally observe in our staff, even after many years." He glanced at Mrs. Jenkins. "I am told you possess a natural talent for aiding customers with superb choices and that you have exceptional taste in clothing and accessories."

"Thank you, Mr. Field." Charlotte hoped their session would soon end. She feared his praise would soon lead to a complaint. Long ago she had learned that words of praise were usually followed by words of correction.

From somewhere beneath his desk, Mr. Field pushed a buzzer. The door opened and several people filed into the office carrying a vast assortment of clothing and accessories. There were gowns, shirtwaists, skirts, woolen coats, fur-lined capes, along with a variety of scarves and jewelry. "I'm not one to simply trust the word of managers or supervisors, even ones so valued as Mrs. Jenkins or Mr. Selfridge. Therefore, Miss Spencer, I thought we would put you to a test of sorts. You don't mind, do you?"

Fear clutched at her belly. She shouldn't have eaten break-fast. Charlotte stole a quick look at Mrs. Jenkins. The older woman provided no assistance. Her features were fixed in a stoic expression that would offer no help with Charlotte's deci-sion. Apparently Mr. Field didn't expect a response, for he was hastily directing the placement of the clothing and accessories throughout his office.

When he was satisfied with the arrangement, he dismissed everyone except Charlotte and Mrs. Jenkins. "Now, Miss Spen-cer, pretend I am a male customer and I approach you to request assistance selecting clothing for my wife. From the items in this room, I would like you to choose two complete ensembles."

Charlotte considered Mr. Field's request before offering a response. "Before I selected any items, I would ask if you could furnish me with a likeness of your wife—a photograph or paint-ing. If not, I would ask for her complete description so that I might choose colors and styles most becoming to her figure. Next I would ask you about your wife's social obligations and activities in order to choose items that would prove most use-ful." Charlotte stepped toward one of the gowns and then looked at Mr. Field. "Though her husband might think this gown lovely, a woman who does not attend the opera or formal balls has no need of such an item. No matter the beauty of the fabric, she would surely be annoyed with him if he purchased this gown for her, don't you think?"

Mr. Field appeared to weigh her response and then agreed. "I like this idea. Follow me, ladies. If we can find a gentleman shopper, we shall put Miss Spencer's theory to the test."

Though he didn't find a gentleman amidst the aisles of

finery, Mr. Field was not deterred. He bid them wait while he walked outside. Soon he returned with a gentleman in tow. "This is Mr. Flynn. He has agreed to be our candidate. I've told him that you will choose items for his wife. He has agreed to return with Mrs. Flynn later this afternoon. She will assess your choices."

The man nodded his agreement. "You also said my wife could keep all of the items free of charge."

"If you supply Miss Spencer with the information she needs to select the ensembles, and the two of you return and answer our questions later today, the items will be hers to keep—without charge."

The man beamed. "When do we start picking out?"

Charlotte drew near the man and requested he join her in the dress salon on the second floor. "There is a small office where we may converse without interruption. If you like, I'd be pleased to request coffee and a few pastries delivered for your enjoyment while we talk."

Mr. Flynn followed on her heels, obviously delighted he'd been chosen for the task at hand. Once situated in the office with his coffee and a cinnamon bun, Charlotte proceeded. As she'd expected, he had no photograph or other likeness of his wife. He did proudly mention an oil painting of his wife that hung on their living room wall—one that had been painted by a family friend when his wife was a young child. Though it could be of no assistance to her, Charlotte agreed the painting sounded quite lovely.

Mr. Flynn detailed his wife's social commitments, which primarily centered upon church, her reading club, and an occasional afternoon tea. As he finished his refreshments, Mr. Flynn pointed to one of the clerks outside the small office. "She looks much like my wife—same size and hair color." Charlotte signaled to the clerk, who entered the office. Mr. Flynn bobbed his head. "Except my wife's eyes are hazel instead of blue. Does that help?"

"Indeed, it does, Mr. Flynn. Based upon the information you've given me, I'll make some choices I believe your wife will enjoy." She escorted him to the front door. Once he departed, she set about shopping, all the while wondering if Mrs. Flynn would prove as agreeable as her husband.

After choosing a final piece of jewelry, Charlotte assembled the items, pleased with her choices. Given the sparkle in Mr. Flynn's eyes as he had talked about his wife, Charlotte returned to fifth floor and made one final selection. Her task now completed, she returned to her duties in the accessories department.

Once she'd finished assisting her customer, Mrs. Jenkins joined Charlotte behind the glove counter. "Mr. Field was impressed with your ideas this morning. I trust Mr. Flynn cooperated in the process." She straightened a pair of kid gloves while she spoke.

"He was most helpful, although a picture of his wife would have proved an added benefit. He did offer detailed information, and I'm now anxious to meet his wife. I do hope she will be pleased with the selections. Will you accompany me to Mr. Field's office later this afternoon?"

She nodded. "He said that he will send for us when we're to join him."

The remaining hours passed slowly, and Charlotte thought

three o'clock would never arrive. When she hadn't been summoned by three-thirty, she wondered if Mr. and Mrs. Flynn had failed to arrive, and when the atrium clock chimed to announce the arrival of four o'clock, her spirits drooped to a new low. Would Mr. Field consider her a failure and discharge her from his employ if the Flynns didn't reappear? The effect upon Priddle House would be dramatic. Mrs. Priddle had come to rely on Charlotte's weekly paycheck to help cover expenses—especially now, with so few of the women working outside of the house.

Her gloomy thoughts persisted until Mr. Field's assistant finally appeared at four-thirty and spoke to Mrs. Jenkins, who then signaled Charlotte. As the two of them made their return to Mr. Field's office, Charlotte touched Mrs. Jenkins's arm. "Have the Flynns returned?"

"I have no idea, my dear, but we shall soon find out." Mrs. Jenkins tapped on Mr. Field's door; at his response, the two of them entered.

Charlotte saw that Mr. and Mrs. Flynn had indeed arrived. Both of them appeared pleased. Mrs. Flynn was attired in one of the suits Charlotte had chosen, and it seemed a perfect fit. With her husband's detailed description as well as the comparison to one of the salesclerks, Charlotte would have recognized Mrs. Flynn without an introduction. She was a comely woman who appeared somewhat uncomfortable in her current role.

Mr. Flynn pointed to the suit. "It's perfect, don't you think, Miss Spencer?"

Charlotte glanced at Mr. Field. She wasn't certain whether she should speak or let him take charge.

He nodded.

"The color is perfect," she said. "Would you mind standing up, Mrs. Flynn? I'd like to see the flow and length of the skirt on you." The woman rose from the chair, walked across the room, and turned in a circle. She'd obviously already performed for Mr. Field. "The suit is a lovely choice for you. Your husband proved an expert advisor."

Mr. Field cleared his throat, and Mrs. Flynn seemed to realize she should return to her husband's side. "Mr. and Mrs. Flynn are both pleased with your choices, Miss Spencer." His eyes suddenly sparkled as he leaned across his desk and looked directly at Mrs. Flynn. "What if I told you that you could exchange any of these selections for something else of like value in the store, Mrs. Flynn? Tell me which items you would exchange and why."

Startled, Charlotte wanted to object. Mr. Field's offer to Mrs. Flynn hadn't been a part of their original agreement. Was he unhappy because the woman had been pleased by the selections? Had he wanted her to fail at the task? Confusion and fear assailed Charlotte while she watched Mrs. Flynn assess the selections.

"If I were choosing for myself, I would not change one thing. I am pleased with every choice, but I would be much happier purchasing items for my children instead." Her eyes filled with a mother's longing, and she picked up what had been Charlotte's final selection. "And these will bring my family the most delight. I truly cherish this gift more than any." She ran her fingers over the pages of sheet music. "Our family enjoys singing, and all of us play the piano—I suppose my husband told you that."

Mr. Flynn shook his head. "When we passed by the tearoom, I heard the music and mentioned your talent playing the piano—nothing more. Apparently Miss Spencer realized the joy music brings to our family."

The remark seemed to please Mr. Field, for he nodded approvingly. Then, before Mr. and Mrs. Flynn left his office, he generously offered them a matching amount to purchase clothing for their children.

"You performed your assignment very well, Miss Spencer. Please return to my office next Monday morning at nine o'clock, and we will discuss your new duties."

Charlotte followed Mrs. Jenkins out of the office, uncertain what her new duties might entail, but Mrs. Jenkins assured her she'd likely be offered a position that paid more money—perhaps a supervisory position or a new position created due to the influx of customers for the Columbian Exposition.

Though Charlotte doubted she'd be considered for a new position, Mrs. Jenkins waved her index finger back and forth. "That's not an outlandish idea, you know. If Mr. Field believes you can offer his customers a unique service, he will create such a position for you. Mr. Field has progressive ideas when it comes to merchandising, and he wants to offer his customers every possible amenity. Even though the country is teetering on the brink of depression, it is through these special services that he believes his store will continue to show excellent profits." Mrs. Jenkins continued her brisk stride as they returned to the accessories department. "Because of your ability to serve his customers, Mr. Field has taken a particular liking to you, and that is a very good thing, Charlotte."

Charlotte wished she didn't have to wait until Monday to discover what Mr. Field had in mind, and she mentioned that fact during their evening prayer time. Mrs. Priddle brushed aside the complaint with an admonition that Charlotte should develop a modicum of patience and offer a prayer of thanksgiving that God had sent her an easily satisfied woman such as Mrs. Flynn. Charlotte wanted to rail against Mrs. Priddle's assessment and tell her that Mrs. Flynn hadn't been a woman with low expectations. Rather, it had been Charlotte's astute taste in clothing and accessories that had been the cause of her success. But Mrs. Priddle would no doubt consider such a retort prideful and send her upstairs for prayer and reflection, which would result in a missed piano lesson for Fiona.

So she bit her tongue and remained silent, for she couldn't disappoint Fiona again this week. The girl's piano lesson had been cancelled last week due to a special meeting at the church, and Fiona wouldn't want to miss another lesson this evening. The weekly lessons had become the highlight of the child's life. Each night she practiced on her paper piano. With her lesson scheduled for tonight, the girl continued to stick to Charlotte's side like paper glued to a wall. Charlotte wouldn't disappoint her.

CHAPTER TWENTY

Pullman, Illinois
May 18, 1893

Fred bounded downstairs and stopped in front of the hallway mirror. He straightened his tie and called to his mother, "I'm off for Chicago." Before he could exit the door, she scuttled toward him like a prize contender racing for the finish line. Wisps of gray hair stood on end and waved in the breeze. There was little doubt he'd offended her with his attempt to leave without first sitting down for a cup of coffee.

Wiping flour-smudged hands on her frayed apron, she came to a halt in front of him. "Don't you attempt to depart this house with no more than a few words hollered down the hallway. You know better, young man."

Her words reminded him of his early childhood years. "Yes, Mother, but I don't want to miss my train."

The longcase clock struck seven in Westminster chimes, and Mrs. DeVault shook her head. "There's plenty of time before the next train to Chicago departs. And just what business do you have in Chicago this morning?"

This conversation was going to prove uncomfortable. "I'm going to see Ellen Ashton."

His mother folded her arms across her chest and frowned. "Why? You're no match for a woman like Ellen Ashton." Her features softened. "Not that I don't think any woman would be blessed to have you as a husband, but Ellen Ashton hails from a different world than ours, Fred. She's from a family of money and social status. Why would you even consider pursuing a woman like her?" His mother flicked an imaginary speck from his jacket. "Those facts aside, Olivia has a much more pleasant personality."

"And how would you know that, Mother? You've never even talked to Ellen. If you did, I believe you'd find her quite personable and very kind."

His mother's frown returned. "I still believe you need to resolve your differences with Olivia."

Fred searched unsuccessfully for an answer that would satisfy his mother. "We're not going to resolve this matter before I leave. Besides, with Olivia traveling the rails and my work schedule, I don't know when I'll have an opportunity."

"You could *make* an opportunity if you truly wanted to. And she's been back home since last Friday." His mother placed her hands on her hips. "Am I correct in assuming your trip to Chicago is pleasure rather than business?"

Fred backed toward the hall tree, intent upon retrieving his hat. "A little of both, I suppose."

"Perhaps I meddle too much, but—"

"*Mother!*"

She waved her hand. "I know, I know. Not another word.

I'm returning to the kitchen to complete my bread baking."

After a fleeting kiss to her cheek, Fred watched his mother head off toward the baking that awaited her in the other room. The longing howl of a train whistle announced he had little time to spare, and he hurried out the door and down the front steps. He could have set his mother's mind at ease regarding his relationship with Ellen Ashton, but the less she knew about his involvement with the unionization movement, the better. If anyone inquired about his frequent trips to Chicago, she could easily say that he was calling on a lady friend. Besides, Bill Orland's presence in Chicago provided excellent justification for his journey.

Not that anyone had actually inquired, but Mr. Ashton had explained the necessity of always having an answer at the ready. *"When you least expect it, you'll be called upon for a detailed response. You must be prepared, Fred."* He'd heard that comment from both Mr. Ashton and Ellen several times.

Should anyone begin questioning his mother and she actually knew the truth, she might slip up. Fred couldn't take that chance. There was always the possibility she might unintentionally disclose information when visiting with her friends. He remained confident that maintaining secrecy would prove best for both of them.

The train lurched to a halt, and Fred made his way down the aisle. He stepped off the train, entered the Van Buren Street station, and ambled across the massive concourse. The sounds of hurried footsteps, urgent shouts, and beckoning train whistles echoed through the cavernous depot. Yet he didn't feel a sense of urgency, merely a desire to keep Mr. Ashton informed. He hoped the older man would be pleased to see him. The news he carried to Chicago wasn't pressing, but Fred had detected subtle changes in attitude among many of the workers. Deeper feelings of dissatisfaction had begun to surface since the company's investigation into the fire. The focus upon workers as the possible culprits had resulted in feelings of bitterness and resentment. And the ongoing economic downturn throughout the country had increased speculation of lowered wages and layoffs, both matters of constant concern and discussion among the Pullman employees.

He exited the massive depot and strode toward Mr. Ashton's office. Perhaps the older man would chide him for another visit to his office, but he hadn't specifically told him to stay away—merely to be careful. Immediately Fred glanced over his shoulder. He should have been watching to see if he'd been followed before now. On the other hand, company spies wouldn't believe a romantic liaison existed unless he called upon Ellen. That was what he was telling himself as he opened the front door of the Ashton law office.

As Fred entered, Montrose Ashton turned and an annoyed look crossed his face. He held his unlit cigar in the air and then continued his conversation with Ellen. A few moments later, he turned to face Fred. "What brings you here this morning?" He craned his neck and peered over Fred's shoulder as though he expected to find someone lurking outside the doorway.

Fred shook his head. "I wasn't followed."

"No offense, Fred, but you're no expert on such things. An entire parade could follow you, and I doubt you'd notice."

Fred didn't argue. He'd learned he couldn't match wits or intelligence with Montrose Ashton. He took a step closer to Ellen's desk. "In order to reinforce the idea that Ellen and I are involved in a romantic relationship, I thought I should call on her at least once a week. And since I work in the evenings . . ."

Ellen looked up from the notes on her desk. "I thought we agreed at the train station that I would come to Pullman."

Fred grinned and clasped a hand to his heart. "I couldn't wait to see you." He tipped his head toward Mr. Ashton and whispered, "That's in case some unseen person is listening through the keyhole in the front door."

Ellen giggled, but Mr. Ashton remained stoic. "Don't take this matter lightly, Fred. Men much less involved in unioniza-tion than you have gone missing." He chewed on the tip of his cigar. "They're likely decaying in the depths of Lake Michigan."

"Father! There is no need for your morbid talk. And Fred's point is well taken. A couple in love would use every opportu-nity to see each other."

Vindication coursed through Fred's veins. Ellen had come to his rescue. He squared his shoulders and met Mr. Ashton's steely-eyed gaze. "I do have news of some recent developments. It isn't of earth-shaking proportions, but I did want to keep you apprised of any changes that might help us sway more of the workers toward unionization."

Mr. Ashton nodded toward his office. "Let's go in and sit down." He tapped his daughter's desk as he passed by. "Ellen, check outside and make certain Fred wasn't followed."

The command lessened Fred's sense of confidence. Appar-ently Mr. Ashton hadn't completely agreed with Ellen's assess-ment. Fred could only hope she wouldn't discover someone lurking nearby. If so, Mr. Ashton would consider him a com-plete incompetent.

Once he and Mr. Ashton had discussed the latest happenings in Pullman, the older man dismissed him. "Take my daughter for a stroll, and then be on your way." He brandished his unlit cigar through the air like a baton. "And next time listen to what she says. Unless it's an emergency, don't show up unexpected or uninvited. Do I make myself clear?"

"Yes, sir. Completely."

"Ellen!" The older man's voice boomed throughout the office. "Lock the door on your way out."

Ellen strode into her father's office. "I'm certain everyone within a half-mile radius heard that command, Father. There's no need to holler." She leaned down and kissed his weathered cheek. "I'll return shortly."

"Not too soon." He winked. "Remember, you're a woman in love."

After she secured her hat in place, the two of them left. Ellen grasped Fred's arm, and they walked toward State Street. "I'm anxious to hear if Olivia has returned home." Ellen gazed at him expectantly.

"I understand she returned home last Friday, the same day that I first visited your father's office."

Ellen frowned. "I'm surprised she hasn't contacted me. You're certain she's been back since then?"

He grinned. "Absolutely. My mother reminded me of that particular fact shortly before I left home this morning."

"Yet *you've* not spoken to her?"

He might as well clear the air. He was weary of tiptoeing around his relationship with Olivia. He offered a quick explanation of their tenuous relationship and hoped Ellen would move along to another topic.

The bow on Ellen's hat wobbled to and fro as she shook her head. "I see. Well, from my personal observations as well as my conversations with Olivia, I can tell you that she has no interest in Mr. Howard. Of course she must converse with him regarding her work duties. And you must remember that Olivia has no one else to depend upon for her livelihood. You can't expect her to treat Mr. Howard with disdain. She fears losing her job. Surely you can understand her predicament."

Fred had ceased listening to Ellen's rebuttal. Instead, he was watching their reflections in store windows as they passed by. They were being followed. He tugged Ellen toward the door of a bookshop. "I want to see if they have a book my mother has been interested in reading."

She frowned as he pulled her along. Once inside, she withdrew her hand from the crook of his arm. "Why are you shouting?"

"We're being followed. I hoped the man would follow us inside so you could get a look at him."

Ellen balanced on tiptoe and retrieved a volume from one of the dusty shelves. She flipped through the pages and then handed the book to Fred before continuing toward the front window. For all intents and purposes, she appeared engrossed as she perused the leather-bound selections. Fred decided she was quite good at this. Any onlooker would believe her only interest was the discovery of a specific title.

Several minutes passed before she returned, bearing another tome for his review. She handed him the book. "Open the pages and pretend to be reading." She pointed a gloved finger to a line of type. "That's the same man who followed us the last time you were here. The note you sent me after your return to Pullman said he went into the administration building after you returned. Correct? He's surely a spotter for the company."

Fred flipped the page of the book and turned to face Ellen, hoping to gain a better view outside. The man was looking at items displayed in the window. "No. He may be the same height and build, but that's not the same man. His hair is a different color, and he doesn't have a mustache."

Ellen removed the book from his hands and snapped it shut as the man entered the store. The well-dressed gentleman appeared to be an absorbed patron, completely uninterested in the two of them. Without hesitation, he strode to the store owner and began to chat.

Fred grinned. "You see? He's not at all concerned about us."

"We're leaving; follow me." Ellen placed the book on a shelf as they departed the store. Fred hurried after her.

He'd need to pick up the pace in order to keep up with Ellen's brisk stride. When he finally came alongside her, he laughed. "Is this a race?"

She yanked on Fred's arm and stepped into an alleyway. "Just remain silent and wait." The whispered command was followed by a fearsome warning glance. She motioned him to move close to the building. With their bodies pasted against the brick and mortar, they remained side by side, blended into the shadows, listening to the sound of approaching footfalls.

Ellen poked his arm as the man passed by the alley. The moment he passed by, his footsteps ceased. Ellen swung around and pulled Fred into an embrace. "Kiss me!"

Fred leaned down and kissed her full on the lips, but his eyelids remained at half-mast. He watched the man take several backward steps and look in their direction. Finally satisfied, the man continued down the street. Fred lifted his head. "He's disappeared from sight."

Ellen straightened her hat. "He'll be waiting down the street. Mark my word."

Fred wasn't convinced the man was actually following them. "I doubt that. We've surely proven we're no more than a young couple in love."

They were nearing Marshall Field's huge dry-goods store when Ellen poked him in the side. "There he is—standing near the entrance."

"Why don't we walk right past him and go inside the store? If he wants to follow us, we should at least let him do a bit of shopping for his wife."

Ellen laughed and shook her head. "The doorman would stop me before I could set foot inside. I'm banned from Mr. Field's wondrous establishment."

"Banned?" Fred thought he'd misunderstood. "But why?"

"Mr. Field has issued orders that any customers known to be affiliated with unions should be immediately escorted from his store by house detectives. Though I don't belong to a union, nor does my father, we are much too closely associated with the unions to be permitted in Mr. Field's domain." She shrugged her shoulders. "I suppose you could say I've been relegated to those who must shop at the Boston Store."

He frowned. "Boston Store?"

Ellen chuckled. "Yes, the Boston Store. There's a little song about shopping at Mr. Field's establishment: 'All the girls who wear high heels, they trade down at Marshall Field's; All the girls who scrub the floor, they trade at the Boston Store.' The tune is a prime example of the class distinction between those who can afford to shop in Mr. Field's store and those who cannot. In my case it's a distinction of not adhering to Mr. Field's beliefs. Shopping elsewhere is a small price to pay, wouldn't you agree?"

"Absolutely. Why don't we go and enjoy an ice-cream soda at the confectionery. Unless you're banned from there, too." He grinned. Arm in arm, they crossed the street to Kranz's Viennese Confectionery Shop.

While the two of them enjoyed their sodas, they continued their discussion of Mr. Field and his strident policies. A short time later they departed for the train station. So did the man who had been following them for the last hour.

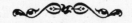

CHAPTER TWENTY-ONE

Pullman, Illinois
June 5, 1893

Chef René greeted Olivia with a halfhearted smile when she reentered the kitchen after a hectic morning in the downstairs baking kitchen. Both Fanny and Edna had taken ill, and though Fanny had made an early morning appearance, Chef René had immediately sent her home. Ailing employees were not permitted in the kitchen—a rule of management that was strictly enforced by Chef René.

"I see you have survived the rigors of the baking kitchen. Let us hope that at least one of the women is well enough to return tomorrow."

Olivia fully agreed. Though she enjoyed baking pastries, decorating cakes, and creating fruit and flowers from marzipan, spending hours kneading and mixing dough for the loaves of bread and fresh rolls served with each meal in the hotel was not among her favorite chores. "I'll say a special prayer for both of them this evening."

Chef René chuckled. "You had best begin now. I'm sure they're not the only ones needing God's attention." Olivia grinned as he swiped his hands on a smudged green-and-white dish towel that hung from his waist. "I almost forgot. Mr. Howard stopped by to talk to you this morning. When I explained we were short of help and you were assisting in the baking kitchen, he asked that I have you stop by his office later this afternoon when we're not so busy."

"And when might that be?" Olivia inquired while glancing around the kitchen.

Beads of perspiration lined his forehead and glistened in the sunlight streaming through the east window of the kitchen. "Perhaps you could go now, before we begin preparations for the evening repast?"

Evening repast? With the foreign dignitaries arriving for the Columbian Exposition, Chef René was beginning to take on a few airs of his own. The thought amused her, for Chef René's delectable cuisine was enough to impress even the most demanding critic. Olivia removed her flour-dotted jacket and toque and hung them in the hallway closet. "I doubt I should be gone for long. Especially since Mr. Howard realizes we are short of help."

The chef returned to the open cookbook he'd placed on the counter a short time earlier. "I shall not depend upon what Mr. Howard does or doesn't know about our staffing difficulties. I will know you have returned when I see you enter the door."

She couldn't argue with his response. If Mr. Howard wished to detain her, neither Olivia nor Chef René could object. It was simply the way of things in Pullman. Given the time of day, perhaps he wouldn't be busy. Unless a dignitary or unexpected stockholder arrived in town late in the day, Mr. Howard seemed to conduct his meetings during the morning.

The scent of fragrant climbing roses greeted Olivia when she exited the back door and ran down the stairs. The heady perfume was nearly as exhilarating as the sumptuous smells that filled Chef René's kitchen each day. The June sun warmed her back, and she crossed the street with a spring in her step, pleased for the return of summer and the leafy trees and blooming flowers that accompanied the season.

Mr. Howard's clerk, Mr. Mahafferty, looked up from beneath hooded eyelids and pointed Olivia toward a chair. Had the office walls been crumbling around him, Olivia doubted the man could muster a jot of enthusiasm. He appeared locked in the doldrums of life, a man simply performing a role in which he'd been cast. She thought him rather sad and was reminded of a gloomy morning months ago when Mrs. DeVault had explained the fullness of life that is gained through knowing Jesus. The older woman had read a Scripture passage: *"The thief cometh not, but for to steal, and to kill, and to destroy: I am come that they might have life, and that they might have it more abundantly."* Mr. Mahafferty needed to read that Scripture so that he might live his life more richly.

Before Olivia could mention either Mrs. DeVault or the Scripture, the man pushed back his chair and excused himself. "I'm expected to take notes at a meeting in another part of the building. Mr. Howard will be with you shortly."

Olivia thanked him, but after he'd departed, she decided to jot down the passage on a piece of paper and leave it on his desk. Whether Mr. Mahafferty ever read the Scripture or not would be entirely up to him—and God. She stepped to the other side of the room and sat down behind the desk. Swallowed up by the high back and deep seat of the large chair, Olivia took up the pen and wrote *John 10:10* on a sheet of paper.

She had replaced the pen in its ebony holder when the door latch leading to Mr. Howard's office clicked, and she heard his voice.

"We haven't yet completed our discussion, Geoffrey."

Olivia held her breath. Once the door snapped shut, she would return to the chair across the room. But the door didn't close. Muffled voices drifted into the room. She remained fixed in the large chair behind Mr. Mahafferty's desk, afraid to move yet afraid to remain in the chair. What if Mr. Mahafferty returned and found her sitting at his desk? What if Mr. Howard walked out and thought she had intentionally hidden there in order to eavesdrop? Her hands quivered as the men continued to talk, Mr. Howard's voice growing louder by the minute.

"I want to know exactly *why* you're so certain there is nothing more than a romantic liaison between Fred DeVault and Miss Ashton."

Olivia perked to attention at the mention of Fred's name.

"Quite frankly, I'd stake my life on the fact that he's a union organizer. I don't believe his meetings in Chicago are purely romantic in nature."

A man laughed, followed by the sound of chair legs scraping across the floor. Olivia scooted farther down in the chair.

"This isn't a humorous matter, Mr. Townsend." Mr. Howard's anger shot through the air like a pistol report. "Do you not realize the danger these demon unions present to our stockholders? Why do you think you've been employed by this company? Certainly not to laugh and make light of serious situations. I doubt Mr. Pullman would be pleased with your attitude."

Mr. Townsend? Wasn't that the name of the man who'd been in the Pullman depot when Mr. Howard met her train after her unaccompanied trip to New York? Mr. Howard said the man had previously worked for a competitor but was considering a position with Mr. Pullman.

"Your veiled threats and self-righteous words might impress Mr. Pullman, but my investigations have uncovered more than you might imagine, Mr. Howard. If I were a man in your position, I'd think twice about going to Mr. Pullman or the stockholders with a report that *I'm* not performing in their best interest."

Olivia wished she were somewhere else. Anywhere but in this reception office hearing these two men level charges against each other.

"Exactly what are you implying, Geoffrey? If you've discovered another matter of concern, I don't see it in this report."

Olivia could hear shuffling papers, and she pictured Mr. Howard riffling through page after page of paper work to corroborate his rebuttal.

"Does the idea of improper job assignments prod your memory, Samuel?"

"What are you suggesting? I haven't the slightest idea what you're talking about."

The earlier anger she'd detected in Mr. Howard's voice had been replaced by a slight tremor. Did he have something to fear?

"No need to divulge all of the gory details. Let's just say that I believe we're both men who open the door when opportunity knocks. Whether compensation is slipped under the table or arrives in a pay envelope, it's all the same to both of us. Right?"

Though Olivia strained toward the door, she didn't hear Mr. Howard's response. She wasn't certain if he had replied at all, for her thoughts were interrupted by the sound of Mr. Townsend's scornful laughter.

"No need to worry overmuch, Samuel. For now, we need only resolve the issue of Mr. DeVault and Miss Ashton. I want to reaffirm my earlier conclusion that what is occurring between them is no more than a lovers' tryst. Believe me, had you seen them together—a young couple locked in passionate embraces, kissing, walking arm in arm while lovingly gazing into each other's eyes, you would agree that Mr. DeVault's sole purpose for visiting Ashton's law office is to woo this young woman. In all my years I've never observed a labor uprising being planned while enjoying an ice-cream soda or in a flower mart while selecting roses."

Hearing Mr. Townsend blithely relate the assignations caused bile to rise in Olivia's throat. She swallowed hard. Surely Mr. Townsend's information was erroneous. Yet hadn't she seen Ellen and Fred together with her own eyes? She silently chided herself for holding out hope that Fred might still care for her. How could she even consider such a thing!

"Perhaps you're correct, but I don't want any blunders. I'm the one who hired you, and I'll be held accountable if your findings prove inaccurate."

The sound of scraping chairs and footfalls signaled the meeting must be drawing to a close. Blood pulsed fiercely through Olivia's veins, pounding in her head. She must do something, *now*. Yet if she stood up, one of them would see her. After a quick glance toward the floor, she slid downward and folded herself into the deep kneehole of Mr. Mahafferty's oak desk. Her disappearance occurred none too soon, for she'd barely tucked the fullness of her skirt beneath her when the two men passed by the desk, still talking in hushed tones.

After waiting several minutes, Olivia peeked around the edge of the kneehole before slowly climbing from beneath the desk and scurrying to a chair on the other side of the room. When Mr. Howard returned to the office, she hadn't had time to digest the distressing information she'd overheard only moments earlier.

His jaw went slack as he entered the room. "Olivia! Where did *you* come from?"

She forced a demure smile. "Why, the hotel, of course. Chef René said you stopped by the kitchen earlier today and wanted to see me. Did I misunderstand?"

Obviously bewildered, he shook his head. "No, no. You understood correctly."

Before he could question her further, Mr. Mahafferty returned, and Mr. Howard directed her into his office. Olivia brushed a piece of carpet fuzz from the cuff of her shirtwaist in a forced attempt to remain nonchalant. "If this isn't a good time for you, I can return later."

She hoped he'd accept her offer, but he shook his head. "Now is fine. I merely wanted to give you fair warning that you'll likely be going back out on the trains within the next week or so." He shuffled through the papers on his desk. When he looked up, he appeared surprised to see her still sitting across the desk. "As soon as I'm certain, I'll let you know."

Obviously she'd been dismissed, though he hadn't actually declared an end to their brief meeting. When she reached the door of his office, she glanced over her shoulder. "If at all possible, I'd prefer to remain in Pullman. With all the extra visitors in town due to the Columbian Exposition, my help is greatly needed in the kitchen." When he didn't immediately respond, she continued her pursuit. "Do you think my request might meet with a favorable response?"

He batted the air as though swatting a bothersome fly. "I don't have time to further discuss the matter. I said I'd let you know."

The anger in his voice startled her. He'd obviously forgotten that she had come here at *his* directive. From the conversation she'd overheard, she knew they both had matters of greater import to worry about this day.

Chicago, Illinois
June 12, 1893

Mrs. Jenkins hurried to Charlotte's side. "Mr. Field sent word he wants to see you in his office—alone." She stepped close and lowered her voice. "Has there been some problem of which I'm unaware?"

Charlotte shook her head. Mr. Field had cancelled their previously arranged meeting without fanfare. There had been no explanation, merely a message from Mr. Field's clerk stating the Monday morning meeting had been cancelled. Though she'd been disappointed, Charlotte had continued working behind the counter and hadn't expected to hear anything further from the store owner. "Except to say hello when he's walking the floor each morning, I haven't talked to Mr. Field since the day we went to his office and I shopped for Mr. Flynn's wife." Mrs. Jenkins's frown didn't relieve the queasiness that had suddenly taken up residence in the pit of Charlotte's stomach. "Do you think I'm going to be terminated?"

Mrs. Jenkins offered a weak smile. "I see no reason. You've been an excellent employee. Our sales are increasing every week, and I've not heard of any complaints." The older woman patted her arm. "If it's bad news, I'll do what I can to help you secure a position at the Boston Store. It won't pay nearly as well, but it will be honest work, and I know one of the supervisors. Now hurry along. You mustn't keep Mr. Field waiting."

Charlotte thanked Mrs. Jenkins for her kind offer, though she wondered how meager the clerks' wages must be at the Boston Store, for she thought the salary paid by Mr. Field was miserly—as did all of the other clerks. The gossip that circulated throughout the store indicated the company partners and managers were paid quite handsomely, although Mr. Field kept them in a state of perpetual apprehension and fear with his cold and abrupt behavior. During lunch last week, one of the salesclerks in the furrier department had confided that Mr. Field always announced bonuses and promotions at the annual company dinner. Last year Mr. Field had surprised one of the managers with an announcement he was accepting the man's resignation from the company. Charlotte wondered if Mr. Field would also be accepting her resignation in the next few minutes.

She tapped on the door and waited to be acknowledged. Perhaps her years of learning proper etiquette and social skills required of nobility could be of assistance if she must persuade

Mr. Field to keep her on his staff. On the other hand, she could set aside all pretenses and tell him the truth: she needed this job in order to help pay bills and purchase groceries for herself as well as the other women at Priddle House. Yes, she'd simply be honest and let God do the rest.

Charles Sturgeon, Mr. Field's clerk, led Charlotte into the sparsely decorated office. Her employer's austere surroundings were becoming familiar. Mr. Field remained stoic as she approached. Not one hair of his perfectly trimmed white mustache twitched. "Sit down, Miss Spencer." She'd barely settled in the chair when he leaned across his desk and offered her an envelope. "This was personally delivered to me by a valued patron whom you recently served in the accessories department. The letter is sealed, but the patron did advise me that your service went beyond expectation; that you, Miss Spencer, extended the gracious assistance that continues to make Marshall Field and Company renowned for its merchandise and service."

Mr. Field's gaze remained fixed on the envelope. There was little doubt he desired to know the contents, but Charlotte tucked the missive into the pocket of her skirt. She preferred to read the letter in private. Her heart flip-flopped as she wondered if Mrs. Pullman had taken time to write a thank-you note. The woman had appeared most pleased with the assistance Charlotte had offered with the evening bag selection. Likely that was the reason Mr. Field remained interested in the letter.

Employees knew of the solidarity that existed between Mr. Pullman and Mr. Field. The men were titans of business as well as neighbors, each living in an elegant mansion on Prairie Avenue. Mr. Field was said to wait frequently at the end of the block for Mr. Pullman. With their carriages following behind them in case of inclement weather, the two would stroll down Michigan Avenue to the Pullman Building, where Mr. Field would stop for coffee before walking on to his mammoth retail store. And unless otherwise occupied, the two would often join their counterparts for lunch at the Chicago Club, where reserved seats awaited them at the millionaire's table. Occasionally they would be joined by Robert Todd Lincoln or General Phil Sheridan—if not for lunch, then later in the evening at Mr. Field's mansion for a game of poker.

She scooted to the edge of the chair, hoping to be dismissed, but Mr. Field shook his head. "There is another matter I wish to discuss with you, Miss Spencer."

She swallowed, fearful of what might follow. Mrs. Jenkins had told her Mr. Field's employees could never be completely comfortable with the man and his sudden changes in disposition.

"Have you heard many stories about me, Miss Spencer— about my rise to wealth and fame?"

"Mrs. Jenkins speaks highly of you, Mr. Field. She tells me you are an astute businessman."

He smiled and tented his fingers beneath his chin. "I am also a good judge of character, Miss Spencer. I am a man who believes it is impossible to completely erase one's personal history. Our past is reflected in how we shape our future." He leaned back in his chair. "I am the son of a hill farmer, but I was determined to make my mark in this country. Although I have achieved my goal, I remain a farmer's boy." He narrowed his eyes. "You, Miss Spencer, are not the daughter of poverty. You bear the mark of wealth and nobility."

She stiffened at the remark. "I live at Priddle House and—"

He shook his head. "No need to defend yourself. I do not intend to investigate your past, Miss Spencer. I have observed in you the qualities I need to expand services in my store. Are you interested?"

"Yes, I believe so." Charlotte couldn't imagine how many more services Mr. Field could add to the variety already afforded his customers. Why, he had even hired interpreters to assist foreign customers who had come to Chicago to attend the Columbian Exposition. The idea had proved opportune, and word had quickly spread that language was no barrier in Mr. Field's fine establishment.

"You recall your test from several weeks past?"

She nodded, uncertain where their conversation might lead. Would this be her assignment to a supervisor's position? She wasn't certain she would have the ability to manage salesclerks with the talent and insight of a woman such as Mrs. Jenkins. Conversely, she dared not refuse a position that would garner higher wages.

"After much consideration and several meetings with my managers and a few of my trusted business partners, I have decided to add a new service for my customers. Beginning next week, Marshall Field and Company will offer the expertise of a personal shopper. You, Miss Spencer, will be our first employee to carry this title." He made the announcement with a flourish generally reserved for the entire staff.

She wasn't certain how to respond. Did he expect a host of questions or an effusive thank-you? Perhaps both would be in order. "I am grateful you've offered me this opportunity, Mr. Field, and I will do my utmost to provide the type of service your customers have come to expect." She met his steady gaze. "Have you created a narrative of what the position will entail?"

Mr. Field tapped a sheet of paper lying atop his pristine desk. "Indeed I have, Miss Spencer. In much the same way you assisted Mr. Flynn, you will provide services for customers who feel unqualified to select an item either for themselves or for a gift. Some of my customers are occasionally unable to visit the store due to time constraints or for other reasons. You would make selections for them, as well." He picked up the piece of paper and handed it to her. "I don't believe you will find any of these duties beyond your abilities. I have noted your new salary at the bottom of the page. If you have questions, you may schedule an appointment with my clerk."

His brief nod indicated that she had been dismissed. Before she could turn the doorknob of the carved mahogany door, Mr. Field stopped her. "Mr. Sturgeon will escort you to your office on the second floor. Please advise him of any specific items you may need to perform your duties."

Office? She would have an office? "Yes, I'll do that. Thank you, Mr. Field." That she was to have a personal office came as a complete surprise. Was she supposed to work at the accessories counter when she wasn't busy shopping for wealthy customers, or was she to sit in her office? If that was so, her days would pass at a snail's pace. She hoped Mr. Field's list of instructions would address that issue, for she doubted there would be many customers seeking her assistance. Women *enjoyed* shopping!

CHAPTER TWENTY-TWO

Once Mr. Sturgeon departed Charlotte's second-floor office, she sat down at the mahogany desk and grazed her palm across the hand-tooled, tobacco brown leather tabletop. How had this happened? One minute she had been a salesclerk working behind the glove and evening bag counter, and a short time later she occupied a personal office on the second floor. Though her first thought had been to hurry downstairs to the accessories department and speak with Mrs. Jenkins, Charlotte held back, worried Mr. Field might unexpectedly appear at her door. What would he think if he discovered the office vacant? She unfolded the description of her new duties and carefully read the list.

Tracing her finger down the page, Charlotte stopped at number six. *You will meet with department supervisors as you deem appropriate. Each supervisor will be notified of your new position and will lend complete cooperation in the performance of your duties.* She wondered if the supervisors had already been notified. Had one of Mr. Field's infamous memoranda been delivered while she was in his office? She read through the list several times, arranged the items on her desk, and then stared at the closed door. Now what? She couldn't sit here for the remainder of the day.

After jotting down her whereabouts, Charlotte placed the piece of paper atop the desk and crossed the room. She momentarily admired the elegant Aubusson covering most of the wooden floor and wondered who had made the choice. Though all of the stylish furniture and appointments were to her liking, she considered the office unnecessary, and should Mr. Field inquire, she would tell him so, but such a statement would likely be considered untoward on her first day.

Charlotte pulled her heavy office door closed behind her and returned to the familiar aisles of the first floor. Mrs. Jenkins spotted her rounding the corner and hurried forward. She grasped Charlotte's hands between her own. "I am so very proud of you, my dear."

"Then you've received Mr. Field's notification?"

Mrs. Jenkins released Charlotte's hands and led her back toward the accessories department. Though congratulations were in order, Mrs. Jenkins couldn't be away from her assigned post. "Yes. The message was delivered shortly after you departed for Mr. Field's office. I couldn't have been more pleased. And you have an office of your own! You are the first woman to achieve such an honor." She tipped her head closer to Charlotte's ear. "Until now, only managers have been afforded the privilege of having an office. Perhaps this bodes well for other women in Mr. Field's employ."

For the sake of the female employees, Charlotte hoped so,

although she had her misgivings. Only a handful of women supervisors could be counted among Mr. Field's three thousand employees. Motivated young men were Mr. Field's employees of choice, the ones whom he preferred to mold and groom as future managers and partners. He expected them to rise quickly to the top. For that reason, he paid them higher salaries than the rest. Still, he expected loyalty from all who labored within the walls of his wholesale and retail emporiums. Though he paid the remainder of his employees much lower wages, he sought to win their allegiance with amenities rather than money. A cost-effective method he'd cultivated long ago.

"I truly don't know how I'm to keep busy all day. I had hoped I could return to work in accessories and fulfill these newly acquired duties when the need arose, but it doesn't appear that will be the case. I shall truly miss working behind one of your counters, Mrs. Jenkins."

The older woman beamed. "You've made me very proud, and it's not as if we won't see each other. And now that I'm no longer your supervisor, we can even enjoy an occasional lunch together."

"I would be honored."

Mrs. Jenkins rearranged several pairs of gloves while Charlotte continued to express her concerns over a lack of customers needing her assistance. The older woman laughed and tucked a graying strand of hair behind one ear. "If Mr. Field has given you an office and assigned you to the position, rest assured he has already made certain there is a need. If I know him as well as I think I do, he's most likely already contacted possible customers and has a list of clients awaiting you. I would guess he's merely giving you a brief time to adjust before you are flooded with work. Now, you had best introduce yourself to all of the supervisors and managers. I'm certain there are many who don't know you."

Charlotte heeded the older woman's advice. When she had finally completed her rounds, she stopped to enjoy a cup of tea in the music room. At least she'd managed to fill several hours with the obligatory stops in each department. She enjoyed a sip of the hot brew. This had been a most eventful day. Her thoughts returned to her earlier meeting with Mr. Field when he had summoned her into his office to deliver a message. She slipped her hand into her pocket and withdrew the forgotten missive she'd received earlier in the afternoon.

Though she'd at first considered Mrs. Pullman the likely author, on second glance the handwriting appeared more masculine. Mr. Flynn, perhaps? Not likely. Mr. Flynn wouldn't spend his hard-earned money on such expensive stationery. Her interest piqued, Charlotte carefully opened the thick envelope and withdrew the letter. She immediately detected the money inserted within the folds of the page. Without counting the amount, she looked for the signature. *Randolph Morgan!*

She returned to the beginning of the letter, her gaze flitting down the page of script.

> Dear Miss Spencer,
> I wish to thank you for the kind assistance you offered my family during our recent visit to the accessories department of Mr. Field's fine establishment. You exceeded all expectations with your readiness to aid both my daughter and my wife. Your willingness to serve them in a most delicate manner was greatly appreciated.
> Though I do not know your circumstances and I do not

wish to offend you in any manner, I am enclosing a small sum as a very poor substitute for my immense gratitude.

Sincerely,
Randolph Morgan

He'd been most cautious. Although he was obviously thankful she'd not embarrassed him or made a scene in front of his wife and children, he'd carefully avoided incriminating himself in the note. While chords of Mozart wafted through the music room, Charlotte counted the money. Not a small sum, yet she doubted any amount of money would erase Randolph's personal guilt or her own pain. The best thing would be to slip the letter and money back into the envelope and send it back by return mail. Or would it?

Charlotte shoved the envelope and its contents into her pocket, and after a brief stop in her office to see if anyone had left her a message, she went to the fourth floor. Mr. Henretti greeted her with the eagerness of an abandoned puppy. "Back so soon? How may I assist you?"

"I'm interested in the prices of pianos. I'd like to inspect your least-expensive model."

He grimaced. "I doubt a customer who is using your services as a personal shopper would be interested in our cheapest offering, Miss Spencer."

"Trust me, sir. I know what I am looking for."

Mr. Henretti begrudgingly led her to the rear of the showroom and pointed to two models. "These would be our least expensive, but you'll find the tone won't compare with that of the others. At least let me show you some of our finer instruments."

Olivia shook her head. "No, that won't be necessary. Thank you for your assistance."

The befuddled supervisor followed her across the room while pointing over his shoulder. "Did you wish to make a purchase? Although I don't recommend either of the two less-expensive pianos, I'll bow to your wishes."

Mr. Henretti followed close on her heels, and when she came to an abrupt halt, he crashed into her backside. His apologies were both profuse and long-winded. He finally scurried away when she mentioned he'd left his workstation unattended. She exhaled with relief when she reached the quiet of her office. Though she was pleased to be away from Mr. Henretti, she remained disappointed that she was unable to afford any of the pianos on the fourth floor. Even the least-expensive instrument cost more than she'd received from Randolph Morgan.

She sat down and contemplated the matter. A visit to the Boston Store might produce better results. Surely it would have a piano she could afford with her recently acquired funds. She would go after work this evening.

A short time later the door to her office opened, and Mr. Field stood in the entrance. "There you are. I stopped down an hour ago but found you missing."

In answer, Charlotte picked up the note she'd left on her desk, but he waved his hand.

"I saw your note. Visiting with the department heads was an excellent idea." He sat down on one of the chairs opposite her desk and removed a folded piece of paper from his inside pocket. "I have customers interested in your services. They'll forward information to you personally, by mail or through one of their employees."

Charlotte scanned the rather lengthy list. Mrs. Jenkins had been correct: Mr. Field had assured himself there were customers prepared to avail themselves of her services. "I look forward to assisting them."

"I liked the idea of your leaving a note on your desk when you leave, since you have no secretary or clerk taking your appointments. You should continue the practice so that the supervisors will have some idea where to locate you in the store. Beginning tomorrow the newspapers will carry information regarding our new service. I hope we'll soon be keeping you much busier than even I imagined." He pulled the chair forward and rested his arms on her desk. "Mr. Henretti tells me you were in his department shopping for a piano." He tugged on his white mustache. "His most inexpensive model, I believe."

Word traveled fast. Mr. Field's managers didn't lose any opportunity to keep him apprised of every movement. "Yes. Funds are quite limited for that particular purchase, and I don't believe we can accommodate the customer."

"You know my motto, Miss Spencer."

"Indeed. Give the lady what she wants. But in this case, the lady doesn't possess adequate funds. I believe a purchase at the Boston Store would prove more appropriate."

"And the customer would be someone with whom I am acquainted?"

Charlotte hesitated. "Not exactly. Well, yes and no."

His brow furrowed. "Well, which is it, Miss Spencer?"

"The piano is for a young girl named Fiona who lives at Priddle House. I was planning the purchase as a gift. Piano lessons have been most difficult for Fiona."

"How so?"

His interest surprised her. Likely because he knew Mrs. Priddle, she decided as she quickly explained the paper keyboard she had made and Fiona's weekly lesson at the church. "The girl appears to have talent, and she's exceedingly motivated to learn. When she isn't finishing her school lessons or completing her chores, she's practicing on her paper keyboard."

"The girl certainly deserves better than a piece of paper to learn on. How much are you willing to contribute toward the piano, Miss Spencer?"

"One hundred dollars."

Mr. Field nodded. "I believe with your employee discount you can afford one of our pianos, Miss Spencer. I'll see to the matter. Tell your young protégé she may expect delivery tomorrow. You may pay Mr. Henretti your one-hundred-dollar contribution toward the girl's gift."

"Thank you, Mr. Field. I do appreciate your kindness."

He stopped and turned when he reached the office door. "If you truly appreciate my help, then you will keep this matter to yourself, Miss Spencer. Should word circulate among the employees, they would all expect drastic reductions on items they wish to purchase. I would soon find myself in financial ruin."

"I'll not say a word." Charlotte wondered how Mr. Field would explain the purchase to Mr. Henretti, especially given the fact that she was expected to pay one hundred dollars toward the item. On second thought, she decided Mr. Field would likely not explain anything, nor would he expect to be questioned by an employee. She hoped Mr. Henretti would grant her the same courtesy.

———

Though Mrs. Priddle had been exceedingly pleased to hear of Charlotte's promotion and increase in pay, she pulled her aside after supper. "You are now making enough money that you won't need to remain at Priddle House any longer." Her weathered face creased with worry.

The woman didn't need to say what she was thinking. Charlotte had already considered the matter. With her increased salary, she could well afford to move to a boardinghouse or even rent a small house for herself. But the residents of Priddle House would suffer without her income. Only one additional resident had moved into the house since Charlotte's arrival. And that young woman was expecting a child before the year's end. Locating employment for her would be impossible. Although one wouldn't know it from the hordes of shoppers and the visitors attending the Columbian Exposition, the depressed economic condition throughout the country had caused a substantial decrease in philanthropic gifts and not merely to Priddle House. Charitable organizations throughout the country were suffering.

"If it isn't against the rules of Priddle House, I would prefer to remain here. I'll continue to contribute all of my wages except the weekly allowance you've assigned for my expenses."

Tears clouded Mrs. Priddle's bright blue eyes, and she turned away until she had regained her composure. "I suppose we could permit you to stay with us if that's your choice. Needless to say, your income is of great assistance. I do believe that given the amount of your financial contribution, your weekly allowance should be increased. With this new position, you may need a few new clothes and some money to eat your lunch with the other managers from time to time."

"Thank you for your thoughtfulness. I'll agree to accept whatever allowance you deem best." Charlotte's acceptance of the advice seemed to please Mrs. Priddle, for she situated herself next to Charlotte on the worn divan later in the evening. The older woman opened her Bible and began to read the fourteenth chapter of Matthew, the story of Jesus multiplying the loaves and fishes. The older woman patted Charlotte's arm. "Jesus is using Charlotte to help provide for us, just as He used the loaves and fishes to feed the multitude back in Bible times. Her increased wages are going to help us feed even more needy folks." Charlotte was embarrassed, but Mrs. Priddle appeared not to notice. She beamed her smile around the room and continued to pat Charlotte's arm.

Fiona clapped her hands, but Charlotte's frown brought the girl's applause to a quick halt. She didn't want their thanks. Indeed, if any of them should learn of the child she'd abandoned, they'd likely run her out of town on a rail. Her discomfort deepened when Mrs. Priddle suggested each of the women offer a brief prayer to thank God for sending Charlotte to Priddle House. By the time they'd all finished, Charlotte's cheeks burned hot with mortification. She almost wished she hadn't told Mrs. Priddle of the promotion and increase in her wages. With all she'd endured throughout their Bible-study time, Charlotte decided against mentioning the piano. She didn't want to be heralded as someone special. She merely wanted to blend into the fabric of Priddle House, at least for the present.

The next morning Charlotte departed for work with the ladies gathered near the front door to give her a send-off befitting a conquering hero. The entire matter had become absurd.

If Mr. Field hadn't already made arrangements for delivery of the piano, she'd cancel the order. No doubt the musical instrument would once again make her the center of attention, not what she had intended when arranging for the purchase. Charlotte knew she really wouldn't cancel the order, even if she could. She'd given momentary thought to using the funds toward the purchase of her passage back to England, but she wasn't yet prepared to desert her son or to face her parents. Moreover, Fiona deserved at least a jot of happiness, the true unadulterated bliss of receiving a very special and unexpected gift.

Charlotte well remembered the first time she'd felt that excitement. She'd been a very small girl, and her father had been gone for several weeks. When he returned home, he carried a box under his arm that contained a beautiful doll. The gift had been unexpected, for she merely longed for her father's return home. That particular doll had remained her favorite throughout the years. She had packed the doll in white linen and stored it in a drawer of her chest in Lanshire Hall.

First things first, she decided upon entering the store. Before going to her office, she bid the elevator operator good morning and rode to the fourth floor, where she located Mr. Henretti. "I want to make my payment before beginning my daily duties." She retrieved the money from her purse and carefully counted the bills. The piano remained exactly where it had been yesterday afternoon. Either it would be loaded onto a truck later this morning, or they had another stocked at the warehouse, and this model would remain on the floor for display purposes.

She'd been in her office only a short time when Mr. Field

appeared. He had a well-dressed gentleman in tow, a visitor who had arrived in town on business and wanted to surprise his wife with a special gift for their anniversary. Mr. Field introduced Charlotte and then turned the man over to her care. "I told Mr. Lowe you were the person who would help him make the perfect choice."

Helping Mr. Lowe had proved more difficult than anticipated. The man knew little about his wife's likes and dislikes and freely admitted he had no idea how she filled her spare hours, nor did he seem to care. As for a description of the woman he'd been married to for twenty years, he seemed at a total loss. He merely portrayed her as average. Average height, average weight, average brown hair, and Mr. Lowe remained uncertain if his wife's eyes were brown or green. Attempting to gain knowledge of decorating preferences had yielded even fewer impressions of Mrs. Lowe's taste. In desperation Charlotte finally selected two items, both from the accessories department. She could only hope Mrs. Lowe would be pleased with the evening bag and gloves. If not, Charlotte was certain Mr. Lowe would absolve himself of all responsibility for the choices, and Mr. Field would be promptly notified.

When she departed for home, Charlotte realized she'd not taken time to eat her lunch. After spending far too much time with Mr. Lowe, she'd received requests for assistance from several supervisors. By day's end, she'd not even completed her rounds to each of the departments. Her feet ached as if she'd walked every square inch of the store, and she was thankful for her ride home in the delivery wagon.

Charlotte spied Fiona pacing the length of the front porch when the wagon neared Priddle House. The delighted prancing could only mean one thing: the piano had arrived. The moment the girl gained sight of Charlotte, she flew down the porch steps, her hair flowing behind her like a silk scarf on a spring breeze. "Charlotte! You'll never guess what has happened. Just wait until you see." Fiona grasped her hand in a viselike grip and hurried her into the house. The girl extended her arm in wild abandon toward the east wall of the parlor. "Look! It was delivered today. Mrs. Priddle says not to get overly excited because we may not keep it, but I think we should, don't you? Isn't it lovely?" Fiona's words tumbled over one another like a cascading waterfall.

The girl continued her rambling, but Charlotte failed to hear anything further. Her gaze settled upon the beautiful piano and stool. This was not the piano from the rear of the fourth floor, not the least-expensive model she had chosen. Instead, it was one of the finest. The setting sun shone through the west window and danced across the black-and-white piano keys. Fiona slid onto the stool and perched her short fingers above the keyboard, obviously prepared to offer a brief recital for Charlotte's enjoyment.

Before Fiona's hovered fingers could descend upon the keys, Mrs. Priddle scuttled into the room, her face as tightly knotted as the bun on her head. "Fiona! Do not touch that piano." The older woman's features slightly softened when tears pooled in the girl's eyes. "I must talk to Charlotte in private. Go upstairs and finish your school lessons."

Longing shone in the girl's eyes as she slowly headed to the staircase. Mrs. Priddle waited until Fiona was out of earshot and then motioned Charlotte toward the divan. She closed the pocket doors leading to the hallway and dining room. Apparently this would be a serious discussion.

Instead of sitting beside her, Mrs. Priddle pulled a bentwood chair across the room and stationed it directly in front of Charlotte. The older woman sat on the wickerwork seat and scooted the chair forward until they sat knee to knee. "We need to have a talk—a *truthful* talk." Mrs. Priddle pointed a thin wavering finger toward the piano. "About that."

Charlotte waited. She didn't know why Mrs. Priddle thought it necessary to emphasize the fact that she wanted to hear the truth. Had she uncovered her secret past? "What would you like to know?"

"Everything! The deliveryman said that an employee of Marshall Field and Company had purchased the item and given this address for delivery. Exactly how would you have the necessary funds to purchase this piano? Have you done something illegal that could place Priddle House in jeopardy? You know the rules, Charlotte."

Charlotte folded her hands in her lap and met Mrs. Priddle's unwavering stare. "I assisted a customer. He returned, met with Mr. Field, and stated he had been pleased with the help I'd afforded. He left a thank-you note and enclosed a tip for the service I rendered."

Mrs. Priddle narrowed her eyes. "What *kind* of service did you perform that a man would give you enough money to purchase such an item?"

A wave of anger surged in Charlotte's chest. Mrs. Priddle must think her no more than a common harlot. "Your accusatory tone and the look in your eyes speak volumes, Mrs. Priddle. I can tell you it's not what you've imagined. The gentleman *and his family* came into the store. I assisted both the wife and daughter as they made choices in the accessories department. He is a wealthy customer who apparently wanted to do something to help a poor workingwoman."

Mrs. Priddle's shoulders wilted. "I apologize, Charlotte. Please forgive me for my judgmental behavior, but I was startled when the piano arrived. There's no doubt it carried a dear price." She shifted her attention to the instrument. "Do you realize how many bills could have been paid with that amount of money?"

Charlotte nodded. "I do. But no amount of money could replace the joy this piano has brought to Fiona's heart." She grasped Mrs. Priddle's aging hands between her own. "I believe the piano will prove to be a sound investment in both Priddle House and Fiona's future."

A smile slowly formed and Mrs. Priddle nodded. "I believe you are correct, my dear. Indeed I do."

CHAPTER TWENTY-THREE

Pullman, Illinois
Early July 1893

Olivia stepped off the train, weary from yet another excursion on the rails. Her plea to Mr. Howard had gone unheeded, and she'd been traveling for the past ten days. He had promised this would be her last journey unless something unexpected should arise. The man consistently added a caveat to his assurances, providing him with an escape clause Olivia had come to dislike. Fortunately, she did not need to concern herself with finalizing her notes. This trip, she had strictly adhered to what she'd been taught by Mr. Howard on her first journey on the rails and had maintained the notes throughout the journey. Although she still didn't keep the minute details he preferred, her notes could be presented to him upon request.

Beginning tomorrow, she hoped her work would remain within the confines of Hotel Florence, where she could do what she loved most: create culinary delicacies alongside Chef René. No more sleeping in swaying beds at night or jotting down the names of stations where food was tossed to waiting friends and family, where men loaded crates of oranges grown on family plots, and then pocketed the money when the fruit was squeezed and the juice sold for breakfast or in a mixed drink in the library car. And no more making note of the trains where she'd seen employees betting on a game of whist or drinking from a flask during the nighttime hours. The infractions were numerous, and though she had documented only the most flagrant abuses, there were many smaller ones she intentionally ignored, like the porter who boarded his wife and children for a free ride in order to celebrate an anniversary. How could she fault a man for a desire to be with his family? Especially when his job permitted so little time at home. Mr. Howard wouldn't approve of Olivia's pick-and-choose method, but this evaluator position wasn't the job for which she'd been hired. When Mr. Howard and Mr. Pullman assigned her to the rails, they'd been aware her expertise was in the kitchen. Surely they didn't expect her to have the same mentality as someone with the ability to sniff out the shortcomings of others—someone like Mr. Howard. The thought gave her pause, and she recalled her first impressions of him when she'd arrived in Pullman.

He had changed from the kind and gentle man she'd met on that sunny day in the spring of 1892. Or *had* he? Was the man she'd met back then genuine or merely a façade of the real Mr. Howard? She couldn't be certain, but with all that she'd seen and heard over the past months, Olivia believed all pretenses had been stripped away to reveal a skeleton of a man she could never respect.

She must continue to heed Mr. Howard's authority as her superior in the workplace, but beyond that, Olivia intended to maintain a distance, even if it required moving from her comfortable rooms in the Barneses' home. With her journal tucked beneath her arm, she left the train station. She would deliver her notes to Mr. Howard's clerk after depositing her bags at home; then she could enjoy a visit with Chef René. She was anxious to discover all that had happened while she'd been away. No doubt the chef had been overworked; she hoped his existing heart ailment hadn't worsened during her absence. Prior to her departure, she'd expressed her misgivings to Mr. Howard, but he'd pointed to the doctor's discharge as support for his position. He hadn't been worried over Chef René's welfare. His primary concern had been Olivia's return to the rails.

With the journey behind her, she hoped to set aside the anger she'd harbored toward Mr. Howard since her departure. *If* she found all was well with Chef René. Otherwise she might not be so quick to forget. Thankfully, Mrs. Barnes wasn't at home, or she would have been detained for hours. Olivia placed the cases in her room, removed the pages from her journal, and placed them in an envelope. Then she hurried down the stairs and across the street to the administration building. Mr. Mahafferty sat hunched over his ledgers at the large oak desk. She wondered if he'd ever discovered the Scripture notation she'd placed on his desk.

"Something you need, Miss Mott?"

"Good afternoon, Mr. Mahafferty." If he'd seen the envelope in her hand, he gave no indication. "I have a delivery for Mr. Howard."

He had already returned his attention to the ledgers. "He's in Chicago for the afternoon."

What good fortune! She wouldn't have to speak to him. "I'll

leave this with you, then. If you'd see that he receives it, I'd be most appreciative."

He didn't look up, just nodded his head in a lethargic movement.

She reached the door and then stopped as she turned the knob. "You might consider reading John 10:10, Mr. Mahafferty, the part about having a more abundant life." Before he had a chance to respond, she was out the door and down the hallway, feeling a sense of satisfaction that she'd perhaps thrown out a rope to a drowning man.

"Olivia!" With her palm cupped against her forehead to shield the bright July sun, Olivia stopped and squinted into the distance. A man was coming from the direction of the train depot, and her thoughts took flight as she observed the tall lanky figure running toward her. *Mr. Howard?* She sucked in a breath and continued to stare. *Please—not him. Not now*. This was the time she'd reserved for her visit with Chef René. Keeping her eyes fixed upon the approaching man, Olivia resumed a slow pace toward the hotel. He waved his hat overhead. "Olivia, wait! I need to speak with you."

She noted the shock of sandy hair as the man drew closer. *Matthew Clayborn!* They hadn't spoken to each other since her initial solo trip on the rails. Olivia quickly turned and walked toward him, waving her handkerchief with unbridled enthusiasm.

He slowed to a walk, and she clapped her hands with enthusiasm. "What a perfect surprise for my return home. I've been out on the rails for the past ten days. I can't tell you how many times I've thought of you when I was out there." She pointed in the direction of the railroad tracks.

. Perspiration beaded Mr. Clayborn's forehead. He was obviously out of breath, but she thought that he could at least smile and say hello. Instead, he offered a curt nod. "I was here earlier in the week, and Chef René told me you were traveling. News I found most disheartening."

His words surprised her, for he'd made no attempt to contact her previously. From his somber look, she didn't know whether to be flattered or fearful. "Exactly why did you find the news of my absence discouraging? Other than your having to make a return trip, of course." Once again, she smiled.

He didn't. "Because I knew what you were doing out there on those trains. And that you would continue to ruin the lives of people I care about, people I consider friends." He enunciated his words, shooting them forth like arrows aimed at a target, and there was no doubt she was that target.

"What are you talking about?" She took an involuntary backward step.

He immediately moved forward to fill the space. "You know exactly what I'm talking about. Don't feign ignorance with me!"

His lanky frame towered over her. Clearly Mr. Clayborn intended to intimidate her. Thus far, he'd succeeded, but his haughty manner and obtrusive behavior were growing tiresome. Why didn't he merely speak his mind? She squared her shoulders and placed her hands on her hips. "If you don't care to explain your ridiculous allegations, you can stand here and shout to the wind. I'm going inside to visit with Chef René."

She stepped to one side, but he grasped her arm. "I'm talking about your employment as a spotter for Mr. Pullman. I'm a newspaper reporter who should be able to separate the wheat from the chaff, but this time I was taken in. I've got to admit that you're good at what you do. You had me completely fooled. You're a treacherous fraud."

She pulled free from his grasp. "My position is exactly what I told you. I'm an assistant chef at the hotel. Surely Chef René confirmed that much when you were here last week."

His hands were balled into tight fists. "I don't doubt you work for Chef René *when* you're in Pullman. It's when you're riding trains that you present a threat. You with your notebook, taking down information to report to the company. Acting like an innocent and using me to gain introductions so you could report any misdeed you might observe." He kicked a stone with a vigor that sent it sailing across the park. "How could I have been so stupid as to have been taken in by the likes of you? Because of you, Chef Richmond and three other men working in that dining car have been fired. And I bear responsibility, too. I'm the fool who introduced you to those men."

"Your allegations are completely unfounded. I am *not* a spotter. I've heard talk of spotters and spies, but I truly don't believe such a position even exists with the Pullman Palace Car Company. My sole duty when traveling on the rails is to discover cost-saving methods for the company—nothing more and nothing less. I am an advisor. For you to believe I had anything to do with Chef Richmond's discharge is outrageous. First of all, I thought him an excellent chef and was delighted to meet him. I hadn't heard of his discharge until this moment. I've not even seen him since I traveled with you."

"Of course you haven't. He was let go two days later—due to a report to managers that items were being loaded in and out of the kitchen door, items that shouldn't have been unloaded from the kitchen." He tapped his index finger to his temple.

"Does that stir up any memories for you, Miss Mott?"

She truly wanted to march off and tell him to leave the premises, but his words struck a chord. Her notes had mentioned using the rear door of the dining car to load linens rather than through the kitchen door as a time-saving possibility. But surely they wouldn't have fired the chef over such a simple comment. Mr. Clayborn sensed her confusion and continued with his barrage until she stomped her foot. She hadn't meant for her foot to land on top of his shoe. But it had. His verbal attack came to an abrupt halt while he hopped around and pointed toward his foot.

"I apologize. Totally unintended." He didn't appear to believe her, but there was little else she could say to convince him. If he didn't believe she wasn't a spy, he wouldn't believe she hadn't intended to harm him. "Oh, bother! Come and sit down on the bench. I don't believe your foot could possibly hurt all that much." He hobbled after her and sat down. Olivia shook her head in amazement when he actually removed the shoe and began to rub his foot. "What a baby you are. I cannot imagine what you would do if you were faced with genuine pain."

His eyebrows shot upward, and he pointed to his foot. "This *is* genuine pain. I think you may have broken a bone. If I remove my sock, I'm certain you'll discover my foot is already discolored."

"Don't you *dare* remove your sock, Mr. Clayborn. It's scandalous enough that you're sitting in a public park without your shoe." She waved toward his unshod foot. "There are *rules* in Pullman, you know."

"Oh, we certainly wouldn't want to break a rule, now, would we, Miss Mott? Someone might be watching and report us to

Mr. Pullman. And if anyone knows about reporting, it would be you." He leaned closer. "Wouldn't it?"

"We're not going to accomplish one thing until you cease your accusations and explain in a calm and understandable manner exactly what has occurred and why you believe I'm to blame."

Mr. Clayborn exhaled a deep sigh that seemed to say she should already understand. He gently slipped his shoe back on his foot and, in a slow and methodical manner, told her of the recent firings that had occurred. "I've traced them back, Olivia. The majority began with that first train ride you took with Mr. Howard and a porter who served you tea. Seems it took him two minutes over the allowable time to serve you. He no longer works for the company. He has a wife and five children who are dependent upon him. They're hungry, Miss Mott."

"When Mr. Howard mentioned the porter's slowness, I argued that he'd been very prompt and kind. My reports have never been directed toward the men and their performance. I've merely attempted to do what I was told—find ways to save the company money. How could you think so little of me, Mr. Clayborn?"

"You are either completely naïve or an expert in deceit. I can't decide which." He leaned down to tie the laces of his shoe.

"I don't know what I can say or do that will prove the truth of what I've told you. But at least you need not worry about me in the future. I was promised this would be my last venture on the trains."

Mr. Clayborn straightened and looked directly into her eyes. "The company bigwigs realize you've been nabbed as a spotter, and you'll not be able to gather much useful information in the future. You see, Miss Mott, the porters and waiters may argue among themselves, but if a spotter is on their train, they don't hesitate to pass the word. They're not accustomed to a woman in that position, so they were slower to figure you out. To tell you the truth, I believe you have the dubious honor of being the first."

"You honestly believe I was sent out on the trains for the sole purpose of having people discharged?"

He shook his head. "No, but you weren't sent out there to locate cost-saving methods, either. If you furnished an occasional suggestion that could save the company some money, fine and dandy. I'm sure they put it to use. However, they were using your notes to gauge how well the employees performed their jobs, or if they misappropriated any company property. All reports that reflect poorly on an employee's performance or use of company property results in reprimand or discharge—usually the latter."

The thought that she'd been used as a pawn to spy upon fellow employees was more than Olivia cared to believe. Surely Mr. Howard wouldn't have placed her in a position in which she could have found herself in danger. Then again, if it served his purpose, perhaps he would. With what she'd recently overheard in his office, there was little doubt she didn't know him nearly as well as she'd thought. She wondered if she could trust her judgment about anyone. Possibly Mr. Clayborn couldn't be trusted, either.

"I'm planning to write a series of articles for the newspaper. I've already received approval from my editor."

"Exactly what kind of articles?" He'd interrupted her

thoughts with his unexpected announcement, and her voice had trembled. She was certain the articles would deal with Mr. Pullman and the railcars in some manner or form, but that certainty didn't diminish Olivia's desire to hear exactly what he had in mind. Was Mr. Clayborn going to throw her to the wolves in order to print a good story that might garner his publisher's accolades?

"About the treatment of the Pullman employees working on the trains—primarily the porters. I won't use your name, but I am going to divulge the company's tactics and the names of the men who have been fired—Chef Richmond, for one. A connection might be made back to you, but I'll try to avoid the possibility."

It was just as she'd suspected, though how could she object? She didn't want to lose her job, but if it would help bring about change for the employees, she couldn't ask him to remain silent. Mr. Clayborn would need time to gather information and write the commentary. She would have time to begin assessing possibilities for future employment. Obtaining work in a Chicago restaurant or hotel would probably prove futile given Mr. Pullman's influence. She shuddered at the thought of leaving everything familiar. None of the cities she'd visited while traveling the rails had appealed to her, and she'd not return to England.

"I believe I should attempt to walk on this foot before it becomes so swelled I'm unable to make it back to Chicago."

Olivia had completely forgotten his injured foot. "Oh, of course. We could stroll down to Lake Calumet if you like."

He grinned. "I'm not certain I can make it quite that far, but we can walk in that direction. The breeze off the lake should be refreshing."

Olivia couldn't agree more. The afternoon was warm, and given his recent announcement, she'd rather Mr. Howard didn't observe her in Mr. Clayborn's company. Once the articles were in print, Mr. Howard would connect the two of them, and her fate would be sealed. A train whistled in the distance, and she unconsciously glanced toward the depot. Mr. Howard could return at any time.

A tinge of guilt assailed her as Mr. Clayborn limped along beside her. She wondered if Dr. McLean might have a cane in his office. He lived nearby, but stopping to see the doctor could prove a fatal error. He might mention Mr. Clayborn to Mr. Howard, and she couldn't take that chance. "Would holding my arm help to steady you?" She bent her elbow and angled her arm toward him.

"Why, thank you, Miss Mott." He placed his arm atop hers and firmly grasped her wrist.

She hadn't expected him to accept her offer. Nor had she expected him to lean quite so heavily on her arm. At this rate, she doubted either of them would have the required stamina to walk to the lake. They inched their way toward a small rise that overlooked a grassy clearing in the distance. Once they arrived at the top of the knoll, the going should become less strenuous for Mr. Clayborn. If he didn't want to proceed further, they could rest in the valley below. There were hand-hewn tables and benches that the town residents used for Sunday afternoon picnics. They could sit and enjoy the breeze without venturing to the lake.

When they finally reached the top of the hillock, Mr. Clayborn stopped and wiped the perspiration from his forehead. He nodded toward the valley. "Looks like they're enjoying the shade, the cooler breeze, and each other."

Olivia stared into the distance, where a man and woman were sitting at one of the tables with their heads close together. A couple in love, sharing a few moments alone, Olivia decided as they continued onward. Minutes later, the man and woman turned. She couldn't be certain, but it looked like—no, surely not. Yet it was! *Fred and Ellen!* How could they? She gasped and lowered her arm. Too late, she realized she'd been remiss in her duty to help Mr. Clayborn maintain his balance. His foot slid on the grassy slope, and he tumbled downward with a piercing yelp.

Fred and Ellen hurried toward them. Olivia frantically looked back and forth between Mr. Clayborn's supine body and the approaching couple. She longed to run in the opposite direction, but her feet remained firmly planted.

Ellen immediately dropped to her knees. "Matthew! What in the world happened?"

Olivia didn't know which she found more confusing: the fact that Ellen knew Mr. Clayborn's name or the fact that Fred and Ellen were openly courting in Pullman. Mr. Clayborn and Ellen continued to chat like long-lost friends. Olivia thought she might actually faint.

She swayed, and Fred grasped her around the waist. "Are you ill?" She shoved at his arm, but another wave of dizziness washed over her, and Fred grasped her waist more tightly.

Concern shone in his eyes. At least she thought it was concern, but who could know with Fred. Perhaps it was simply the way of Americans! She hadn't experienced this problem in England. If people didn't like you in her country of birth, they might not speak the words, but their opinion was clear. With a faint sniff of the air, her countrymen would raise their noses and pass by without a word. She could now appreciate their haughty attitudes, for at least they didn't act like a friend one minute and a betrayer the next. Except for those of noble birth, who did whatever pleased them. Here in America, people *acted* like friends, but she could never be certain. That had been her experience thus far. Except for Martha and Mrs. DeVault, of course.

She tipped her head and looked into Fred's eyes. Her pulse quickened, and she forced herself to look away. "I'm feeling faint—the heat, I think." She pointed a wobbly finger toward the sun as though he wouldn't understand.

He grinned. "Yes. It is quite warm. And you're entirely correct: the sun is to blame for all this heat. Why don't I help you to one of the benches where you can sit down, then I'll return and assist your friend."

She ignored the questioning tone of his final comment. Why should *he* care if Mr. Clayborn was her friend, an acquaintance, a business contact, or a complete stranger? She attempted to shake herself free of his hold. "I can make it on my own."

"Do let him help you, Olivia. I don't believe I can care for two invalids at once."

Ellen's words were immediately followed by a charming smile that annoyed Olivia even more than Fred's attempts to tug her toward one of the distant benches. She pulled against Fred's arm. Making certain to avoid Ellen's gaze, Olivia turned her attention toward Mr. Clayborn. "I am terribly sorry. Did you further injure your foot?"

He grimaced. "Perhaps a little. Why don't you go and sit down. I'll join you in a moment."

Mr. Clayborn obviously needed the assistance of someone much stronger than Ellen to help him to his feet. And it had become clear that Fred wasn't going to release her until she did as he requested. "Fine. I'll go and sit down if that will make you all happy."

Once she'd settled on one of the wooden benches, Fred hastened back up the hill. While he assisted Mr. Clayborn, Ellen raced toward Olivia with the wild abandon of a ten-year-old.

She plopped down beside Olivia and pulled her into a warm embrace. "It's so good to see you. The moment I stepped off the train, I asked Fred if you'd returned, and he said he didn't think so. I'm so pleased to discover he was wrong." She gulped a breath of air. "When did you arrive?"

"Earlier this afternoon." She wanted to ask why Ellen cared, but first things first. She wanted to know how Ellen happened to know Mr. Clayborn's name. "Do you know Mr. Clayborn?"

"Matthew? Oh yes. We've been friends for years. He writes for the *Chicago Herald*. He's interviewed my father numerous times for his news articles. As newspaper reporters go, Matthew is one of the best. He attempts to write an unbiased, truthful story. He's a refreshing change from most reporters. We've gone to dinner on several occasions, but I don't think our relationship could ever move beyond friendship. We differ on too many issues."

"And you and Fred? From all appearances, the two of you

have discovered you agree on all issues. Even to include matters of the heart."

Ellen reared back as though she'd been slapped. "What are you insinuating, Olivia? Fred and I aren't romantically involved. Do you truly believe I would do such a thing?" Pain laced her words.

Olivia would have to give Ellen her due. She was quite the actress, but Olivia knew better. She'd not be swayed. "Yes, I do believe you'd do such a thing. In fact, I *know* you would. I saw you kissing Fred in broad daylight on the platform of the Van Buren Street train station in Chicago. Would you care to deny that also?"

Ellen shook her head. "No. I'll not deny what you saw, but I'd like the opportunity to explain."

"Yes, please do explain. This is quite interesting," Mr. Clayborn said. He sat down and propped his leg on the bench.

Olivia didn't notice the men return while she was making her accusations, and a rush of heat flamed her already warm cheeks. Once again she felt as though she might swoon. How long had Fred and Mr. Clayborn been listening? When would she learn to control her tongue? Fred stood with folded arms across his chest and was staring at her.

Ellen touched her hand. "Olivia? Will you let me explain?"

"I'll listen to what you have to say." Her tone was cold and flat and filled with a healthy portion of self-righteous indignation.

After swearing Mr. Clayborn to secrecy, Ellen began by explaining that she and Fred had begun to visit during Martha and Albert's wedding reception. "Mr. Howard had engaged you in conversation, and Fred was aware of my father's affiliation with the union movement."

Olivia gasped. "Your father is a union organizer?"

"Not an organizer, but he strongly believes in unions as a voice for the working people of the country. For that reason he lends his legal expertise to the unions when needed. The capitalists consider him a force to be reckoned with. From time to time they've made our lives somewhat uncomfortable." She smiled. "My father doesn't mind discomfort nearly so much as I do."

Olivia now began to understand why Mr. Howard and Fred had shown interest in Ellen during the reception, albeit for opposing reasons. And it explained why Mr. Howard had been visibly shaken when he'd seen her in the possession of one of Mr. Ashton's business cards last year. The Earl of Lanshire, stockholder in the Pullman Palace Car Company, had selected a lawyer who was involved in unionization. Yet how could he have known? He likely went into Chicago and chose a name from the city directory. Mr. Ashton's name would have been near the top of the listings. The idea was downright humorous.

The hair on the back of Olivia's neck prickled when Fred and Ellen described the man who'd been following them. What was Fred thinking? More important, was he thinking at all? He'd voluntarily placed his job and his mother in jeopardy. Though she longed to interrupt and question his sanity, she held her silence.

After nearly an hour of discussion, Mr. Clayborn removed his watch from his pocket. "Seems there's more to this story than time permits. I must return to Chicago on the next train. Care to accompany me, Ellen?"

"Yes, but there may be someone watching Fred and me. We can't be certain. Why don't we all walk to the station? Fred can bid me farewell." She glanced at Olivia. "It will require a kiss. And then we can be on our way."

Olivia forced a smile and nodded. How could she disagree? They'd just explained the seriousness of their situation. Why, then, did everything within her shout in protest?

CHAPTER TWENTY-FOUR

Chicago, Illinois
July 6, 1893

The piano notes hung in the air as the residents of Priddle House ended their final hymn of the evening. Once Charlotte had settled on the divan, Mrs. Priddle opened her Bible. They'd been studying passages from the book of Isaiah for nearly a week now. Charlotte didn't know why Mrs. Priddle had decided to change their routine, but last week she'd abruptly announced they were moving from the book of Matthew to the book of Isaiah. Nobody questioned her decision.

Mrs. Priddle fanned through the whisper-thin pages of her Bible and then looked at her audience over the top of her wire-rimmed spectacles. "Open your Bibles to Isaiah, the forty-ninth chapter." Lips pursed, she waited until they ceased rippling through the pages.

After a brief nod that signaled she would begin, silence reigned. Other than the occasional shuffle of feet or turn of a page, quiet ruled during Scripture reading. Mrs. Priddle stopped long enough for a sip of water and then continued with the fourteenth verse. " 'But Zion said, "The Lord hath forsaken me, and my Lord hath forgotten me. Can a woman forget her sucking child, that she should not have compassion on the son of her womb? yea, they may forget, yet will I not forget thee. Behold, I have graven thee upon the palms of my hands; thy walls are continually before me." ' "

Charlotte clutched her waist and stifled a gasp. The passage struck like a sharp blow to the midsection. Did Mrs. Priddle know about the baby she'd left in Pullman? Is that why the gray-haired matriarch had chosen to read from the book of Isaiah? While Mrs. Priddle continued reading, Charlotte studied the older woman's every move. If Mrs. Priddle knew Charlotte had a son, she'd given no indication. She didn't lift her eyes from the Bible for even a scant peek in Charlotte's direction. No. There was no possible way Mrs. Priddle could know about Morgan. Yet why had she chosen to read from the book of Isaiah this week when only last month she'd told them they were going to study the entire book of Matthew before selecting a book from the Old Testament?

Mrs. Priddle preferred to move back and forth—a book from the Old Testament, then a book from the New Testament. She said it gave balance to their studies. Charlotte didn't know about balance, but she preferred the New Testament, maybe because she didn't like the harshness found in the Old Testament. There were all those plagues, and the passages that told of God's retribution made her *very* uncomfortable. They reminded her too much of the sin in her own life. Not that the New Testament didn't reveal her sin, too. But Jesus was in the

New Testament, and she'd much rather study about Him and about forgiveness and grace.

Still, the question remained: Why had Mrs. Priddle ceased their study of Matthew and selected the book of Isaiah? *Because God knows your secret.*

Her heart pounded against her chest in a rapid cadence. Surely everyone in the room could hear the hollow thumps. But no one turned in her direction, not even Mrs. Priddle. The remaining Scripture and the discussion that followed passed in a fog. She didn't hear a word. Her only thought was to flee the room.

Had Mrs. Priddle changed her schedule at God's direction? Because He knew about her past and wanted her to understand that He knew? That didn't make any sense. Her thoughts had now become as incoherent and confused as her life.

The moment Mrs. Priddle closed her Bible and indicated the study had ended, Charlotte jumped to her feet and excused herself. "If you have no objection, Mrs. Priddle, I have a busy schedule tomorrow and would like to retire early." Charlotte noted Fiona's sad eyes, but even the young girl's desire to learn another tune on the piano couldn't deter Charlotte this evening.

Mrs. Priddle waved toward the stairway. "Go along, my dear. Do be quiet so you don't waken Sadie."

Before Mrs. Priddle could change her mind, Charlotte raced up the steps. The baby's soft snores rose and dropped in quiet rhythm while Charlotte quickly donned her nightgown. Though the room was stifling, she pulled the sheet over her head, the method she'd adopted as a child when attempting to hide from her mother or nursemaid. But a thin cotton sheet hadn't concealed her from her mother, and it didn't hide her from God, either. *I know you, Charlotte, and I know what you have done.*

In her sweltering white-sheeted cocoon, Charlotte accepted the fact that God had knowledge of every sin she'd ever committed. But surely there must be mortals guilty of more significant transgressions than her own. Why would God consider her a choice for His attention? *Because I love you.*

She lowered the sheet from her head and wiped the beading perspiration now dotting her upper lip and forehead. How could God love her? Unlike Ruth, whose husband had run off, Charlotte had given birth to a child out of wedlock. Even worse, she'd run off like a thief in the night, leaving her infant behind. What kind of woman committed such atrocities? Certainly not one that God could love. She had attempted to mend her ways. Each week she deposited her wages in the Priddle House coffers. Even Mrs. Priddle admitted they couldn't get along without her financial contributions. And there was Fiona. The old Charlotte would have completely ignored Fiona, even considered her an outright nuisance. The new Charlotte had shown compassion and love. She had done her utmost to nurture the girl. During her stay at Priddle House, Charlotte had worked with diligence to erase the sins of her past. Wasn't that enough? Why must she endure these feelings of guilt?

She tossed and turned in the heat of the room but pretended to be asleep when Ruth and Fiona came upstairs later in the evening. She didn't want to talk. Her thoughts were enough to contend with this night.

Although none of her customers could have found fault with her service the next day, Charlotte's thoughts didn't stray far from the Scripture she'd heard the previous night. Whether selecting an exquisite Persian cashmere shawl for the wife of a wealthy businessman or offering condolences to a grieving widow while locating black mourning attire, Charlotte's guilt continued to nag at her. If only Mrs. Priddle had selected some other passage to study.

A knock at her office door halted any further thought of Mrs. Priddle. A beautiful young woman, escorted by Mr. Field, entered the room. Charlotte pushed away from her desk, but Mr. Field waved for her to remain seated. "I've brought someone who needs your assistance, Miss Spencer."

The woman looked vaguely familiar. Likely someone she had observed shopping in the more-expensive fur or dress salon. From her jewelry and attire, there was no doubt the young woman had either been born or married into wealth. She smiled demurely and sat down in one of the velvet-covered chairs across the desk from Charlotte.

Without fanfare Mr. Field sat down in the matching chair. "May I introduce Lady Eugenia of—"

"Birmingham."

Mr. Field's eyebrows raised several notches on his forehead, and Eugenia slanted a narrow gaze in her direction. "Have we met?"

What had she done? "I believe one of the clerks may have mentioned that your mother visited the store earlier in the week, saying she possessed exquisite taste in lace and fabric. Am I remembering correctly?" Charlotte had personally observed the Countess of Heathbrier purchasing the items last week, but she had been careful to avoid the woman. Though their families had seldom attended the same social functions back in England, there were events of court at which they saw one another. And the Countess of Heathbrier would recognize Charlotte. Lady Eugenia was younger than Charlotte by at least six years, and the two of them hadn't seen each other for years.

Eugenia's shoulders relaxed. "Oh yes. Mother was quite pleased with her purchases. And that day proved delightful for me, as well. With Mother away for the afternoon, I was able to stroll the Midway, and I even rode the Ferris wheel." She batted her lashes at Mr. Field. "Don't you dare tell on me. Mother would likely swoon if she knew I'd been walking the Midway Plaisance unaccompanied."

He touched his index finger to his lips. "Your secret is safe."

"What a magnificent ride! Have you been?" She glanced back and forth between Charlotte and Mr. Field.

When both of them indicated they'd not had the pleasure, the young woman scooted to the edge of her chair and, with a burst of excitement, insisted upon relaying the many details. Charlotte didn't think Mr. Field appeared overly enthralled with the topic, but she commented in the appropriate places and did her best to focus upon Eugenia's commentary.

When the girl stopped talking long enough to catch a breath, Charlotte seized the moment. "And how may I be of assistance to you with your shopping experience, Lady Eugenia?"

Eugenia was surprisingly silent for a moment. Charlotte wondered if the girl even remembered why she'd come seeking her assistance.

It was Mr. Field who came to Eugenia's rescue. "Lady

Eugenia is in need of a gift for a dear friend who will soon marry."

Eugenia beamed. "Quite right, Mr. Field."

Mr. Field nodded toward Charlotte. "I'm going to return to my duties, and I'll leave you in the capable hands of Miss Spencer."

Before either of the women could offer an objection, he strode from the room. Not that Charlotte could blame him. She'd like to escape the chattering young woman, too. She eyed Eugenia and wondered if she'd ever been as self-indulgent and carefree as this young woman. Of course she had. Before she'd met Randolph Morgan, she'd been a silly twit of a girl. She picked up a pad.

"You're from England, Miss Spencer?" Eugenia folded her hands in her lap and stared across the desk.

Charlotte pushed away from her desk and stood. "I was born in England, but Chicago is now my home." She strode across the room with a determined step and held the door open for the younger woman. "Shall we?" Charlotte waited until Eugenia crossed the threshold and then closed the door. "Do you have some idea what your friend might enjoy? Shall we look in the clothing department, or do you think a lovely piece of jewelry or perhaps some crystal would better suit her?"

Eugenia continued to stare at her with an intensity that had become increasingly uncomfortable. "Are you perchance related to the Earl and Countess of Lanshire? Their surname is Spencer. You somewhat resemble the countess."

A quivering sensation settled in the pit of Charlotte's stomach. "I'm flattered by the comparison, but I doubt you'd find a relative of nobility working in Chicago."

Eugenia placed her fingertips over her mouth and giggled. "How silly of me." Yet her brows knit into a frown as she continued to stare at Charlotte. "But there is a definite resemblance. I'm certain my mother would agree. It's a shame we're departing for home in the morning. Otherwise, I'd insist Mother come in and meet you. I know she'd concur."

Charlotte's stomach settled at the news. "I do hope you'll have a safe journey. Now, about the gift?"

Eugenia sauntered through the crystal department, looking at several vases and an array of stemware. Up and down the aisle, again and again. The girl was completely indecisive. Each time Charlotte attempted to steer her toward another department, she'd wave a finger and pick up yet another vase or candy dish. When Charlotte had finally marched back and forth as many times as she could possibly withstand, she clutched Eugenia's arm. "If your friend were purchasing a gift for you, what would you like to receive?"

Eugenia giggled. "I would prefer something for myself. A scarf, gloves, or—"

"What about an evening bag? We have some particularly lovely arrivals that I'm certain would please your friend."

"Oh yes!" The girl clapped her hands together like a small child. "Where are they?"

"If you'll follow me." With a slight wave, Charlotte led the way.

The girl's incessant chattering continued until they came to a halt in the accessories department. Mrs. Jenkins was busy tying and arranging silk scarves in a lovely display but hurried forward to greet Charlotte. "May I be of assistance, Miss Spencer?" Thankfully, Mrs. Jenkins hadn't addressed her as Charlotte. Eugenia wouldn't be deterred if she discovered Charlotte's name an exact match with that of the Earl and Countess of Lanshire's daughter. Scheduled departure or not, the girl would return with her mother in tow. And there would be no deceiving the countess.

"Mrs. Jenkins, this is Lady Eugenia. She is seeking a gift for a dear friend and has decided an evening bag would please her. I mentioned we've had some lovely selections this season."

The evening bag proved a success, and the purchase was completed in record time. Charlotte sighed with relief and headed toward her office. The fear of being discovered had served to momentarily assuage her guilt, but when a mother carrying a tiny baby passed by, the feeling returned with a vengeance. Perhaps if she talked to Mrs. Priddle . . . *No!* How could someone such as Mrs. Priddle ever understand? The perfect little woman would be horrified beyond repair.

Yet could she continue to plod through life with this mantle of guilt weighing her down? If she could be assured that Morgan was flourishing and doing well without her, perhaps that would help. She ripped a sheet of paper from her notepad and considered the idea. She should offer financial assistance! Why hadn't she thought of that before? With the increased allowance from Mrs. Priddle, she could send money for Morgan's care. She could arrange to send the funds each week. Her burden seemed lighter now that she'd developed a plan.

Mr. Field appeared in her office doorway holding his ivory walking stick in one hand and black homburg in the other. "I trust you were able to assist Lady Eugenia?"

"Yes. She settled on a lovely evening bag for her friend—and one for herself, as well."

"Excellent. I was certain you could help her make the proper choice."

"Mr. Field." Charlotte summoned her courage. "May I request a slight change in schedule?"

He arched his brows. "Exactly what do you have in mind?"

"I'd like to leave two hours earlier than usual today. I don't have any appointments scheduled. And I'd be willing to have you decrease my wages for the time away from work. Or if you prefer, I could come in early or forego my lunch breaks."

"If you don't have scheduled appointments, I suppose I could permit a change this one time. You may come in an hour earlier than usual the next two days in order to make up the time. But don't spread word to the other employees. I don't want to make this a practice. If anyone asks, say you'll be away on business. Don't elaborate!"

"I won't. And thank you so much, Mr. Field."

He saluted with two fingers and marched off without a reply. She glanced at the clock and then checked the contents of her purse while silently chiding herself. She counted out the coins and sighed with relief. Although she'd have only a few cents to spare, there was enough to cover a round-trip ticket to Pullman.

Once her decision was made, Charlotte completed her paper work, walked through each department, and visited with the supervisors. She returned to her office in time to collect her belongings and post a message on the door indicating that she had departed for the remainder of the day—on business. She passed through the aisles of fabric and was nearing the front door when she glanced up and froze in place. She couldn't believe her eyes. The Countess of Heathbrier and Lady Eugenia had entered the store and were turning toward the fabric section, obviously headed toward the elevator for a visit in her office. Charlotte veered to the left, passed through the footwear section, and made a hasty retreat out the rear doors. She stopped long enough to catch her breath and utter a prayer of thanks that Eugenia would fail in her attempt. She hoped the mother and daughter would depart on schedule tomorrow.

The two women haunted her thoughts as she rode the train to Pullman. With many visitors arriving from abroad to attend the Columbian Exposition, she should have been prepared for such a circumstance. Yet how did one plan for something like this? She could do little to prevent the possibility of being discovered. There were some things in life for which one couldn't be prepared, she decided as the train neared Pullman.

Charlotte stepped off the train and entered the familiar depot, hesitating only a moment before walking out the door. Her palms turned sweaty as she crossed the street and slowed her gait. Children played in the park while their mothers sat on benches visiting with one another. She crossed to the opposite side of the street. She hadn't made many acquaintances while living in Pullman, but one of the ladies from church might recognize her. She wouldn't take that chance. She'd come for only one reason: to check on Morgan's welfare.

She turned onto Watt Avenue and gathered her courage before advancing up the front steps. Through the screen door, she could hear sounds of a baby. She stepped to the window and peered inside. *Morgan!* How he had grown during these past months. Her heart swelled at the sight of him. His hair had turned blond, and his cheeks had grown round and plump. She stepped inside, careful to be quiet, for she didn't want to startle him. The baby sat on the floor playing and gazed upward when she entered. He smiled, his chubby cheeks pink from the afternoon's warmth.

Charlotte stooped down beside him. "Hello, Morgan. You don't remember me, but—"

Without warning, a buxom woman with hair flying in all directions rounded the corner, stopped, and shrieked. Charlotte lost her balance and fell backward while the baby sniffled and then wailed with alarming gusto. With an accusatory glare, Charlotte regained her balance. "Now look what you've done. You've made him cry. And who are you?"

The woman glared in return. "*Who am I?* Who are *you*, and what are you doing in my house playing with my little girl?"

"Your baby? This flat belongs to Olivia Mott and—" She stopped short. "Girl?"

The woman leaned down and lifted the child from off the blanket. "Yes. This is my little Dorrie. And you're needing to be changed, aren't ya?" she cooed at the child. Her eyes turned cold as she glared at Charlotte. "You haven't said what you're doing in my house."

"I'm acquainted with Olivia Mott. I stopped by to see her."

"Well, you could have knocked, you know." The woman's features softened as she leaned down to change the infant's diaper. "Miss Mott moved out of here a long time ago. She's living in a place over near the hotel somewhere. I'm not sure where, but if you stop by Hotel Florence, they could give you her address. You may even find her at work."

Charlotte backed down the hall and out the front door while offering her profuse apologies.

She stumbled down the front steps and was nearing the corner when Mrs. Rice charged toward her. "So you've finally returned, have you? What kind of a woman are you to take off and leave your baby in my care, never giving a second thought to anyone other than yourself?"

Charlotte attempted to sidestep Mrs. Rice, but she immediately extended her folded umbrella and blocked Charlotte's path. "I don't want to argue, Mrs. Rice. Please move your umbrella."

Mrs. Rice bent forward from the waist and shook her finger beneath Charlotte's nose. "You're an evil woman, leaving your baby with no one to care for him. *Now* you return! Now that your baby is gone and you don't have to care for him. God metes out special judgment upon women like you."

Charlotte pushed the woman aside and raced down the street toward the train station, Mrs. Rice's condemnation ringing in her ears. Evil! That's what she was.

CHAPTER TWENTY-FIVE

Pullman, Illinois
July 12, 1893

With his lightweight cap pulled low on his forehead and shoulders hunched forward, Fred turned only a fleeting glance toward the row house where Albert and Martha resided. The two men saw little of each other these days. With their opposing work schedules and Albert's marriage, their paths seldom crossed. Albert had distanced himself from the men who promoted unionization or supported changes within the car works, and that included Fred. There was little doubt Albert's withdrawal from his friends had been at Martha's insistence. Like many of the women who lived in Pullman, she feared not only the loss of income but also their displacement from the Pullman community.

Meeting with the other men had proved difficult for Fred, as well. His hours coincided with those of few of the workers. He'd had to rely on one or two trusted men to aid in building a strong voice for their unionization efforts. After this morning's meeting, he believed a strong foundation of support now existed. More and more men were speaking out against their low wages. Opportunities for promotion had become nearly nonexistent, with higher-paying positions being filled by virtual newcomers, men who had little experience or talent for the jobs. The longtime employees were expected to train the recently hired men, which further served to fuel their anger. Although several of the men, including Fred, thought the practice strange for a man such as George Pullman, who had previously hired only highly skilled workers, they were daily faced with this recent procedure.

Fred hurried up the front steps and called to his mother as he entered the house. He yanked off his cap and hung it on the hall tree.

Mrs. DeVault appeared at the kitchen door. "Your food is growing cold. Where have you been? You're going to be late to work if you don't hurry."

He shook his head and grinned. "I told you I was going over to the training center. I have plenty of time to eat and still arrive at work on time." Leaning down, he pecked her on the cheek and continued into the kitchen. "Smells good in here."

She arched her brows. "Doesn't it always?"

He laughed and helped himself to the chicken and dumplings. "Not when you're cooking cabbage."

"I can't argue with you on that account." She sat down and joined him at the table while he offered a prayer of thanks for their meal. "So how were things over in Kensington this morning?"

He shrugged. "Same as usual. We're not having much luck getting many of the fellows hired. Hard to figure out what's going on with the hiring practices right now. Things aren't what they used to be in that respect."

"Well, you men need to learn a little patience. Things can't always go the way you want. The management's not going to keep the employees informed about why they've changed things, but I'm sure there's a good reason."

He gave her a sidelong glance. "I know you want to believe everyone and everything is good, but it's not always that way. There are decisions being made over at the car works that aren't sound, and some are downright flawed. I know you don't want to hear negative comments about the company, but that's just the way it is."

His mother didn't comment. Probably just as well. He didn't want to have an argument before leaving for work. Nothing would be resolved, for neither one's mind would be changed. Fred finished his meal and carried his plate to the counter. He hoped when the time arrived, there would be a sufficient number of workers willing to do what was right, even if it meant they must suffer. For now, he had a core group of men willing to strike whenever necessary. At least he hoped so.

While strolling along the shore of Lake Calumet with Fred last Sunday afternoon, Olivia thought she and Fred had finally resolved their differences. After he had detailed his relationship with Ellen's father, she understood the necessity for Fred's behavior with Ellen. Not that she agreed with his involvement in unionization or strikes. She thought the risk too great, and she'd told him so. He'd been surprisingly willing to listen to her, but she knew he hadn't changed his opinion. She hadn't changed hers, either. But Olivia felt certain his invitation to attend the Columbian Exposition today indicated they had set aside their past differences.

She grasped his arm as they walked down the front steps outside the church. Mrs. DeVault scurried to her side when they reached the sidewalk.

"I'm glad I caught up with you before you left." She bowed her head close to Olivia's ear and lowered her voice. "I've already told Fred this, but I want you to know that several ladies in my quilting group mentioned that there are scantily clad belly dancers and natives from other countries who are bare to the waist—*women*. Can you imagine?"

Olivia shook her head. "No. I truly can't. It's going to be exciting." Mrs. DeVault frowned. Obviously that wasn't the answer she'd anticipated. "Thank you for the warning. I'll be careful to avoid any such sights."

Mrs. DeVault nodded her approval. "Good. And make certain Fred does the same."

Other than twisting Fred's head in the opposite direction, Olivia wasn't certain how she was supposed to comply with Mrs. DeVault's order, but she didn't argue. If they didn't hurry, they'd miss the train and be delayed for another half hour.

Even with an entire afternoon and evening, they'd not have sufficient time to visit the Midway and all of the exhibit buildings. She'd overheard many of the hotel guests discuss the exquisite sights, and most of them returned every day for up to a week. The fact that the country was in the midst of an economic downturn didn't seem to deter visitors. They continued to arrive from all over the country in huge numbers, filling the hotel every night. She could only assume Mr. Pullman was delighted, for completion of his four luxurious Colonnades had met with the same success. Reminiscent of Renaissance Italy's loggias, the four semicircular buildings with their graceful colonnades and arches defined and enhanced the newly reconstructed Market Hall. Not to mention the added income the twelve fine apartments brought to Mr. Pullman.

Olivia's excitement heightened as the train came to a halt at Terminal Station directly outside the fairgrounds. They stepped off the train, and she grasped Fred's arm, pleased he would be her escort for this exciting occasion. She pictured the two of them quietly talking about the pleasures of this day for years to come.

"I'm certain you'll be pleased to know that Ellen and Matthew Clayborn are going to accompany us. They plan to meet us at the Columbian Fountain."

She stopped midstep, yanking Fred to an abrupt halt.

He arched his brows. "Are you unhappy about that?"

For a brief moment she considered stomping her foot. What was wrong with Fred? Didn't he realize this was supposed to be their time together? More important, why did he want Ellen along? "I'm genuinely surprised you didn't mention Ellen and Mr. Clayborn before now. To be honest, I had hoped we could spend the day alone together."

He nodded. "Yes, but Ellen and I must keep up appearances. I haven't seen anyone following us today, but I can't be certain. If we're being watched, and I don't meet Ellen, questions will naturally arise. Being alone with you would ruin the impression that I'm in love with Ellen."

Olivia recalled the conversation she'd overheard between Mr. Townsend and Mr. Howard while she was hiding in Mr.

Mahafferty's office. Geoffrey Townsend was already convinced Ellen and Fred were in love, but Fred didn't realize that he and Ellen had achieved their goal. There would be no reason for the investigator to continue his pursuit. She briefly considered revealing the information. But what would Fred think of such behavior! Hiding in the kneehole of a desk wasn't something she'd proudly relate to anyone, especially Fred. Would he believe her or think the information was merely a trap she'd concocted with Mr. Howard? Her recently renewed ties with Fred remained too weak for such a test.

They proceeded onward, swept into the crowd of bustling travelers as they navigated their way around the white Corinthian columns inside the terminal and passed beneath the massive coffered arches that heralded their entry onto the fairgrounds. "You do understand, don't you?"

Olivia detected a note of concern in his voice. "Yes, I do." And she did understand, but it didn't lessen her disappointment. She forced a smile. "We'll all have a wonderful time."

As they exited the terminal, Olivia stopped and stared at the magnificent white Administration Building that centered the Grand Plaza. The edifice alone covered nearly three acres of ground. An octagonal dome encased in aluminum bronze rose from the uppermost tier of the main structure and glistened in the warm afternoon sunlight. To the east she could see the Columbian Fountain and the Grand Basin with the golden Statue of the Republic at the far end and Lake Michigan in the distant horizon. A brief glimpse was enough to confirm that the White City was everything Olivia had imagined and more. Her excitement mounted as she stepped into this magical kingdom.

Though crowds swarmed around them, Olivia could hear a

band playing lively tunes at the northeast corner of the Grand Plaza. The Manufacturers Building loomed to the rear of the Columbian Fountain, centered with magnificent carvings of sea nymphs and animals with the head and torso of a horse and a tail resembling a huge fish. Electric fountains flanked either side of the grand centerpiece. If she didn't see another thing, Olivia would count this day most memorable.

"*Here* you are! We've been looking all over." Ellen stepped between the two of them and grasped Fred's arm. She waved her free hand in the air. "Matthew's on the other side of the fountain. Wave at him, Fred. You too, Olivia."

Fred and Olivia joined in, and soon Mr. Clayborn jogged to Olivia's side, panting for breath. "It's much too warm to be running around. I'd prefer taking a dip in that fountain. What do you think? Would I get in trouble?"

Olivia giggled. "Given the number of guards patrolling the grounds, I daresay they'd toss you out on your ear or perhaps lock you up somewhere."

Mr. Clayborn casually looped her hand into the crook of his arm. "It's good to see you, Olivia. Have you been here long?" He leaned close to her ear as he spoke.

She leaned away, dismayed by his familiar behavior. "No. We've come here directly from the terminal." As he once again stepped closer, Olivia attempted to withdraw.

He smiled broadly and placed his hand atop hers. "We're supposed to be a couple who enjoy each other, Olivia. We must keep up pretenses. Perhaps you should follow Ellen's lead." He tipped his head toward Fred and Ellen.

She couldn't deny they appeared the young couple in love. Ellen, in her pale yellow organza dress and matching parasol, was hanging on Fred's every word while smiling at him like a woman struck by Cupid's arrow. If Olivia didn't know better, she'd actually believe they were smitten with each other. Little wonder they'd been able to deceive Mr. Townsend. Their behavior was enough to make her once again question if they might truly be in love.

As if reading her thoughts, Ellen suddenly turned and motioned them forward. "Come talk to me, Olivia. What do you think of this grand fair the city of Chicago has created?"

"I'm truly captivated. I've never seen anything that compares. It's so huge, I doubt anyone could see even one-fourth of it in an afternoon. Little wonder the hotel guests return day after day for an entire week."

Ellen shook her head. "We can come back again. I'm surprised you haven't been here before now. The fair's been open since the first of May."

"One needs both time and money to attend the Exposition. I'm afraid I'm one of those lacking on both accounts." She grinned. Perhaps a smile would ease the sharpness of her reply.

Ellen frowned but quickly brightened. "In that case, we'll let you take charge. What would you like to see?"

"I'm told there's an entire train of Pullman cars as well as a replica of the town of Pullman in the Transportation Building. I'd like to see those."

Fred leaned forward, a frown on his face. "Of all places, why would you want to see those? You've been out on the rails traveling in Pullman cars, and we live in the town."

Ellen patted Fred's hand. "Do stop, Fred. I think it would be fun to see those exhibits, too. I've not visited the Transportation Building on my previous visits. What else would you like to see, Olivia?"

There was little doubt Fred hadn't been pleased with her choice. "What about the Ferris wheel? Do you think we could see it?"

"Yes! Not only see it, but we'll take a ride. My treat. It's out on the Midway Plaisance. We'll take one of the electric launches through the lagoon, visit the Midway, and then explore the Transportation Building. If there's someplace else you want to see along the way, we can stop. What do you think?"

Before any of them could either agree or object, Ellen led the way toward the south end of the lagoon. She purchased the tickets and handed one to each of them. They waited in line only a few minutes before boarding the next launch. Their boat slowly moved through the water, allowing them a view of the wooded island and then the vast Manufacturers Building.

Ellen nodded toward the building. "They say this is now the largest building ever constructed. When we come for our return visit, we'll eat at the German restaurant inside. The food is quite wonderful." As they rounded a bend farther down the lagoon, Ellen pointed out the conical roofs and graceful lines of the Fisheries Building in the distance and then the domed U.S. Government Building with its many elegant pavilions and pylon entrances. Water branched off from the lagoon and separated the two uniquely different buildings. Ellen had obviously visited numerous times, for she offered knowledge regarding nearly every structure along the way.

They disembarked at the grand landing along the eastern

entrance of the Woman's Building and climbed several stair-
cases before finally reaching the ground level.

From their distant vantage point, they could view the Ferris
wheel. The towering apparatus appeared to touch the clouds,
and Olivia wondered if she would have the courage to step
inside the contraption. Ellen pointed out the sights as they
strolled along the Midway. They passed Hagenbeck's Animal
Show, and Ellen promised they would go inside after their ride
on the Ferris wheel if time permitted. The show promised lions
riding atop the backs of horses, and tigers that rode veloci-
pedes—something Olivia would surely like to see. There was a
Japanese Bazaar and a Javanese Settlement, a German Village
and Cairo Street, where Olivia saw the dancers she'd been
warned against, but it was the camel rides that captured her
attention. Ladies and their admirers were actually riding atop
the huge beasts that trotted down the narrow passageway of the
make-believe street.

Mr. Clayborn pointed toward one of the camels. "Would you
like to ride?"

She laughed and shook her head. "I would never try such a
thing, but it's great fun to watch the others take such risk. I
believe the Ferris wheel will prove as much excitement as I can
manage for one day."

They continued toward the Midway, where the Ferris wheel
loomed in the distance. Ellen came alongside Olivia and
grabbed her hand. She tugged her forward, and the two of them
followed Mr. Clayborn and Fred into the wood-veneered car.
Forty plush-covered swivel chairs awaited the passengers, along
with space for an additional twenty people who would stand

throughout the ride that would make two full revolutions and six stops.

Olivia inhaled a ragged breath. "This is as large as one of Mr. Pullman's railcars."

Ellen nodded. "Exciting, isn't it? The ride takes a full twenty minutes, so relax and prepare yourself." A guard was stationed in each car, and Ellen explained that the uniformed official would lock their door before the ride began. "The newspaper said the committee required mesh be placed over the large windows to keep hysterical women from leaping to their doom." Ellen giggled. "The men I've seen look every bit as frightened as the women. Don't you agree?"

Olivia shrugged and held her breath. At the moment, she couldn't think of anyone's fear but her own. The wheel made one stop on the ascent and then stopped at the very top. The fair unfolded below in an astonishing panorama. This view was the same sight afforded the birds now winging through the skies. Olivia savored every moment until they finally reached the ground and stepped out of the car. The ride had been amazing. She only wished she had been sitting next to Fred instead of Mr. Clayborn.

They continued down the midway and then boarded the electric launch back toward the Transportation Building. The sun was setting low in the sky. The afternoon had passed far too rapidly for Olivia. Ellen suggested they eat supper after their visit to the Pullman exhibits. "We must stay until after dark. Every building and exhibit is outlined in white lights. It's a beautiful sight."

Olivia glanced toward Fred. She didn't want to consent unless he was in agreement. But Fred wasn't listening to their conversation. He was walking toward a familiar-looking gray-haired man. As the man drew closer, she noticed the unlit cigar in his hand. *Ellen's father*. Had this invitation to the Exposition been nothing more than a scheme to meet with Mr. Ashton?

Mr. Ashton waved his cigar in the air. "Good to see you again, Miss Mott. I trust all is going well for you."

"Very well, thank you. I'm truly surprised we encountered you in this vast place—and among all these people." Olivia cast a sidelong glance in Fred's direction.

Mr. Ashton's rich baritone laugh resonated in the warm afternoon breeze. "You are an astute young lady, Miss Mott. I thought perhaps you and Matthew might enjoy some time alone while I visit with Fred and Ellen."

Fred nodded. "Of course." He patted Mr. Clayborn on the shoulder. "You and Olivia go on without us."

Olivia folded her arms across her waist and frowned. "But we were going to visit the Pullman exhibits."

"I can see them another time, Olivia. When you've completed your tour, Ellen and I will meet you out here, and the four of us will go to supper."

As easily as that, she had been dismissed. Olivia took Mr. Clayborn's arm and walked toward the beckoning golden arch of the Transportation Building. Well, so be it. She and Mr. Clayborn would tour the exhibits, and she *would* enjoy every one of them.

Fred watched Olivia and Matthew walk away. There was little doubt he'd offended her. He hadn't wanted to, but his talk with Mr. Ashton must be private. Telling her of his plans in advance would be foolhardy. The slightest slip of the tongue could alert others. He wanted to mend their relationship, but he couldn't take unnecessary chances.

Mr. Ashton walked alongside Fred as they sauntered past the Transportation Building. "What's so important that we needed to meet today, Fred?"

"I think we've made genuine progress in gaining enough men who are willing to join the union and strike." He made the announcement with whispered bravado.

Mr. Ashton stopped in his tracks. "That's good to hear, Fred. However, the eyes of the world are on Chicago right now. The last thing we want to do is get everyone riled up during the Exposition. We had enough naysayers who said Chicago wasn't a fit city for the fair. We want to achieve our goal, but not at the expense of the city as a whole." His bushy eyebrows knit in concern. "We want change to come, but we don't want to embarrass the United States. We want the country on our side when we finally make our move."

Fred nodded. "I understand the wisdom of what you're saying."

"Why don't you give Fred some specific directions, Father? What should he tell the workers if they become restless with simply waiting?" Ellen collapsed her parasol and looped the umbrella's tasseled cord around her wrist.

Mr. Ashton ran his fingers through his thick white hair. "You must tell the men that you've thought this over, and although valid grievances exist against the company, this isn't the proper time to make a move. Perhaps shortly after the Exposition closes, but not before then. Have you gained enough trust that they'll listen to you?"

"I think so. Some of them are anxious to strike right now, while others are fearful. I believe I can convince them we must wait." He spoke with more certainty than he felt. While most of the men would be relieved, there were some who would resist—the very men he counted on to convince the unenthusiastic workers a strike was necessary.

"I like you, Fred. You're dedicated to the cause, and I believe you'll have no trouble convincing the men what is best." Mr. Ashton slapped him on the shoulder. "You might advise the men to begin saving their money so they'll be prepared in the event of a future strike. Tell them you're acting as our liaison, and we'll do our best to keep them advised."

CHAPTER TWENTY-SIX

Chicago, Illinois
Late July 1893

Following the evening meal, the residents of Priddle House took their usual places in the parlor. Since her encounter with Mrs. Rice in Pullman, Charlotte had done her utmost to keep up appearances. She assisted customers with her usual zeal, listened to department supervisors' suggestions and offered ideas, completed paper work in her usual timely fashion, helped Fiona with her schoolwork and piano lessons, and attended the nightly Bible studies and weekly church services—all with a forced smile and an aching heart. This evening she longed to be alone with her thoughts.

Mrs. Priddle had taken her chair in the parlor and was preparing for their nightly Bible study. Charlotte gazed at the woman with her hands folded in her lap and her clear blue eyes shining with serenity. Only a halo was needed to complete the picture. God surely must be pleased with Mrs. Priddle.

"If you have no objection, Mrs. Priddle, I believe I'll go

upstairs and rest." Charlotte avoided looking directly into the woman's piercing gaze.

The older woman shook her head. "We all grow weary from time to time, Charlotte. You'll be fine once we get started." She motioned toward the piano as the others began to filter into the room. "Go and play for us, Charlotte."

Fiona perched beside her at the piano and watched intently while Charlotte's fingers slid over the ivory keys. When she'd struck the final chords of the last hymn, the two of them took their usual places on the divan. While Mrs. Priddle gave the Bible lesson, Charlotte's mind wandered, her thoughts a jumble of scattered vague memories, a self-reflection and condemnation of her life. Mrs. Priddle said God loved her, but how could He love someone so selfish? All her life Charlotte had done what pleased herself; she'd expected others to do what pleased her, too. Mostly, they had. Except for Randolph Morgan, who had walked into her life, turned it into a shambles, and then retreated to the safety of his home and hearth.

Fiona's sharp nudge jostled Charlotte from her private thoughts. She glanced at the girl and noted the other women were now departing the room. "Want to help me with my lessons?"

"Not tonight, Fiona. You go on upstairs. I want to visit privately with Charlotte for a few minutes." Mrs. Priddle's announcement was met with a frown, but Fiona jumped up from the divan and scurried up the steps. The older woman waited until the girl was out of earshot and then moved to sit beside Charlotte. She placed a work-worn, wrinkled hand atop Charlotte's smooth youthful hands. "You've not been yourself of late. Won't you tell me what has happened? I can't help you if you won't let me inside that wall you've built around yourself."

Mrs. Priddle's eyes shone with warmth and encouragement. There was little doubt the matriarch of Priddle House wanted to help. But how could Charlotte possibly confide in this perfect woman? Mrs. Priddle would likely swoon if she knew the depth of Charlotte's sin. She stared at the faded multicolored rug, unable to force the words from her lips.

The older woman lifted Charlotte's chin with her aged finger. "Do you think I have always been a God-fearing woman, Charlotte? Is that why you fear telling me what has happened? You believe what you have done will cause me to drop dead from the shock?"

Charlotte bobbed her head. "Or at least cause you to faint."

With a smile and a faraway look, Mrs. Priddle settled back into the corner of the divan. "Let me tell you about myself, Charlotte. I'm not the same woman you would have met years ago. I, too, was young and carefree once upon a time. The boys thought me quite pretty in my day." A faint tinge of pink unexpectedly colored her cheeks. "That was back in the day when I thought you could believe everything a young man told you. My parents were good people. They reared me in a fine home with strict Bible teaching, but I was a rebellious young girl who wanted to have fun and spend time with the boys. There were several I liked a lot, but I was particularly fond of one young fellow."

The older woman's voice had taken on a distant softness. Not wanting to miss a word, Charlotte leaned in closer. "And was that young man Mr. Priddle?"

Mrs. Priddle's gray eyebrows rose high on her forehead. "Mr. Priddle? Oh no. I didn't marry Mr. Priddle until many years later. I was a disobedient and foolish girl who didn't heed the lessons I was taught from an early age." Her jaw tightened. "Needless to say, my parents were devastated when they discovered I was going to have a child. I was scared out of my wits—afraid to tell them yet not knowing what else to do."

Charlotte frowned. "Why didn't you tell the young man? You could have married."

The sparkle disappeared from the old woman's eyes. "He said he doubted it was his child, and then he skedaddled out of town." She laced her thin fingers together. "Probably for the best. He wouldn't have been a good husband or a good father to the child."

"What happened to your baby?"

"My parents sent me to a home in Philadelphia—a place for girls like me. They wanted to hide their embarrassment, and I didn't blame them. I didn't want to remain at home, where I'd be the topic of local gossip. My baby was given to a good home, or so I was told. They didn't give me much information, just that I'd given birth to a healthy boy and they had a family anxious to give him a home. I hope he's had a good life. I still pray for him every day."

Charlotte didn't pray for Morgan. The idea her infant son might need her prayers for protection and safety hadn't ever entered her thoughts.

Mrs. Priddle wiped a tear from her cheek and smiled at Charlotte. "You see, Charlotte? None of us is perfect. Sometimes it takes hard lessons before we turn our lives around. Even worse is the fact that we hurt others in the process. My parents never did get over the pain I caused them. I believe they felt like failures for the rest of their lives, yet my behavior wasn't due to anything they had or hadn't done for me. They had always attempted to teach me right from wrong, but I wouldn't listen. I had to learn my lessons the hard way, and learn them I did. I'd like to tell you I changed as soon as that baby was born, but I didn't. I blamed everyone but myself. I remained in Philadelphia, and eventually my behavior brought me to my knees. I finally accepted that I was the one at fault, that I had made those bad decisions and I needed to ask for God's forgiveness."

"And that was it? From that day on, everything was fine?"

Mrs. Priddle laughed. "Not quite, my dear, but it was much better. I wrote my parents a letter and asked for their forgiveness. They asked me to return home, but I knew it wouldn't be a good thing—for them or for me. I didn't have any real training and didn't know what to do with myself. The pastor at the church I attended said they needed workers at one of the mission houses the church sponsored. I lived and worked in that mission house until the pastor asked if I might be interested in moving to Chicago. I met Mr. Priddle after I moved to Chicago. Although we never had children of our own, we had many good years together." Mrs. Priddle glanced toward the dining room. "I believe the others have all gone upstairs. Shall we go to the kitchen and have a cup of tea?"

Charlotte nodded. "Thank you for sharing your story with me, Mrs. Priddle. I won't say a word to the others."

The older woman glanced over her shoulder and smiled as she led the way into the kitchen. "I know you won't, Charlotte. I believe you understand that some things are best shared only when they'll help another heal."

While Mrs. Priddle filled the kettle with water and set it on the stove to boil, Charlotte lifted the cups and saucers from the cupboard. Perhaps Mrs. Priddle *could* help her decide what she should do. When they sat down at the table a short time later, Charlotte slowly stirred cream into her tea.

She stared into the tiny whirlpool created by the stirring motion. "Do you remember when I was late returning home from work?"

Mrs. Priddle nodded. "Yes. A couple of weeks ago. You missed your supper, and we had to keep it warm in the oven."

Charlotte nodded. "I left work early that day. I had Mr. Field's permission," she hastened to add. Mrs. Priddle nodded her approval and Charlotte continued. The older woman didn't interrupt as Charlotte related why she'd gone to Pullman and what events had followed. She appeared neither shocked nor surprised to hear Charlotte had been born into a family of wealth and nobility, stolen her mother's jewelry, coerced a maid, told more lies than she could even remember, threatened Randolph Morgan, given birth out of wedlock and, worst of all, abandoned her infant. Charlotte drew in a ragged breath. "Do you think Mrs. Rice was telling the truth about my baby? I mean, that he's gone?"

"I have no way of knowing, my dear, but there's certainly that possibility."

Tears welled in the corners of Charlotte's eyes. She didn't want to cry. "What should I do, Mrs. Priddle?"

The old woman patted her hand. "If you haven't asked God to forgive your sins, that's the first step. Once you've asked God's forgiveness, you must forgive yourself, Charlotte. You can't change your past. What's done is done. You'll not move forward until you accept that fact. Then you must prayerfully decide what is best for you and for your child."

Charlotte picked at a thread along the edge of the table-cloth. "You think the baby will have a better life without me?"

"I truly don't know what is best for you or your baby, but God does. He will direct your path if you ask Him to do so."

A short time later Charlotte thanked Mrs. Priddle for her kindness. She bid the older woman good-night and then climbed the stairs. The matriarch's kiss remained warm on Charlotte's cheek as she walked down the hallway and into the darkened bedroom. Moonlight streamed through the curtains to form a lacy pattern across the floor. She quietly changed into her nightgown. Fiona shifted and turned as Charlotte slipped into bed. She closed her eyes and asked for God's forgiveness and direction. Now she must trust that He would lead her.

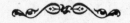

CHAPTER TWENTY-SEVEN

Early August 1893

Charlotte patted her cheeks and forehead with a lace-trimmed handkerchief. Rather than admit to frenzied nerves, she blamed the August heat and humidity. She closed her eyes and rested her head against the back of the upholstered seat while continuing to blot her face and neck.

"You ill, lady?"

She forced her eyes open. A concerned conductor peered down at her, and she shook her head. "It's just the heat. I'm fine."

"Won't be long now."

Charlotte had barely closed her eyes when the man returned with a fan. He spread open the tight folds and thrust it into her hand. "Maybe this will help." He glanced about the coach. "Nobody else appears too warm, miss. You sure you're not sick?"

"I'll be fine." She waved the fan in his direction. "Thank you." The conductor hovered in the aisle, obviously uncertain.

She rapidly fanned herself, then forced a smile. "See? Much better."

"If you say so." He didn't appear convinced, but at least he quit staring at her and continued down the aisle.

The breeze helped. She closed her eyes again and wondered if this would be as difficult as she expected. Mrs. Priddle had bid her good-bye with a departing admonition to keep a stiff upper lip. Charlotte wasn't certain what was meant by the expression. How did one keep her upper lip stiff? She clamped her upper lip between her teeth and wondered if that was how one produced the desired effect.

"You *sure* you're feeling well, miss?"

She popped open her eyes and released her lip. Not surprisingly, the man was staring at her as though she'd lost her mind. She nodded. "Perfect, just perfect."

He gave one final glance over his shoulder as he continued toward the rear of the coach. Perhaps coming here today was a mistake. She should have given the matter further thought, but more time wouldn't change anything. Instead of this continual vacillating, she needed to gain resolve and move forward with her plan.

With three short blasts of the whistle, the engineer announced their train had reached the outskirts of Pullman. Charlotte leaned back and inhaled a deep breath. *Everything will be fine. Everything will be fine. Everything will be fine.* She silently repeated the refrain as she stepped off the train and entered the depot. Church bells pealed in the distance, a reminder to any who might have considered sleeping in on a Sunday morning. Residents who regularly attended the Greenstone Church would soon begin to exit their homes and head down the streets of Pullman. Charlotte lowered her veil, squared her shoulders, and lifted her chin. *Dear Lord, give me courage.*

As she neared the church, Charlotte slowed her step. A group of congregants had gathered outside. She strained forward and searched the crowd for any sign of Olivia. After leaning against the thick trunk of a maple tree, she lifted a corner of her veil to permit a better view and a bit more air. Even with the slight breeze off the lake, the air remained heavy. Some of the crowd began to filter indoors. Perhaps Olivia had arrived early and already gone inside. Oh, this was a bad idea. She should turn around and go back to Chicago where she belonged. Where she belonged? She nearly laughed aloud. Where *did* she belong?

Charlotte dropped her veil into place as a young couple carrying a toddler advanced. Dressed in their Sunday finery, they smiled and nodded to her. She turned and continued watching as they strolled down the street. Suddenly she glimpsed a green-and-white silk frock and broad-brimmed hat with matching ribbons that signaled Olivia's approach. Charlotte would have recognized her former gown and hat anywhere. She'd never particularly liked the wide stripes, but from a distance, the effect was quite striking. If she hurried, perhaps she could intercept Olivia before she reached the church.

The heels of Charlotte's shoes clicked out a rapid beat as she hurried down the sidewalk. She waved, but Olivia had already turned toward the church. With a sinking feeling, Charlotte stopped short and watched Olivia climb the steps and enter the wide front doors. She had hoped to talk to Olivia outside before the services began and then return to Chicago.

Strains of organ music continued to waft from the doors, indicating the preacher hadn't yet taken his place. If she went inside, she might still have time to talk to Olivia. She climbed the steps, nodded at the usher, and whispered where she'd like to sit. If he recognized Charlotte, he gave no indication. When he arrived at the fifth pew from the front, he stopped and gave a firm nod.

Olivia narrowed her gaze, and Charlotte lifted the veil from her face.

"Charlotte!" Olivia exclaimed in a hushed whisper.

Mrs. Rice slapped her hand on the back of the pew. "See there! I *told* you she was still around. You should be ashamed coming into the house of God. Why, it's an affront that a woman like you would dare to darken the doorway."

Charlotte turned and nodded. "Good morning to you, Mrs. Rice. So *very* nice to see you once again."

Fire danced in the older woman's eyes. She stiffened until her back was straight as a broomstick. "You see, Olivia? She hasn't changed a lick—still acts like a Miss Fancypants."

Mr. Rice grunted an unintelligible remark at his wife. The older woman leveled one final glare at Charlotte before she leaned back and folded her arms across her chest.

Mrs. DeVault leaned forward and welcomed Charlotte with a warm smile. "It's good to see you, my dear. You must join us for the noonday meal."

Charlotte thanked her for the invitation before sitting down next to Olivia. She tipped her head as close as her hat would permit. "I hope you're not too angry with me, Olivia."

Olivia shook her head. "No. I'm most pleased to see you looking so well. Mrs. Rice told me you had been in town, but I wasn't certain if she was telling the truth. When I asked how I could contact you, she said you wouldn't tell her."

A sharp chord sounded from the pipe organ, notification that conversations cease and the congregants stand in preparation for the first hymn. Charlotte's response must wait awhile longer, especially now that Reverend Loomis had taken his place on the dais. She well remembered his rule about silence during Sunday morning services. Besides, Mrs. Rice's angry words had been enough for one morning. She wouldn't risk the preacher's wrath, too.

The sermon was likely very good, but Charlotte didn't hear a word. She wondered about her son and where he was. Apparently, Mrs. Rice had been truthful when she said he was gone. Otherwise Morgan would be here in church with Olivia. She longed to know all the particulars of her baby's whereabouts, but after waiting for nearly a year, she could wait a short while longer. Somehow it didn't seem possible she'd fled from Pullman so long ago. And yet tomorrow Morgan would be a year old. She wondered who would help him celebrate his special day. A year ago she hadn't considered the day of his birth to be special. Rather, she had wished to die. Now she was pleased she hadn't. Strange how much life could change in a short time. Morgan's life had been changed by her decision, too. She hoped her decision hadn't proved tragic for him.

Olivia tugged at her sleeve, and Charlotte rose to her feet for the benediction. The moment the organist struck the first chord of the postlude, Olivia wrapped Charlotte in a warm embrace. "I'm so pleased you've come back. Please say you'll stay the entire day so we may find out all that has happened with you."

"I can remain for the afternoon, but I must be back to Chicago by seven o'clock."

"So you're living in Chicago?"

They exited their pew and had turned to walk down the aisle when Mrs. Rice dug her fingers into Charlotte's arm. "You got your nerve coming into this church, you sinful woman."

Mrs. DeVault and Fred bustled to Charlotte's side, but Charlotte shook her head. "You go on, Mrs. DeVault. Olivia and I will join you and Fred shortly. Mrs. Rice and I need to have a few words."

Mrs. DeVault frowned, but she grasped Fred's arm and the two of them continued down the aisle. Mr. Rice seized the moment to shoo his children from the opposite end of the pew and follow them toward the vestibule.

Mrs. Rice tilted her head to one side and released her hold on Charlotte's arm. "Well? What have you got to say for yourself, Charlotte?"

Charlotte met the woman's angry scowl with what she hoped was an engaging smile. She had prayed God would give her the strength to act upon her newfound faith and speak in kindness and love.

She took a deep breath. "I wanted to tell you that I've asked for and received God's forgiveness for my sins. I know that my actions were reprehensible when I was here. Although I cannot change the past, I do want you to know I have acknowledged the depth of my wrongdoing. If you can find it in your heart to do so, I'd be grateful for your forgiveness, also." Charlotte lightly touched the woman's hand. "And I want to thank you for the care you provided Morgan during my absence." She gently squeezed the woman's hand.

Mrs. Rice appeared dumbstruck. The earlier anger that had shone in the older woman's eyes was now replaced by a look of bewildered surprise.

"Thank you for considering my request, Mrs. Rice." Charlotte grasped Olivia's elbow, and the two young women headed for the rear of the church.

Before they departed, Olivia glanced over her shoulder. "Mrs. Rice hasn't moved an inch. I believe your words have rendered the poor woman speechless."

"Well, that wasn't my intent, but I do think she was taken aback," Charlotte said with a grin. After weaving through the crowd of visiting church members, Charlotte gathered the courage to inquire about Morgan.

"He's gone to England with your parents." Olivia twisted her handkerchief through her fingers.

"What?" Charlotte clasped a hand to her chest. "How? Please tell me everything."

Olivia led her to one of the unoccupied park benches, where the two of them sat in the shade of a leafy old oak. Nearby, a small garden of rosebushes scented the air with sweet perfume. Charlotte doubted Olivia's story would be as pleasant as the fragrance of these summer blooms. Folding her hands in her lap, Olivia detailed the story of Charlotte's parents' visit to Pullman, the confrontation over the stolen jewels, and, of course, young Morgan's birth.

"And my parents? How were they? How did they react to news of the baby?"

"They both appeared in good health." Olivia hesitated. "If either of them was experiencing illness, I doubt they would have confided in the likes of me. As for the baby, your father was more difficult to convince than your mother. Though he never said as much, I believe he initially thought I might be lying in an attempt to situate the child in a life of wealth and nobility."

Charlotte understood. Many was the time an unwanted child would be left on the doorstep of England's nobility by mothers hoping to give their children a better life. Charlotte knew that nearly all such children ended up in orphan asylums, a fate far worse than remaining with their mothers. Fear constricted her throat. Had her parents taken Morgan to England and then placed him in an asylum? Would they have done such a thing to avoid embarrassment?

"Did my parents finally accept the boy as their grandchild?" In spite of her fear, she must know the truth.

Olivia chuckled. "Your mother was easily convinced, and her love for the boy was obvious that first evening."

"You believe he has remained in their care? They didn't plan to give him to . . ." She faltered and then continued. "They didn't give him to someone *else*?" She couldn't bring herself to ask if they'd mentioned an orphan asylum.

Olivia reached forward and clasped Charlotte's hand in her own. "Your mother had grand plans for little Morgan. I've had only one brief note from her since they left, but you are welcome to read it. The letter arrived approximately six months ago. Although she said she would continue to keep me informed of Morgan's welfare, I've heard no more since then. I'm certain she's quite busy." She squeezed Charlotte's hand. "I'm also a reminder that your whereabouts remains unknown. They were distraught by your disappearance."

The clock tolled the hour, and Olivia jumped to her feet.

"My! I didn't realize the time. Mrs. DeVault will wonder what has happened to us. Come along. We can continue our conversation on the way, and we'll have the rest of the afternoon. We're all anxious to know how you've fared over the past year."

Sun splashed across the streets and rooftops in jagged designs, and the two women strolled arm in arm along the flower- and tree-lined sidewalks as though time had never separated them. "Tell me what has happened between you and Fred. And what of Samuel Howard?"

Olivia arched her brows. "I know you thought Mr. Howard a better choice for me, Charlotte, but trust me when I say that he isn't. As for Fred . . ." She shrugged and tipped her head to one side. "I continue to hope. He found our list of lies. He finally seems to have forgiven me, but he's cautious. He may never completely trust me again."

Charlotte shook her head. "I'm sorry to hear that. The fault is largely mine, but you shouldn't marry someone who doesn't trust you. I'll pray that God will open his eyes and he'll see what a fine woman you are, Olivia."

"Pray?" Olivia stared at her as though she'd sprouted a set of wings. "I noted a difference in you, but I didn't realize how much you'd changed."

As they approached the tenement, Mrs. DeVault appeared at the front door and waved them up the steps. "Come along before our meal grows cold." The smell of roasted chicken wafted through the open door to greet them. Mrs. DeVault scuttled ahead and motioned Fred toward the dining room. "I've got corn and fresh green beans, along with your favorite, Fred, mashed potatoes and gravy."

Fred followed her cue and fell in behind Olivia. "It was good to see you in church this morning, Charlotte. I trust you've been well."

Mrs. DeVault pointed toward the dining room chairs. "You can ask your questions once we've said the blessing."

Questions and answers spilled atop one another throughout the afternoon, some more poignant than others. Mrs. DeVault had been particularly concerned over Charlotte's welfare once she departed Pullman. The older woman shook her head when Charlotte explained how she'd shifted from pillar to post before eventually making her way to Priddle House.

Mrs. DeVault wiped away a tear. "Even in those terrible circumstances, God was drawing you to Him, Charlotte."

"I suppose you're right, Mrs. DeVault. Unfortunately, my behavior caused pain and suffering to many people, especially to my son. How I wish I could change what I've done."

"Most of us wish we could change something in our past. Though we can't change things, we can learn from our mistakes and do better in the future. I'm pleased to see that you've already chosen a new path for your life. I'm proud of you, my dear. And now that you've learned about young Morgan's whereabouts, you're faced with decisions for your future—and his."

Charlotte knew Mrs. DeVault was correct. Her parents and her son deserved more from her. "I know I've caused my parents great distress, and I should have contacted them long ago. I attempted to convince myself they would forgive me and welcome me back, yet my fear of rejection was stronger than my desire to reunite with them."

Mrs. DeVault cupped Charlotte's chin between her palms. "By and large, we parents are a forgiving lot. I believe you need to set your parents' minds at ease and let them know you are alive and well. Trust me, they'll be grateful to hear from you."

"Mrs. DeVault is right, Charlotte. Your father made provision for your return before they sailed for London. He employed Montrose Ashton, a solicitor with an office in Chicago, to handle the arrangements for your return should you be located. I have his card." Olivia fetched her reticule from the hallway table and withdrew the worn business card. "I've kept this card with me at all times, hoping one day I'd find you."

Charlotte took the card and tucked it into her skirt pocket. Guilt washed over her anew as she considered the pain and worry she'd caused by her thoughtless actions. Not only to her parents but to Olivia and Mrs. DeVault, who had lovingly cared for Morgan after she'd selfishly fled her responsibilities.

Discovering her parents had provided a home for Morgan and even arranged for her return to England was more than she could have imagined. Yet she realized that if her problems had been so easily resolved a year ago, she wouldn't have changed. And she wouldn't have met Mrs. Priddle or Fiona. Most important, she wouldn't have met her Savior and truly been forgiven. Had she returned to England back then, she'd still be a selfish, immature young woman. What was it Mrs. Priddle said? God's timing. We must wait upon God's timing. She couldn't be certain, but possibly now God's timing had arrived for a reunion with her parents and son. Prayer would be needed before she made a final decision. She would pen a letter to her parents this very evening, advising them of her safety and begging their forgiveness.

Charlotte rested her head against the back of the seat and listened to the train wheels clack along the rails. This day had been eventful and exhausting. She realized her decision to return to London should be a simple one. Everything dear to her was in England. Or *was* it? She loved her parents and Morgan, but what of Mrs. Priddle, Fiona, and the other residents of Priddle House? What would happen to them? Mrs. Priddle had admitted they were dependent upon Charlotte's income. Contributions to the house had become nearly nonexistent since the economic depression had spread throughout the country. Not that Mrs. Priddle was one to actively seek such funds. She held to the theory of self-sufficiency. Leaving Mrs. Priddle with a shortfall of funds didn't seem the Christian thing to do. If Mrs. Priddle had realized the possible consequences for Priddle House, she might not have encouraged Charlotte's visit to Pullman. No, that wasn't true. Mrs. Priddle was the most selfless person Charlotte had ever known. She wrapped her fingers around the card in her pocket and wondered if this Mr. Ashton might provide the solution to her concerns.

The train hooted three short blasts. She'd soon arrive at the Chicago depot. Charlotte closed her eyes. *Lord, please grant me wisdom to make the proper decision.*

CHAPTER TWENTY-EIGHT

Chicago, Illinois

As she neared the house, Charlotte caught sight of Mrs. Priddle sitting on the front porch with her mending basket near her side. Wisps of gray hair played about the woman's head like a half-blown dandelion. She glanced up from her stitching, offered a welcoming smile, and nodded toward the empty chair.

"Too hot inside. I decided to come out here and do a bit of mending before Bible study. Sit down and tell me about your visit." She formed the torn edges of the chemise into a thin seam before slipping her needle into the cotton fabric. "You're looking a bit pale. Did the heat get to you, or is it the news you heard while you were in Pullman that's got you upset?"

Charlotte dropped to the chair. "I suppose it's some of both. My father and mother have taken Morgan back to England."

"Good! It's comforting to know the child has been well cared for, don't you think?"

"Yes, of course. I'm most thankful they accepted him, but I do find myself facing a difficult decision."

Mrs. Priddle inspected her handiwork and gave a firm nod. After securing the stitches with a knot, she broke the thread and folded the chemise. "Tell me about this decision of yours."

Mrs. Priddle bent down and retrieved one of Fiona's stockings from her mending basket while Charlotte began to detail all she'd learned earlier in the afternoon. The older woman offered an occasional comment or word of encouragement.

Finally Olivia leaned back in the chair and sighed. "Now you've heard the extent of it, and I'm left to decide whether to call upon this Mr. Ashton or merely pen a letter to my family and tell them of my whereabouts."

"What's the harm in calling upon this Mr. Ashton? Since your father made arrangements with him rather than with Miss Mott, perhaps the lawyer has some additional information for you."

Charlotte smiled at the older woman's assessment. "He wouldn't have conducted *any* business with Olivia. She had worked as a scullery maid in the kitchens of Lanshire Hall. My father would have considered such dealings with a woman to be completely inappropriate, especially with someone of a lower class."

"Dear me, such a thought never occurred to me. I suppose you're correct. In any event, it can't do any harm to go and talk to the man. Meanwhile, you should write to your parents."

"If I return to London, what will happen to Priddle House? I realize others contribute to the expenses, but . . ."

Mrs. Priddle adjusted her darning egg beneath a hole in one of Fiona's stockings. Her blue eyes sparkled like brilliant sapphires. "'Tis true your financial aid will be sorely missed if you leave, but if it's God's will for you to return to your homeland, then He'll provide the means for us to survive. He always has. Of course, some times He's done better than others." She chuckled and inserted her needle into the lisle stocking.

Charlotte rubbed her temples. "And what of Fiona? If I leave, I fear my departure will break her heart. She's suffered so much loss in her young life. If only I wouldn't have allowed her to form an attachment to me."

"No. Think of what both of you would have missed if you'd done such a thing. The girl has flourished since you arrived. She's gained confidence, too. Why, I believe it won't be long before she'll be able to play the piano in church on Sunday mornings." The old woman shook her head and laughed softly. "Probably with fewer sour notes than what we hear every week, too." A fat robin pecked at the ground before flying to a nearby branch. "Fiona understands the loss of a mother's love. If you decide to go, she'll understand that your son needs you."

Charlotte wasn't certain Fiona would so quickly understand. However, she would pray and wait upon God's answer. In the meantime she'd write to her parents and consider a visit to Mr. Ashton.

A week later the letter to her parents had been written and posted, but a visit to Mr. Ashton had yet to occur. Charlotte had used every excuse she could think of to forestall an appointment with the lawyer, and then Mrs. Priddle had taken the matter in hand. She arranged a date for the appointment, carefully scheduling a time late in the day in order to avoid any excuses from Charlotte. Mrs. Priddle had even insisted she would accompany Charlotte. Though the matriarch had stated she merely wanted to provide additional strength, Charlotte knew the woman's true intent. She was going to ensure the visit to the lawyer occurred as scheduled.

Only a slight rearrangement of her work hours would be necessary, and Mrs. Priddle had personally contacted Mr. Field with the request. She hadn't mentioned where they were going, only that Charlotte's presence was necessary at an important meeting that affected Priddle House. After receiving the request, Mr. Field had called Charlotte to his office. His curiosity had been evident. Before he granted permission for an early departure, his questions had skirted the fringes of an outright inquiry. Thankfully he'd stopped short of asking for exact details. She didn't want Mr. Field scouting about for her replacement when she'd not yet decided whether she would return to London.

As she passed the ladies' salon, Charlotte glanced into one of the full-length walnut-framed mirrors. She hesitated for a moment, pressed a few strands of hair into place, and proceeded downstairs to the State Street entrance.

"*There* you are! I thought perhaps I was going to have to come upstairs and fetch you." Mrs. Priddle grasped Charlotte's arm and tugged her forward. "Hurry along. I have a carriage waiting to take us to Mr. Ashton's office."

"You don't need to accompany me, Mrs. Priddle. Surely there are matters of greater importance requiring your attention."

"Nonsense!" Mrs. Priddle thumped the tip of her ancient parasol on the sidewalk. "Come along now, or the driver will think I've deserted him."

There was little use in arguing. Mrs. Priddle was determined, and there would be no changing her mind. With forced resignation, Charlotte settled onto the worn leather carriage seat and stared straight ahead.

"No use getting yourself in a snit, young lady. You've been dragging your feet about meeting with Mr. Ashton ever since you returned from Pullman. You can't make a wise decision until you have all the facts." She wrapped her weathered hand around the parasol handle. "I don't look forward to having you leave us, but let's find out what arrangements your father made with this man."

Mrs. Priddle was correct. If Charlotte could have avoided this meeting, she would have. She'd been praying over her decision, hoping for a quick and precise response, something resembling a bolt of lightning. Thus far, that hadn't occurred. Mrs. Priddle said an answer to prayer didn't usually rain down like manna from heaven. Sometimes God expected folks to do a little of the legwork on their own. No doubt Mrs. Priddle considered this appointment some of Charlotte's necessary legwork.

"Finally!" Mrs. Priddle shook her head. "That carriage driver must have taken the long way around. I thought we'd never get here."

Charlotte thought the carriage ride hadn't taken nearly long enough, but she wouldn't argue. She pulled a coin from her reticule and handed it to the driver. "You may as well go on. I believe we'll be a while."

He tipped his hat, offered a clipped thank-you, and flicked the reins.

Charlotte forced aside the foreboding that weighed heavily on her chest. An instant decision wasn't required just because she'd come here today. Simply speaking with Mr. Ashton wouldn't necessitate her immediate return to London.

Mrs. Priddle marched ahead of her and pushed open the front door of the lawyer's office. A bell jingled, announcing their arrival. An attractive young lady sat at a large mahogany desk and was reading from a thick leather-bound volume. She looked up and glanced back and forth between the two of them. "You must be Mrs. Priddle and Miss Spencer." She smiled warmly. "My father is expecting you." She pushed away from the desk. "I'm Ellen Ashton. Olivia's friend."

"Pleased to make your acquaintance, Miss Ashton." A clock in the far corner struck the half hour, and Mrs. Priddle snapped to attention. "We're on a rather limited time schedule."

A slight blush rose in Miss Ashton's cheeks, and she stepped from behind the desk. "Oh, indeed. Right this way." She led them into the adjacent office and stepped to one side. "Father, Miss Spencer and Mrs. Priddle."

The broad-shouldered, white-haired attorney jumped to his feet when they entered the room. Unlike Mr. Field, this man would be considered well groomed yet somewhat disheveled at the same time. He offered a slight bow and made a sweeping gesture toward the chairs opposite his desk. "Do sit down, ladies. I am most pleased to make your acquaintance—especially you, Miss Spencer." He waited until they were seated and then dropped into his large brown leather chair. "Your parents will be overjoyed to hear that you are alive and well."

"I've already written to my parents, Mr. Ashton. They should receive my letter any day now." His bushy eyebrows knotted, and she wondered if he had planned to take credit for locating her whereabouts. "You find that information distressing?"

His thick white hair remained firmly in place when he shook his head. "Not at all. I'm merely surprised that you wrote to your parents but didn't immediately come to my office once you learned your father had contacted me."

Apparently when she'd made this appointment, Mrs. Priddle had provided considerable detail. "I'm not certain when I will return to London. I plan to wait for a response from my parents first."

Mr. Ashton tented his fingers and rested them beneath his chin. "Nevertheless, your father did leave instructions with me and money to pay for your return voyage. Is that why you've come, Miss Spencer? For the money? If so, let me advise you that I have strict instructions regarding use of the funds."

Silly man! Did he think she wouldn't know that her father would place stipulations on his money? "I have no doubt my father gave you explicit guidelines, Mr. Ashton. He guards his money well."

"Better than his daughter, I fear." Mr. Ashton frowned and lowered his eyelids to half-mast.

"I didn't come here to discuss my father's attributes or failings, Mr. Ashton. Exactly what instructions did he give you?"

Mr. Ashton turned the key of a bronze-and-silver humidor and removed a fat cigar from the wood-inlaid depths of the box. He passed the length of rolled tobacco beneath his nose and inhaled deeply. Still holding the cigar in one hand, he pushed back and opened the center drawer of his desk.

He withdrew a long envelope, closed the drawer, and leaned forward, waving the sealed envelope. "He asked that if and when we met, I should first have you read this letter."

Charlotte picked up the letter opener lying on his desk and

slid it beneath the seal. From the corner of her eye, Charlotte saw Mrs. Priddle inch forward on her chair.

The older woman pointed a finger toward Mr. Ashton. "I hope you aren't planning on lighting that smelly wad of tobacco in my presence, sir."

Mr. Ashton laughed and shook his head. "My daughter doesn't permit smoking in the office. I've given up the habit, but I still enjoy the smell of fine tobacco."

While Mr. Ashton and Mrs. Priddle continued their discussion of cigars, Charlotte scanned her father's letter. He'd made arrangements with Mr. Ashton to purchase first-class passage for her return voyage home. The letter didn't state if her father had turned over the funds prior to his own departure or if he arranged to reimburse the lawyer once Charlotte boarded a ship. She needed to speak with him alone.

"I don't think we'll be much longer, Mrs. Priddle. Perhaps Miss Ashton could assist you with securing a carriage while I finish my business with Mr. Ashton."

Mrs. Priddle pursed her thin lips. "If you want to speak privately with the man, just say so, Charlotte. I won't be offended."

Charlotte laughed. "I'd like to speak to him privately, Mrs. Priddle."

She pushed up from her chair. "You see? That wasn't so difficult." She circled around the chair and departed to the outer office, careful to close the door behind her.

Mr. Ashton leaned back in the leather chair and locked his fingers behind his thick cap of hair. "Your father read the letter to me before he sealed it in that envelope, Miss Spencer. What questions do you have?"

"Did my father leave the funds with you, or did he arrange

for your reimbursement at a later date?"

The lawyer unlocked his fingers and dropped forward in his chair. "So long as you have a ticket, what difference should it make to you, Miss Spencer?"

"I trust our conversation will be held in confidence?"

"Of course. I'm an attorney, Miss Spencer."

"I understand. That's why I inquired." She didn't permit him to defend his fellow solicitors, but she knew whereof she spoke. She'd met enough of them in England, and many could be bought for a small price. "I've already informed my father that I will not leave until I am certain there are adequate finances for the operation of Priddle House during my absence."

"During your absence? You plan a return to Chicago?"

"I'm not certain what my future holds, but one thing is certain: I will not leave Chicago until proper funding arrangements are in place for Priddle House. The loss of my wages will place great financial strains upon Mrs. Priddle, and providing monetary aid is the least I can do."

Mr. Ashton rubbed his forehead. "Your *wages*? You *work*, Miss Spencer?"

"Yes. I am employed by Marshall Field."

The lawyer paled. Indeed, his complexion virtually matched his white hair. "I do hope you didn't tell anyone at work that you were coming to my office, Miss Spencer. If so, you'll not have a job come morning. Mr. Field considers me an enemy. My daughter and I are not permitted inside his establishment. You see, I represent some of the unions and their members. Men like Marshall Field and George Pullman consider me a traitor and a pariah of the upper class." He grinned. "I doubt your father realized that fact when he took me into his confidence."

Charlotte had heard rumors of employees being fired because of union affiliation. She also knew that the doormen had a list of people who were banned from the store, but she'd heard nothing concerning lawyers. Perhaps she could sneak a look at the names tomorrow morning and see if Mr. Ashton was actually listed. She had her doubts, for Mr. Ashton's office didn't reflect a man of power or means, certainly not someone that Marshall Field or George Pullman would fear.

"Since my father conducts business with Mr. Pullman's company, I would think you should have told him."

Mr. Ashton shrugged. "If this had anything to do with your father's interest in Mr. Pullman's company, I would have sent him elsewhere, but your parents had already scheduled their departure and had little time to spare. As to your question regarding payment of your passage, your father will reimburse me for the costs. Since your whereabouts were unknown, we agreed reimbursement would be the best method. As set forth in the letter, I am not to furnish money that will help you remain in this country."

Charlotte nodded. "Yet it doesn't prohibit the disbursement of additional funds that would permit my departure."

Mr. Ashton laughed. "Perhaps you should consider becoming a lawyer, Miss Spencer. You appear to have a knack for turning disadvantage into advantage, but we both know that the extra money you're requesting isn't truly necessary for your passage."

"No, but it is necessary before I will board a ship. As I stated earlier, Mr. Ashton, I've written to my father and advised him of my whereabouts and my concern for Priddle House should I leave." She slipped her hands into her lace gloves. "I'll simply await his reply. Thank you for your time, Mr. Ashton."

After returning to Priddle House the previous evening, Charlotte had prayed and wrestled with her decision. Though she didn't realize that she'd finally fallen asleep, sometime near the break of day she had awakened with a clear thought of what she must do. She waited until Mr. Field completed his morning rounds before approaching his office. Before she knocked on the door, she uttered a silent prayer.

Mr. Sturgeon bid her come in and immediately ran a finger down the page of his leather-bound appointment book before he looked up. "I don't see your name on my list, Miss Spencer." The clerk turned his head toward the door as if she'd been dismissed. Did he truly believe his simple comment would send her rushing from the room?

"If Mr. Field is not currently occupied, would you please inquire if he has a moment to speak with me?" She crossed the room, sat down, and folded her arms across her waist. Charlotte was well aware Mr. Field was alone. She had seen him return to his office, and no one had entered since that time. She pretended not to notice the clerk's glare as he passed by her and tapped on Mr. Field's door.

Moments later, he stood in the doorway, staring above her head. "You may go in." As she stepped beside the clerk, he bowed his head. "Mr. Field has a *scheduled* appointment in twenty minutes."

Good! Their discussion would be brief. Mr. Field wouldn't have sufficient time for one of his infamous interrogations.

CHAPTER TWENTY-NINE

August 20, 1893

Carrying a loaded tray, Martha entered the hotel kitchen, her lips tightened into a perfect seam. Since their wedding, Olivia had spent little time with Martha and Albert. With her schedule riding the rails, and the newly married couple enjoying their evenings alone, the only time Olivia seemed to see Martha was at the hotel. Martha tapped the silver-domed serving tray and gave a fleeting heavenward glance. "Mr. Pullman's in a terrible mood. Didn't eat a thing and said to take the tray out of his office."

Olivia shrugged. "Perhaps he ate breakfast before he left Chicago this morning." She took the tray and signaled for one of the kitchen boys.

Martha nudged Olivia's arm. "There's quite a row going on upstairs. Did you know Mr. Howard came running over here about ten minutes ago?"

With an exaggerated wave, Olivia motioned several of the kitchen boys toward the dining room. "You'd think those young

361

fellows would routinely perform their work without my forcing them from task to task each day, wouldn't you?" She waited until the boys departed the kitchen. "I'd guess there are some mechanical problems over at the car works and Mr. Pullman arrived to resolve the matter."

Martha shook her head. "No. I heard Mr. Pullman shouting about an—"

"Olivia! I need to talk to you in Chef René's office—*immediately*," Mr. Howard interrupted in a loud voice, then turned and stalked out of the kitchen.

The combination of Mr. Howard's clenched jaw, creased forehead, narrowed eyes, and angry command caused Olivia's stomach to roil. She cast a questioning glance in Martha's direction before scurrying from the kitchen. Mr. Howard stood just inside the door of Chef René's office with a newspaper tucked under his right arm. The moment she crossed the threshold, Mr. Howard closed the door with a decisive bang. He stormed around the desk and, with a resounding whack, slapped the newspaper onto Chef René's desk.

Resting his hands on the desk, Mr. Howard arched forward until they were nearly nose to nose. His jaw twitched. "*Well!* What do you have to say for yourself, Miss Mott?"

She took one step backward. "About what?"

The newspaper snapped beneath his palm. "About this!" He pointed to the bold-print typeface looming above a lengthy article on the first page.

From the headline, the article clearly had something to do with Mr. Pullman and his unfair treatment of porters and dining car employees. She reached for the newspaper. "I know nothing about this article. If you give me a moment to read, I'll be better able to answer your questions." With trembling hands, she sat down and focused her attention upon the column.

The article carried Matthew Clayborn's byline. A wave of nausea washed over her. Mr. Howard paced around the office in wide circles, finally dropping into the chair beside her. He leaned across the narrow expanse between them. "Please don't insult me by feigning ignorance, Olivia."

She folded the paper and laid it on the desk. "I can only tell you the truth. I had nothing to do with the publication of this piece. I have no idea why you would even think I had any involvement."

His eyes darkened. "Did you *read* the article? I'd have to be a complete fool not to realize you supplied information for this piece. And you have been observed keeping company with Matthew Clayborn."

"Truly? And when might that have happened?"

He folded his arms across his chest and leaned back in the wooden chair. "If memory serves me correctly, you were seen with him on at least one occasion here in Pullman and on another occasion in Chicago. I don't have time for this pointless deception. Mr. Pullman is a busy man, and he wants answers."

"You have jumped to conclusions, Mr. Howard. I won't deny that I know Matthew Clayborn, but I did not supply him with information for his news article."

"News?" He thumped his index finger atop the paper. "*That* isn't news. It's garbage! A smear campaign of the worst sort. Clayborn is an activist who inevitably sides with the unions. He uses this sort of tactic at every turn. The man is a critic of the worst sort, always filling his so-called news articles with inaccuracies. And you've allied yourself with him."

Olivia glanced toward the hallway. If he didn't lower his voice, the guests seated in the dining room would soon be a-twitter. "I haven't aligned myself with him. I don't understand how you can make such statements. You've just condemned Mr. Clayborn for writing inaccuracies, yet you're falsely accusing me without validating the facts."

"Any fool can see that the men who were fired are the employees listed in your reports."

His lips continued to move, but Olivia didn't hear another word. Mr. Howard didn't realize that he'd unthinkingly admitted exactly what Mr. Clayborn had understood all along. They *were* using her as a spotter. Her position riding the rails had nothing to do with detecting cost-saving methods or the betterment of services offered the passengers. She'd been duped into doing exactly what they had hoped, acting as a spotter who would go undetected by the railcar employees. Mr. Clayborn had told her of occasions when spotters had been physically harmed after being identified. If Mr. Howard truly cared for her, why would he permit her to be placed in such a precarious situation? And now he was accusing her of giving Mr. Clayborn information to print in the newspaper. He continued waving his finger under her nose like an angry parent. How dare he act so self-righteous!

She squared her shoulders and met his heated stare. "Just one moment. I have something to say before you continue with this tirade."

His mouth gaped open. She was pleased her unexpected interruption had surprised him.

"You have just admitted that you intentionally misrepresented my position riding the rails. You told me my position was to assess the services offered in order to save money and find ways to better serve the passengers. In truth, I was working as a spotter, wasn't I? While I thought I was actually assessing methods to offer a higher level of services, you were using my reports and turning them against the employees—discharging men based solely upon my notes."

"Well, I trust you didn't place any half-truths in your reports. And if those men had been satisfactorily performing their duties, they would still be employed."

His pompous reply merely fueled Olivia's anger. "So you *do* admit you misrepresented my position!"

"Mr. Pullman has implemented several of your suggestions. We'll need additional time to analyze whether your ideas will improve services or save money for the company."

"Oh yes. We wouldn't want Mr. Pullman or his stockholders to suffer any losses."

"Your disdainful tone isn't becoming, Miss Mott. I'll confess that your position was somewhat misrepresented. But other than using spotters, we've found no other method effective against employee abuses. The porters have learned to identify the male spotters we send out. We knew none of them would be suspicious of a woman."

His unemotional response fueled her outrage. "Perhaps if you paid the workers a decent wage, they wouldn't be forced to resort to such tactics in order to support their families."

He shook his head. "There are no excuses for stealing."

"Or lying?" She folded her hands and rested them in her lap. She could play his game.

Mr. Howard shifted in his chair. "There is a difference between a slight misrepresentation and an actual lie."

"I disagree. If you are going to brand the dining car attendants as thieves for giving leftover food to their hungry relatives, then you are guilty of more than a simple misrepresentation. Even now you continue to accuse me of slandering the company by furnishing information to Mr. Clayborn. Another *misrepresentation?*"

Mr. Howard leaned forward and rested his arms across his thighs. "If you didn't, who did?"

"Have you considered the workers who were fired? I would guess they'd be pleased to have their story told. Who has listened to their complaints? Certainly not Mr. Pullman." She tapped her finger on the newspaper. "This article certainly captured his attention—and very likely the interest of his stockholders, too."

"No doubt. And that is exactly why we are investigating this matter. We want to determine the truth. I find it difficult to believe that all of the men referred to in this article traveled to Chicago in order to speak with Matthew Clayborn."

Olivia didn't believe Mr. Howard was seeking the truth. It seemed he'd already determined she was the guilty party. She'd been accused and convicted before ever speaking a word. He didn't want to believe she hadn't participated in the news article. Strange. She'd not heard him deny the truth of the article, only his concerns about how Mr. Clayborn had obtained the information.

"I can't speak for those former employees or for Matthew Clayborn, but I do know that he travels extensively and has grown familiar with many of the porters and dining car attendants. I know this because I traveled on the same train with him on my initial solo journey to New York. He observed many of the same incidents that I noted in my first report to the company." She drew in a ragged breath and gathered her courage. "Although many told me I was foolish, I continued to believe the company cared about its employees. Your betrayal saddens me, for you've proven otherwise."

He frowned. "I don't know what has come over you, Olivia."

Was it anger or disgust she detected in his brooding stare? She couldn't be certain. But there was little doubt she had crossed the line.

"I'm not certain who or what you've been listening to, but I have several ideas. Be that as it may, I'm beginning to think you no longer value your employment here in Pullman." He edged a bit closer.

"Are you threatening to discharge me?" She had hoped to sound defiant. Instead, her voice cracked, and the question fell flat.

"Whether you remain employed will depend upon you and your future choices." He stood and took a step toward the door. "I will expect a full report setting forth anyone you have talked to who might be involved in this attempt to malign Mr. Pullman."

His sanctimonious attitude proved more than she could bear. "I wonder what Mr. Pullman would think of your recent employment tactics?" She clenched her fists in an effort to maintain her courage. "Do you believe he would approve of the money you're taking in exchange for certain job assignments?"

Mr. Howard stepped away from the door. His complexion seemed to pale, but she couldn't be certain in the dim light of the chef's office. "It would appear that *you* are now jumping to conclusions, Olivia. Do you have proof of these accusations, or is this another unsubstantiated story that will carry Matthew Clayborn's byline in the newspaper?" He dropped to the chair beside her.

Olivia ignored the reference to Mr. Clayborn. "How I discovered your deceptive practices is immaterial. The significant question is: What now, Mr. Howard? You've misled all who know you—workers, friends, Mr. Pullman. I suppose the only one you've failed to deceive is God. It's difficult admitting our failings to others, but realizing God's disappointment is so much greater, don't you think?"

Mr. Howard turned away. A suffocating silence pervaded the office, but she knew this conversation was far from over. She waited, expecting she would soon see his eyes glisten with remorse and hear an admission of inexcusable wrongdoing. He would feel the same frightened desperation she'd experienced when confronted with her own deception almost a year ago. He would likely plead for forgiveness. The wait seemed interminable.

When he finally swiveled around and met her gaze, his eyes shone with a cold, hard anger that startled her. Could he see her tremble? Instinctively, she looked at her hands. Outwardly they weren't shaking, but white-hot tremors coursed through every inch of her being.

She detected the familiar tic in his jaw. "You can't prove your allegations, Olivia. If it is your intent to reveal your accusations to Mr. Pullman—he's upstairs—feel free to air your supposed findings to him. I would remind you, however, that I have been a valued employee for many years. Mr. Pullman has never questioned my loyalty to him or to this company. On the other hand, you are an employee known for your deception and lies. After all, you came into our employ under false pretenses. If required to defend myself against you, I will point out your past offenses."

He turned his hands palm-side up and gently lifted his arms up and down as though attempting to balance a scale. He didn't need to say any more. He'd made his point. This man was a total contradiction, and his behavior frightened her.

As if reading her thoughts, he patted her hand. "I'm the same Samuel you've always known, Olivia. By most standards, I've lived a moral and decent life. But circumstances do change. Even you must admit that occasionally a situation occurs that will force one to do things that are totally out of character. That's what happened to you, wasn't it?"

He was turning the tables, and Olivia's level of discomfort continued to rise. "Yes, but when challenged with my misdeeds, I asked forgiveness and have attempted to refrain from lies and deceit."

"Have you? Or have you merely exchanged one behavior for another?"

She arched her brows, stunned by the question. "What do you mean?"

"You say you've given up your lies, but when confronted with this newspaper article, you immediately attempt to slander me and ruin my career."

Her mouth dropped open. There was no doubt he was on the attack, but how could she do battle with such a skilled tactician. Should she even try? "I do believe I could prove the validity of the accusations I've made. It is not my intent to slander or ruin your career, Mr. Howard. Instead, I had hoped you would see the error of your ways and remedy the situation."

He leaned back in his chair and extended his right leg full

length. His smile appeared less than genuine. "You are, I believe, an altruistic young lady, Olivia. Because of that, I'm willing to extend an olive branch. I'll pursue the possibility of a reinstatement of the porters and dining car attendants who were discharged. No promises, of course."

"I'm certain the men would be grateful."

His forced smile disappeared into a frown. "What are you willing to offer in return, Olivia? This is a peace negotiation, is it not?"

"I have nothing to offer you, Mr. Howard."

He snorted. "Of course you do. When the porters are reinstated, you can assure me that Matthew Clayborn will print an article that tells the entire incident was no more than a misunderstanding between employees and their employer. He can report that once Mr. Pullman became aware of the error, he immediately reinstated the workers."

"But that's not true. Besides, I don't think Mr. Clayborn would ever agree to such a tactic."

"How do you know unless you ask? Let him weigh his own decision. He does say that he wants these men to have meaningful work so they can support their families, doesn't he?" Mr. Howard didn't wait for her response. "I'm giving him the opportunity to help them. You should let him decide."

Olivia hesitated for a moment and then shook her head. "No, I don't believe Mr. Clayborn would do such a thing. It's not in his character."

He laughed. "But you're not always the best judge of character, are you?"

"I suppose not, but . . ."

He tented his fingers beneath his chin. "It appears we have

a number of issues before us, Olivia. While you have unfounded allegations about my hiring practices, I have years of loyal service on my side. Should I discharge you, and you speak to Mr. Pullman—if he would even deign to see you—he would consider your allegations no more than that of a disgruntled employee wishing to malign the supervisor who terminated her employment. Given the content of the article in today's paper, I don't think he would consider your discharge surprising."

Olivia inhaled a ragged breath and feared where all of this would end. "If you decide to terminate me, there is nothing I can do. Except—"

"Except what, Miss Mott?"

She took a moment to muster her courage. "I do recall that a Mr. Townsend is familiar with your hiring practices."

Mr. Howard lurched forward. "Have you been eavesdropping, Olivia?"

She swallowed the lump in her throat. "I don't intend to divulge how I happen to know of Mr. Townsend or how much more I know."

Her statement contained more bravado than anything else, but it had been enough to capture Mr. Howard's attention. She could see the concern in his eyes as he contemplated her words.

"So you know Frank Townsend, do you?"

Mr. Howard was toying with her. "You mean *Geoffrey* Townsend?"

He momentarily wilted but quickly regained his composure. "Sometimes it's wiser if you know less rather than more, Olivia."

Once again he was on the offensive. She tightened her hands into two fists and awaited the attack.

"We are going to have to come to some resolution very soon. I suppose the easiest way would be for me to remind you of several more people you may want to consider. I know you are quite fond of Fred DeVault and his mother." His lips curved in a condescending smile. "She *is* a sweet lady, isn't she?"

Olivia stiffened. "They have nothing to do with any of this."

"We won't argue that point. However, I know you would be burdened with guilt if Mr. DeVault happened to be discharged and his poor mother had to leave her home. I seem to recall that you told me how much she enjoyed living in Pullman. Wasn't it Mrs. DeVault who feared ever having to move from our fair city?"

She inwardly seethed. Why had she ever told him anything about Mrs. DeVault? Did he plan to dredge up every word Olivia had ever spoken and use it against her?

"How could you entertain such a thought? Fred is a good employee. And his mother doesn't deserve your retribution. They have done nothing to you or this company. They live here quietly and abide by the rules."

"*Do* they? You may be speaking the truth where Mrs. De-Vault is concerned, but that isn't true of her son. He's a trouble-maker. He thinks I know nothing of his rebellious activities, but there are people who tell me most anything that goes on in this town—even in Kensington, Miss Mott."

"*Kensington?*" She stared at him dumbfounded. "The train-ing center? You call helping men learn a trade a form of rebel-lious activity?"

"I'm certain you know there's more than teaching that takes place inside that building. And if you don't, I suggest you ask Mr. DeVault. I'd wager he'll know exactly what I'm talking about. His activities are suspect." He tapped his index finger to his temple. "Think *union*, Olivia. He needs to cease such activities."

Her heart beat at an alarming pace. Had someone reported that Fred was conducting meetings at the training center?

Mr. Howard swiveled around and vacantly stared at the ceiling. An uneasy silence stretched between them like a yawning abyss.

She uttered a silent prayer. If only she knew what to do. Just when she thought she could no longer withstand the overpowering confines of the room, Mr. Howard faced her.

"It seems we have reached an impasse, my dear Olivia."

She wanted to scream that she wasn't his "dear," but she silently stared at him with her hands folded in her lap.

"We both possess knowledge that, if used, could create tragic circumstances for the other. Would you agree?"

She nodded.

"In addition, I would suggest that my power to create such misfortune and heartbreak far outweighs your own. While you are controlled by a loving concern for others, I am not belabored by such sympathies. We must decide what we will do, Olivia. *I* propose we leave this room with an agreement that what has been said within the confines of this office remains between us. Your position with the company will be secure so long as your lips are sealed."

"And Fred?"

He shrugged. "So long as he gives up his foolish activity."

"I truly need time to pray and ask God's guidance before giving my word. May I have until tomorrow?" She looked up at him.

"I don't think your prayers will help. But if you give me your word that none of this conversation will be repeated to anyone until I have your decision, you may have until tomorrow."

"I promise," she said. "And I'll pray for you, too, Samuel."

"You need not bother. I've passed beyond a point where prayers will help me." His eyes clouded.

An inexplicable wave of sadness washed over her—a deep sorrow for the man that Samuel Howard had become. If only she could shed a ray of light into the darkness that surrounded him. She reached across the short distance between them and touched his hand. "The Bible says that whoever commits sin is the servant of sin. But it also says: 'Ye shall know the truth, and the truth shall make you free.'" She stood and walked across the room. With her hand on the doorknob, Olivia turned to him. "We never reach a point where God won't forgive us, Samuel. He'll forgive you and redirect your path, if only you'll ask."

Chef René's Blanquette de Veau

1 leek
2 carrots
1 onion
1 clove
1 oz. butter
1 ½ Tbsp. oil
2 ½ lbs. veal cut into pieces
flour
1 bouquet garni
2 egg yolks
¾ cup sour cream
Juice from ½ lemon
Salt and pepper

Peel the leek and cut into thin slices. Peel carrots and cut them into rounds. Peel onion and push clove into it. Heat butter and oil in a large pot. Place on low heat and cook veal slowly without allowing it to brown. Add salt and pepper to taste. Sprinkle meat with flour. Mix well and cook 2 minutes. Add just enough hot water to cover the meat. Add carrots, leeks, onion (with clove), and the bouquet garni. Cover and let simmer for 1 hour and 15 minutes. Remove the meat and put on a plate (cover to keep warm). Strain cooking liquid from vegetables and put the liquid back on the stove. Cook several minutes over high heat to reduce the liquid. Reduce heat to low. In a bowl mix egg yolks and sour cream. Add the lemon juice, salt, and pepper. Pour the mix into the cooking liquid, stirring constantly with a whisk. Do not let mixture boil. Pour the sauce over the meat. Stir and serve. The classic accompaniment to blanquette de veau is white rice or steamed potatoes. You may also add the vegetables you strained from the liquid back into the mixture before serving.

Chef Richmond's Duchess Potatoes

6 medium potatoes
¼ cup butter
Pinch nutmeg
⅛ tsp. white pepper
1 tsp. salt
2 Tbsp. milk
1 egg, lightly beaten
1 egg yolk, lightly beaten
1 egg beaten with 1 tsp. cold water (glaze)

Boil potatoes and allow to cool, then peel and mash to measure four cups. Beat butter, nutmeg, pepper, salt, milk, egg, and egg yolk into the potatoes. Meanwhile, preheat broiler. Fill a pastry bag fitted with large rosette tip with the potato mixture and press out onto a lightly greased baking sheet, forming 12 spiral cones about 2 ½ inches in diameter. Or simply spoon potatoes into 12 mounds. Brush lightly with egg glaze. Broil five inches from heat three to five minutes until lightly browned. Serves six.

Mrs. DeVault's Apple Cake

4 cups sifted flour
4 tsp. baking powder
2 tsp. cinnamon
2 cups sugar
1 cup orange juice
1 cup oil
4 eggs
1 tsp. vanilla
4–6 cups thinly sliced apples
Mix together an additional ¾ cup sugar and an additional 3 tablespoons cinnamon

Sift together flour, baking powder, and cinnamon. In a separate bowl mix eggs, sugar, oil, vanilla, and orange juice. Slowly add dry ingredients and mix. Pour half of the batter into a greased angel food cake pan. Top with half of the apples followed by half of the sugar and cinnamon mixture. Repeat layers and bake at 350° for 1 hour and 15 minutes or until cake tester comes out clean.

Orange Pound Cake Loaf

1 cup butter, room temperature
1 ½ cups sugar
4 eggs
1 ½ cups all-purpose flour
1 ½ tsp. baking powder
2 Tbsp. grated orange zest
2 Tbsp. orange juice
½ cup chopped pecans
½ cup chopped dates

Grease a 9x5x3-inch loaf pan; dust with flour. In a large bowl beat butter. Add sugar gradually, beating until light and fluffy. Add eggs, one at a time, beating after each addition. In a separate bowl stir together flour and baking powder. Gradually beat flour mixture into the butter and egg mixture just until blended. Stir in orange zest and orange juice. Fold in pecans and dates. Pour batter into prepared loaf pan. Bake at 350° for 45 to 55 minutes, or until cake tests done. Cool in pan on a rack; remove from pan to rack to cool completely.

ACKNOWLEDGMENTS

Special thanks to:

Linda Beierle Bullen and Mike Wagenback of the Pullman State Historic Site, who answered my many questions and provided me with their excellent insights, as well as tours of the hotel, car works, and the town of Pullman.

Members of The Historic Pullman Garden Club who hosted a tea and book signing at the Hotel Florence to celebrate the release of this series and to Linda Beierle Bullen for her excellent promotional efforts for the event.

Tony Dzik for his outstanding photographic services.

A MESSAGE TO MY READERS

Dear Reader,

I hope the POSTCARDS FROM PULLMAN series whets your appetite for further exploration into the life and times of the residents and community of Pullman, Illinois. As you continue to read this series, or perhaps in between each release, you may want to visit the town or check some Web sites to learn more. If you have the opportunity to visit, I would encourage you to do so. The residents of the town are proud of their community, and restoration is an ongoing process.

I would suggest you consider visiting the second weekend of October, when the Historic Pullman Foundation and the Pullman Civic Organization cosponsor the annual Historic Pullman House Tour. The Pullman State Historic Site, which includes the Hotel Florence and the Pullman Factory, is open that weekend for tours. In addition, tours of the Greenstone Church are available. You may learn more about the scheduled events throughout each year by going to *www.pullmanil.org* and clicking on "Programs" and then "Calendar." Walking tours of the town are conducted on the first Sunday of the month from May through October.

More information on the Pullman era is available at the following Web sites: *www.pullman-museum.org* and *www.chipublib.org/008subject/012special/hpc.html*.

There are numerous books of interest regarding both Mr. Pullman and his community.

While researching for his series, I visited Pullman and have developed a deep love for the history of the town and its people. I hope you will experience the same pleasure.

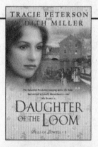

Looking for More Good Books to Read?

You can find out what is new and exciting with previews, descriptions, and reviews by signing up for Bethany House newsletters at

www.bethanynewsletters.com

We will send you updates for as many authors or categories as you desire so you get only the information you really want.

Sign up today!